REBELLION'S
FORGE

Audio Books

A Land Divided
A Wounded Realm
Rebellion's Forge
Blood of the Cross
The Last Citadel

K. M. ASHMAN

THE BLOOD OF KINGS: BOOK THREE

REBELLION'S FORGE

THOMAS & MERCER

Published by Thomas & Mercer, Seattle

www.apub.com

Amazon, the Amazon logo, and Thomas & Mercer are trademarks of Amazon.com, Inc., or its affiliates.

ISBN-13: 9781503942271
ISBN-10: 1503942279

Cover Illustration by Alan Lynch
Cover design by Lisa Horton

Printed in the United States of America

MEDIEVAL MAP OF WALES

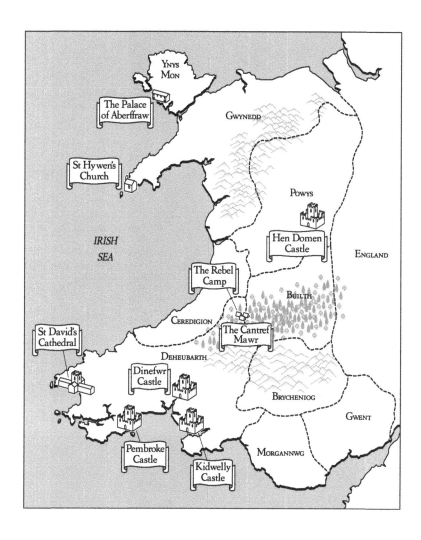

Though the borders and boundaries of early Wales were constantly changing, for the sake of our story the above shows an approximation of where the relevant areas were at the time.

Character List

Although correct pronunciation is not really necessary to enjoy the story, for those who would rather experience the authentic way of saying the names, explanations are provided in italics.

THE HOUSE OF ABERFFRAW

Gruffydd ap Cynan: King of Gwynedd – *Gruff-ith ap Cun-nan*
Angharad ferch Owain: Married to Gruffydd – *Ang (as in hang) Harad*
Cadwallon ap Gruffydd: Oldest son of Gruffydd
Cadwaladr ap Gruffydd: Second son of Gruffydd
Gwenllian ferch Gruffydd: Daughter of Gruffydd
Adele: Angharad's maid – *Ad-Ell*

The 'll' can be difficult to pronounce in Welsh, and is formed by placing the tongue on the roof of the mouth, while expelling air past the tongue on both sides. Non-Welsh speakers sometimes struggle with this – audible representations are available online.

Cynwrig the Tall: Ally of Gruffydd – *Cun-rig*
Osian: Warrior of Gruffydd – *Osh-an*

THE HOUSE OF TEWDWR

Hywel ap Rhys: Oldest son of Tewdwr – *How-well*
Gruffydd ap Rhys: Youngest son (known as Tarw) – *Tarr-oo (roll the letter 'R')*
Nesta ferch Rhys: Daughter – *Nessa or Nest-A*
Henry FitzHenry: Nesta's son
William FitzGerald: Nesta's son
Emma: Maid of Nesta

THE HOUSE OF POWYS

Cadwgan ap Bleddyn: Prince of Powys – *Ca-doo-gan*
Owain ap Cadwgan: Son of Cadwgan – *Ow-ain*

HEN DOMEN

Baldwin de Boulers: Castellan of Hen Domen Castle
Sir Broadwick: Knight of Henry

OTHER CHARACTERS

Henry Beauclerc: King Henry of England
Gerald of Windsor: Nesta's husband
John Salisbury: Constable of Pembroke

PLACE NAMES

Aberffraw: *Ab-er-frow*
Brycheniog: *Brick-eye-knee-og*
Deheubarth: *Du-hi-barrth (roll the 'R')*
Dinefwr: *Din-e-foorr (roll the 'R')*

Gwynedd: *Gwin-eth*
Hen Domen: *Hen-doe-men*
Mynydd Carn: *Mun-ith Ca-rrn (roll the 'R')*
Powys: *Pow-iss*
Ynys Mon: *Un-iss Mon*

Prologue

The year is AD 1109 and an uneasy peace exists between the two countries of England and Wales. Henry Beauclerc is on the throne of England and is married to Matilda of Scotland.

The years since the Norman invasion have been very difficult for the Welsh as not only have many been subject to the harsh law of the English Crown but they have also suffered at the hands of fellow Welshmen, who often fight amongst each other, seeking to restore the power and glory of the old kingdoms within the borders of Wales.

Nesta ferch Rhys is the daughter of the last king of Deheubarth, Rhys ap Tewdwr. Rhys was killed at the battle of Brycheniog several years earlier. Deheubarth is an enormous kingdom covering the south and west of Wales and was traditionally the stronghold of many Welsh kings, but since the death of Rhys it has become controlled by the English.

As a girl, Nesta was taken to Westminster to live at court, and she is now married to Gerald of Windsor, at the request of King Henry, despite having given birth to the monarch's bastard son after a passionate affair. The union is no more than a marriage of convenience, and though Nesta is still in love with Henry, she is powerless to resist the arrangement and lives in Pembroke Castle along with Gerald, who has been appointed the castellan. The marriage is seen as a politically astute move as to have a Welsh princess married to one of the English king's most trusted knights will be seen as a conciliatory gesture towards the people of Wales.

The rebellion that lasted many years has petered out and an uneasy peace has descended on the country, though small pockets of resistance remain. The mood is calm though tense, but as there is very little organised opposition, the English and their allies control most of south and east Wales via strategically placed castles.

In the south, the English control Gwent, Morgannwg, Deheubarth and Brycheniog. Powys in the north-east is ruled by Maredudd, a vassal prince who answers to the English Crown, while Ceredigion in the west is ruled by his brother, the rebel Cadwgan ap Bleddyn. The only true Welsh monarch left in Wales is Gruffydd ap Cynan, king of Gwynedd, a kingdom that stretches from the border with England in the east to the west coast of Wales.

In Ireland, Nesta's younger brother, Tarw, has been brought up by King Murcat. Tarw was sent to Dublin as a boy to escape the aftermath of war after the battle of Mynydd Carn, a bloody conflict that saw five Welsh kings fight each other for control of the country. His older brother, Hywel, was captured in the months leading up to the battle and kept captive for many years, suffering terrible torture and castration at the hands of his captors. When Tarw finally had a chance to rescue his brother from Hen Domen Castle, a brutal knight by the name of Sir Broadwick pursued them across Powys, and though the two young men escaped, it was not before the death of their mother at the hands of Broadwick's men.

Tarw nurses an anger at how his father's kingdom has been dismantled and the way his family have been devastated by the English and vows to one day return to Wales to win back his father's lands. Hywel now resides within the sanctuary of Saint David's Cathedral, not only to heal from a lifetime of abuse but also to keep him away from the murderous hands of Sir Broadwick.

———

In the north, Gruffydd ap Cynan has finally settled in as king of Gwynedd, and though he maintains a strong standing army, he enjoys the many benefits that peace with the English brings. His sons are growing up to be fine young men and his daughter, Gwenllian, is turning into a beautiful, yet strong-willed, young woman. Being brought up in a predominantly male household, Gwenllian is heavily influenced by her brothers and sees herself as an equal to any man. Much to the frustration of her parents, she sees her future as fighting the English in a quest to free Wales, but as she is only twelve years old, they allow her to continue her training in the hope that she will eventually see the futility of her dreams and will one day marry.

Pembroke Town

November 1st, AD 1109

Nesta walked through the busy market, humming to herself and pausing occasionally to browse the wares as she passed. Her two sons, Henry and William, chased each other between the stalls, brandishing wooden swords and squealing in delight at the fruitless attentions of their breathless nanny as she tried to keep them in check. The calls of the stallholders battled for sovereignty with the chatter of the peasants, while caged sheep, geese and pigs added their own sounds to the overall bedlam, the steam from their bodies rising wisp-like into the frosty autumn air. The smell of hot ale tempted even the most resolute of men, and a table before the communal bakery groaned under the weight of freshly baked bread.

Despite the throng, Nesta walked easily along the lane, untouched and unflustered, the crowd opening before her like a furrow before a plough. Many villagers nodded in deference, for not only was she the wife of the local castellan, Gerald of Windsor, she was also the daughter of Rhys ap Tewdwr, the last king of Deheubarth.

Behind her walked Emma, her maid, and two armed men, knights from the castle on the hill, for although the country was enjoying an unprecedented period of peace, there was always the faint chance of a brigand desperate to make a name for himself.

'My lady,' ventured a voice from one of the stalls, 'the blessings of our God be upon you this day.'

Nesta looked over and saw a short woman standing before a stall containing several rolls of fabric. The woman had her hair tied back with a bright rag of green silk that matched the friendly green of her eyes. Her face was weather-worn though friendly, and Nesta was drawn to her beaming smile.

'And on you,' smiled Nesta, turning slightly to walk towards the woman. She looked down at the assorted rolls of cloth on the trestle table. 'You have a wide range of silks,' she said. 'How are you in possession of such bounty?'

'My husband was a merchant working out of the docks at Bristol, my lady,' replied the woman, 'but he lost his life when his ship foundered last autumn. Bristol is no place for a woman and child with no man to protect them, so as I was born and raised in Dinefwr, I returned home and now live with my family on their farm. This silk is the only thing my husband left me of any value, and I hope to raise enough money to apprentice my son to a tradesman.'

'I'm sorry for your loss,' said Nesta. 'How old is your son?'

'This will be his sixth year so I need to make the arrangements soon otherwise he will drive me mad with his antics.'

'I know what you mean,' laughed Nesta, looking over to where her own two sons were chasing a chicken between the stalls. 'I have one the same age.' She returned her attention to the silk. 'Tell me more,' she said, 'for our family are soon to attend a celebration in Cardigan, and I'm sure our castellan would have his lady looking the best she can on such an auspicious occasion.'

The woman grinned before unrolling an arm's length of blue silk.

'I understand this colour is very popular in the courts of King Henry, my lady, and would be certain to turn the castellan's head.'

Nesta paused at the sound of the king's name. She hadn't seen him for over a year, and despite her now being wed to Gerald, she still had a soft spot in her heart for the father of her first child.

'Really,' she said, the smile returning to her face. 'Well, if these silks are good enough for the ladies of Westminster, then they are certainly suitable for the ladies of Gerald's household. However, I would prefer a colour with more passion. Do you have such a thing?'

The stallholder moved some of the silk on the table, retrieving a smaller bolt of fiery red. 'What about this?'

'Perfect,' said Nesta. 'Though I will need the full bolt.'

'Of course, my lady,' said the woman. 'It is one of the more expensive pieces though.'

'How much?'

'Six silver pennies.'

'You do realise you are talking to the castellan's lady,' said one of the knights from the side, 'a woman of royal blood descended from one of your own kings? I suggest it would look good on you if the silk was a gift?'

'I wouldn't hear of it!' exclaimed Nesta. 'I have never taken anything from my own people without fair recompense and I do not intend to start now. Six silver pennies, you say. Emma, pay the woman.'

'Four is a fairer price,' said Emma over her shoulder.

'Six is a fair price,' said Nesta, 'and I will hear no more of it.'

Emma reached inside her cloak for the purse of coins she carried on behalf of Nesta but her face furrowed when she found the pocket empty.

'Is there a problem?' asked Nesta.

'My lady,' said Emma, patting at her cloak, 'I fear I do not have the purse . . . I . . .'

'Pickpockets,' growled the knight, looking around, his hand moving to the hilt of his sword. 'I knew it was a mistake coming into this viper's nest.'

'My lady,' said Emma, her face dropping, 'I am so sorry.'

'Be calm, Emma,' said Nesta. 'It is not your fault.' She turned to the two knights. 'Do either of you have the asking price about your person?' Both men shook their heads. 'Such a shame,' she said, placing the cloth back on the stall, 'it would have made such a beautiful dress.'

'Please take it, my lady,' said the woman. 'I have every trust you will fulfil your side of the bargain when next we meet.'

'No,' said Nesta. 'You need the money and I would not deny you the income. When I return to the castle I will send one of the servants back down with the coins, and if it is still for sale, I will gladly take it off your hands.'

'Thank you, my lady,' said the woman with a nod of her head. 'May God go with you.'

'My lady,' cried a voice from across the market. 'Young William has had a fall.'

Nesta walked quickly through the crowd to find the nanny kneeling beside her eldest son.

'Is he all right?' she gasped, dropping to her knees.

'He has a cut on his head that's quite deep,' said the nanny, wiping away the blood, 'but nothing that won't heal. We need to get him back to the castle and summon the physician. Something tells me there may be a little sewing to do.'

'It's time we got back anyway,' said Nesta, standing up. 'The sun is almost at its highest and Gerald wishes to see me before noon.' She turned to one of the knights. 'Sir Howell, could you carry William back to the castle with all speed? We will follow right along.'

The knight nodded and scooped the sniffling boy into his arms.

'You will have a fine scar when that heals,' he boomed, looking at the wound. 'Many of my fellows would be proud to wear such a badge of honour. Now, where's your sword?'

The little boy stopped crying and pointed into the dirt.

'Pass this young man his weapon,' said the knight with a wink, 'for though he is wounded, he is still a soldier.'

Emma retrieved the toy and gave it to William.

'Nothing to worry about,' she said, as the knight strode away. 'He'll be back to normal in a few hours.'

'My lady,' someone called. Nesta turned to see the stallholder approaching with the bolt of red silk in her arms. 'Take this silk with you.'

'Good lady,' replied Nesta, 'I have already told you that I cannot take your wares without suitable recompense, though the gesture is greatly appreciated. Now, please allow me to proceed.'

'No, you don't understand,' said the woman. 'Your gentleman friend has paid in full, and he gave me an extra penny to bring it over to you.'

'Gentleman friend?' asked Nesta, looking around. 'And who, pray, may that be?'

'The handsome gentleman in the black jacket,' said the woman. 'He is just over there.' She turned and pointed over to the stall but her arm fell back to her side. 'Oh,' she said with disappointment, 'he was there not a few moments since.' She quickly scanned the market place but to no avail.

'And did this gentleman have a name?' asked Nesta.

'No, but he did leave a message.' Her voice lowered and she tiptoed up to whisper in Nesta's ear. 'He said, "There is no satchel big enough to contain the value of a stolen kiss."'

For a moment Nesta frowned in confusion but then the light of realisation dawned in her eyes.

'Do you know the man?' asked the woman, who was watching Nesta carefully.

Nesta looked away. 'No, he is surely a simpleton with dreams beyond his reach.'

'On the contrary, he seemed very well bred and his purse was heavy with coin. A handsome fellow, young and full of vigour.'

'A noble bearing does not preclude the disease of idiocy,' said Nesta. 'What sort of man pays a small fortune for a gift yet disappears like the mist before gratitude can be expressed?'

'I don't know, my lady, but if you wasn't a married woman, I would suggest a heartbroken suitor.'

'Nonsense. Like I said, a simpleton with ideas of grandeur.' She turned to her maid. 'Emma, take the lady's silk. We will have our new dresses after all for if this stranger wishes to let good coin pass through his hands like river water, who are we to judge? Good lady,' she continued, turning back to the woman, 'if you should see this man again, please thank him on my behalf but suggest he keeps his distance. His intentions may be innocent but my husband has a temper second to the devil himself. Now, I wish you good day.'

'Good day, my lady,' said the woman and she watched as the princess walked back towards Pembroke Castle.

'So,' said Emma, catching up with Nesta, 'who was he?'

'Who?'

'You know who,' said Emma. 'The lovesick suitor.'

'I have no idea,' said Nesta, her gaze never leaving the path before her. 'Nor do I wish to know. I am a married woman with eyes only for my husband.'

'If that is the case, why did you blush like an unfrocked bride on her wedding night?' said Emma, glancing around to make sure she was not overheard.

'I'm sure I have no idea what you mean,' said Nesta, increasing her pace. 'Now, we will hear no more about it.'

Emma smiled and allowed Nesta to pull away from her, knowing full well that her mistress was lying.

Nesta continued walking up to the castle, her mind spinning and heart racing. Though it had been three years since she had seen him, she had no doubt who the mysterious man was, the one person in the world who had made her feel like a lovesick girl even though they had talked only once. That man was Owain ap Cadwgan, the son of the most feared rebel in Wales.

The Outskirts of Builth

December 16th, AD 1109

The sun trickled down through the bare branches of the forest canopy, lighting the fallen autumn leaves like a rich tapestry of golds and reds. Birds had long since flown south and nothing stirred for leagues around, as if waiting for the inevitable snow. An uneasy silence lay heavy on the woodland glade.

Eventually it was broken by the approaching sound of cart wheels, ploughing through the winter-crisp leaves. Voices spoke quietly and the occasional cough gave witness to an approaching body of men.

'I'll be glad to get to the castle,' said one from the seat of a covered wagon. 'Get this damn journey over with.'

'You're not alone,' said the man at his side. 'I hate this route more than any other.'

'Have you been to Hen Domen before?'

'Once – and, to be honest, it wasn't a good experience. The man in charge is nothing but a bastard.'

'Baldwin de Boulers? He's not so bad. I've served under worse.'

'No, not him. I'm talking about Broadwick, his first knight. He treats us commoners as nothing more than slaves.'

'Such is life, my friend. There are the haves and the have-nots. We unfortunately are the have-nots. Learn your place, keep your mouth shut and hopefully we will live to see old age.'

'Yeah, I understand that but we are all supposed to be on the same side. The last time I was there he had us cart masters cleaning out the latrines until the next caravan was ready to go. I may be lowly born, but cleaning other people's filth is a job for slaves and the condemned, not allies supplying much-needed succour to the garrison.'

'So who is he, this Broadwick?'

'An English knight famed for his ruthlessness,' said the first man, 'and like I said, a bastard of the highest order. Keep your distance, your eyes lowered and carry out any task issued without complaint and we just might get back out with our thumbs intact.'

'It sounds like we may be safer out here,' sneered his companion.

'Oh, I don't know about that. There are too many places to be ambushed as far as I'm concerned, and we should have at least twice the number of guards for this amount of wagons.'

'And since when are you a master of strategy?' said a horseman, riding up alongside the cart.

'Sir Julian,' stuttered the first man. 'I did not realise you were so close. I meant no criticism of your men, but was just observing that perhaps the castellan of Hen Domen is expecting a lot from so few.'

'Leave the worrying to me,' said the knight. 'You just make sure these two disease-riddled mules live long enough to deliver your load. We have already lost far too much time and any more delays will see every one of you forfeit your price.'

The cart master was about to respond when the wagon in front slowed to a halt. He reined in his own team and watched as the knight rode forward to meet the sergeant-at-arms running back along the wagons.

Behind the sergeant, a body lay amongst the detritus, its arm stretched out as if reaching for a discarded sword. Another two lay nearby, their bodies contorted into the grotesque shapes that battle often brought, and an abandoned horse stood untethered in a clearing, uncaring about the brutal ways of man.

The remains of a fire smouldered between a circle of stones, and the carcass of a burned rabbit still hung over the embers, the scorched black flesh no longer any good to man or beast. Smoke rose unchallenged by any breeze, slicing the clear winter air like the hottest knife through butter, and the smell of death lay like the heaviest fog.

Julian reacted immediately. He was a seasoned veteran of many conflicts, and his first instincts were to secure his command's security.

'Cavalry to the flanks,' he shouted. 'Archers, string your bows. I want two on each cart.' He turned to the sergeant. 'Move your command forward and secure the clearing.'

'They are already deploying, my lord,' said the experienced soldier.

Julian reached to the side of his saddle and untied his helmet. Men ran to their posts and the sounds of shouting filled the air. Swords were unsheathed and pikes lifted from the racks on the sides of the wagons. Within moments, the caravan guards were in position and satisfied his men would not be caught cold, the knight walked his horse forward to the scene of the conflict. He dismounted and looked around the clearing, counting the bodies, his breathing shallow to avoid taking in the familiar stench of death.

'It looks like they were ambushed,' said the sergeant-at-arms, walking amongst the victims. 'I reckon there were archers on both sides of the track. These men stood no chance.'

Sir Julian looked around the clearing, his eyes taking in every aspect of the one-sided battle. He was no stranger to death and did not fear its embrace, but to be cut down by cowards from the safety of the trees was no way for any man to die.

'Look for survivors,' he said. 'And see if you can find any colours. I need to know who these men were.'

Robson called a squad of men to search the dead, tasking them with checking each corpse for any evidence of identity.

'My lord!' someone shouted. 'Over here.'

Robson ran over and stared down at a dead man lying on his back. The throat gaped wide open and a frozen scream was still evident on the victim's grey face, but despite the blood soaking the corpse, the sergeant could still clearly see the emblem on the dead man's surcoat – two golden lions on a red background.

'In the name of Jesus Christ,' said Robson, crossing himself, 'it is the royal emblem. This man was a knight of King Henry.' He looked around nervously. The sight of so many dead already made his men uneasy but the fact that someone had actually had the nerve to attack a column under the protection of the Crown made their own situation all the more precarious. Sir Julian joined Robson at the body and stared down coldly.

'Do you know him, my lord?' asked Robson.

'No, though his colours are of Hereford. I assume he was out here on a similar task as I, as protection for merchantmen going about their legal business. It looks like they were struck down by overwhelming numbers.'

'Welsh brigands?' suggested Robson.

'Welsh, yes,' said Sir Julian, 'but brigands? I think not.' He bent over and retrieved an arrow from the leaves, rolling it carefully between his fingers before examining the goose feathers and staring along the shaft.

'This arrow was made by an expert fletcher,' he said, 'and is recently made. I would wager that any others we find are of similar quality.'

'Why is that important?'

'Because brigands won't waste good coin on arrows when their old ones can be used over and over again. Whoever attacked this caravan wasn't concerned with collecting the arrows, which means they are already well stocked. That can mean one of two things: either it is a well-equipped army, which we know is highly unlikely, or it is the next most dangerous thing.'

'Rebels?' ventured Robson.

'Rebels,' confirmed the knight.

'But all rebel bands disbanded when Henry signed the treaty with Gruffydd.'

'Gruffydd does not rule all of Wales,' said Sir Julian, standing up and looking around the nearby treeline. 'His reach extends through Gwynedd and Ceredigion and as far east as Powys, but there are many minor nobles who would gladly turn against Henry again given the chance.'

'To do so would invite a terrible retribution,' said the sergeant.

'Only if they were caught,' said Sir Julian, but before he could continue, another voice called out from amongst the trees.

'My lord, this one's still alive.'

The knight ran over and squatted down alongside a badly wounded man. A rope tied him in a sitting position against a tree but his hands were free and pressed tightly against his own stomach. Sir Julian moved the hands slightly and grimaced when he saw they were the only thing holding in the victim's innards.

'This has been done with purpose,' said Sir Julian quietly. 'It is a slow way to die and whoever did it knows that it cannot be undone.' He turned his head. 'Bring me a flask of water, quickly.'

One of the soldiers handed over a goatskin and Sir Julian held it to the lips of the semi-conscious man.

'Here,' he said quietly. 'There is nothing we can do for you, my friend, but I will not see you thirsty as you pass.'

The man lapped gratefully as the water ran down his chin into his beard. His eyes flickered open and he gazed at the knight.

'Can you tell me who did this?' asked Sir Julian. 'Do you know who they were?'

The man's eyes closed as his lips tried to form the words.

'I can't hear you,' said Sir Julian. 'Here, have some more.' He poured more water into the man's mouth but the victim turned his head away, groaning in pain as the previous water pushed his stomach into voids that should not have been there.

'I know you are in pain,' said Sir Julian, 'and I will end your life quickly should you so wish, but if there is anything you can tell us, please do so.'

The man looked at him again and once more his lips formed words, though still indistinct.

'Again,' said Sir Julian, placing his ear near to the man's mouth.

The man strained and spoke for the last time before his head fell forward onto his chest. His hands relaxed, and as they fell away, his steaming innards poured through the gaping wound into his lap. Sir Julian pushed himself away and got to his feet.

'What did he say?' asked the sergeant.

'I'm not sure,' said Sir Julian. 'It sounded like *"stay here"*.'

'Why would he want us to stay here?'

'He was very indistinct,' said Sir Julian. 'I may be mistaken . . .'

Sir Julian stared at the soldier for a moment, his face frozen as he realised exactly what the man had said.

'*Still here*,' he gasped. 'Whoever did this is still here.' He drew his sword and spun around. 'To arms!' he shouted. 'It's a trap.' But even as his foot soldiers drew their own weapons, the unmistakeable sound of willow slicing through the air confirmed his worst fears and three men fell to the ground, their bodies pierced with arrows.

'*Take cover*,' screamed the knight. 'Sergeant, recall the cavalry.'

Robson gave the order and the sound of a horn echoed through the trees. Panic ensued as the guards sought cover from the deadly hail of arrows. More men screamed as shafts of willow and steel smashed into their bodies, their chainmail useless at such short range. Sir Julian's horse fell, snorting in pain as a dozen arrows thudded into its flesh, and it lay on the floor shaking violently, its eyes wide with fear as it died in excruciating pain.

Out in the forest, horsemen tasked with securing the perimeter heard the horn and turned their mounts to head back, swords drawn and shields to the fore. But as they rode, the undergrowth came alive as armed men emerged from beneath the detritus to hurl themselves at the horses, their blades hacking at the beasts' legs. Animals fell everywhere, throwing their riders to the ground to be slaughtered by the assailants, and any man who managed to get to his feet lasted only moments as archers picked them off one by one.

Back in the clearing, Sir Julian and the rest of the English soldiers were pinned down. Arrows fell amongst them, and each man desperately found whatever cover he could behind the trees and the tangled undergrowth. The enemy seemed to be concentrated on the higher ground where the forest climbed away and shadowy figures moved constantly between the trees, changing positions to better their chances of a kill. The forest seemed alive with attackers, and the screams of wounded men echoed between the trees. The knight knew they were at risk of being picked off by the archers and the only thing they could do was try to escape the clearing. Some men would fall but hopefully many would make it through.

He looked to his left. Robson and five other men lay hidden from the attackers' line of sight and in a good position to retreat. On Julian's right flank, the rest of his command were in a more precarious position and unlikely to be able to withdraw without incurring serious casualties.

'Listen,' he hissed to Robson. 'I want you to take the men to your left and head for the wagons. Keep low and run as if the devil himself was on your heels. Stop for nothing, and if you make it, task the drivers to ride as hard as they can to clear the treeline. At least in the open the enemy will be denied the cover of the forest and our own archers will have targets.'

'What about you, my lord?' asked the sergeant.

'I will take the rest of the men and attack the enemy closest to us.'

'But they have archers well deployed.'

'I know, but they will have time for only one volley. If God is with us, most of our men should survive and give you a chance to escape, but I don't know how long we can last. For all we know there could be hundreds of them out there.'

'Then let us all take the fight to them.'

'No, we need to get those wagons to Hen Domen. I gave my word I would see them arrive safely, and if it is God's will that I die in the process, then so be it. You just focus on getting back to the wagons. Those of us who survive will meet you where the river bends a few leagues south of here. Make sure you protect the wagons but wait one day, no more. If we are not there by then, you must assume we have been killed and take it upon yourself to complete this task in my name. Now, enough talk. Brief your men quickly, and prepare to move.'

Robson crawled through the undergrowth, passing on the knight's orders to those ordered to retreat. As he went, Sir Julian looked around, desperate to find better cover. A few paces behind, a small stream cut into the forest floor offering a limited amount of protection from the archers above. Carefully he crawled backward, followed by the rest of his men, each keeping as low as he could amongst the undergrowth. As the last man slid down the bank Sir Julian gathered them around to give his orders.

'It is time to show your mettle, my friends,' he said. 'On my word, we will break cover at the far end of this bank and head for the slope before us. Those of you without shields, stay close behind those who do, but as soon as we are amongst them, break away and wreak havoc with your swords. I believe the enemy are light on men-at-arms, else they would have already assaulted us. However, whatever we find, it is important you keep going. Stop for no man – friend or foe. At all costs, we must get through them and muster on the ridgeline. Those of us who survive will reassess when we get there. Understood?'

A mumble of acknowledgement came back from the twenty men and Sir Julian adjusted his grip on the hilt of his sword.

'Let us wait no longer. The odds might be against us, but I believe God is on our side. If the wagons escape due to your actions in the next few minutes, I will personally guarantee a reward to every man who survives. Ready?'

'Aye,' said the men, and after a deep breath Sir Julian got to his feet, holding his shield before him.

'Men of England,' he shouted, 'in the name of the king, *advaaance!*'

With an almighty roar, the knight's men burst from cover and ran towards the higher ground. Immediately they were met by a hail of arrows but though two fell, each with an arrow embedded in his face, most were protected by their shields. Encouraged by their success they sprinted forward and were amongst the trees within moments. Enemy archers broke cover and retreated up the hill, surprised at the aggression from their victims, and it wasn't long before the first ambusher fell to Julian's sword.

'*Keep going!*' he roared, and buoyed by the sight of their first enemy blood, the foot soldiers renewed their efforts. Some of the ambushers turned to fight but they were no match for the English, and many fell, victims of cold steel and stout hearts.

'*Withdraw,*' echoed a voice from the trees, and the rest of the enemy turned to flee up the hill. Julian's head spun around to see a man astride a horse higher up the slope. With renewed vigour he pushed himself harder, confident that even though he may be tired from the climb, should he manage to reach this rebel leader his training and lifetime's experience in warfare would see him emerge the victor. With his men close behind him, he neared the top of the wooded hill, the sweat pouring from beneath his helmet. The arrows had long since stopped, and though he had lost several men, the bloodlust raged in his veins and he pushed up the last climb to emerge into another clearing. With his lungs almost bursting from his chest, he planted his sword in the ground before him, leaning on it as he caught his breath. One by one his men joined him, each gasping after the arduous climb.

Before them, the few archers who had survived the counter-attack ran wildly across the clearing, desperate to reach the safety of the trees on the far side. Having no archers of his own, Julian was unable to drop them from afar, but he was not about to give up the chase.

'After them,' he shouted, picking up his sword, 'before they have a chance to reorganise.' As one the men leapt forward and pursued the running men, but they hadn't reached halfway when Sir Julian stopped dead in his tracks. He held up his hand, his chest still heaving from the exertion of the chase. His men gradually slowed to a stop and stared in alarm at the sight before them. The escaping enemy had reached the trees but as they disappeared from view, a new line of archers appeared. Each one stepped forward, their bows loaded with arrows, and took aim at the men in the centre of the clearing.

Julian's heart sank, knowing he had been outmanoeuvred. The men to his front outnumbered his own two to one and though he would accept those odds in a fair fight, the fact that they were archers meant he wouldn't be able to get anywhere near them before his own men were cut down.

He looked back the way they had come but another line of armed foot soldiers over a hundred strong were running across the treeline to his rear, effectively cutting off any chance of escape. His own men looked around frantically, seeking an escape route, but their search was fruitless and within moments they were completely surrounded by the far superior force.

Julian stood firm, staring at the forest to his front as the enemy commander emerged from the treeline. The knight cursed, realising he had been tricked. Whoever this man was, he had cleverly used himself as bait, knowing that the Englishman would see him as a prize worth pursuing. And he had been right, for despite his years of training, Sir Julian had walked into a very simple trap.

'Well,' he roared, holding his sword out from his body, 'what are you waiting for?' He turned around slowly, shouting at the surrounding circle of men, each staring back at him in silence.

'This is what you wanted, isn't it? The blood of Englishmen.'

Again there was silence, and Julian began to get angry.

'*What are you waiting for?*' he shouted again. 'If you are hoping we will beg for mercy, you wait in vain, for I assure you we will all die of thirst before that day comes. Kill us if you have the nerve. End it here in cold blood, safely distant from any risk of injury.'

When there was still no reply, he planted his sword in the ground before undoing his chinstrap and casting his helmet to one side. He drew his knife and cut through the side straps of his chainmail shirt before lifting it over his head and throwing it to the ground. His linen undershirt followed and he was soon bare-chested under the afternoon sky. Picking up his sword he turned again to face the silent man upon the horse.

'You,' shouted Julian. 'You deem to lead these men. Face me like a man and I will fight you bereft of armour or sword. I will even discard my knife if you so wish, yet bid you come armed as you are. What say you, stranger, are you a man or be you a sheep?'

Silence fell around the clearing and the man upon the horse leaned down to talk into the ear of a sergeant. The man nodded and ran over to a team of archers, passing on his leader's instructions. Seconds later, another fifty archers notched arrows into their bowstrings and took aim at the men before them.

'And there's your answer,' laughed Sir Julian sarcastically. 'Any soldier worth his salt can take down a man in battle but it takes a special type of coward to kill an unarmed man from a distance. Do your worst, coward, but have your men watch carefully as we fall for there will be no fear nor subservience displayed on this field.'

The horseman raised his hand and Julian swallowed hard. Despite his defiance, he had been bettered and he knew he would soon face God for his final judgement. The knight was not afraid to die but there was an unexpected sadness at the method. His warrior heart yearned for the death in battle his creed sought, yet here he was, about to die no better than a stag in a hunt.

'So be it,' he said eventually. 'Do your worst, Welshman, the time for parley is over.' He discarded his sword and tilted his head back, his arms outstretched, inviting the thud that would inevitably arrive to end his life.

The man on the horse paused a moment longer before bringing his hand sharply down and the air around him filled with arrows. Volley after volley followed, the glade filled with the screams of dying men as shields were splintered by the iron-tipped missiles. Finally, the man raised his hand again and the field fell silent as the deadly rain came to a halt. The rider urged his horse forward accompanied by six of his men, coming to a stop above the body of Sir Julian.

'Get up,' he said quietly.

For a few moments there was nothing, but eventually the cowering knight got to his knees, astonished he was still alive.

'Replace your shirt,' said the rider, as Sir Julian gazed at the men surrounding him. A few still remained alive, groaning from non-lethal wounds, but any hopes of mercy quickly disappeared as the rebels opened their throats with hunting knives.

'Why?' asked the knight, his face ashen with shock. 'Why kill all my men but leave me to live?'

The rider didn't answer but turned to one of the soldiers.

'Ensure he is bound and blindfolded. Bring him to the camp tonight.'

'Aye, my lord,' said the soldier, and the rebel commander rode away to the treeline, closely followed by the rest of his army.

'Who is he?' asked the English knight, gazing after the disappearing leader. 'Why has he spared only me? Is it to claim a ransom?'

'Ransom,' laughed the soldier, tightening a rope around the knight's hands. 'He has no need of English coin, my friend, and I suggest you don't get too excited about your reprieve. If I know him, he already has something very special planned for you.'

'Who is he?' asked Sir Julian again. 'I would know his name.'

'Even if I told you,' said the soldier, 'it would not be one you are familiar with, but I will say this. Before long, everyone will say his name in awe, especially the English. Now, get to your feet, we have a long way to go.'

The Foothills of Snowdonia

December 17th, AD 1109

Gruffydd ap Cynan, king of Gwynedd, sat astride his charger, staring across the foothills of the Snowdonia mountains. Alongside him on their own horses sat his daughter, Gwenllian, and the four Welsh knights acting as their bodyguards. Behind them came Master Perry, the court falconer, and two squires, each carrying a hooded bird of prey.

The past few years had been good to Gruffydd, for despite raising the ire of the English after his successful attack on Ynys Mon a few years earlier, the full-scale assault by Henry's armies never materialised and he was left alone to rebuild his kingdom. His family had joined him from Ireland and they had settled in their ancestral home at Aberffraw, safe in the knowledge that though they could never be complacent, the political situation meant they were as safe as they could be in dangerous times. His sons were growing strong and healthy, and as long as warfare could be avoided, he had no doubt that one day one of them would succeed him as king of Gwynedd.

The company gazed down into the valley. For the past few hours they had ridden over the hills, seeking the open spaces where the hawks could do what they did best, and finally the king held up his hand, bringing them to a halt before a lush valley containing a sky-reflecting lake.

'It looks like we are in luck,' said the king, standing up in his stirrups. 'The lake is calm and ducks abound on its surface. What say you, Master Perry, do you think Diana can earn her keep?'

'Aye, she will do you proud, my liege,' said the falconer, drawing his own horse to a halt. 'I will have her brought forward.'

'No,' said the king. 'Let Gwenllian be the one to set her loose.'

The falconer looked across at the princess, seeing the obvious delight in the girl's eyes.

'Are you sure, my lord?' asked the falconer. 'Diana is known for her fiery temperament.'

'My daughter is equal to any boy her own age,' said the king, 'and I would see her treated the same as my sons.'

'As you wish,' said the falconer. He turned to Gwenllian. 'My lady, have you flown hawks before?'

'No,' she replied, 'but I have seen it done on many occasions. Just furnish me with a gauntlet and I won't let you down.'

'Then tie back your hair, in case the bird gets entangled.'

Gwenllian reached behind her head to secure her long, golden hair, before receiving a gauntlet from one of the squires.

'Why is she called Diana?' she asked as she waited for the ties to be secured. 'Is it not a strange name for a bird?'

'On the contrary, my lady,' replied Perry. 'Diana and Artemis were both goddesses of the hunt. What better names could we have chosen for so lethal a pair of killers?'

Gwenllian waited as Master Perry lifted one of the gyrfalcons carefully onto her forearm.

'Be strong in your stance,' he said when the bird had settled, 'and calm in your manner. Diana is a royal lady and is the king's favourite. However, her beauty belies a feisty nature and she will not suffer fools lightly. If you show fear, or uncertainty, then she will just as likely use her daggers upon your pretty face as upon the game we hope to catch.'

'Daggers?' asked Gwenllian.

'Her talons, my lady. No man has ever borne more lethal a blade.'

'Her plumage is beautiful,' said Gwenllian as the bird exercised its wings, 'and she is heavier than I expected. Where did you get her?'

'I brought her and her brother from the west of Ireland,' replied the falconer. 'And it cost your father a small fortune.'

'It did indeed,' added the king. 'I could have fielded a dozen knights for a year for the same purse, so treat her gently.'

Gwenllian ran her free hand down the bird's back, revelling in its beautiful softness.

'If you are ready, my lady,' said the falconer, 'we can begin.'

Gwenllian nodded, and the falconer manoeuvred his horse beside hers.

'Turn your hand so that the bird faces the lake,' he said, 'and then remove the hood. Wait a few moments for her to see the prey and then lift her up into the air while releasing the tethers in your fist. Ready?'

'Ready,' confirmed Gwenllian, and after taking a deep breath she followed the falconer's instructions. Moments later, the beautiful gyrfalcon swooped down the valley before catching an updraft and rising gracefully into the air, the pure-white plumage shining in the midday sun.

'She's so graceful,' gasped Gwenllian.

'She is,' responded the king, 'but behind that grace and beauty lies inner strength and a lethal instinct.' He turned to face his daughter. 'We live in cruel times, Gwenllian. Perhaps it would be wise to learn from the bird.'

Gwenllian returned his gaze, absorbing her father's words of wisdom. Having three older brothers, she had been brought up in a male-dominated world, but far from seeking the femininity of her mother's company and the rest of the ladies at the palace of Aberffraw, she had embraced the culture of the warrior caste and was growing up into a single-minded young woman. Her sword skills matched those of any boy of her age, and she could better any man with her riding. While other girls learned how to sew and sing in the halls of the palace, she could usually be found with the weapon masters, trying out the bows or practising her skills with shield or blade. Many was the time her mother, Angharad ferch Owain demanded she embrace her femininity, but Gwenllian had steadfastly refused, instead joining her brothers in the daily arms training expected of all men destined to be soldiers. At first her father had forbidden such nonsense, but when it became clear she would carry on behind his back anyway, he realised that if she had her heart fixed on fighting, it was his duty to ensure she was as best prepared as she could be and so he arranged formal lessons from the masters-at-arms. Despite this, Gwenllian was already growing into a beautiful young woman, and he knew that one day she would bring him untold heartache.

'She's seen the prey, my lord,' shouted the falconer, and all eyes turned to see the flock of ducks rise from the surface of the lake. High above, the gyrfalcon floated on the breeze, peering downward, waiting for the opportunity it knew would come. Within moments a lone bird separated from the flock, seeking cover in the nearby treeline, and without hesitation the falcon twisted its body to speed earthward like the truest of arrows.

Gwenllian held her breath, sure the bird would crash into the ground. The duck changed course, desperate to escape the predator, but it was too late, and with a distant thump amidst a cloud of downy feathers both birds fell to earth. The gyrfalcon's work was done.

'Excellent hit,' shouted the king. 'Come, let's see the fruit of her endeavours.' He spurred his horse forward, closely followed by the rest of his party. Within minutes they came upon the scene of the kill. The gyrfalcon pinned the duck to the floor and held its wings out wide, squawking loudly as if inviting compliments on her excellent kill. Perry dismounted and fed the bird a piece of raw flesh from a pouch before replacing the hood and handing her back to one of the squires. Gwenllian picked up the duck, its green-and-silver plumage speckled with blood where the claws of the gyrfalcon had pierced its chest.

'A fine bird, with plenty of meat on the breast,' said the king. 'Place it in your bag, Gwenllian. The flight was yours, as is the prize.'

'If the prize is mine,' said Gwenllian, 'then allow me to present it to my champion.' She turned to the falconer. 'Master Perry, I trust the birds will be fed when we return to Aberffraw?'

'They will, my lady.'

'In that case, this evening Diana will dine on the most succulent of duck breasts. A meal fitting for royalty such as her.' Gwenllian held up the duck and the falconer smiled as he put the bird in his own sack.

'I'm sure she will greatly appreciate the feast,' he said.

'Enough,' said the king. 'Let us regain the high ground. Perhaps there is still time to take a hare before the light fades.'

The group turned to ride up the slope but one of the knights stayed where he was, staring into the distance. The king turned to follow his gaze, as always finely attuned to the ways of his men.

'My lord,' said Osian, the knight in charge of the king's bodyguard, 'it looks like we have company. Look to the left of the hill.'

'A single man worries me not,' said Gruffydd, seeing a lone rider coming towards them, 'but we will see who he is. Come.'

Gruffydd and the other knights led the way, leaving Gwenllian, the falconer and the squires close behind.

'It looks like a monk,' said Gruffydd as the rider got closer.

'Since when does a monk ride a horse as fine as that?' asked Osian, admiring the black stallion.

'A point well made,' said Gruffydd. 'The rest of you, stay here. Osian and I will take a closer look.'

Across the field, the rider drew nearer, his face covered by the deep hood of his drab grey cloak. Gruffydd's hand crept unconsciously to his sword.

'Hold there, stranger,' shouted Osian. 'Who dares cross the land of Gruffydd ap Cynan uninvited, with neither colours nor banner?'

'This land belongs to all of Wales,' replied the man, reining in his horse, 'and I would have parley with this man who calls himself king.' Osian's hand went to the hilt of his sword, but the sound of Gruffydd's laugh made him pause and look across to his king.

'My lord?' he asked, confusion written all across his face. 'I will not allow this man to insult you so.'

'Stay your hand,' said Gruffydd. 'This man's voice is known to me for I have heard his uncouth insults over many a tankard.'

'Indeed,' called the man with a laugh of his own, 'and if I recall correctly, it was usually my purse that was much the lighter after our visits to the tavern.' He reached up and pulled back his hood, making the smile on Gruffydd's face even wider.

'By all that is holy,' said Gruffydd. 'Cynwrig the Tall, my old friend.' He spurred his horse forward, grasping the other man's wrist in friendship.

'My lord,' said Cynwrig. 'It has been a long time.'

'Almost two years,' replied Gruffydd. 'I heard you managed to kill Huw the Fat, so I planned a feast in your honour, but you never returned. I thought you must have been caught and hanged by the English.'

'No, I made good my escape,' replied Cynwrig. 'But for a while I would have welcomed death, such was the weight upon my conscience.'

'Why?' asked Gruffydd. 'I have seen many men fall to your sword. Surely the death of one who was responsible for the murder of your family does not warrant the slightest regret?'

'You would think not, but as he died begging for mercy, I felt a great weight in my heart and decided I never again wanted to see the light of life flee a man's eyes. I wandered for an age, not knowing where my future lay, no better than a beggar, but eventually I was given succour by a priest and everything became clearer. As penance for my violence I would give my life to God, and so I entered the cathedral of Saint David as a novice.'

Gruffydd gazed at the man who had saved his life. 'And now you are a priest?'

'In name only for I have no church. However, I have been sent north by the archbishop to continue my studies at Aberdaron.'

'St Hywen's,' said Gruffydd, his eyes opening with recognition. 'It is the same church that offered me sanctuary during my struggle for the Crown of Gwynedd.'

'I know,' said Cynwrig. 'And it is for this reason I accepted the position. Powys holds too many memories, while St Hywen's still has a link to those I now call family.'

'Those are very kind words, my friend,' said Gruffydd. 'And though my heart is saddened by the loss of a great soldier and close comrade, it is also lightened by the fact you are alive and have a settled mind. I know you are keen to get to your church but first you must accompany me back to Aberffraw and see Angharad once again.' He turned and called out to the rest of the party. 'Gwenllian, come forth and meet an old friend of ours.'

His daughter rode up and nodded in deference to the man of God but showed no sign of recognition.

'I take it you have no memory of him?' laughed Gruffydd. 'This is Cynwrig the Tall, the man who saved my life and treated you as a daughter when you were still a little girl.'

'Forgive me, Father,' said Gwenllian. 'I remember the name for it is oft spoken in our house, but the memories escape me.'

'You were a very little girl,' said Cynwrig with a smile, 'though if I recall correctly, one who could hold her own against her brothers.'

'And still can,' said Gruffydd. 'Time has not softened her temper or eased her ambition for conflict.'

'Really?' said Cynwrig. 'I would have thought you would have softened into a lady like your mother by now.'

'The ways of the ladies at court are like poison to me,' said Gwenllian. 'When I am older, I will ride at Cadwgan's side and drive the English from our land.'

'Really?' replied Cynwrig with surprise. 'And may I ask why that is?'

'Any man who needs this explaining casts doubt on his own heritage,' said Gwenllian.

'Please, humour me. I am interested why someone so young and beautiful harbours so much bitterness and desire for warfare.'

'Just look to our past,' replied Gwenllian. 'Our own stories and tales of our ancestors are rich with valour and pride, yet everything that has gone before is at risk of disappearing from our memories at the whim of a foreign king, himself the son of an invader. What right does he have to tax our people, steal our lands and rob us of our history?'

Cynwrig looked at Gruffydd, amusement on his face. 'Methinks perhaps she has listened to too many tales around the campfires.'

'Oh, she is quite serious, Cynwrig,' said Gruffydd with a laugh. 'My beautiful daughter has grown up with the stories of Mynydd Carn and looks to carry the mantle forward alongside her brothers.'

'The battlefield surely has no place for someone so pretty,' said Cynwrig, 'and I hope there will never be a need for men to die in battle ever again. The treaty seems to be working, and men enjoy the sleep of comfort in their beds, knowing that war is never the answer.'

'I recognise no treaty,' said Gwenllian. 'Our country is occupied, and if the men of Wales seek their beds like frightened dogs, then let them do so. I will honour my father's will as long as I live under his roof but should the day come when Wales needs her people to rise again, I for one will answer that call, treaty or no treaty.'

'You speak the words of foolish men,' replied Cynwrig, his grin turning to a frown, 'yet you are still a little girl. Perhaps when you are a little wiser you may see the world through different eyes.'

'Enough,' said Gruffydd, anticipating his daughter's imminent outburst at Cynwrig's patronising tone. 'Let us leave for Aberffraw immediately and you can tell us more about your adventures over hot ale and cold pork.'

'In that case, lead the way, my friend,' said Cynwrig. 'I look forward to seeing your beautiful wife once more, and a tankard by the fire sounds most inviting.'

Together, the two friends rode north-west towards the wooden bridge spanning the salty straits separating the mainland from the island of Ynys Mon. As they rode, they laughed freely and exchanged stories, both completely unaware that within a few short years, the king's hand would once more wield good Welsh steel against the might of the English army.

The Castle at Cenarth Bychan

December 18th, AD 1109

Nesta stood atop the highest tower of the castle keep, looking down at the village and the river Teifi in the valley below. She knew there would be merriment in the taverns of the village as people arrived from all over Wales to enjoy the festival. Her face eased into a smile at the thought of so much happiness, and the memories of her own happier times came flooding back.

When she was a young girl, Nesta's mother would host grand feasts in the halls of Dinefwr and lords from miles around would travel for days to sample their hospitality without fear of injury. Minstrels would play jolly tunes and Nesta would often creep down from her quarters in the tower to peer from behind tapestries, witnessing the dancing and merriment. Once her mother had spied her and, far from being annoyed, had actually brought her out to sit on her knee. Those were special memories for Nesta and her heart yearned to feel that way again, free and excited for the future rather than trapped in a loveless marriage of convenience.

Her long, dark hair waved gently in the wind and her eyes closed as she smiled softly, enjoying the freshness of the sea breeze blowing in from the coast. Over the next few days, the village would be alive with minstrels, bards and storytellers from all over Wales, each eager to tell their stories of Welsh heroes over many generations. Children would dress up and act out great battles, while poets would regale enthralled audiences with tales of tragedy and heroism in equal measure.

Everyone was excited, for it was the first celebration to be held openly in Wales for many a year without fear of sanctions by the English. Indeed, the new treaty between the Welsh nobles and King Henry meant that it was going ahead with the English Crown's blessing, and Nesta's husband had been invited as guest of honour. Gerald and Nesta had travelled from their home at Pembroke Castle over the previous two days along with two of their sons, Henry and William. The journey had been testing and they had stopped halfway to rest in the manor house of one of Gerald's trusted men before resuming their journey and arriving at Cenarth Bychan earlier that day.

'Mother, let me see,' called a voice. Nesta turned to pick up her son, Henry, holding him tightly as they both peered down into the valley below.

'Are there brigands down there?' asked the boy nervously.

'Yes,' said Nesta. 'You are not to wander from the gates of the castle without me or your father. The nasty men may take you away and feed you to the wolves.'

'Is Hywel a brigand, Mother?' asked the boy. 'Will he feed me to the wolves?'

'Hywel? Don't be silly, Henry, he is my brother and a good man. What makes you say that?'

'Some of the other boys at home said he was a rebel and was sent away to be hanged by Father. They also said Tarw will be hanged if he ever returns from Ireland.'

'Don't you listen to boys who know no better, Henry. Both my brothers are good men and would lay down their lives for you if needs be.'

'So why don't we see them any more?'

'Tarw has returned to Ireland to finish his training with King Murcat, while Hywel resides in the halls of the Cathedral of Saint David.'

'He has been there a long time.'

'Indeed, for he was very ill and though he now fairs much better, he has made a new life amongst the priesthood.'

'Why can't he come and live with us?'

'It is very difficult to explain, Henry. Some people loyal to the king see him as a threat and would have him thrown into a dungeon if he should ever leave, so he is safer where he is. Don't forget, he spent many years as a prisoner and if it wasn't for Tarw, he would have died there.'

'Did Tarw rescue him?'

'He did.'

'That makes him a traitor to the Crown.'

Nesta sighed deeply. Despite her bringing up her children with the stories of their Welsh ancestors, it was obvious that living in an English castle surrounded by soldiers of the Crown was having an effect on their perception of their place in the world, and though, as the son of the king, young Henry's allegiance to England was to be expected, it worried her that his viewpoint would be clouded by misguided loyalty.

'Henry, there are many things you don't understand,' she continued. 'Your father may be the king of England but my father was the king of Deheubarth before he died. That makes both Tarw and Hywel Welsh princes, but the English Crown doesn't agree and worries there may be a war. That is why there are so many soldiers in our country, to stop that war taking place.'

'If there is a war, Mother, which side would we be on?'

Nesta stared at her son, momentarily lost for an answer, but before she could respond, Gerald walked through the doorway behind her.

'There you are,' he said. 'I was beginning to wonder where you were.'

Nesta braced at the sound of her husband's voice and, after taking a deep breath, turned to face him, a false smile upon her face. She lowered Henry to the floor and kissed her son on the cheek.

'Go down to our quarters,' she said, 'and have Emma prepare you for bed. Perhaps we will talk some more of these things on the morrow.'

Henry ran through into the stairwell and disappeared from sight.

'Gerald,' said Nesta when he had gone, 'I thought you were enjoying ale with your men.'

'I was,' said the knight, walking towards her, 'but the weariness of the journey catches up with me. My bed calls and I would have you join me. What brings you up here?'

'I have missed these views,' said Nesta, turning away, 'and was keen to come up here as soon as possible. We should stay here more often.'

'It is truly striking,' said Gerald, 'though the sea is quite far away.'

'We can't compare it to Pembroke,' said Nesta, 'for each place is beautiful in its own right. At home we are almost upon the shore itself, but here you have the majesty of the gorge wed to the green of the landscape. We should appreciate both for what they are.'

'God does indeed paint a pretty picture, Nesta, but I can't help seeing it with the eye of a soldier.'

'In what way?'

Gerald peered over the parapet. Unlike other motte and bailey castles, this one had its tower built against the far wall of the outer defences to take advantage of the steep drop to its rear. The castle had been built two years previously, when Cadwgan and his rebels threatened to overrun the west coast, but after almost losing the castle to an unexpected assault, Gerald had commissioned improvements and a redesign of the inner tower.

'The builders have served me well these past months,' said Gerald over his shoulder, 'and the keep would now be difficult to breach from this direction. Certainly there could be no assault from the river for the climb is too hard, but the front palisade is still weak by comparison. Once the celebrations are over, I will have my architect design stronger walls. I may even see if our finances will stretch to stone rather than timber.'

'Why waste all that money?' asked Nesta. 'Peace now prevails throughout Wales, so surely it is better spent elsewhere.'

'On the contrary,' said Gerald, turning to face his wife, 'it is at times such as these when it is even more important we guard against assault. To do otherwise invites attack from those who see our actions as weakness.'

'Even though there are signed treaties?'

'Treaties can be broken, Nesta. Even tomorrow we put ourselves at risk, and if it wasn't for the instructions of the king we would still be in Pembroke, safely sat alongside our own hearth.'

'What do you mean?'

'I talk of Cadwgan ap Bleddyn. That man alone is responsible for the deaths of hundreds of our countrymen.'

'*Your* countrymen,' corrected Nesta without thinking. 'Do not forget I am Welsh-born.' She stopped suddenly, knowing that she may have overstepped the mark and to do so often invited Gerald's ire.

'And you should not forget you are my wife by the grace of the king!' shouted Gerald. 'And as such you assume my nationality and allegiances. Cadwgan was and still is responsible for the deaths of many on both sides of the Marches, including those born of Welsh mothers. Tomorrow he will be in reach of my blade, yet instead of avenging my comrades, I will be supping wine with him as if we were long-lost brothers. The thought sickens me to the stomach.'

'Cadwgan may have been a rebel, Gerald, but even he now observes the treaty. To dwell on events long past only feeds the embers that still smoulder between the English and the Welsh.'

'Such embers are never extinguished, Nesta, and I would thank you to stay out of the affairs of men. Now, I am away to our chambers and I expect you to follow me. I have a tiredness about me and it would serve you ill to keep me waiting.'

He turned away and walked down the steps leading to their chambers, leaving his long-suffering wife staring out over the woodlands. She closed her eyes and breathed in the sharp winter air, the iciness cutting into her lungs like the sharpest blade.

Memories of her childhood came flooding back again, the happy times when, as children, she and her brother played in the snows outside their father's castle at Dinefwr. In particular, she recalled the excitement when the hunt had gone well and they both leaned over the parapets, eager to see what bounty the hunters' arrows and spears had felled for the table. Any successful hunt was always celebrated with a feast, and the celebrations in the great hall brought a warm feeling of contentment to her.

They were happy days, and often her mother would sit them both on her knee in front of a roaring fire and regale them with tales of their ancestors, of princes and kings and great Welsh battles. A time when all Welshmen served no other masters except those with royal birthright within their own country's borders.

Those days were long gone, and if her mother had told her all those years ago she would one day be locked in a loveless marriage to an English knight while bringing up the English king's bastard son, then she would have run away to Ireland at the first opportunity.

With a sigh she came back to reality and gazed out at the landscape one last time. To keep Gerald waiting invited admonishment and though her husband had never beaten her, his words were as painful as the heaviest club.

It had not always been like this, for the first time they had ever met, in Windsor, they had both been attracted to each other, but after she had fallen for the yet uncrowned Prince Henry they had gone their separate ways. Years later, they were reunited at the whim of the king and despite assurances to the opposite, she couldn't help but think that

Gerald saw her as used goods, only accepting her as his wife to please Henry.

With a heavy heart she descended the steps to their quarters, ready to do her wifely duty. For a few seconds she paused before the door, before regaining the false smile she had worn only minutes earlier. Hopefully he would be quick and fall asleep soon after, as was his wont these days, and though she missed the passion and intimacy she had once enjoyed with the king, at least it meant she would be free to dream of a different time, a different fate.

———

The following afternoon, Gerald and Nesta walked down to the town with their entourage. The streets were alive with entertainers and people laughed freely at the jesters and gaudily dressed dwarves as they executed their routines with skill and no little bravery. Fire eaters performed to child and adult alike, causing jaws to drop in amazement, and the air was alive with music. Minstrels sat at the sides of the streets playing their instruments, hoping for coins to be dropped in the hats at their feet, while wenches enticed already drunk men into their taverns. Whores stood discreetly on the corners, seeking more personal attention from the many newcomers into the town, and pie sellers did a roaring trade, meeting the needs of anyone seeking a cheap meal.

'Well it certainly is lively,' said Nesta as they made their way through the crowd.

'Not what I expected at all,' moaned Gerald. 'I hope the main events have a bit more decorum about them.'

'You worry too much,' replied Nesta, tossing a coin towards a dwarf balancing on the shoulders of a stilt walker. 'And you should enjoy yourself more.'

Gerald grunted in reply but said nothing. Soon they reached the central square and could see a crowd facing a platform containing a trio of performers juggling flaming axes between them. Behind the crowd another platform had been built, this time containing nought but a row of empty chairs.

'It looks like we are early,' said Nesta.

'On the contrary,' said Gerald, 'we are just in time.' Nesta followed his gaze and saw a fat man swathed in a cloak of forest green striding towards them. Though he seemed unarmed, like Gerald's party he was accompanied by a bodyguard of several men, and both sets of warriors eyed each other warily.

'My lord,' said the man, coming to a halt before Gerald and removing his ornate gauntlet. 'Please allow me to introduce myself. I am Simon of Worcester, sheriff of Ceredigion and loyal subject of King Henry. Welcome to our celebration.' He bowed slightly in deference to the knight's higher station.

'I am pleased to meet you, Simon,' replied Gerald, accepting the handshake. 'It is rare that I find a Welshman who swears fealty to an English king as readily as you.'

'My countrymen can be blinkered at times, my lord,' said the sheriff, 'and many need to see the way the world is changing. The quicker they accept Henry's rule without question, the sooner peace will be the norm, not an exception.'

Gerald nodded in agreement but inside he had already decided he did not like this man. Welsh or not, in his experience anyone who denied his own countrymen so easily could never be trusted. His appointment was new, and though his girth and gaudy trappings meant he was obviously well rewarded for his loyalty, the guards around him were evidence he was already unpopular in Ceredigion.

'I understand you slept within the walls of Cenarth Bychan last night,' said the sheriff. 'I trust you found my preparations suitable?'

'Indeed,' said Gerald, 'and the meal was particularly welcome.'

'I'm glad,' said the sheriff. 'Of course, the cost was prohibitive but I trust the king will issue recompense in due course?'

'You will be compensated from my own purse,' said Gerald. He turned away, keen to cut short the conversation. He beckoned Nesta forward. 'This is Nesta ferch Rhys, my wife.'

'Of course,' said the sheriff, taking Nesta's hand and kissing it gently. 'I recall dining at your father's castle many years ago, my lady, and a little girl appeared from her chambers, upset at all the noise. It seems that little girl has matured into a very beautiful lady.'

'Thank you, my lord,' said Nesta. 'Unfortunately I have no recollection of you.'

'No, it was a long time ago and before . . .' He stopped, realising the conversation was not going the way he had hoped.

'Before what?' asked Nesta innocently.

'Before the good sheriff changed allegiances,' smirked Gerald before the fat man could respond. 'Now, is there somewhere we can get a drink?'

'Of course,' said the sheriff. 'I have a tent situated behind the viewing platform. I'm sure you will find everything to your satisfaction.'

Simon of Worcester led the way, and for a while Gerald endured his company, listening to tales of how efficient he was in the administration of the king's estates. However, the ordeal finally became too much and the castellan sought out the company of his own bodyguards, preferring the familiar shared tales of battles long fought, as was the wont of all soldiers.

Eventually a messenger entered and spoke quietly to Simon, who then turned to Gerald. 'My lord, may I have a word?'

Gerald nodded and joined Simon to one side of the tent. 'What is it?'

'My lord, I know you are aware we have other guests today and I am informed they will be here momentarily.'

'You speak of Cadwgan, I assume?' said Gerald.

'I do, and I want to check with you regarding the seating arrangements. In the circumstances, do you want me to seat him at the far end of the seats, away from you and the Lady Nesta?'

'And why would you do that?'

'I am aware that you hold no respect for Cadwgan, and thought you may see it as an insult to be seated next to a man who once ravaged the north of this country with his rebel army.'

'Sheriff, you are correct in assuming I have no allegiances with this man, or indeed intend any friendship. However, the king himself asked for this meeting to go ahead in the interests of the treaty. So, despite my reservations, I will do as I am bid by my monarch and treat this man as a fellow guest. Nothing more, nothing less. Do as you will with the seats, I have no interest either way.'

'Of course, my lord,' said Simon, and he bowed slightly before walking away. 'My friends,' he said, clapping his hands and raising his voice to be heard, 'the main activities are about to commence, so if you will please accompany me, it is time to be seated.' Everyone made their way outside and was shown to their seats.

Before them the crowd had increased in size and vendors carrying trays of food and ale forced their way between the throng, their voices filling the air as they tried to sell their wares. The stage was now empty and all the earlier performers had disappeared, their frivolity done for the day. Nesta gazed around the crowd as Simon sought to re-engage Gerald in conversation, drinking in the splendour of the spectacle. Slowly she scanned the crowd, taking in the smiling faces, most of whom had obviously endured times of hardship and war. At last they could sleep in peace, no matter how precarious.

Nesta's gaze suddenly stopped and she stared in shock at a group of men making their way towards the stage. In all there were twelve warriors, each dressed in the leather armour common amongst the Welsh knights, and at their forefront were two men, one markedly older than the other. Nesta assumed correctly that this was the famed rebel, Cadwgan ap Bleddyn, now walking as free as a bird amongst the villagers, fully aware that under the terms of the treaty he was free from any threat from the king's men, but it was the younger man that had made her gasp aloud. He was at least a head taller than any of his comrades and his unkempt fair hair made him stand out from the crowd.

As she watched, the man lifted his head and met her stare across the sea of people between them. For a second she held his gaze, sharing the moment of recognition, but as the colour raced to her cheeks, she turned her head away, her heart racing, yet feeling sick to her stomach.

'My lady, are you well?' whispered Emma, seeing her mistress's distress.

'Yes,' stuttered Nesta quickly. 'Though it seems my goblet runs dry. Please arrange a refill.'

'Wine?'

'No, please could you get some honeyed water?'

'Of course,' said Emma, and she turned to summon a servant.

Nesta's mind worked furiously. If she was correct, the man across the square was none other than Owain ap Cadwgan, the rebel who had helped her family release her brother from captivity several years earlier, and though she had met him only once, he was one of only two men who had ever made her heart race with desire.

'Nesta,' said Gerald, turning to his wife. 'You look like you have seen a ghost. Are you well?'

'Of course,' said Nesta, though deep inside she was shaking like an autumn leaf. 'I believe the wine has had an unfortunate effect on my stomach, but I have requested some water. Please do not fret on my account.'

'The wine is the best available in these parts,' blustered Simon, 'and cost a pretty penny. I'm sure it must be something else.'

Gerald ignored him and leaned forward.

'If you want to return to the castle, just say and I'll have them bring a cart.'

'I'll be fine,' said Nesta. 'We are here now and should not miss the performance.' She leaned forward and whispered into Gerald's ear.

'Besides, as odious as the man is, he has gone to a lot of trouble on our behalf. It would be rude to retire at so early a juncture.'

Gerald smiled, pleased his judgement of the sheriff was obviously shared by his wife.

'So be it,' he said, 'but not a moment longer than is needed.'

Nesta nodded and turned to accept a goblet of water from Emma.

'Ah,' said Simon, looking up, 'it seems the remainder of our guests have arrived. My lord, may I introduce Cadwgan ap Bleddyn, prince of Powys, and his son, Owain.'

Gerald rose from his chair and nodded slightly, acknowledging the two men's presence and station.

'This, of course,' continued Simon, 'is Gerald of Windsor, castellan of Pembroke Castle and second to Henry himself.'

It was Cadwgan's turn to bow slightly, as did Owain, but markedly no man extended the hand of friendship.

'Sir Gerald,' said Cadwgan, 'it is an honour to finally meet you, especially as you are obviously held in so much esteem by the king of England.'

'And it is intriguing to meet the man who led our forces such a merry dance over the last few years,' said Gerald.

'An outcome aided by our landscape,' said Cadwgan.

'Indeed,' said Gerald, 'but let us hope those days are behind us and that we can become friendly, if not friends.'

'As a fellow knight, I agree with your sentiment, Sir Gerald.'

Gerald was about to comment that he saw Cadwgan as no knight, but just a rebel with an unrecognised title, when he felt Nesta squeeze his arm, and he put the thought to the back of his mind.

'Are these your men?' he asked, nodding towards the rest of the warriors.

'Just a precaution, and no more than your own, I would suggest,' said Cadwgan.

'Indeed,' said Gerald, 'but I assure you I intend to fully honour the treaty and you are at no risk.'

'In that case,' responded Cadwgan, 'I will take your word and ask my men to withdraw.'

He nodded to one of his sergeants, who led the bodyguard over to the nearby tavern. Far enough away to be unobtrusive yet near enough to be on call.

'Please, shall we take our seats?' said Simon, intervening in the tense conversation.

'First I would be introduced to the lady at Gerald's side,' said Cadwgan. 'Though if truth be told, she needs no introduction, for her beauty is louder than the greatest herald. Do I have the honour of addressing Nesta ferch Rhys?'

'You do,' said Gerald, stepping to one side. 'This is my wife, Nesta.'

Cadwgan took Nesta's hand and kissed it gently.

'My lady, I am honoured to meet you at last. Your father was an inspiration and Deheubarth is extremely lucky to have a Tewdwr to look up to.'

'Thank you, Lord Cadwgan,' said Nesta, 'but it is my husband who rules Deheubarth on behalf of the king, not I.'

'Perhaps on the royal parchments,' said Cadwgan with a smile, 'but in my experience, the lady of the house often has the last word behind closed doors. Is that not the case, Sir Gerald?'

'Something like that,' said Gerald.

'This is my son,' said Cadwgan, turning to indicate Owain at his side. 'I believe you have met?'

'Once, many years ago, and for a moment only,' said Nesta. 'It is good to see you again, Owain.'

'And you, Lady Nesta,' said Owain, and he kissed her hand gently.

Despite her exterior being the model of decorum and calm, inside Nesta's heart was racing as fast as if she was running a race. Quickly she turned away.

'Shall we sit?' she asked, desperate to hide her blushes.

Gerald and Cadwgan took the two centre seats, while Nesta sat at the end of the line alongside her maid. Just as she settled, Owain followed her over and coughed gently to attract her attention.

'My lady,' he said, 'would it be improper to request I sit alongside you? I know no one else here and feel that due to our previous meeting, albeit ever so short, at least we may have something in common.'

Nesta hesitated but before she could decline, Emma got to her feet and made way for the prince.

'You can have my seat,' she said. 'I will sit on the bench.'

'Emma . . .' started Nesta.

'My lady, I am fine,' replied Emma. 'My lord, please be seated.'

'Thank you, Emma,' said Owain with a disarming smile. This time it was the maid's turn to blush.

'What do you think you are doing?' hissed Nesta under her breath as the handsome man sat at her side.

'Just waiting to enjoy the celebrations,' replied Owain, 'the same as you.'

Nesta glanced across and met his gaze. Again her heart skipped a beat and for once she was lost for words. Owain was without doubt the most handsome man she had ever met and like many women before her, she was instantly in his thrall.

⌣

'So,' sighed Gerald, turning to Simon. 'What are we to expect as entertainment this fine day?'

'Unfortunately, my lord,' whispered Simon, leaning forward, 'the entertainment is distinctly Welsh in flavour. You will understand that if I had my way, there would be far more minstrels with tales of Henry's triumphs, but alas, I am tasked with keeping these people happy so I had to make allowances.'

'It is their day, is it not?' asked Gerald.

'I thought the flavour would be offensive to you,' said Simon, 'bearing in mind your heritage.'

'Remove such things from your mind, Simon. My wife is as Welsh as any person here and will no doubt relish such entertainment. So please tell me what we can expect.'

'Well,' replied Simon, 'there are several minstrels with songs of the Welsh princes and a bard with an ode to Hywel Dda. I believe there is a short farce about the traitor Meirion Goch but the main event is a recital about the battle of Mynydd Carn. It has been especially commissioned by the lords of Ynys Mon in deference to Gruffydd ap Cynan and is said to be a truly wonderful piece.'

'It sounds wonderful,' said Nesta, but she glanced towards Gerald. Though it had been made clear that this was a celebration of all things Welsh, the constant reference to local heroes and battles must have been hard to take. However, Gerald was unperturbed and as the final guests took to their seats, the entertainment started.

'It's good to see you again, Nesta,' said Owain after a few minutes.

'And you,' said Nesta without turning. 'Are you well?'

'No, actually,' said Owain, 'I am quite ill.'

Nesta turned quickly to face him. 'Really? I am sorry to hear that, Master Owain, prey tell what ails you.'

'An affliction as deadly as any blade or lance, and many men have fallen to its ravages. Luckily there is a cure.'

'What is this disease?' asked Nesta, intrigued. 'And what is the nature of the cure? Perhaps I can help. I have access to an excellent physician.'

'You could indeed help, Lady Nesta, though I am beyond the aid of even the finest physician. I have a broken heart, which can only be fixed by the love of a good woman.'

Nesta stared at Owain, her eyes narrowing in suspicion. 'Master Owain, are you jesting with me?'

'On the contrary,' he said, 'I am deadly serious.'

Something touched Nesta's fingers between their chairs and she glanced down to see Owain's hand seeking out hers. Instantly she snatched her hand away and glared at him.

'What do you think you are doing?' she hissed. 'Are you mad?'

'Completely,' he said. 'Nesta, you have been in my thoughts since the day we met and I knew we had to meet again. Unfortunately, the war prevented that, but now we are at peace, the opportunities have come more frequently.'

'You are talking nonsense,' said Nesta. 'This is the only time I have seen you since that day I paid you for your aid in releasing my brother.'

'You may not have seen me,' said Owain, 'but I have seen you on many, many occasions.'

'What do you mean? Explain yourself.'

'Well,' said Owain, 'first of all, I would like to compliment you on your beautiful dress. Red is certainly your colour. Did you buy it here?'

'No,' she replied, 'as you are well aware.'

'Just a little gift. I would have approached but you were heavily guarded.'

'Owain, what is all this about?'

'All will become clear, Lady Nesta,' he replied. 'But can I just say that when I first saw you all those years ago, I thought your beauty would never be surpassed. However, I was wrong. The vision before me today makes the young woman who refused me a kiss pale into significance.'

Nesta blushed again but was lost for words. Never had she reacted in this way to any man and she had no idea how to respond.

'Thank you,' she stuttered, 'but we should watch the presentations.'

'Of course,' said Owain, and he smiled again before turning to face the performers on the opposite stage. Once again Nesta felt his fingers brush hers, but this time she left her hand where it was.

———⌣———

For the next hour or so, everyone's attention was taken up by the various artists on the stage, and for a while, Nesta was distracted, her worries forgotten as she revelled in the colourful tales about her heritage. Finally, the event came to a close and she climbed down from the viewing platform, leaving Gerald to bid their farewells to their host. Patiently she and her maid waited for him to finish, and stood talking quietly about the excellent entertainment they had just witnessed.

'My lady,' said a voice, and Nesta turned to see Owain ap Cadwgan standing behind her.

'Owain,' she said, glancing around. 'Did you enjoy the recitals?'

'Indeed I did, but there is something I would discuss with you. Do you have a moment?'

Nesta paused before turning to her maid. 'Emma, could you bring me a flask of that excellent honeyed water you found earlier? I would take some back to the castle for my bedtime drink, such was its flavour.'

'Of course, my lady,' said Emma, and she disappeared into the crowd, leaving Owain and Nesta alone at the side of the stage.

'So, how can I help you?' said Nesta.

'Nesta, we don't have much time so I will be straight with you. I want you to come away with me.'

Nesta's mouth opened slightly in astonishment. '*What?*'

'I know it sounds ridiculous, but it makes complete sense,' continued Owain. 'You are a princess of Deheubarth and I am a prince of Powys. We should be together.'

Nesta shook her head slowly. 'You are truly mad, and I will pretend this conversation never took place. Now, if you will excuse me, I have to return to my husband.' She turned to leave but Owain grasped her arm.

'Wait,' he said, and he spun her around to face him.

'Owain, please release me,' she said quietly.

'Please, just hear me out.'

'There is nothing to discuss, Owain. I am with Gerald, that's all there is to it. Now let me go before I call for help.'

'Go ahead,' he said, releasing her arm. 'Call out and accuse me, if you dare. Men will die here and the treaty will be broken, and for what reason? Just because you wouldn't listen to a few words. Remember, I helped save your brother, so at least have the decency to hear me speak.'

Nesta paused before turning to face him again. 'Owain, I will be forever grateful for your part in Hywel's rescue but that does not give you leave to pursue a course of conversation uncomfortable to me. I would appreciate it if you allow me to leave.'

'To go where?' asked Owain. 'Back into the arms of an Englishman?'

'Gerald is my husband and his bloodline is none of your concern.'

'Oh, but it is,' said Owain. 'I have watched you both and listened to the way you talk. Your face lights up whenever anyone discusses this land or our heritage, while his is creased with scowls and disdain. How can you bring yourself to live with such a man, when the Welsh blood in your veins runs as fierce as mine?'

'The wars are over, Owain, and Wales is at peace. Gerald is a good husband and I would have no man speak ill of him.'

'Do you love him?'

'*What?*'

'Do you love him?'

'Of course I do,' said Nesta. 'He is brave and loyal and would die rather than see me or my children hurt.'

'So you love him as you would a guard dog.'

'Of course not. I mean, yes but . . .'

'Nesta, be true to yourself,' said Owain. 'I truly believe you would die for this country if necessary, yet the fire in your eyes is but embers compared to what it used to be. Break free from this unholy union and take your place back amongst the royalty of Wales where you belong.' He grabbed her by both arms and looked deeply into her eyes. 'Meet me tonight outside the walls of Cenarth Bychan. Ride away with me under the stars and I will see those embers flame with passion.'

'*What?*' Nesta asked again.

'You heard me. For an age I have tried to fight the memory of you, losing myself in lakes of ale. I have sought solace in the arms of the most beautiful women in Wales, yet each one is unfit to even walk in your shadow. I have tried, Nesta, I really have, but I have finally admitted defeat and know I must have you at my side.'

'This is ridiculous,' said Nesta, glancing around to ensure they were not overheard. 'I am a married woman, Owain, and the fact that I am in the company of my husband is an insult to us both.'

'I didn't want it to turn out this way,' said Owain, 'but you are a hard woman to approach. I have tried on several occasions over the past few months but your castellan has you guarded like the most coveted treasure. But enough talk, Nesta. Embrace the person you are and make the break before it is too late. Just imagine the loyalty we could command – you a princess of Deheubarth, and me a prince of Powys. Together we could rival the house of Gruffydd ap Cynan himself and take our place as a truly royal union, born of Welsh kings and descendants of Hywel Dda. Even Henry himself would have no choice but to acknowledge our claim.'

'*You are truly mad*,' gasped Nesta, her heart racing. 'There can never be anything between us.'

'But there can,' said Owain. 'You were a free spirit once, Nesta, and can be again. Come with me tonight and we will make a life together in the wilds of Snowdonia. Our castles will be the mountains and our towns will be the forests. We will drink the purest water and eat the fruits of God's bounty. I mean it, Nesta. You are better than this. You should be as free as a hawk, not some Englishman's plaything.'

'You have lost your mind,' said Nesta, pulling her arms away once more. 'We have met only twice but your arrogance is astounding. Why do you think I would even be interested in you?'

'Because I see it in your eyes and on your face. I hear it in the tone of your voice and feel it in the fire of your touch.'

'Then you are drunk from the ale still upon your breath,' said Nesta. 'You are a stranger to me, Owain, and your arrogance borders on insult.'

'Really?' asked Owain as he looked again into her eyes. His hand reached out and touched her neck gently. His voice lowered. 'Then tell me you don't feel it, Nesta, and if I see the truth in your eyes, I will walk away, never to return.'

Nesta hesitated.

'Well?' he continued.

'Owain, this has gone on enough. Your ardour is flattering but you talk of things that cannot be. Perhaps if things were different, there may have been a chance, but alas, we are where we are. The fight against the English is over and my place is at Gerald's side, for it is there that I can best serve my people.'

'As the wife of an English castellan?'

'If needs be. I am flattered, but lives such as you seek are found only in the songs of minstrels. As much as it hurts me to say it, I fear a free Wales is an ideal we can no longer reach. The best we can hope for is a measure of self-rule, yet beholding to the English Crown.'

'Then what about us?'

'There is no us, Owain, nor can there ever be.'

'You just said that if the situation was different we may have had a chance. What did you mean?'

'I meant that the things you speak of do indeed pull at my heart, but alas, they can never be.'

'What if I can change things, Nesta, what if I make it all possible?'

For a moment she hesitated, imagining herself at this handsome man's side, riding across a free Wales. She held his burning gaze, desperate to reach out, to return the passion in his eyes, but reason tempered her desire and she breathed deeply as she came crashing back to reality.

'Perhaps in another life, Owain, but I fear this one can deliver no such dreams. Now, I suggest you be gone before my husband sees your unhealthy interest and has you flogged in the street.' She turned away and walked over to the group of men now talking to her husband.

Owain stared after her, his pulse racing. He had been with many, many women over the years but never had any affected him the way she did. For a few moments he considered calling after her, but realising her mind was set he turned and disappeared back into the crowd.

'Gerald,' said Nesta, interrupting her husband's conversation.

The castellan turned and frowned when he saw the look on his wife's face. 'Nesta, you still look unwell.'

'My head aches,' she said, with a tear in her eye. 'Please take me back to Cenarth Bychan.'

The Forests of Montgomery

December 18th, AD 1109

Fifty leagues away, Sir Julian lay blindfolded in the bottom of a cart, his hands tied securely behind his back.

The last two days had been a nightmare for the knight. In addition to the shame of being allowed to live while the rest of his command were slaughtered, he had been tied naked to a tree and beaten remorselessly until he had collapsed through exhaustion and pain. Finally, his captors had cut holes in a stinking sack and forced him to wear it in lieu of clothing, stripping him of all dignity before throwing him into the back of a cart amongst the filth of the previous occupants – a dozen pigs meant for market.

Four guards sat on boxes in the cart, taking turns to keep him awake and in pain. The sacking was sodden from the ice and snow, and he shivered uncontrollably.

'Water,' he croaked.

'Shut up,' said a voice, and he received a kick in the ribs for his trouble.

'Give him a drink,' said a quieter voice. 'We need him alive.'

'A few hours' thirst never hurt any man,' said the first voice. 'If I had my way, I would stick him right now. Just say the word.'

'You know our orders,' said his comrade. 'Now give him a drink, and while you're at it, give him some bread from your satchel.'

Despite some further grumbling, Julian felt himself getting dragged into a sitting position. A few moments later he felt the trickle of water on his upper lip and he opened his mouth wide, gulping at the much-needed drink. All too soon it stopped, but before he could risk asking for more, a fist of bread was forced between his teeth.

'Eat,' said the voice. 'And be quick about it. I have hungry dogs outside who are more deserving of this bread.'

Despite almost choking, Julian chewed as quickly as he could, swallowing hard as the last of the bread disappeared.

'Water,' he said again hopefully.

'No more for you,' said the original voice. Without warning, a hand grabbed his hair and he was thrown back to the floor, sliding across the cart and smashing his face against a box.

Laughter burst out from the other guards and Julian decided to lie still. Despite his predicament, he carried no serious wounds and was still quite strong. As long as he could maintain that state, there was always a chance of escape, but the mood his captors were in, they were far more likely to cause him injury should he protest. For the next hour or so he lay still in the freezing mud, wishing for the hellish journey to come to an end. The occasional kick from one of the guards ensured he stayed awake and he listened carefully to their conversations, hoping to pick up any information about where they were or where they were going. Eventually the cart ground to a halt and the sound of voices outside raised his hope that they were at last at their destination. Sure enough, he heard the back flap being pulled open and the tailgate being lowered.

'Get him out,' said a voice.

'Yes, my lord,' said the familiar voice of one of the guards.

'And put a blanket about him,' said the first man. 'If he dies before Diafol sees him, you will take his place.'

'Of course, my lord,' said the guard, and moments later Julian was dragged from the cart to stand ankle-deep in a pool of water on the track. Unseen hands untied his bindings, but though he rubbed his wrists gratefully, his relief was short-lived as they were retied before him. As promised, a heavy blanket was thrown around his shoulders and he clutched it tightly, relishing the heavy warmth it brought.

'I'll take him from here,' said a new voice. A hand pushed against his back. 'Start walking, Englishman.'

Julian stumbled through some undergrowth before being placed against what felt like a tree and secured to the trunk with a sword belt tied tightly around his chest. Although he could hardly breathe, it was a far more comfortable position than the floor of the cart and he allowed himself the luxury of thinking he may actually survive. After all, why would they go to all this trouble just to have him killed?

One of the guards removed his blindfold, and as Julian blinked to focus his eyes, the remaining guards walked into the forest, where the light from many campfires sent dancing shadows amongst the trees. When all the guards had gone, the knight strained against his bonds, testing to see how secure they actually were, but to no avail. Again and again he tried but it was pointless, the leather strap just cut deeper into his flesh with little sign of loosening.

'You're wasting your time, shiny man,' said a quiet voice, and Sir Julian's head spun to see a warrior unlike any he had ever seen standing just a few paces away.

Julian looked the strange man up and down. The warrior's hair was long and matted and a similarly unkempt beard hung to his chest. His face was smeared with ash and the few teeth remaining in his head were nothing but blackened stumps. Around his upper body hung a heavy cloak made from the pelt of a highland wolf and his legs were clad in a pair of plaid leggings. In his hand he grasped a long spear, tipped with a huge iron bodkin, while from a belt around his waist hung an unsheathed sword and a curved dagger.

'Do you like my knife, shiny man?' asked the warrior, drawing the smaller blade. 'I took it from the dead hands of a Saracen outside Antioch.' He drew the flat of his knife across his palm, before allowing the curved tip to nick his skin. 'Do you know of the Saracen, shiny man? Do you know how they have perfected the art of disembowelment while keeping their victims alive for the buzzards to fight over their entrails? Have you ever been in one of their stinking pits with your comrades' bones as carpets and nought but your own filth to eat. No? I thought not. Your armour was far too shiny to have seen any real conflict.'

'Don't judge me on my appearance, wastrel,' snarled Julian. 'I have heard the tales of the crusade and would gladly have taken the cross had I been called, but it was not in God's plan. My place was here, serving my king. I have fought and bettered many men in combat. Men far more worthy than yourself.'

'What do you call combat, shiny man?' asked the warrior, licking the blood from his palm. 'Riding a destrier while clad in full chainmail, chasing down peasants forced into combat with nought but their scythes for weapons? Is that how you win your spurs these days, by slaughtering the weak in the name of a foreign king?'

'Henry is the rightful king of all Britannia,' said Julian, 'including this godforsaken country you call Wales.'

'A French-born son of a French noble who invaded our country and put a weak king to the sword. Is that what it takes to be a rightful monarch? If so, I would wager there could be many such kings in the future.'

'William may have been French,' spat Julian, 'but Henry is English-born.'

'Or so they claim,' responded the warrior.

Julian was about to retort but had second thoughts, realising he was being taunted by this strange man and there was no way he was ever going to win the argument.

'Lost for words, shiny man?' said the strange man, taking a step forward. 'Let's see if I can loosen that tongue for you.' Without warning he leapt across the space between them and rammed Julian's head back against the tree. Before he could even struggle, the knight felt the razor-sharp edge of the Saracen blade against his throat and he froze in fear.

'What's the matter, Englishman,' hissed the warrior, 'don't you like the look of me? Am I not pretty like your own men, with shiny chain-mail and pretty colours upon their tabards?'

Sir Julian held his breath, waiting for the blade to cut into his flesh, but just as the warrior seemed to brace for the cut, a voice echoed from the trees.

'Dog, put him down.'

The warrior snarled, his eyes glaring wildly and his breath fetid in the face of the prisoner, but he didn't move.

'Dog,' said the distant voice, 'you've had your fun, now leave him be. Diafol is ready to see him.'

The warrior paused a moment longer before easing the pressure on his blade. He stepped half a pace backward but did not take his eyes off the English knight.

'Don't think this is the end of it, shiny man,' he said, 'for if I know Diafol, you will soon be wishing it was my knife that sent you to meet your God.' Before Julian could answer, the warrior lunged forward and slammed his forehead into the knight's face, shattering the bone in his prisoner's nose.

'*Dog!*' shouted the voice again. 'I told you to leave him. Why did you have to do that?'

'Because it made me feel better,' growled the warrior, watching the blood pour from the Englishman's nose. 'Be good, shiny man,' he said. 'See you later.' Before he walked away, he reached out and caught a pool of the knight's blood in his palm before rubbing it over his own face.

Sir Julian looked up, relieved to see the warrior disappearing into the trees. The pain in his nose was excruciating and he could feel more blood running down the back of his throat. He coughed violently, spitting globules of phlegm and blood onto the floor as another two guards approached to release him from his bonds.

'Who was that madman?' gasped Julian.

'Oh, that was just Dog,' said one of the men. 'He likes to have a bit of fun with the prisoners before we hand them over to Diafol.'

'His mind is set in the sewers of hell,' spat Julian, 'and he will surely burn in Satan's fires.'

'I don't think that will worry him much,' said the guard, throwing the restraining belt to one side. 'It would not be anything he hasn't experienced tenfold in the Holy Land.'

'That man took the cross?' asked Julian incredulously.

'I don't think there was any religion involved,' said the second man, 'he just likes to kill for money. Now start walking, Englishman. Diafol has demanded your presence and he doesn't like to be kept waiting.'

'Diafol is a strange name,' said Julian as he staggered forward at the point of a spear. 'I have never heard it spoken before.'

'It is not a name,' said the guard behind him. 'It is more of a title and comes from the old language.'

'What does it mean?' asked Julian, walking towards the distant fires.

'The Devil,' said the guard, 'and a truer title was never held by any man.'

The Forests of Ceredigion

December 19th, AD 1109

Owain ap Cadwgan sat on a forest log, staring into the glowing embers of the campfire. The moon was high in the winter sky and a cloak lay around his shoulders, keeping away the worst of the chill. Several of his most trusted men also sat around the fire, sharing tales of conquest, both military and sexual, while passing around various containers of wine and ale. Despite the scene being comforting and familiar to the rebel prince, Owain was quiet, and avoided being drawn into the usual banter between men of arms.

His thoughts were full of Nesta. Ever since their first meeting several years earlier, he knew she was something special. At first he had tried to dismiss her from his mind, and though his life as a wanted rebel meant there were often more life-threatening situations to concern him, seldom did more than a few days go by without the thoughts of her flooding back to haunt him. He wasn't sure why he was so obsessed. Yes, she was beautiful, but he had shared a bed with many even fairer, and it wasn't even that her manner was courteous, for on the few occasions they had talked she had been dismissive to the point of rudeness.

No, there was something else, a hidden fire that burned behind her eyes, a smouldering passion that just waited to be set free. Deep inside he now knew that his ardour was pointless, and despite his approach at the celebrations, she had made it clear that she would never leave Gerald to be with him.

His fists clenched with frustration. If only she would give him a chance, he would do everything in his power to become the man she dreamed of, no matter what the cost. He leaned forward again and stirred the embers of the fire, his mind a maelstrom of thoughts that he now knew could never be.

Behind him, one of his men emerged from the shadowy forest and hurled an oversized branch onto the fire, causing a fountain of sparks to rise into the surrounding trees.

'Bedwyr, in the name of God watch what you're doing,' shouted one of the other men. 'You could have set my beard aflame.'

Men alongside him laughed at the outburst, but leaned back to avoid the onrush of heat released from the disturbed fire.

'Shut your mouth and pass the ale,' said Bedwyr, dropping down onto the log alongside Owain. One of the men passed the skin, and after taking several gulps Bedwyr turned and offered it to Owain.

'Not for me,' said Owain. 'I think I'll seek my tent.'

Bedwyr sighed deeply and stared at the man he had ridden alongside since they were boys.

'This isn't right, Owain,' he said eventually.

'What isn't?'

'The way you are acting. If I didn't know you better, I would suggest you are pining for that English wench like a motherless calf seeks the cow.'

'She isn't English, Bedwyr,' said Owain. 'She is as Welsh as you and me. More so, in fact, for she is descended directly from the line of Hywel Dda and as such her veins run with the blood of kings.'

'She has slept with at least two Englishmen that I know of,' said Bedwyr, 'and one of those was Henry himself.'

'Be careful where you go with this, Bedwyr,' said Owain, the frustration he felt inside now evident in his voice, 'for I will hear no ill spoken of Nesta. Few can dictate the circumstances in which they find themselves and she was a prisoner in Windsor for many years. For all we know Henry forced himself upon her.'

'You are fooling no one, Owain,' said Bedwyr, taking another draught of ale. 'She was a willing partner, even whelping an English brat. In my eyes it makes her a whore, nothing less.'

Without warning, Owain's right hand lashed out and he caught his friend across the mouth with the back of his fist. Bedwyr tumbled backward from the log and scrambled to his feet, wiping the blood from his mouth. His eyes burned with anger and he turned to face Owain, who was also on his feet, glaring at his comrade. The rest of the men got to their feet in shock, but realising there was about to be a fight, formed a circle around the two men, already making wagers about the outcome.

'So is this how it is going to be, Owain?' asked Bedwyr. 'That you put the name of a woman you hardly know above the advice of a friend who has fought alongside you since childhood?'

'I warned you to stop,' growled Owain, 'but you wouldn't listen. She is a princess, Bedwyr, and should be alongside us in the fight for freedom.'

'She is nothing more than a woman,' said Bedwyr slowly, 'and such women can be bought in every village in every county across the whole of Wales. A worthless title does not make her any different to the rest.'

'She is different,' said Owain, his voice rising in frustration, 'but I wouldn't expect you to understand.'

'Understand what? She is the wife of an Englishman with two children sired by Englishmen living in an Englishman's castle. Open your eyes, Owain, she no longer cares about this country and has sold her soul to the enemy.'

'She is the daughter of Rhys ap Tewdwr!' shouted Owain.

'*She is a whore!*' roared Bedwyr at the top of his voice.

Owain lashed out again, catching Bedwyr across the jaw with his fist. Bedwyr staggered backward but stayed on his feet. With a bellow of aggression, he charged his comrade, knocking him to the floor. For the next few minutes, both men fought furiously, much to the delight of their comrades, each cheering on their favourite. For a moment it looked like Bedwyr would emerge the victor but as he clamped Owain around the neck from behind, Owain slammed his head back into Bedwyr's face, making him cry out in pain. Before Bedwyr could respond, Owain spun around and knocked him to the floor, before drawing a knife from his boot and pressing it against Bedwyr's throat.

All the cheering stopped and silence fell amongst the trees as the rebels realised what was happening. Fights often occurred in the rebel camp, but never did they end in the serious injury of one of their own.

'Owain,' shouted one of the other men, 'what do you think you are doing?'

'*Keep to your own business,*' roared Owain over his shoulder, his eyes wide with rage. 'This is between him and me.'

Bedwyr lay motionless, the knife pressing against his throat, but his face showed no fear. Instead he stared coldly into his friend's manic eyes.

'Remove the knife, Owain,' he said calmly.

Owain's eyes flared wider and he leaned forward, increasing the pressure, drawing a slight line of blood. Spit hung from his mouth and his teeth clenched.

'Owain,' said Bedwyr again. 'Remove the knife.'

Before Owain could do anything, a boot kicked the prince in the side of the head and he fell sideways into the mud. Two men grabbed him and lifted him up against a tree, while a third held a sword to his throat. The rest of the men gathered around, shocked at how close their leader had come to killing one of their own. Bedwyr hauled himself from the floor and picked up Owain's knife, before pushing his way through the men.

'Get out of my way,' he said, and the sword-bearer moved aside, leaving Bedwyr standing face to face with the restrained prince.

'Release him,' said Bedwyr.

'My lord, he is still in a rage,' said one of the men. 'He could attack you again.'

'Release him,' said Bedwyr again, and he watched as Owain wrenched his arms free.

The two men stepped to one side, but within seconds Bedwyr drew back his arm and sent the knife spinning towards Owain's head.

'*Bedwyr, no,*' shouted a voice, but it was too late and the knife found its target.

Everyone gasped and stared at Owain, the knife still quivering in the tree alongside his head. The prince didn't move but could see the hilt quivering so close to his temple he could feel the vibrations in the air.

Everyone knew the miss had been deliberate and for a few moments there was silence, before the air was filled with the roar of laughter mixed with relief. The men walked back to the fire, knowing the fight was over, but Owain and Bedwyr just stared at each other, neither willing to break the other's gaze.

'Well,' said Owain eventually, 'are we done here?'

'No,' said Bedwyr, 'we are not. You almost killed me over a woman and now expect to walk away unchallenged. What is this obsession, Owain? Why does it consume you like a starving dog?'

'I cannot explain it, Bedwyr. It is like a thirst that won't go away.'

'But you can have any woman you want, willing or otherwise.'

'I cannot have *her*, Bedwyr, and therein lies the problem. All my life I have had what I wanted, when I wanted, yet to her I am nothing but a scavenging dog skulking around her ankles.'

'Owain, I have known you all my life, in foul mood and in fair. I have fought alongside you in battles too many to recall and seen you kill men without a second thought, but never have I seen you react as quickly or as savagely at the mere mention of a name. What is it about this woman that raises the berserker within you?'

'I know not. The sound of her name makes my heart race, and to hear someone pour scorn on her virtue brings a red mist down upon me. The mere thought of her haunts my every dream and not a day goes by without me thinking how I can make her mine. I have no reasons that make sense, but that is the way that it is.'

'Like an itch that won't go away?'

'Something like that, yes.'

'Then in that case I suggest that itch needs to be scratched.'

'What do you mean?'

'I mean, I have never seen you like this before, and if even the sound of her name makes you react like the devil himself, then you are at risk of becoming a liability to yourself and the rest of our men.'

'Are you suggesting you take the role of leader, Bedwyr?' asked Owain, his voice dangerously low.

'No, on the contrary, I will always follow you, but this situation needs to be sorted out once and for all.'

'And how do you suggest we do that?'

'Do you want this woman?'

'You know I do.'

Bedwyr stepped forward and drew the knife from the tree. He spun it in the air before catching the blade and offering the weapon back to Owain, hilt first.

'Then let's go and get her, Owain. Let's reclaim this Welsh princess and bring her back to where she belongs.'

Cenarth Bychan Castle

December 20th, AD 1109

Nesta knelt at her bedside table, her arms folded in prayer. Behind her, in the giant bed they shared, slept Gerald, his breathing regular and deep beneath the sheepskin covers. A hearty fire burned in the stone hearth, sending flickering light bouncing off the other three walls and keeping the worst of the winter cold from their room. Nesta finished her prayer and looked up at the sleeping form of her husband. For a few moments she imagined that it was Owain sleeping beneath the furs and not Gerald, and though at first she was shocked at her own thoughts, she allowed the scenario to play out in her mind. Was it so bad to allow herself a momentary dream of happiness? Would God in his infinite wisdom be so cruel as to punish her for her wanton thoughts, or would he recognise them for what they truly were, nothing more than a momentary dream for something that could never be? With a sigh she got to her feet and stood at the side of the bed to remove her robe.

Outside the night was silent, interrupted only occasionally by the call of an owl or the lonely howl of a distant wolf, a sound far rarer than it used to be and sure to send shivers down the spine of any shepherds and farmers in the valley. Two Irish hunting hounds lay on a moth-eaten rug at the foot of the bed, one fast asleep while the other gnawed quietly at the remains of a deer bone, desperate to reach the marrow inside.

Nesta was about to get into the bed when something made her stop and look towards the dogs. The one with the bone had stopped gnawing and his ears twitched as he stared at the window. A low growl crept from deep within his throat and the second dog stirred from his slumber, lifting his head in curiosity but soon lowering it when nothing more threatened the silence.

'Lie down, Giant,' whispered Nesta. The wolfhound looked at her for a few seconds, his tail wagging to hear his name, but soon returned his attention to the bone. On the far side of the room a door creaked slowly open and Nesta looked up to see Emma entering the bedchamber carrying a candle.

'*Emma!*' whispered Nesta in surprise. 'What brings you here?'

'My lady, you made me jump,' replied Emma. 'I thought you would surely be fast asleep, so I was going to check on the boys. That wolf is making the most unholy of noises and I thought they may be afraid.'

'Thank you, Emma,' said Nesta, 'but those two could sleep through the mightiest battle and still wake up demanding their breakfast.'

'Shall I just check, my lady?' said Emma, glancing towards the side door. 'Besides, it's a very cold night and you know what Master William is like for kicking off the furs. I'll just go and tuck them in and then retire to my own room.'

'Thank you, Emma,' said Nesta with a smile. 'That is very good of you. You see to the boys and perhaps we could sit awhile and share some warmed wine. Sleep evades me anyway.'

Emma disappeared into the boys' quarters, while Nesta poured the contents of a flask into a pot, placing it on the embers at the edge of the fire. She added another log to either side and poked at the coals before standing up and retrieving a robe from the side of her bed.

'My lady, you shouldn't have done that,' whispered Emma, returning to the room. 'I would have seen to it.'

'Nonsense,' said Nesta, walking back across the room. 'It doesn't hurt anyone to dirty their hands occasionally. Do the boys sleep soundly?'

'Like the dead,' said Emma, 'though it is mighty cold in there so I added a few furs to keep them warm.'

'If it gets any colder,' said Nesta, taking a seat by the fire, 'I'll allow them to stay in here until we leave for Pembroke. Please, be seated.' She indicated the empty chair opposite her. Emma glanced at the sleeping form of Gerald.

'Don't worry about him,' said Nesta, seeing Emma's concern. 'He is full of wine and will sleep until dawn.'

Emma nodded and sat down. She had been Nesta's mother's maid for many years, but after Gwladus had been killed by an English arrow, Nesta gave the servant a position in her own household. She soon proved to be invaluable and not only was she a reliable maid, she had also become Nesta's closest friend.

'Will you be glad to get back to Pembroke, my lady?' asked Emma, smoothing the head of the dog now settling at her feet.

'If truth be told, I will,' said Nesta. 'This place is very beautiful but it is nothing compared to Pembroke, and the cold seems to find its way into every corner.'

'That is the beauty of a stone-built castle,' said Emma. 'The walls are solid, whereas these timber ones groan and creak as if they are in pain.'

'A truer word was never spoken,' replied Nesta with a sigh, 'and sometimes I wonder if it is the creak of the boards or the moans of the dead that keep me awake.'

'Spirits?' laughed Emma quietly. 'I have no time for such superstition.' As if mocking her statement, the moan of the wind whistling through the palisades whispered through the room and both dogs jumped up, their hackles rising.

'Giant,' hissed Nesta. 'Settle down. You too, Eldred.'

'They are truly beautiful animals,' said Emma, stroking Giant once more.

'They are,' said Nesta, 'and would die to protect us, if necessary.'

'Let's hope it never comes to that,' said Emma. She leaned forward and peered into the pot. 'I think the wine will be warm enough by now. Shall I serve?'

'I'll fetch some goblets,' said Nesta, standing up.

'My lady, let me,' said Emma.

'Stay where you are, Emma,' said Nesta. 'You work hard enough.' She walked over to the table by the shuttered window and picked up two ornate goblets, but before she turned around she paused, her brows knitting as she listened intently.

'My lady,' said Emma, looking across the room, 'is something wrong?'

'No,' said Nesta eventually. 'I just thought I heard something.'

'I hope it's not those wolves,' shuddered Emma. 'Now they *do* give me the shivers. I'd rather spirits over wolves any day.'

Nesta returned to the chairs by the fire and Emma poured the drinks. For a while they sat in silence, savouring the rich flavour of the full-bodied wine and allowing its warmth to seep deep into their innards. Together they sat quietly, princess and maid, enjoying a rare few moments of closeness as they shared stories from their youth. The sound of Gerald snoring quietly in the bed and the warmth of the dogs at her feet were strangely comforting and Nesta found herself nodding off in the warmth of the fire. Eventually Emma replaced her goblet quietly on the small table and leaned forward to put the last of the logs on the fire.

'Are you going?' asked Nesta, opening her eyes.

'I need my bed, my lady,' said Emma, 'as do you. I'll have some more logs brought up before I retire, for these flames are making no headway against the cold.'

'Don't worry yourself,' said Nesta, stifling a yawn. 'I will retire to the warmth of the bed. Just arrange for the fire to be banked up at first light.'

'Of course, my lady,' said Emma, 'and thank you for the wine.'

'Say nothing of it,' said Nesta.

Emma curtsied in deference and had turned to leave when both dogs jumped to their feet, their hackles rising and growling deeply.

'What's the matter with these dogs?' sighed Nesta. 'If they awaken Gerald, there will be hell to pay.'

'Giant, lie down,' hissed Emma, reaching for his collar, but before she could grab him both dogs started barking and ran across the room, jumping up at the shutters on the window.

'Giant!' scolded Nesta. 'Get down.' But her remonstrations were useless. Both dogs stood on their hind legs, barking wildly.

'What's going on?' grunted Gerald, sitting up in the bed. 'Nesta, why all the noise and what's Emma doing here?'

'My apologies, my lord,' said Emma, tugging at Giant's collar. 'I was just leaving.'

'What's the matter with the dogs?' asked Gerald, frowning in concern.

'I know not, Gerald,' said Nesta, pulling at the second dog. 'They just went wild.'

For a moment Gerald stared at the two dogs. They had been bred from pups to defend him and he trusted their protective nature.

'Let them go,' he said, getting up from the bed.

'My lord?' asked Emma.

'Release the dogs,' repeated the castellan. 'They are only doing what they are trained to do.' He reached for a robe and tied the belt around his waist before walking over to the window. The dogs bounced wildly by his side, and he unbolted the shutters before pushing one open to peer outside.

The blast of cold wind and sleet was instantaneous, causing tapestries to flap on the walls. Gerald bent his head against the wind and peered out. The weather meant he could see hardly anything, but just at the bottom of the motte he could see the glowing embers of the sentry's brazier.

'Is everything as it should be?' shouted Nesta, pulling her robe tighter around her.

'I think so,' replied Gerald, over the wind, 'but I can't see much.'

Nesta walked over and joined her husband by the window. The wind caught one of the shutters and pulled it from Gerald's hand, slamming it wide open against the wooden wall of the tower.

'Damn it!' shouted Gerald, and he leaned out to grab the shutter. He pulled it shut and began to make his way towards the door.

'Where are you going?' asked Nesta.

'The dogs are unsettled about something,' said Gerald, 'and I trust their instincts. I'll just go down and check the guard. Lock the door behind me.'

———

Down in the bailey, Owain ap Cadwgan leaned against the wooden palisade, waiting as the last of his men crawled over the defences and lowered themselves to the ground.

'*Owain,*' whispered Bedwyr, appearing through the snow, 'the outer gatehouse is taken. There were but two guards on duty, and one of those was asleep.'

'And this Gerald is supposed to be one of Henry's best knights?' sneered Owain. 'What sort of man leaves his castle in the hands of so few men?'

'One who trusts a treaty perhaps?' suggested Bedwyr.

'Then he is a fool,' said Owain. 'Send ten men to the barracks and secure the rest of the guard. Try to take them peacefully but if they fight, put them to the sword.'

'Understood,' said Bedwyr, and he gave the necessary orders.

Owain turned to stare up at the motte. So far the assault had gone far easier than he could have hoped. The outer palisade had been guarded by only two men patrolling along its ramparts, and two well-aimed arrows had seen them fall. After that it was a simple case of using a scaling ladder to better the defences, and soon fourteen of his men were inside the bailey, while a further ten waited outside with the horses. He knew he had been lucky and the current treaty was partially responsible for the weak defences, but in his eyes that was no excuse. This was an English castle deep in enemy territory. Put simply, this Englishman deserved everything he was about to get.

'We have to be quick and get to the gates of the tower,' he continued when Bedwyr returned. 'If they bar the entrance before we get there, we don't have the strength or the time to mount a siege. Bring the rest of the men and follow me.'

'Aye,' responded Bedwyr, and moments later the rest of the armed party scrambled up the steep bank of the motte, keeping out of sight of the arrow slits alongside the great door. When they reached the tower they sidled along to the first aperture, and Owain ducked down to pass it without being seen.

He stepped out in front of the door and knocked hard on the oak with the hilt of his knife. For a few moments there was no response and he struck the door again, gratified at the sound of an inner door being opened.

'Who is it?' asked a male voice, heavy from his interrupted sleep.

'It's the captain of the guard,' shouted Owain. 'Open the door quickly, I need to speak to Gerald.'

'The master will be asleep. What is so important that won't wait until morning?'

'The castle is at risk,' replied Owain, glancing at Bedwyr. 'I need to brief him immediately.'

'At risk?' said the gatekeeper. 'Are you sure?'

'There is movement in the trees outside the palisade. I need Gerald to agree that a patrol should go and investigate.'

'Of course,' said the voice. 'I'll bring the master.'

'Gatekeeper,' shouted Owain, 'I am in the teeth of the storm out here, at least let me in to wait out of the wind.'

The sound of the raging storm outside gave the gatekeeper some sympathy to those still on duty. He pulled back the two heavy bolts and pulled the door slightly inward to peer through the crack, but as soon as it moved, the door crashed open and Owain's men burst into the tower, knocking the gatekeeper to the floor.

'Tie him up,' said Owain, taking the bunch of keys from the frightened man's belt. 'Bedwyr, you and two men come with me. The rest of you, check for any more guards. Lock anyone you find in the kitchens.'

'This is too easy,' said Bedwyr. 'Where are the guards?'

'I suspect most are down in the barracks,' said Owain. 'This tower is not meant to be garrisoned and has been designed to act as a last resort in the event of a siege.'

'So where is Gerald?'

'The quarters must be up there,' said Owain, nodding towards the stairs. 'All we have to do is walk on up and surprise him.'

'Then what are we waiting for?' said Bedwyr. 'Let's go.'

Two flights of stairs up, Gerald pressed himself against the wooden wall, aghast at what was unfolding down below. Dressed only in his robe, he was unarmed and knew he would have no chance against two fully armed warriors. Silently cursing, he turned and ran back up the stairs to his quarters.

'My lord, are you all right?' said Emma, as he burst into the room.

Gerald closed the heavy door and dragged the two wooden security bars across before turning to face his wife and the maid.

'The castle has been compromised,' he said. 'We are under attack.'

'*What?*' gasped Nesta. 'But that is impossible. We have heard no sounds of battle.'

'It looks like they used subterfuge and trickery,' spat Gerald, running over to open one of the shutters. 'Wake the boys and get them dressed.' He peered down into the bailey but there was no sign of anyone. Emma ran into the boys' room, while Nesta stood with her back against the locked door, staring in horror at her husband.

'I knew these damned Welsh couldn't be trusted,' he snarled, slamming the shutter shut. 'Curse this treaty.'

'What are we going to do?' she asked, her fear evident in her voice.

'I'm not sure,' said Gerald, getting to his feet. 'Obviously we have been attacked, and as far as I can make out, the castle has fallen. I knew I should have bolstered the defences.'

'Are any of our men alive?'

'I don't know. I fear the worst but what I don't understand is why now? What possible reason could they have to break the treaty, and why here in this unimportant backwater?'

'It's very quiet out there,' said Nesta. 'Perhaps you are mistaken?'

'No,' said Gerald. 'I heard them myself. As we speak they are making their way up here. I suspect they are checking the other rooms as they come, so we have moments only.'

'For what?' asked Nesta.

'I don't know,' said Gerald, as he pulled on his leggings. 'But I will promise you this, I will sell my life dearly in the defence of you and the boys.'

The sound of the heavy door handle turning slowly made them both turn and stare.

'*Damn*,' muttered Gerald, pulling on his jerkin and reaching for a knife on the tray that held the remains of their supper.

'Where is your mail?' asked Nesta.

'In the armoury,' said Gerald, 'along with my sword and anything else of use.'

The door rattled again, though this time with much more force.

'What should we do?' asked Nesta.

'There's not much we can do,' said Gerald, 'but I need time to think.'

'Gerald of Windsor,' shouted a voice from outside, 'I know you are in there. Open this door and face me like a man.'

Gerald glanced at Nesta before speaking. 'I am here, stranger. Who is it that storms a castle of the king and breaks a truce between countries?'

'A truce is only valid between agreed parties,' said the voice, 'and my name is on no such document.'

'Are you a king, stranger?' asked Gerald. 'For treaties are the domain of such people.'

'I am no stranger, Gerald,' said the voice. 'We shared wine only a day ago. I am Owain, son of Cadwgan, the true heir to the throne of Powys, and I know my father is not a signatory to this so-called peace treaty.'

Nesta's hands flew to her mouth in shock, instantly realising why the Welsh prince was there.

'That is because your father was and still is a rebel,' replied Gerald, 'and is a prince in name only, as are his brothers. They are mere vassals of Robert de Belleme and have no claim to kingship.'

'Ha!' exclaimed Owain. 'And you wonder why Welshmen take up the sword against you. Who are you to decide who should rule in our country, Englishman? Are Welshmen with lineages that stretch back as far as men can recall to be denied by second-generation Frenchmen? I think not, and as long as I, and people like me, have breath in our bodies we will lean against your tyranny.'

'What do you want, Owain?' shouted Gerald. 'Why have you come here?'

'Oh, that's easy,' said Owain, glancing at Bedwyr, 'to take you into custody and claim ransom from the false king.'

'You have betrayed your family and your country,' snarled Gerald, 'and Henry will pay no ransom.'

'Oh, I think he may,' said Owain. 'After all, we will have the woman he once loved, his first knight and his bastard son. I think he will pay a pretty price for all three.'

Gerald grimaced, knowing that Owain was probably right.

'You would see peace destroyed and your own people slaughtered?'

'Their hearts are already dying,' replied Owain. 'At least this way I may reignite the passion in some who still toil under your yoke. Now, enough talk. Open this door and nobody will be hurt.'

Gerald turned to Nesta. She was silent but the astonishment was clear on her face. Inside, her heart was in turmoil, consumed with both fear and excitement. After the last few years of being emotionally ignored, the thought of Owain risking everything to be with her set her pulse racing, and yet it was tempered with fear for her children's safety.

'He is surely a madman,' she ventured, her voice shaking.

'Obviously,' said Gerald, striding across the room to open the travel chests, 'but whatever the reason, he will get no surrender from me.'

'What are you looking for?'

'Anything I can use as a weapon.'

'Surely you are not going to fight him?'

'*What else can I do?*' shouted Gerald, causing Nesta to step back in fear. 'Just surrender to these common rebels like a scared woman? Even if he is true to his word and he spares our lives, the shame alone would do what his sword did not. If I am to die, Nesta, it will be in battle and not as a frightened child.'

'Listen to yourself,' said Nesta. 'You talk of *your* honour and *your* shame and yet your thoughts exclude the safety of those two little boys in that room. Does not *their* safety mean anything to you?'

'*Of course it does,*' roared Gerald, 'but I have no other options. You don't understand, this is the business of men.' He started pacing the floor like a caged animal, his thoughts consumed with how he could escape Owain's grasp.

'If I can just hold them off until morning,' he said to himself as he walked, 'the supply wagons will be here and will realise our predicament. If they summon the sheriff, he and his men can be here within hours.'

A heavy banging came on the door, stopping Gerald in mid-stride.

'Gerald,' shouted the voice.

'What do you want, rebel?' asked the knight, returning to the door.

'What I want is for you not to do anything stupid,' said Owain. 'We both know you are trapped in there. There is nowhere to go, Gerald, all your men are in captivity. Open this door and all this will soon be over. Before the month is out, you can be back in Pembroke and I will be substantially richer. It is a small price to pay for your lives.'

'It will take you all night to break down this door,' said Gerald, 'and by then the morning patrols will be here.'

'Oh, I have no doubt our time is limited,' replied Owain, 'and that is why we have to burn this place.'

'*What?*' gasped Nesta, picking herself up from the floor. 'What is he saying?'

'He wouldn't do it,' said Gerald, turning to face his wife. 'He wouldn't dare.'

'What's it to be, Gerald?' called Owain. 'A short captivity and then freedom to pursue me across the length and breadth of Wales seeking revenge, or the death of you and your family in an inferno of heat and unimaginable pain?'

'If I was to open this door, how do I know you will not strike down both me and my family anyway?'

'You don't,' said Owain, 'except that you have my word as a Welsh prince.'

'It means nothing to me, rebel,' replied Gerald, 'and like I said, to me you are no prince. Just a common criminal like your father.'

'In that case, you leave me no choice but to force your hand. Remember, I gave you the option, and now you and your family must face the consequences. You will go down in history as the knight that allowed the king's son to be burned alive.'

Nesta stared at her husband, seeing his eyes wild with panic. Despite his stubbornness she knew he was in a terrible position. He could not fight them as he had no weapons, to surrender would render him a coward, yet to do nothing meant they would all surely die. He was a man trapped in his worst nightmare.

'Open the door, Gerald,' she said quietly. 'Perhaps we can negotiate terms.'

'If I open that door, he will kill all of us.'

'No,' said Nesta, 'I don't believe he will.'

'What makes you say that?'

Nesta considered sharing her suspicions but thought better of it. Gerald was a jealous man and if he suspected any sort of attraction between Nesta and Owain, he would see them all burn before opening the door.

'I don't know. But if he claims to be of princely blood, perhaps I can appeal to our mutual royal status. Don't forget, I was a princess of Deheubarth, and in the eyes of many, still am. Surely he would back off from killing me and the boys?'

'Even if he did, I can't see him freeing me after having gone to so much trouble to sack the castle.'

Nesta thought furiously. There had to be a way out of this situation. Finally, her eyes lit up as the answer came to her.

'You must escape,' said Nesta. 'Leave us here, and when you are gone I will open the door. Not even this rebel's son would dare kill a woman born of Welsh kings.'

'There is no escape, Nesta,' said Gerald. 'The windows are too high and even if I survived the fall, Owain's men now occupy the bailey.'

'At the front, yes, but at the back the walls of the tower drop straight down into the gorge.'

'A fall I would never survive.'

'From the window perhaps, but the drop from the garderobe is no more than the height of three men.'

'The garderobe?' sneered Gerald. 'You expect me, a knight of Henry, to crawl through other men's waste to drop into a cesspit?'

'Yes, I do,' said Nesta, grabbing his arm. 'If it will save your life and that of your family, I expect you to do that and more.' She stared into his eyes. 'Oft you have told me about the filthy conditions of the battlefield, of the terrible sacrifices that you and men such as you had to make in the name of the king. What is so different now? If you stay here, we could all die, but by swallowing your pride, you could save your sons' lives and live to seek retribution.'

'And if I do this, what about you?'

'I will wait as long as I can before opening the door, and give you as much time as possible to escape. When I can wait no more, we will surrender to this prince and throw ourselves at his mercy.'

'You do know he may kill you?' said Gerald.

'He may, but I don't think he will.'

'At the very least, he will take you away and hold you to ransom.'

'One which the king will gladly pay,' said Nesta.

Gerald resumed his pacing, his mind racing furiously. 'If I do this, I can rally my forces and seek you out within weeks. Whatever fate befalls you and the children, I will avenge you. Whether it be in this life or the next, I will find this man and I will cut his heart from his chest.'

'I know,' said Nesta. 'But enough talk. You must make your escape while you still have the time.'

Gerald nodded and turned away. He strode to the back of the room, pulling aside the tapestry that led to the garderobe. Nesta followed him through and watched as he wrenched the wooden seat from the toilet bench. The hole underneath was just big enough for a man to fit through and it sloped away at an angle, designed to drain away any human waste to the outside of the tower wall.

'Be brave, Nesta,' said Gerald. 'I promise I will return to free you and the boys.' Without another word he allowed himself to slide forward, pushing his hands against the sides of the chute to control his descent. Seconds later he sat on the edge of the drop, pausing for a few moments before dropping into the darkness. She stayed a few moments longer before turning and walking back into the main room.

'Emma, take the boys into the other room,' she said. 'Stay calm and everything should be all right. I just need to talk to this man and find out exactly what he wants.'

Emma did as she was told and shut the door behind her. Nesta walked over to the main door.

'Owain,' she shouted, 'it's Nesta. Do you promise that no harm will come to me or my children?'

'You have my word,' said Owain.

'That's not good enough, Owain. Do you swear before God?'

'Just open the door, Nesta. No harm is going to befall you or your children.'

'Swear it, Owain.'

For a few seconds there was silence, before Owain gave her the assurances she needed.

'Nesta ferch Rhys, I hereby swear before almighty God that no harm shall come to you or your children this day, or any day that your safety lies in my hands. Is that good enough?'

Nesta sighed with relief. 'In that case, we accept your terms, but may the Lord have mercy on your soul if you speak falsely.'

She walked across the room and tied the dogs to the bed before returning to the door, waiting as long as she could to gain Gerald the time he needed to escape. Finally, she knew she could stall no more and with a deep sigh pulled back the bolts.

Owain's men burst in brandishing their weapons, pushing Nesta against the wall in their eagerness to secure the tower. Behind them walked Owain, his own sword hanging menacingly from his fist. He gazed at Nesta silently, taking in the image of the woman who consumed his every waking thought.

'He's not here,' said Bedwyr, returning from the search.

Owain turned to Nesta.

'Where is he, Nesta?' he asked. 'Tell me quickly and all this will be over.'

'He's not here,' said Nesta. 'He has made his escape.'

'How?'

'The method is irrelevant, just accept that he has long gone. Now tell me, Owain, what exactly is it that you want?'

For a few moments, Owain returned her stare, but then turned and barked out fresh orders.

'Search the tower again, he might be hiding.'

Again the men spread out, this time looking under the beds and behind the tapestries for any hidden doorways. Owain joined the search and went through to the quarters where Emma and the boys were waiting silently on the bed.

'Leave them alone, Owain,' said Nesta, following him through. 'They are innocents in all this.'

'Indeed,' said Owain, 'and fine boys they are too. One day they will grow up to be fine knights.' He ruffled the two boys' hair before turning to face Nesta. 'Just like their father.'

Nesta held out her arms and both boys ran over to her, wrapping their arms around her legs.

'I hope you are happy with yourself,' said Nesta. 'All these men dead, heaven knows where my husband is and two very frightened little boys, to say nothing of the treaty you have probably just caused to be ripped up.'

'Only two men have been killed, Nesta, the rest are prisoners and will be left with food and water. By noon tomorrow, they will be free.'

'So what is this all about?'

'You know what this is about,' said Owain. 'I need to be with you and nothing is going to stand in my way.'

Nesta stared as her suspicions were confirmed. The thought that this man had taken a castle to reach her was both stupid and exciting at the same time.

'There was no need for any of this, Nesta,' continued Owain, taking a step towards her and touching her face. 'You had the easy option but turned me down flat.'

Nesta turned her face away from his touch but her heart raced at the contact.

'Emma, take the boys into the solar. I will be out shortly.' When the door closed, she spun around to stare at Owain.

'Are you mad?' she gasped. 'You did all this just because I rejected your advances?'

'I suppose I did,' said Owain, touching her face again, this time without rejection. 'You see, Nesta, this is far more than an infatuation, for no other woman under the sun could have made me act this way and besides, didn't you say if circumstances were different we may have had a chance?'

'Yes, but I didn't mean this. Do you realise what you have done? My oldest child is the son of Henry himself. By attacking him you have attacked the king himself, and he will never let you get away with it.'

'I have to admit I did not realise your children would be here, but what is done is done and it will all work out in the end.'

'You attacked the king's castle, Owain,' said Nesta, walking away from the prince, 'and forced his first knight to flee for his life. Surely even you can see the madness in such an action?'

Owain tilted his head back and sighed heavily before returning his gaze to Nesta.

'The situation is not ideal, Nesta, but I had no other choice. At least this way we can be together and nobody can hold you accountable. As far as everyone is concerned, you were abducted and will be with me against your will. Only we will know the truth of the matter.'

Nesta looked around the room with exasperation. No matter how much she tried to explain the foolishness of the situation it seemed the man was obsessed, yet despite her frustration, Owain's single-mindedness sparked feelings deep inside that she had not felt for many years. Feelings of being wanted, of being desired, of being *alive*!

'Your ardour is very flattering, Owain, yet only moments ago you were threatening to burn me alive.'

'It was a bluff,' said Owain. 'I could no more hurt a single hair on your head than fly to the moon.'

'So if Gerald had stood firm?'

'I would have left before dawn but luckily for me, it seems my subterfuge worked.'

'This is the most ridiculous thing I have ever heard,' said Nesta as he walked towards her again, but inside her heart was already racing.

'It is indeed ridiculous,' agreed Owain. 'Mad, stupid, reckless and anything else that you may choose to call it, but ultimately it is right.' He stopped behind her and gently touched her neck, sending shivers down her spine.

She spun around and stared into his eyes.

'It isn't right, Owain. Men have died for this . . .' she struggled to find the words, 'this farce.'

'It is no farce, Nesta,' said Owain, reaching up and putting his hand on her cheek. 'A tragedy perhaps, but one that will have a glorious outcome.'

'You may have started another war.'

'If so, it won't be the first time men have fought wars over a beautiful woman.' He leaned forward to kiss her but she turned her head away. He pulled her head gently back towards him, and could see the fire in her eyes.

'Don't fight it, Nesta. This was meant to be.'

'No—' she gasped, but before she could say any more, he kissed her gently on the lips and this time she did not pull away.

'We can't . . .' she said, her words hoarse.

'We can do anything,' said Owain, kissing her again but with more passion.

'But my boys . . .'

Owain took a step backward and shouted over his shoulder without taking his eyes from Nesta.

'*Bedwyr?*'

'Yes, my lord,' came the response from the other room.

'Take the prisoners back to camp and treat them well. I will join you soon enough.'

'Yes, my lord,' said the voice, and Owain stepped back towards Nesta.

'Now, where were we? Oh yes . . .' He took her head in both hands to kiss her deeply and this time she responded in kind, submitting completely to the feelings that raged inside her.

'What am I doing?' she gasped, pulling herself away. 'This cannot happen.'

'Don't fight it, Nesta,' said Owain, taking her hand. 'As God is our witness, this was meant to be.'

Nesta didn't answer, but without taking her eyes from his entrancing green gaze, she allowed herself to be led over to the bed.

Outside, Bedwyr led the two young boys down the motte steps and through the outer gates of the palisade. Behind them, two guards dragged a struggling Emma down the steps.

'Where is she?' cried Emma, fighting against her captors. 'What is that horrible man doing to her?'

'To the victor the spoils, lady,' sneered one of the men. 'Now if I was you, I'd stop struggling and get on that cart. We have a long way to go and something tells me your mistress won't be joining us for a long time yet.'

Hen Domen Castle

December 25th, AD 1109

'Lady Sybil,' said Baldwin de Boulers, looking up as his wife entered the great hall of Hen Domen Castle. 'You look radiant as usual.'

'Thank you, my lord,' said the woman walking briskly towards him, closely followed by four ladies-in-waiting. 'I just hope these wonderful cloaks are warm enough to keep out the chill of the winter snow.'

The castellan smiled and looked across at the other man in the room. 'If not, then I will personally ensure our first knight here is denied any wine or ale until next Christmas, for it is he that arranged the gifts.'

'A fate worse than death itself,' responded Broadwick, a look of mock horror on his face.

'I would worry not, Sir Broadwick,' smiled Sybil. 'The linings are amongst the finest I have ever felt.'

'Recently harvested from young otters, my lady, and the ruffs are from the wool of our finest sheep.'

'They are certainly a wonderful gift and you have my full appreciation.' She held up her hand for the knight to kiss before turning her attention back to her husband. 'So, Baldwin, are we ready?'

'Would you like some warmed wine first?' asked Baldwin. 'It will warm your innards before you go.'

'No, let's get this done,' said Sybil. 'The quicker it is over, the quicker we can return and start our own celebrations.'

'Indeed,' said Baldwin. 'And I hear the feast will be like none we have ever tasted outside of France. Isn't that true, Sir Broadwick?'

'I understand the steward and his cooks have been very busy, my lord,' said Broadwick. 'I think you will not be disappointed.' He turned to a squire standing near the door. 'Bring the master's cloak and instruct the captain of the guard we are about to leave.'

'Yes, my lord,' said the squire, and he disappeared through the doors.

'Are all the preparations made?' asked Baldwin quietly.

'Nothing has been left to chance, my lord,' said Broadwick, his voice low so as not to worry the lady of the castle. 'Every person in the village knows that if there is even the slightest hint of protest while you walk amongst them, then every man, woman and child will be hung from the palisades before nightfall.'

'Good,' said Baldwin. 'These rumours of unrest make me uneasy, and despite the treaty, I have no faith in anything our so-called king puts his name to.'

'Ready?' asked Sybil, walking over and interrupting their conversation.

'Of course,' said Baldwin, his voice rising in exaggerated excitement. 'Let's go.'

Together, Baldwin de Boulers, trusted castellan of Hen Domen Castle and his wife, Sybil de Falais, made their way out of the keep. Down in the bailey, all the servants and squires stood waiting, each well wrapped against the cold Christmas morning, and amongst them all stood the portly abbot of Shrewsbury Abbey.

'It seems our abbot does not prescribe to the notion of the humble monk,' said Baldwin to Broadwick under his breath as they descended the steps.

The knight looked at the abbot with ill-disguised contempt. The so-called humble man of God was adorned in a thick cloak of purple wool, decorated with an enormous golden crucifix upon the back and lined with the fur of a winter-white sable. On his head he wore a gold-embroidered mitre granted to his monastery by the Pope himself, and in his hand he held a bejewelled staff, topped with a golden crucifix.

'I still think he exceeds his station,' growled Broadwick. 'Just say the word and he will disappear, and I can assure you his replacement will be much more agreeable to your direction.'

'He is a powerful man, Broadwick, and has the ear of the king himself. Let him play his games at the moment, and when the day of reckoning comes, as it inevitably will, I shall gladly watch as you set your hounds upon him and his like.'

'Father Abbot,' said Baldwin as they reached the bottom of the steps. 'Welcome to Hen Domen. The blessings of Our Lord be upon you.'

'And on you, Master Baldwin,' replied the abbot. 'And thank you for attending our simple service in person. It will mean a lot to the poor of the village.'

'My pleasure,' said Baldwin. 'If you are ready, perhaps we can proceed.'

'Of course,' said the abbot, and he took his place alongside the castellan. Behind them came Sir Broadwick and Lady Sybil, followed by a group of six monks wearing their traditional grey habits. A donkey-drawn cart trundled behind, its contents covered with a heavy linen sheet, and the whole procession was followed by a detachment of forty horsemen, ready to deploy at a moment's notice should they be required.

The column approached the gates in the palisade and as they swung open, fifty men marched out, forming the advance guard. Baldwin and his entourage followed them onto the road and together they made their way towards the village a few hundred paces away.

'Sir Broadwick,' said Sybil as they walked, 'I have been meaning to ask you, why are the nearest houses of the village so far away from the castle?'

'There used to be houses almost under the walls themselves,' said the knight, 'but I had to have them removed to provide clear fields of fire for the archers on our palisades. People naturally move closer to the shadows of castles, especially in times of trouble, but to allow such expansion provides cover for would-be attackers. That luxury has to be denied them and such actions are warranted for the greater good.'

'I see,' said Sybil. 'And was some sort of compensation made for those who have lost their livelihoods and their homes?'

'Times are hard for all of us, my lady,' responded Broadwick, 'and our focus has to be aimed at providing protection against the rebels. What use is a house if you are to be killed by an attacker's arrow?'

'On the contrary,' intervened the abbot over his shoulder, 'to die in your own home is a luxury coveted by many men.'

'Perhaps so, but it is not in the country's interest to waste money on such things. Besides, I'm sure the king would look kindly on any support the abbey is able to offer.'

'We have given succour to all that need it. However, even our finances are limited,' said the abbot.

Broadwick glanced again at the rich accoutrements of the abbot but decided not to comment. Today was not a day to argue about such things.

'Well, here we are,' said Baldwin eventually.

The column stopped at the beginning of the main street leading into the village. On either side of the road, the peasants waited patiently, most forced into attendance at blade-point by the soldiers standing amongst them.

'Let's get this done,' said Baldwin, and they stepped forward, walking slowly along the lines of people. Baldwin took one side of the street, while his wife took the other, engaging in light conversation and passing on their Christmas greetings. As they walked, the monks came behind, handing each child a single copper penny and anointing them with the blessings of Christ. Most pennies were immediately confiscated by the parents, painfully aware that one penny, carefully spent, could feed a family for a week.

Slowly, they made their way to the centre of the village and Baldwin climbed up onto a small platform, set up especially for the occasion. His family and servants stood behind him, and he held his hand up for silence as the crowd gathered in.

'People of Montgomery,' he said, 'the blessings of our Lord Jesus Christ be on you this day.'

'And upon you,' murmured the crowd.

'As you know,' said Baldwin, 'I have been castellan of Hen Domen and constable of Montgomery for almost four years so have grown an affinity with this village. This tradition of gifting a penny to the children was started my predecessor, Earl Belleme, many years ago and I am very happy to see it is growing in strength as a local tradition. However, the earl, by necessity, has to spend most of his time on his estate in Normandy, so let us not forget that these lands now come under my responsibility and as such, it is my duty to ensure you, the people, thrive as much as possible. To this end, we have come here today, not just to share your Christmas celebrations, but to bring a gift to every household, one that will help you feed and clothe your children for many years, as well as provide a source of income.'

A murmur of approval rippled around the crowd, and Baldwin waved his hand, giving a signal to the cart master at the back of the square. The man led his donkey forward and tied the harness to a hitching rail before pulling the covering from the cart, revealing the piles of cages beneath. The people strained to see the contents, with those behind standing on tiptoe to see what was happening.

'Rabbits are a tasty addition to any pot,' said Baldwin. 'However, they also breed incredibly quickly and their young can produce their own offspring within months of being born. If managed correctly, two rabbits can be the source of a never-ending supply of meat, as well as providing warm fur for your garments or bedding.' He turned and took the hand of his wife, bringing her up beside him. 'As a gesture of goodwill,' he continued, 'my wife and I intend to donate one male and one female rabbit to every lawfully married couple in this village.'

Many of the people started talking, excited at this unexpected gift.

'My lord,' said a voice, 'may I ask a question?'

'Of course,' said Baldwin.

'What about those of us who do not have a wife or husband. Will this grant be available to us?'

'No,' said Baldwin. 'However, there is nothing to stop you buying one from those who breed theirs successfully. That is the beauty of such a venture: it also creates a market.'

'But what if they die?' asked another voice.

'There is always that risk,' said Baldwin, 'as well as, of course, the temptation to just eat your rabbits as soon as times get tough. So to encourage good care and responsibility there will be a list taken of all recipients and a subsequent toll of one fully grown rabbit per household, paid to the castellan and the abbey twice a year. The first toll will be payable at the Easter celebration, while the second will be paid every Christmas morning. It is a small price, and if your animals are looked after, easily affordable. However, if you are unable to pay this nominal toll, you can elect to pay a fine of one penny in its place, collected twice annually, as already discussed.'

'Is this not just another tax?' asked a man.

'On the contrary. If you look after the animals, and breed them well, it is a path to food, warmth, and perhaps a little wealth.' He looked around the crowd with a wide smile on his face. 'So, we will now retire to continue our Christmas celebrations at the castle. The abbot here will leave his monks to record those who wish to take advantage of our generosity. I bid you goodbye, and may God go with you.'

He turned to go, but before he could leave, a commotion at the back of the crowd made him pause.

'What's happening?' asked Sybil, peering towards the far side of the square.

'It looks like a latecomer to the celebration,' said Baldwin, seeing a horse-drawn cart slowly entering the square.

'Hold him there,' shouted Broadwick.

'No,' said Baldwin. 'This is Christmas after all, let him come forward.'

'It may be a trick, my lord,' said Broadwick.

'I am well guarded,' said Baldwin, 'and besides, it is important that I am seen to be sharing the spirit of Christmas. Let him come.'

The crowd parted, allowing the horse to walk right up to the platform. A man sat slumped forward upon the horse's back, and it quickly became obvious that he was tied to the saddle.

'My lord,' someone shouted, 'he is badly wounded.'

'Cut him down,' said Broadwick, and within moments the crowd carried the man up onto the platform.

'Father Abbot, are any of your monks healers?' said Baldwin.

'Brother Neil,' said the abbot, looking around, 'attend this man immediately.'

The monk ran over and knelt by the man, cutting away the last of his bonds.

'What is wrong with him?' asked Sybil from behind her husband.

'I don't know,' said Baldwin quietly. 'He is still alive but has passed out. It looks like he has bandages about his feet and hands.'

The monk looked up at the abbot and spoke quietly. The abbot's eyes widened in shock and he turned to the castellan.

'My lord,' said the abbot, 'you are incorrect. This man does not have wounds to his hands and feet for he does not have any. All have been cut off and the wounds sealed with boiling pitch.'

'What?' Baldwin choked. 'What sort of devil would do that to another man?'

'There is more,' said the abbot. 'Whoever did this also took his eyes and tongue.'

Sybil's hand flew to her mouth and the crowd gasped with shock. Never had they heard of any man being treated so, whether criminal or enemy.

Baldwin regained his composure. 'Will he live?' he asked.

'I don't know. It looks like he was of healthy stock, a fact that has kept him alive so far, but we need to get him to a physician as soon as possible.'

Sir Broadwick stepped forward and knelt beside the victim. Despite the grime and blood on the man's face, the features were instantly recognisable and the knight looked up at Baldwin in shock.

'I know this man, my lord.'

'Then name him, Sir Broadwick, for no man should be treated so.'

'He is one of our own, my lord. It is Sir Julian of Shrewsbury. He was sent on your behalf to Brycheniog a month ago to guard a supply wagon and bring it back to Hen Domen. Whoever did this must have attacked the column and sent this man here as a message.'

'This is Sir Julian?'

'It is, my lord, though he is in a pitiful state.'

'*Who would do such a thing?*' roared Baldwin, his façade of caring nobility temporarily discarded. 'I will have them skinned alive for this.'

'My lord,' shouted a voice, 'wait, there is more.'

All heads turned to the monk still kneeling at the wounded man's side. He had opened the victim's shirt, revealing a horrible wound.

'What other indignity could this poor man possibly endure?' asked Baldwin.

'My lord, there is a name burned into his chest.'

'What does it say, monk?' asked Baldwin, fearing the worst.

'It says, *Y Diafol*, my lord,' said the monk, looking up. '*The Devil!*'

As the castellan and his guests returned to the castle, Sir Broadwick and his men dispersed the villagers, all thoughts of celebrations and rabbits forgotten. The mutilated victim was placed on the back of the cart accompanied by two of the monks, while one of Broadwick's men led them all back to the castle. Several of Baldwin's cavalry rode out to see if they could find the person who had obviously brought the wagon as far as the village, but with no luck. Whoever it had been was long gone. Broadwick rode behind the wagon, deep in thought, when he suddenly reined his horse in.

'Hold,' he shouted at the two monks sat in the back of the wagon. 'Good brothers, those sacks at the front of the cart, have you or anyone else checked what they contain?'

'I think not, my lord,' said one of the monks.

'Then cut one open,' replied Broadwick. 'Perhaps there is a clue as to who is responsible for this outrage.'

The monk stood up and walked over to one of the four sacks. Broadwick threw him a knife and he cut through the ties, causing the contents to roll out onto the deck of the wagon.

A gasp of horror escaped the monks as they looked into the sightless eyes of several heads, each bearing the signs of a brutal and bloody decapitation. For a few moments, silence ensued, broken only by the sound of one of the monks retching over the side of the cart.

'This is truly the work of the devil himself,' said Broadwick quietly. 'Bring them to the castle for burial.'

'Who are they?' asked one of the monks.

'If I am not mistaken,' said Broadwick, 'these are the heads of Sir Julian's men. Whoever was responsible must have captured and killed every one.'

The monk gingerly replaced the heads in the sack and the cart resumed its tragic journey, complete with grisly cargo. Broadwick paused for a few moments before staring up at the forested hills in the distance.

'I don't know who or what you are, Diafol,' he said quietly to himself, 'but as God is my witness, you will pay for this.'

Several leagues away, a dirty bearded man peered down from the treeline, invisible to anyone in the village below. He had delivered the cart as instructed but felt no compassion for any of the victims. Death was like a brother to him, and a few more wasted souls meant nothing.

'Come,' said a voice behind him, 'it is time to go.'

The man got up from his haunches and spat on the grass.

'Goodbye, shiny man,' he sneered, staring at the distant cart as it entered the gates of Hen Domen on the far side of the valley. 'I'll see you in hell.'

Windsor Castle

January 15th, AD 1110

King Henry stood at a table alongside two of his trusted military advisors, Robert Fitzhamon and Gilbert Fitzrichard. Robert stood tall, almost half a head taller than the king, and was clean-shaven with short, cropped brown hair, while his comrade was somewhat shorter, his jet-black hair trimmed straight in line with his jaw. Both men had first-class military pedigrees and both were descended from nobles who had accompanied William in 1066.

On the table before them lay the latest available charts of all the Welsh lands west of the Marches, from Ynys Mon in the north to Cardiff in the south. Carved wooden figures representing units of men lay dotted across the maps, with by far the greatest density along the border between England and Wales. Small carved towers represented all the known fortifications, both English and Welsh, and any routes passable by a large body of men were clearly marked, along with rivers and major mountain ranges.

The walls of the map chamber at Westminster were adorned with beautiful tapestries, while colours of all the allied barons throughout the country hung from the rafters. Armed soldiers stood along the walls, each adorned in richly coloured garments, and despite the glint upon their pikes and swords, their weapons were no less sharp than those of the most battle-weary of veterans.

The oaken map table stood atop a rich red carpet, which led away to the door of the chamber, a luxury experienced in many of the rooms attached to the king's chambers. Against one wall, a table flanked by two servants stood laden with fruits and sweetmeats, along with flasks of wine and ale.

'Tell me, Robert,' said Henry, turning to Fitzhamon, 'why is it that despite the truce negotiated with the princes of Wales, we still need so many resources to protect the supply wagons between my castles?'

'My lord,' said Robert, 'though the peace is indeed observed by the recognised monarchs, they seem to be unwilling or unable to deal with the growing amount of rebels who still pursue a dream of independence from England.'

'Am I to assume Cadwgan is behind these continued attacks?'

'On the contrary, my lord,' said Robert. 'Cadwgan is of a much quieter disposition these days, as is his firebrand son, Owain.'

'Really?'

'Yes, my lord. Even though Cadwgan was one of the worst rebels during your brother's reign, these past few years have seen him settle down on his ancestral lands under the wing of Gruffydd ap Cynan.'

'And what of the Welsh king?'

'He too enjoys the trappings that peace brings. The threat as I see it is not from those who are used to the responsibilities that kingship brings, but from those not old or wise enough to know better.'

'So who are these ghosts who cost my treasuries so much?'

'Nobody really knows,' said Robert, 'though there seems to be an upsurge in support for one who calls himself Diafol.'

'And do we know who he is?'

Fitzhamon glanced across at his comrade, his eyes conveying the awkwardness he felt inside. As an advisor, his role was to keep abreast of all information across the realm, and especially any that concerned potential threats to the Crown. However, despite his army of spies and informants across the country, information regarding the identity of Diafol was non-existent.

'No, my lord, not yet.'

Henry stared in shock. He was not used to failure by his closest advisors.

'Why not?' he asked. 'Are you not furnished with enough resources to find out? Is the treasury not generous in such matters?' His tone lowered as if in warning. 'Are you not clear in the role expected of you?'

'Yes, my lord, but you have to understand, this is no ordinary foe. He strikes like a viper, then disappears as quickly as a startled hare. Not even his own men know his true name.'

'How can this be?'

'It seems he assembles bands of mercenaries each time he wishes to carry out an attack. As soon as it is complete, the attackers are quickly paid off and disperse before any retribution can be sought. There are no permanent armies to target, just rumours and devastation wherever they have had footfall. We have caught several of those responsible for attacking our columns but no name has been forthcoming.'

'Somebody must surely know?'

'Perhaps, but despite the attentions of our best torturers, it seems that nobody actually knows who he is.'

The king stared at Fitzhamon, causing the knight to lower his gaze, knowing that the king would see it as a failure.

'Sort it out, Robert,' said Henry simply, before turning back to the map. 'So where does this leave us?'

Gilbert Fitzrichard cleared his throat. 'My lord, as far as I am concerned the only option is to increase our presence throughout the country. Bolster our forces in the main population centres and construct fortifications along all the trading routes. These can be supported by the Marcher lords, who will be able to respond at a moment's notice.'

'What you are suggesting is almost a full-scale invasion,' said Henry.

'If that's what it takes, then so be it,' said Gilbert. 'We have endured this constant attrition for far too long, and it is about time these Welsh pretenders realise they will kneel before the Crown or suffer the consequences.'

'I don't know,' said Henry. 'My father and indeed my brother invaded Wales on several occasions and always found themselves chasing shadows across inhospitable terrain. The last thing we want now is an all-out war, especially as Gruffydd has signed the treaty. It is his growing influence that worries me the most. Perhaps these minor attacks are the price I have to pay.'

Before anyone could answer, a knock came on the door and a servant entered, crossing the room to talk to Henry.

'My lord,' he said, 'there are two men waiting to see you. They say they have ridden hard for three days and have news that won't wait.'

'Can't you see the king is busy, James?' said Fitzhamon. 'Tell them to come back tomorrow.'

'Of course, my lord,' said the servant.

'Wait,' said the king. 'Did these men state their names?'

'Yes, my lord. Gerald of Windsor and John Salisbury.'

'Gerald of Windsor is here?' said the king, his brow lifting in surprise. 'What has brought him halfway across the country without notification?'

'He didn't say, my lord.'

'Whatever it is,' said Fitzhamon, 'it will be nothing that can't wait until morning. Perhaps, my lord, you should see them on the morrow.'

'Nonsense,' said the king. 'Gerald is an expert on Wales and his arrival is most opportune, though why he has brought his constable intrigues me.' He turned to the servant. 'Bid them come through, James. His counsel regarding all matters Welsh is always welcome.'

'Of course, my lord,' said the servant, and he backed out of the room. Two minutes later, Gerald of Windsor and his constable entered the room, both pausing to incline their heads before walking up to the table.

'Gerald,' said the king, 'it has been a long time. What brings you here with such urgency?'

'My lord,' said Gerald, kissing the king's hand, 'I come bearing the gravest news. Your castle at Cenarth Bychan has fallen to the rebels and has been burned to the ground. Some of my men were slain and my wife and children abducted.'

Henry's smile slipped and he stared at the knight.

'My son has been taken prisoner?' he asked. 'How?'

'By trickery and subterfuge, my lord. They attacked under the protection of the treaty in the dead of night. We were guests of the sheriff of Ceredigion at the time and suspected nothing untoward. Indeed, we were guests of honour at a cultural celebration hosted by the Welsh, so we anticipated no problems whatsoever.'

'Some of your men were killed,' said Fitzhamon, 'the rest were captured, yet you escaped.'

'I did and will bear the weight of that knowledge for the rest of my life. The situation changed so quickly, I found myself trapped in my quarters with death at the door. At the point of defeat, I used the garderobe to escape.'

'Really?' said Fitzhamon, his brow raised in surprise. 'A novel way to escape a building, I would suggest.'

'When the life of yourself and your family is at risk, all options are considered,' replied Gerald. 'If I had remained, I could have been killed and there would have been no witness to this atrocity. In such circumstances, perhaps the rebels would have seen no need to keep hostages. At least by knowing I am alive, they held back the blade from Nesta and the boys.'

'Are you sure they are still alive?' asked the king.

'As far as I know. Their bodies were not found in the ruins, but I have no idea where they are or why they were taken. I assume they are to be ransomed, but so far we have received no such demand.'

'Who was responsible for this?' asked Gilbert.

'The son of Cadwgan,' said Gerald. 'Owain ap Cadwgan.'

'Wait,' said the king, turning to Fitzhamon. 'Did you not tell me just a few moments ago that Owain was a model of servitude?'

'The last I heard, my lord, he was busy helping his father run his estates,' replied Fitzhamon. 'If what Sir Gerald is saying is correct, then it could be a problem. Owain is known as a formidable fighter and is able to call many rebels to his banner.'

'My lord, this just reinforces my opinion,' said Gilbert. 'If Owain has once more taken up the mantle of rebel, then it is only a matter of time before the situation deteriorates. Mobilise the army now before it is too late, else the enemy will have time to build their strength.'

The king turned to Gerald's constable.

'What say you, Salisbury? Your role places you amongst the people of Pembroke. Do you think the Welsh are mobilising for a full-scale war?'

'No, my lord, I do not,' replied Salisbury. 'This Owain is a known firebrand and though his father was once feared across the land, I hear he is not the man he used to be and now prefers politics over warfare.'

The king turned back to Gerald. 'So what of this man known as Diafol?'

'I have heard rumours only,' said Gerald, 'but nothing of any substance. However, Owain now has your son as a hostage and that could provide leverage against the Crown.'

'He also has your wife,' reminded the king.

'Indeed, but my worry is for your son, as well as my own.'

Henry paused and walked around the table. The rest of the men in the room kept quiet, knowing he was deep in thought. Finally, he returned to his place at the maps. 'There is an awful lot to think about,' he announced, 'and the day has been long. We will adjourn this meeting until tomorrow.' He turned to Gerald. 'You and your fellow will be provided with a room for the night. Get some rest and return here tomorrow at noon to share what you know. Before the sun sets tomorrow night, we will make plans not only to rescue your family, but to deal with this burgeoning rebellion.' He turned to Gilbert and Fitzhamon. 'Gentlemen, I bid you good night.' Without further ado he left the map room, leaving his advisors behind him. As they also left to go to their quarters, the servant approached and addressed Gerald.

'My lord, if you follow me I will arrange quarters and some food.'

'Thank you,' said Gerald, his tiredness settling on him like a heavy cloak. 'It has been a long couple of days.'

The following day, Gerald broke his fast in his own room before visiting the stables to arrange fresh horses for the journey home. Despite his forthcoming audience with Henry, he was desperate to start back to Wales as soon as possible.

At noon he presented himself at the audience chambers and was shown through to the map room. John Salisbury and the king's two advisors were already there and they waited quietly, discussing various political events of the past few weeks. Finally, Henry arrived and it was quickly noticed his mood was far from good.

'Gentlemen,' he said abruptly, approaching the table. 'I will be straight and tell you this recent news brought by Gerald has arisen an anger within me. The fact that Gerald's wife has been abducted from beneath his very nose is bad enough, but for the perpetrator to then abscond with one of my sons is an affront to the Crown. As if that wasn't bad enough, to then burn down one of my castles during a period of agreed peace, contrary to all treaties signed by both sides, is almost a declaration of all-out war.' He paused and looked at the four men. 'However,' he continued, 'it is incumbent upon us not to overlook the fact that as far as we know, this crime has been committed by one man and one man only. Consequently it falls to the men in this room to come up with a plan I can present before our barons.' He turned to face Gerald. 'I understand that you want to leave this place as soon as possible and return to oversee the search for your family. However, I beg you to stay a little while longer and brief us as to the latest situation in Wales. Will you do that?'

'Of course, my lord,' said Gerald. 'I am always happy to serve the king, no matter what the outcome.'

'Good, then approach the table and bring us up to date with the political situation.'

Gerald did as he was bid, and lifting up a pointing stick, took a deep breath before starting his briefing. 'My lords,' he said, 'as you know, there is no agreed border between the two countries, though the people of Wales refer to the dyke created by King Offa of Mercia several hundred years ago as the natural boundary between the kingdoms. Most of the dyke is controlled by our barons, and indeed much of the land on the Welsh side is currently in our control.' He pointed to the south of the map. 'Gwent, Morgannwg and Deheubarth are now in our control, as is most of Brycheniog and Builth. Ceredigion, however, is more troublesome. We control the coast up as far as the river Teifi, and indeed had a castle built there to emphasise our claim, but traditionally any lands north of the Teifi have remained under Welsh control. As you are aware, Cadwgan ap Bleddyn currently manages them on behalf of Gruffydd, and though there has been peace for several years, the feeling is one of mutual mistrust.' His pointer slid north into Gwynedd. 'By far the strongest king in Wales is Gruffydd ap Cynan. His rule extends right across the north, from Wrexham to the west coast and down as far as northern Ceredigion. He maintains a standing army of over five hundred men-at-arms but could call upon ten times that amount should it come to war.' He moved the pointer towards the border and the last great tract of land indicated on the map. 'That leaves us with Powys. Officially, this is ruled by the Earl of Shrewsbury, Robert de Belleme, but his continuing argument with the Crown has seen him become less than reliant. When the last king of Powys, Bleddyn ap Cynfyn, died, Belleme allowed Bleddyn's three surviving sons, including Cadwgan, to share Powys between them, as vassals of his estate. Thus they have remained Welsh princes in name but with no route to kingship. However, when Belleme declined Cadwgan's claim to further territorial rights, Cadwgan rebelled and left his lands to be managed by his brother, Maredudd. As we know, Cadwgan became a thorn in the Crown's side, and it was only when the treaty was signed did he step away from the life of a rebel and settle down in Ceredigion at the invitation of Gruffydd. He is quiet at the moment but still commands the respect of the people of northern Wales.'

'We all know of the threat from Cadwgan,' said Gilbert, 'but what about this Maredudd?'

'He seems harmless enough, though it is suspected that he has given shelter and succour to his brother when needed. I don't think he is any great risk and he maintains no standing army that we are aware of.'

'And the third brother?'

'His name is Iorwedd,' said Gerald, 'and he was probably the most powerful of all the brothers.'

'Was?'

'Yes, my lord, he is no longer a threat to the throne.'

'Why not?'

'Because he is imprisoned in Hen Domen Castle, and has been for the last seven years.'

'Interesting,' said the king. He turned back to the map. 'So, it would seem the south is fairly secure up as far as Ceredigion in the west and Builth in the east, while anything further north is controlled by a few powerful Welshmen capable of fielding an army should we march against them.'

'Powys is not a threat, my lord.'

'How can you say that when our supply wagons are attacked on an almost daily basis?' asked Gilbert.

'Because Maredudd is not a warlike man. The main problem seems to stem from this area here.' Gerald leaned forward and circled an area at the centre of Wales encompassing the northern half of Deheubarth and the western edge of Builth. 'This area is heavily wooded and as inhospitable as hell itself. The forests are dense, any open ground is marshy and difficult to cross, and the few paths available are easily defended. A man can ride for several days in any direction without reaching the other side, such are the obstacles. Our patrols steer clear of it as few ever emerge alive, yet when we have taken heavily armed columns into the area to flush out any rebels, we find nought but cold fires and deserted camps. The locals call it the Cantref Mawr and it is a forge of rebellion.' He took a deep sigh and looked up at the king. 'And it is here, my lord, that I fear Owain has taken your son.'

For the next hour or so, the king and his two advisors asked Gerald and Salisbury endless questions about the landscape and politics of Wales, keen to learn everything they could, not only about the terrain but the people they could rely on, should it come to a fight. Finally, the five men sat around a nearby table, drinking warmed wine as they discussed the options.

'So,' said the king eventually, 'what are we to do about this situation?'

'My lord,' said Gerald, 'the whole reason for me coming here was not only to report the abduction of your son but also to beg extra resources to launch a campaign into the Cantref Mawr. Despite the inaccessibility, I think with the aid of some local guides and a strong force I can at least flush Owain out of hiding. By the time it can be arranged, the thaw will be upon us and the weather will be kinder.'

'You would endure the spring rains?' asked Gilbert.

'I would endure the fires of hell, if needs be,' replied Gerald.

'And if you were to succeed, would it not just make this man run to the hills?'

'Perhaps. He certainly couldn't go south, so I expect he would retreat into the forests of Ceredigion and the protection of his father. As signatory to the treaty, Cadwgan has a lot to lose, so I hope he may be convinced to deliver Owain into our custody, especially as Owain's prisoner is a well-loved princess of Deheubarth.'

The king snorted. 'Really?' he asked, a derisive look on his face. 'You really think a former rebel would give up his own son to an Englishman? I would suggest that hell would freeze over before that day comes and anyway, as much as I worry about my son, this has become more than just the abduction. We also have to consider the problem regarding the continued attacks on the supply wagons.'

'I see no other option than to raise an army and campaign into the heart of Wales,' said Fitzhamon. 'Strike at the vipers within their very nests and wipe out these traitors once and for all.'

'A futile gesture,' intervened Gilbert, 'unless . . .' All heads turned to face the advisor as he paused, deep in thought.

'Do you have a plan, Sir Gilbert?' asked the king. 'For if you do, I would be gratified to hear it. The attacks on our supply wagons are costly, but war is costlier still.'

'My lord,' said Gilbert, looking up slowly. 'I think that the arrival of Sir Gerald could be most opportune and though we are grieved by the plight of his family, it may be exactly the opportunity we need.'

'Go on,' said the king.

'Let's go over to the map,' said Gilbert, and they took their places around the map table again, still clutching their goblets of wine. 'If Gerald is correct,' continued Gilbert, 'and it is indeed Owain that abducted Nesta, then there will be some sympathy amongst the Welsh, especially those who support the treaty. Nesta is well loved across Deheubarth and still commands loyalty to her name, so if we send a column into Cantref Mawr, clearly aimed at securing her release, I doubt it would raise many eyebrows.'

'Continue,' said the king.

'So, assuming our men enter the Cantref Mawr, a simple change of direction to the west could see us take Cadwgan by surprise and cut Ceredigion in two, reducing his territories by over half. If he is also squeezed from the north at the same time, he would have to force Owain to hand over the prisoners, but not only that, we will be in an excellent position to launch an attack upon his lands. By using the pretence of searching for this princess of Deheubarth, we can almost march right up to his household unchallenged.'

'That seems a very large operation to find one man,' said Fitzhamon. 'What is to stop this Owain just disappearing into the hills as soon as we arrive?'

'Nothing, but if our intentions include a secondary goal, the cost will be worth every penny.'

'And what would this secondary goal be?' asked the king.

'To eliminate Cadwgan and his influence once and for all. With Ceredigion fully in our control, we can then expand north-east and join with the Marcher lords, not only controlling all the areas threatened by these so-called rebels, but also leaving Gruffydd isolated in the north.

Three quarters of Wales would be under our heel without a single arrow being fired in anger.'

'Maredudd would never allow us to march a column through Powys,' said Fitzhamon. 'He may be quiet but Powys is a big kingdom and blood is thicker than water. No man would stand silent while a foreign army seeks to destroy his brother.'

'I know of one,' said Gilbert.

'Who?'

'The third brother currently imprisoned in Hen Domen. Iorwedd ap Bleddyn.'

'I'm afraid your reasoning makes no sense to me,' said the king. 'Why would Iorwedd turn on his own brother?'

'In return for his freedom,' said Gilbert. 'I think that after seven years as a guest in the dungeons of Hen Domen he would at least listen to what is on offer.'

'And what exactly is that?'

'Freedom, land, riches, whatever you see fit, my lord. We could even throw a title into the deal, perhaps Lord of all Powys?'

'You would give Powys to a criminal?' asked Fitzhamon in surprise.

'In name only,' said Gilbert, 'and of course the title would be non-hereditary, so would revert to the Crown on his death.'

'Which I would imagine,' said Fitzhamon with a smile, 'would be soon after the capture or death of Cadwgan.'

'Exactly,' said Gilbert. He turned to the king. 'Under the illusion we only seek the release of Nesta, the Welsh barons will allow us to ride unhindered through their lands to the west, fearful that Owain could destroy the peace treaty, while Iorwedd places pressure on Cadwgan from the east. Before this year is over, we could be masters of Wales from Gwynedd down to Cardiff and knowing the rest of the country had already bent a knee before the Crown, it would only be a matter of time before Gruffydd himself capitulated.' Gilbert stopped talking and looked around the room. Everyone stood quietly, each turning the plan over and over in his mind, until finally the king spoke.

'I think it can work, but with a slight change. Gerald, you will ride back to Pembroke immediately. However, if this Cantref Mawr is as bad as you say, I fear your strength may be depleted if it comes to an assault on Cadwgan. Therefore, I will grant you the extra resources required, and when the time is right, you will send your men into the Cantref Mawr to seek Nesta, proceeding as Gilbert has indicated.' He turned to Fitzhamon. 'Robert, I want you to join Gerald in Pembroke with a hundred cavalry and another hundred men-at-arms. I will give you dispatches to sequester men from our castles along the coast and you will lead a second column under the guise of rescuing the Welsh princess. As soon as you receive word that Gerald has turned west from the Cantref Mawr, you and your men will ride northward to join him with all haste. That gives us a small army already deep in Ceredigion, and even if Cadwgan realises what is happening, it will be too late.' He pointed to Gilbert. 'While they are preparing in the west, I want you to ride to Hen Domen with all haste and brief the castellan there under the strictest secrecy. If this Iorwedd is agreeable, furnish him with enough funds to raise a small force but supplement it with our own men. Once arranged, send me a message and if everything is in place, we will move against Cadwgan on the first of March. Agreed?'

'Aye, my lord,' replied the four men.

'Good,' said the king. 'Now leave me to my thoughts.'

All four men turned to leave, but as they walked across the room, Henry spoke again.

'Gerald, wait a moment. I would speak to you alone.'

Gerald returned to the table as the men left. Once the door was closed, Henry turned to face him.

'Gerald,' he said, 'you are one of my most trusted knights, yet I have to admit I am concerned about the events you described.'

'In what way, my lord?'

'In several ways. First of all, how could a rebel gain access to one of my castles so easily, even though it was garrisoned by one of my best castellans? In Pembroke, you managed to survive a great siege by overwhelming forces, yet at Cenarth Bychan it seems you rolled over and succumbed without a fight.'

'My lord, we were supposed to be at peace and I anticipated very little threat. My forces were deliberately kept small to avoid antagonising the locals and add credence to the treaty. If I had thought even for a heartbeat we would have been at risk, I would have handled it differently.'

'No doubt,' said the king, 'but the fact remains my son and your wife are now hostages of the Welsh, and that is a situation I cannot contemplate.'

'I understand, my lord, and will move heaven and earth to return him to safety.'

'Him?'

'Your son, my lord.'

'And what about your wife? Would you not do the same for her?'

'Of course, my lord, for they will be together, but my focus will always be on your son.'

Henry sighed and walked around the table to stand before the knight. 'Gerald,' he said quietly, 'I admire your loyalty to the Crown, and your dedication to finding my son is admirable, but let me make this clear. I may be married to Matilda but if circumstances had turned out differently, it would be Nesta sitting alongside me in the throne room, not her. Alas, it was not to be and though Nesta is now your wife, there is still a piece of me that holds affection for her. She is the mother of my son and the woman I once loved. To that effect, I want you to place Nesta alongside my son in importance, for if any harm should come to her, I will hold you fully responsible. Do you understand?'

'Yes, my lord.'

'Good. Liaise with my advisors regarding the details but no matter how long it takes, I want my son and Nesta released. Is that clear?'

'Yes, my lord.'

'Do not fail me in this task, Gerald. Return them both safely and we will overlook your negligence in this matter, but if any harm comes to either of them, then there will be consequences.'

'I understand, my lord,' replied Gerald.'

'Good. Now be gone, you have a lot of work to do.'

As Gerald left the room, the king's aid closed the door behind him. Henry stood over the map, deep in thought. Finally, he turned to the aid. 'Bring John Salisbury to me, but do so in secrecy.'

'Aye, my lord,' said the aid, and he left the room.

Fifteen minutes later John Salisbury returned and acknowledged the king with a slight bow. 'My lord, you summoned me,' he said.

'I did,' said Henry. 'Is anyone aware of your attendance?'

'Only your aid, my lord.'

'Good, then come through.' The two men walked into the inner chamber and the king pointed to an ornate chair. 'Please, take a seat.'

When they were both seated, the king sat back and stared at the constable, remaining silent as one of his servants filled two fresh goblets of wine. When it was done, the king dismissed the servants and the two men were left alone. Salisbury felt uncomfortable but knew it was not his place to ask questions. Finally, the king leaned forward and took a sip of his wine before replacing the goblet on the table.

'Master Salisbury,' he said at last, 'I have heard some good things about you these last few months.'

'You have?' asked Salisbury with genuine surprise.

'Indeed. You may serve across the far side of another country but my eyes and ears are everywhere. They tell me you are a man who has no particular affiliation with anything Welsh. Is that true?'

'I may live amongst them, my lord, but that is in service to you, not through personal choice.'

'I understand,' said the king. 'My spies also say that Gerald is, shall we say, a little *lenient* in the administration of the people of Deheubarth. Is this also true?'

'Again, there is an element of accuracy in that statement, my lord, but as he is married to the Princess Nesta, I suppose it is a delicate role to fulfil.'

'Really?' said the king. 'I would have thought a marriage of convenience should have no bearing whatsoever on the manner of rule in the name of your monarch. Is that not the case?'

'My lord,' replied Salisbury, 'Gerald is a good man and is loyal to you unto death, but if you are asking my opinion on the manner of his servitude, I would have to agree, his stewardship of Deheubarth falls somewhat short of what you may expect.'

'In what way?'

'I would suggest that though there are times when a firm hand may be adequate to maintain the happiness of the people, a mailed fist may be more of a deterrent to those who would wage war against you.'

'So you are saying he is weak?'

'That is not my place, my lord.'

Henry sat back and looked thoughtfully at Salisbury again, sipping on his wine as his mind juggled the information.

'Salisbury,' he said at last. 'My people tell me you are an ambitious man. Is this true?'

'All men aspire to better themselves, my lord. I am no different to them.'

'Good. Then in that case, I have a proposition for you.'

'What sort of proposition, my lord?'

'One that will make you rise to a height that even you may not have envisaged. Does that sound inviting to you?'

'Most certainly, my lord. What do I have to do?'

'Oh, it's very simple, Master Salisbury. All I want is for you to be my eyes and ears within Pembroke Castle. Gerald is to know nothing of this arrangement, and in return, when the time is right, I will ensure you achieve a station far above anything you could ever imagine on your own. These are dangerous times, Master Salisbury, and if the Crown is to keep on top of them, then I need regular information, untainted by misconceived allegiances. Do you understand?'

'Indeed, my lord.'

'Good. Someone will come to your quarters tonight and brief you on how this will work but if you fail me, then perhaps any ambition you currently harbour will disappear along with your life. Do I make myself clear?'

'I will not fail you, my lord.'

'Good, now be gone. We will talk again soon.'

The Palace of Aberffraw

February 10th, AD 1110

Gruffydd ap Cynan stood on top of a hill, breathing in the coastal breeze. It had been two months since he had been reunited with Cynwrig the Tall, and the man who had saved his life had now moved on to seek a life as a priest on the west coast. Gruffydd's hair was now more grey than black and longer than he normally kept it. His body, once taut with muscle formed from the strain of battle, now lay soft beneath his robes, the result of too much ale and too much peace.

Before him lay the dangerous waters separating him from the land of his birth. Though he had seen out his childhood in Dublin, he was a true king of Wales, being the son of Cynan ap Iago and descended from Rhodri Mawr himself. As he contemplated the last few years as the acknowledged king of Gwynedd, he looked down to the beach below, watching his sons and daughter race each other on horseback through the white-topped surf of the Irish Sea. Gruffydd smiled with irony. The sandy yellow shore upon which his children now rode was once soaked red with the blood of Englishmen after he and Magnus Barefoot, the Viking king of Norway, had landed with an army of mercenaries all those years ago to drive the English from Ynys Mon. Many men died that day and though there had been many sleepless nights since, and indeed many more battles, the fact that his children now laughed and exercised on the shore of their own free kingdom made it all worthwhile.

His three sons had grown up to be fine young men and though he had made no choice as to his successor, he knew any one of them would one day make a fine king. Gwenllian, however, gave him cause for concern. Her continued obsession with learning the skills of war caused many sleepless nights for both him and his wife, yet despite all attempts to steer her towards the gentler pastimes usually found with the ladies of a royal court, she steadfastly refused to change her path, wanting only the way of the warrior. Although still young, interests of marriage continued to arrive on almost a weekly basis from suitors throughout Britannia and as far afield as France and Flanders, such was her beauty, but despite the benefits such a union would bring the house of Gwynedd, Gruffydd turned them all away, knowing that to enable such a thing without the agreement of his daughter would break her heart. She was as wild as the gyrfalcons she had come to love over the past few months, free to soar wherever she may choose.

Gruffydd sighed deeply but was interrupted from his musings by the sound of a horse trotting up behind him. He turned and smiled at Osian, his most trusted warrior and right-hand man.

'My lord,' said Osian, reining in his horse. 'My apologies for inter-rupting your walk but Cadwgan has arrived at the palace.'

'Really?' said Gruffydd. 'He is a day early.'

'Shall I bring him out here?'

'No,' replied Gruffydd with a sigh. 'I shall greet him in the great hall. See that he is fed and watered. I will be along shortly.'

'As you wish, my lord,' said Osian, and he turned to ride back to Aberffraw.

Gruffydd waved down at his children, now racing their horses along the sand. It took an age to gain their attention but eventually Gwenllian saw his signal and she led the way back up through the dunes to join her father on the hill.

'It is time to go,' explained Gruffydd when they were all assembled.

'I will go back via the village,' said Cadwallon. 'I have some business there I need to attend.'

'What possible business could you have at such a young age?' asked Gruffydd.

'The sort with long fair hair and a pretty smile,' interrupted Cadwaladr.

'You will leave the girls of the village alone, Cadwallon,' said Gruffydd with a laugh, 'at least until you are another year or so older. Besides, they have a way of distracting young men from their training, and that would never do.'

Cadwallon removed his foot from his stirrup and kicked his brother in the shin for his treachery.

'*Aaah*,' shouted Cadwaladr, and he lashed out in retribution, but it was too late; his brother was already galloping back to the palace, laughing loudly.

'I'll get you for that,' shouted Cadwaladr as he spurred his horse in pursuit.

Gwenllian rode up beside her father and joined him on the journey back, walking her horse slowly beside his.

'You surprise me, Gwenllian,' said Gruffydd as the boys disappeared over the hill.

'Why?'

'I would have thought you would relish the chance for yet another race against your brothers.'

'I have nothing to prove,' said Gwenllian. 'On a level field with equal horses, I will beat any of them nine times out of ten. To win too often puts them in a bad mood and they play tricks on me in retribution.'

'You are a strange girl,' laughed Gruffydd, and they rode awhile in silence.

'Father,' said Gwenllian eventually, 'when you die, will the kingship of Gwynedd go to the eldest or will you share it amongst the boys?'

'That is quite a question, Gwenllian, and truth be told, I have often thought about the matter.'

'So which is it?'

'I said I have thought about it. I did not say I had reached a conclusion.'

'It must tear at your heart to make such a choice.'

'Indeed it does, but it is one I must consider soon for old age is coming towards me like a winter storm.'

'There is an easier answer,' said Gwenllian.

'Which is?'

'You could see Gwynedd have its first queen.'

Gruffydd looked sideways at his daughter, unsure if she was joking, but she was deadly serious. He reined in his horse and stared at her.

'Gwenllian,' he said, 'I know you want great things for this kingdom, and indeed Wales as a whole, but some things cannot be. No country I know of has ever had a woman as a monarch unless she has married a king. Then and only then can she be called queen.'

'It's just not fair,' said Gwenllian. 'I would be a better ruler than any you can mention, yet the opportunity is denied me.'

'I can't change the way of the world, Gwenllian.'

'Then how about just changing the way of Gwynedd?'

Gruffydd smiled. 'Even if it was possible, a woman on the throne of any kingdom would be seen as a weakness and your enemies would swarm to take your crown within days of any coronation.'

'They would not worry me, and they would be dispatched whence they came with their tails between their legs like wounded dogs.'

'Do you know what?' said Gruffydd. 'I believe they would. Anyway, such things are for the future. Don't try to grow up too soon, Gwenllian, just enjoy what we have right now.'

'I know,' she sighed, 'but it is very difficult.'

'I'll tell you what,' said Gruffydd, 'let's race each other back to the palace. I'll even set you a wager.'

'What wager?'

'If I win, you will sit with your mother for one whole day, enjoying her company and showing an interest in her embroidery.'

'I cannot imagine a worse thing,' said Gwenllian, a look of horror on her face.

'I know it will be difficult, but that is my price.'

'And if I win?'

'You can join us for dinner this evening.'

'I don't understand. We eat together most evenings.'

'I know, but not tonight, for I have a very important guest.'

'Who?' asked Gwenllian.

'Cadwgan ap Bleddyn.'

'*The rebel*,' gasped Gwenllian.

'The very same. He has just arrived at the palace and will eat with us tonight. So, do we have a wager?'

'We do,' said Gwenllian, and without waiting for an answer, she spurred her horse to a gallop.

'*Trickery!*' roared Gruffydd with a laugh as he spurred his own horse to pursue his daughter over the dunes and back to the palace of Aberffraw.

———

The rest of the day passed quickly for Gwenllian. First she helped the stable boy groom her horse, before carrying out an hour's sword practice with her brothers. Then she bathed in a wooden tub filled with hot water by the kitchen servants, before donning one of the few dresses she possessed. Finally, her mother's maid tidied her hair, brushing it through a hundred times before leaving it to hang loose about her shoulders.

'We must make you look presentable, my lady,' said the maid, Adele. 'You would bring shame on your father's house should you turn up looking no better than a tavern whore.'

'I don't understand why,' said Gwenllian. 'He is Cadwgan ap Bleddyn, the greatest rebel of our generation. He would be more impressed if I turned up in leggings and a chainmail hauberk, rather than this pathetic finery.'

'On the contrary, his father was a king and Cadwgan is still a prince of Powys. Politeness dictates he is treated as royalty, irrespective of current station. Besides, I hear he has a most handsome son.'

'That is of no relevance to me – unless he wants me to ride alongside him into battle.'

'Oh, Gwenllian,' laughed Adele, turning the girl to face her, 'will you never change?'

'I am happy with who I am. Are you done?'

'I am,' sighed Adele. 'Now go to the great hall but don't forget, you are also representing your father at this feast, so try to act with some decorum.'

'I may not like the frills and nonsense of these sorts of occasions, Adele,' said Gwenllian, 'but I will not dishonour my father.' She leaned over and gave the maid a kiss on the cheek. Adele had been with the family since before Gwenllian was born and was treated as part of the family.

'Go then,' said Adele, 'and enjoy yourself. But remember you are a lady so *try* to act like one.'

Gwenllian poked out her tongue before running out of the room and down the candlelit corridor.

'And walk,' shouted Adele behind her, laughing quietly to herself, knowing that no matter what advice she gave, Gwenllian would do whatever Gwenllian wanted to do.

Gruffydd was standing before the fireplace when Gwenllian entered the hall alongside her mother and the rest of the court ladies. Beside him stood a tall stranger with short black hair and a neatly trimmed beard. Like her father, he was greying gracefully, but despite his well-groomed appearance, Gwenllian could immediately see his face was well weathered and bore the scars of more than one conflict. Around the great hall, a dozen of Cadwgan's men stood talking in small groups along with those of Gruffydd's knights who had been invited to share the meal. All wore clean linen shirts of various colours, but Gwenllian was disappointed to notice that all had surrendered their weapons at the door and none were armed in any way whatsoever.

'Ah,' said Gruffydd, turning to smile at his wife. 'The ladies have arrived.' He took Angharad's hand before turning to his guest. 'Prince Cadwgan, I believe you have met my wife?'

'Many years ago,' agreed Cadwgan, kissing Angharad's hand, 'and can I say, the years have not only been kind but seem to have bestowed you with unnatural amounts of beauty and elegance.'

'You flatter me, Prince Cadwgan,' said Angharad with a smile, 'but please feel free to continue in that manner for the rest of the evening.'

'The truth should never be confused with flattery, my lady,' said Cadwgan. He turned to face Gwenllian. 'And who is this vision from heaven?'

'This is my daughter, Gwenllian,' said Gruffydd.

'Upon my word,' said Cadwgan, 'you have grown into a beauty second only to your mother, and one day will make some prince a very lucky man.'

'My lord Cadwgan,' said Gwenllian with a perfectly executed curtsey. 'I am honoured to meet you and look forward to your tales of battle from the front line of the rebellion.'

'Rebellion?' said Cadwgan. 'My lady, I have not raised a sword for several years, though indeed, the tales of those times can still curdle a man's blood.'

Gwenllian's face beamed but before she could continue, the steward called them to their seats. The room was set up in a narrow horseshoe shape, with just Gruffydd and Cadwgan sat at the top table. Gwenllian sat on the top end of one leg of the horseshoe next to her mother, while her brothers sat amongst the warriors, much to Gwenllian's annoyance. Over fifty men were present at the feast, with Gruffydd's men-at-arms deliberately outnumbering their guests two to one. Gruffydd had learned years ago in the castle of Huw the Fat that no matter how friendly the occasion, a feast was a perfect place for treachery.

'I trust you are hungry, Prince Cadwgan?' said Angharad.

'Indeed,' said Cadwgan, 'and could eat a rotting horse.'

'I think that we can do better than that,' smiled Angharad.

'Horse, boar, stag, I don't mind what meats are served. My hunger will see the bones picked clean.'

'Hmmm,' said Gruffydd, 'if you are expecting red meat, Cadwgan, you may be disappointed.'

'*What?*' roared Cadwgan with mock anger. 'No red meat? How is a man to live?'

'Our meal tonight will have the sophistication of a royal banquet,' said Angharad, 'and though there will be no pigs' heads or legs of venison, I promise you will not be disappointed.' She turned to the steward. 'Let the meal begin.'

A group of minstrels started playing their instruments at the far end of the hall, while a line of serving girls brought trays to the waiting men. Each tray had four clay flasks, each containing a different flavoured wine, from spiced to sweet. Every guest was encouraged to state their preference before being given their own flask to drink. Mead followed along with casks of ale and by the time the first course was served, the hall was alive with high spirits and jovial conversation.

'Ah, here we are,' said Angharad as the serving girls came in with trays of lidded pots, 'the first course has arrived.'

Two of the servants passed out wooden bowls and loaves of bread, while others placed pots along the centre of the tables, one pot between two.

'My lords, ladies and gentlemen,' said the steward loudly, 'the first course is served. Please enjoy spiced plum broth served with the freshest of bread.'

Murmurs of surprise rippled around the room but as it was the first course, everyone soon ladled the soup into their bowls, eating it with relish.

'That was interesting,' said Cadwgan, 'and has certainly whetted my appetite.'

'Good,' said Angharad. 'Do you like losyns?'

'I do,' said Cadwgan slowly, 'but oft wonder what is the point? If a cook is going to make a flour paste, why bake it hard only to boil it again to make it soft. Much better to add butter and make a hearty pastry for a meat-filled pie, if you ask me.'

'Trust me, this will not disappoint,' said Angharad, and she sat back as a servant ladled strips of losyns onto her plate topped with layers of cheese and ham sauce.

Gruffydd tried not to laugh as the prince tried desperately not to exhibit his disappointment.

'It looks lovely,' said Cadwgan with an unconvincing smile.

The rest of the meal was similarly received, with dishes rarely seen by fighting men. Flasks of almond milk were served to wash away the strong cheese taste, and the meal was rounded off with bowls of rice smothered with honey and crushed almonds. By now the ale was flowing freely, and though some still moaned about the lack of meat, most were far too drunk to care, wolfing the food down as if it was the last meal they would ever eat.

Eventually the plates and trenchers were cleared away and the tankards topped up. Storytellers recited tales of Hywel Dda and Rhodri Mawr, roared on by patriotic, though very drunk, warriors, and the evening was wound up with raucous singing and much spilled ale. Tests of strength between the two groups were carefully managed to avoid outbreaks of violence but overall the evening passed by very successfully. Despite the vast quantities of ale and wine sunk by both sides, Gruffydd and Cadwgan had drunk only moderately and both remained sober, knowing their night would continue with private talks long into the early hours.

Gwenllian loved every minute of the feast, laughing at the antics of the warriors and their frequent use of curse words, some of which she had never heard before. Cadwgan told her many tales of the battles over the past few years, and she had listened to the stories of brutality, treachery and honour with fascination, entranced by the lifestyle the rebel prince had led.

All too soon it came to the end of the evening and though she could have listened to the prince for hours, she finally retired to her quarters, laughing at the drunken songs of the rebels as they made their way back to their tents situated just outside the palace boundaries. Cadwgan and Gruffydd remained alone in the great hall and moved to two chairs situated alongside the fire. A servant brought fresh ale and they sat back in comfort to enjoy the quiet, broken only by the crackling of the firewood.

Gruffydd turned to the servant standing near one of the doors.

'Boy,' he called, 'get yourself to the kitchens and bring us a platter piled with whatever meat the cook has ready for tomorrow.'

'My lord,' said the servant, 'my master will be asleep. If I wake him, he will have me beaten.'

'Nonsense,' said Gruffydd. 'If he lays one hand on you, I will make you the cook and him your servant. Quickly now, and slice it thick. Our guest here looks like he will kill himself unless he is fed some sort of animal in the next few minutes.'

'Yes, my lord,' said the servant, and he ran through the door to the kitchens. A few minutes later he returned with a tray laden with sliced pork, half a ham and a whole chicken, along with a loaf of bread fresh from the oven and a pot of salted butter.

'It looks like you found a great treasure trove,' laughed Gruffydd.

'It was for the midday meal tomorrow,' said the boy. 'The cook will have to do something else.'

'You could always have losyns,' said Cadwgan with a smirk, and both men burst out laughing.

'Go to bed, boy,' said Gruffydd, 'and worry not. Tomorrow's lack of midday meal is of my doing, nobody else's. Now be gone.'

The boy ran from the room and both men leaned forward to help themselves to slices of pork, eating silently as the much-missed flavours caused their mouths to water.

'That's better,' said Cadwgan after taking a long draught of ale, 'meat and ale, the true food of kings.'

'Yes,' sighed Gruffydd. 'Please excuse the situation earlier. I fear my wife has been talking to some traders who passed through recently and filled her head with the current trends of royalty. Unfortunately, your arrival coincided with her desperation to try out the latest foods enjoyed by those in London.'

'On the contrary,' said Cadwgan, 'the food was perfectly lovely but perhaps a banquet may not have been the place to try it out, especially one attended by seasoned warriors. Luckily they were too drunk to make a fuss.' He looked down at the plate of meat. 'Still, we have this now so everything is well in the world.'

Gruffydd smiled and stared at Cadwgan for a moment. In his day, Cadwgan had been the most feared man in Wales, roaming the Marches along the border and attacking English interests at will before disappearing back into the hills like morning mist. Several times the English had put a price on his head and many men had died in pursuit of the bounty. Recently, though, he had suffered ill health, so when Gruffydd had signed a treaty with Henry and had been granted stewardship of Montgomery, the Welsh king had negotiated the bounty be removed from his friend's head in return for keeping Cadwgan under his control. Subsequently, Gruffydd had granted Cadwgan temporary lordship of Montgomery in his name, a boon the Welsh prince had gladly accepted.

'You have a lovely family, Gruffydd,' said Cadwgan, 'and should be very proud.'

'I am, and also very grateful,' said Gruffydd.

'Grateful to whom?'

'To God, to the church, even to the English Crown.'

Cadwgan sipped on his ale, eying the Welsh king thoughtfully.

'You surprise me,' he said eventually. 'I never thought I would see you displaying servitude to an English king.'

'Do not mistake gratitude for servitude,' replied Gruffydd, 'and actually, I would have thought your manner would harbour at least a little of the former.'

'Why should I be grateful to the English?' asked Cadwgan. 'They have stolen my lands, imprisoned my brother and made a vassal of another. They have killed my people for as long as I can remember and you expect gratitude? I think not, my friend.'

'All of these things are true, yet it is Henry's hand that signed the document enabling you to see out your days as a free man.'

'My agreement is with you, not Henry,' said Cadwgan, 'and the circumstances leading up to that event were not of my doing.'

'Perhaps not, but you enjoy the benefits so a more measured approach may be called for.'

'I cannot simply remove my memories, Gruffydd,' said Cadwgan with a sigh. 'I have spent my entire life fighting their tyranny and now you expect me to roll over like a beaten dog?'

'I have fought just as long as you, Cadwgan,' said Gruffydd, 'and have seen many friends and family fall to English blades. I spent a large part of my life rotting in a stinking cell, not knowing if each day was my last, but even I can see there is no point in continuing to throw our young men's lives away needlessly. The English Crown can muster an army a thousandfold bigger than any we could ever dream of, yet they allow us the freedom to control our own kingdoms without the threat of war. Surely we should now embrace the opportunity and enjoy the peace it brings?'

'You sound like my brother,' sneered Cadwgan, 'a mere vassal of an unlawful French king.'

'Perhaps, but you should realise the betterment of the people sometimes outranks the needs of the individual.'

'Spoken like a man already beaten,' said Cadwgan.

Gruffydd sighed. 'My friend, don't forget, the reason you are not already dead is because of the amnesty I negotiated on your behalf.'

'Granted, but I would still rather die than bend the knee to an English king.'

'And what of your children?'

'They are men in a man's world, Gruffydd, and need to find their own path.'

'Then you would consign them to a needless death?'

Cadwgan placed his goblet on the table and sat back before staring at the king.

'What is this about, Gruffydd? Why have you summoned me here?'

'You know why, Cadwgan. We need to talk about Owain and the great risk he has placed upon this country.'

'What about him?'

'I want you to give him up, Cadwgan. I want you to betray your son.'

The Palace of Aberffraw

February 10th, AD 1110

Cadwgan looked at the king as if he had grown two heads. 'If I did not know you better, Gruffydd,' he said quietly, 'I would say you were a madman. My mind screams out that you are surely an imposter, yet my eyes tell me you are the same man who stood alongside me in raids throughout the Marches. The proud Welshman who swore to die rather than see the English kill their way through our country. The fabled king who was defeated on many occasions yet always returned to fight for what was right, freedom and family. What happened, Gruffydd? Is it that now you have your own kingdom and the luxury of your family close by, safe behind these impressive stone walls? Or has this so-called treaty poisoned your mind and you now bend the knee with hand outstretched, begging for the king's coin.'

'You talk nonsense, Cadwgan,' said Gruffydd, 'and it is neither of those things.'

'Then what is it, Gruffydd?' shouted Cadwgan, getting to his feet. 'What in God's world led you to believe for a second I would actually betray my own son?'

Gruffydd remained seated and spoke quietly. 'Cadwgan, I know I ask a lot . . .'

'You ask the impossible,' snarled Cadwgan.

'I know I ask a lot,' repeated Gruffydd patiently, 'but I am in possession of certain information that points to an all-out war with Henry, a war we can never win.'

'What is this information that is so important that it makes you ask your oldest friend to tear out his own heart? For that is what it means to me, Gruffydd.'

'Sit down, and I will explain.'

Cadwgan dropped back into his seat and filled his tankard with ale, downing it in one before refilling it again and turning to stare at his friend.

'Well? I'm waiting.'

'Cadwgan, what Owain did at Cenarth Bychan is an act of war, nothing less. He attacked an English castle, taking advantage of weaker defences during a cultural festival, killed two of the guards and abducted the wife and children of one of Henry's most favoured knights.'

'It is nothing compared to what they have done to us in the past,' said Cadwgan.

'I know, but those days must remain behind us. If this treaty holds, then there is a chance we can negotiate some sort of self-governance, but Owain's actions have thrown that possibility into serious doubt.'

'Gruffydd,' said Cadwgan, 'I am more than aware of what Owain did, but you ask me to condemn my own blood when he has done no worse than the deeds of his father. I know the details are different but the effects are the same. I only wish I was well enough to ride alongside him.'

'This is different, Cadwgan. The knight he has wronged is a favourite of the king, a treaty was broken and an English castle sacked, but most of all, the woman he abducted is a favourite of the people, a Welsh princess of Deheubarth, one of our own.'

'She was married to the enemy.'

'Perhaps so, but at least she ensured Gerald treated the people of Deheubarth fairly, and there is a feeling of anger sweeping throughout the population. Owain has made a grave mistake, Cadwgan, he is turning our own people against him.'

'Now it is you who talks nonsense. What true Welshman would turn against one of their own for inflicting pain on the English? If you know of even one, then name him, Gruffydd, for I will call that man a traitor.'

'Iorwedd ap Bleddyn,' said Gruffydd quietly.

'*What?*'

'You heard me,' said Gruffydd. 'Your brother is set to take up arms against you.'

'You must be wrong. Iorwedd would never betray me. Besides, he has been incarcerated in Hen Domen Castle for the past seven years.'

'This is the information I wanted to share, Cadwgan. My spies tell me that Iorwedd has been released in return for bearing arms against you and your son. In addition, he has been promised lands and recognition in Powys, subject to Owain being captured or killed.'

'I don't believe you,' said Cadwgan. 'Iorwedd is still my brother and as loyal as they come.'

'I have no need to lie to you, Cadwgan, but that is not the worst. While Iorwedd recruits men in Powys, Gerald has already mustered his forces in Deheubarth and is set to march north as we speak. There is also talk of a third column under the command of someone called Robert Fitzhamon, but our knowledge is sparse at the moment and we know not where they are.'

'So what are you saying, Gruffydd?' asked Cadwgan. 'Do you think they all intend to march against us?'

'I do, but it gets worse. I have heard that the barons are building their forces in the Marches. If this is true, and those two columns continue up through Ceredigion, then they could be on the borders of Gwynedd within weeks. With your brother already on the move, if that happens we would be squeezed between two overwhelming armies and would stand no chance of driving them back.'

'Is that what this is all about, Gruffydd, the fear of losing your precious kingdom? Because if it is, let me remind you that some of us have already trodden that path and you will find few tears of sympathy shed amongst your peers.'

'If Gwynedd falls, Cadwgan, then any hope of independence for Wales, no matter how small, is gone forever. We are the only independent kingdom that holds any sort of influence when negotiating with Henry. When he wants to talk peace, he comes to me. When he wants to talk trade, his envoys bang on the doors of Aberffraw, and when his head turns to war, then it is my army that stays his arm. Wales needs Gwynedd, Cadwgan, and well you know it.'

'You overestimate your influence, Gruffydd,' said Cadwgan. 'You are a minor king, no more than that.'

'Perhaps, but one who holds the north together and as long as that remains the case, then Wales is at least half free.'

Both men fell silent and refilled their tankards.

'So what exactly is it you want from me?' said Cadwgan.

'I want you to get Owain to hand himself in,' said Gruffydd. 'Get him to release Princess Nesta and her children and I will make personal representations to the king and beg for mercy. The only thing is, it has to be in the next few days for once Henry's forces start marching, there may be no stopping them.'

Silence fell again before Cadwgan shook his head.

'I can't do it, Gruffydd. I can't deliver my son into English hands.'

'Even though your country depends on it?'

'Would you?' asked Cadwgan, turning to face the king.

'That's not a fair question,' said Gruffydd.

'But it is. Look into your heart and answer me truthfully. If you were offered the freedom of our country but in return you had to hand one of your children over to face certain death, what would your choice be?'

Gruffydd returned Cadwgan's stare but did not answer.

'I thought so,' said Cadwgan, getting to his feet, 'and therein lies your answer. We are done here, Gruffydd. First thing in the morning I will return to Ceredigion, and if your prophesies come to pass, then I will be found standing alongside my son, sword in hand.'

'Wait,' said Gruffydd, getting to his feet. 'If you won't hand over Owain, then at least try to get him to release Nesta. Perhaps if you can do that, we may regain the confidence of our own people.'

Cadwgan took a deep breath and paused, staring into Gruffydd's eyes before answering.

'I will see what I can do.'

'Thank you, my friend,' said Gruffydd as he held out his sword arm.

Cadwgan paused again before grasping the king's forearm in friendship. They had been through too much together to fall out now.

'Sleep well, my friend,' said Cadwgan, 'and worry not. Whatever happens, it is all part of God's good plan.'

'Now you sound like a priest,' laughed Gruffydd. 'Get out of here.' He watched as Cadwgan left through a door at the far end of the hall before sitting back in the seat by the fire to finish his drink.

'So,' said a voice behind him, 'how did it go?'

Gruffydd looked up at Osian.

'Not good, Osian,' he said with a sigh. 'I think he may go some way to meet our demands but am unsure.'

'How unsure?'

'Put it this way, tomorrow morning we set about honing every blade in our armouries.' He looked up at his friend. 'I think the English may be coming, Osian, and this time they're coming to stay.'

Cantref Mawr

February 11th, AD 1110

Nesta stood at the door of the thatched hut, staring down to the stream at the bottom of the short hill. Her two boys were playing together, making boats from twigs and leaves before racing them down into the pool where the horses drank. The trees surrounding the small clearing were interspersed with several small huts, along with a pig pen and a cowshed where two cows were kept for milking. Chickens roamed freely and the smell of cooking wafted from the communal hut used by the single men under the command of Owain. There were a few women at the settlement, including two whores who made a good living in one of the huts further into the trees, but Nesta wasn't too bothered. That trade was common in every village, and as long as her boys did not witness anything untoward, then it was no business of hers.

Of more concern was the fact that Emma had been taken back to Pembroke and released in the marketplace. Not that Nesta begrudged Emma her freedom, but it did mean that she alone was now responsible for the safety of the boys, a situation as strange as it was challenging.

'Stay away from the pool, Henry,' she called. 'You could fall in.'

'Leave them be,' said a gentle voice from close behind her. 'They are just having some fun.' A pair of strong arms wrapped around her and Owain laid his chin on her shoulder.

Nesta caught her breath at the sound of his voice and a shiver ran up her spine at his touch. Unlike her husband's, it was firm yet gentle with a promise of safety within his arms, not just the volcanic passion they shared on the cold winter nights but also the gentler, more loving times they enjoyed when a gentle touch was just as exciting as the fieriest embrace. Her eyes closed momentarily as she breathed in his manly scent, but despite her rising desire, her mind dragged her back to the reality of their situation. She knew it couldn't last. If she was some little-known wife of a minor baron, they may have had a chance but as the wife of one of Henry's castellans, and mother of the king's son, there was no way the monarch could let Owain get away with her abduction. Her hand lifted to his cheek and her head turned to face his, their lips meeting gently.

'Happy?' asked Owain.

'For the moment,' she sighed, 'but we are living a lie, Owain. We both know that this is just a dream and one from which we will have a rude awakening any day soon.'

'You fret too much,' said Owain. 'There is no need for this to ever end. You are a princess of Deheubarth and I am the heir to Powys. We are doing no wrong, Nesta, just remember that.'

'And what about the two men you killed to get me here?' said Nesta. 'What should they remember?'

'They should remember to stay dead,' said Owain.

'Owain, I am being serious. We both know we can't live here for the rest of our lives.'

'Why not? We have everything we need, or do you crave the walls of a castle to cement your position?'

'Such things are of no interest to me,' said Nesta, 'but look at this place. It is little more than a hovel in the middle of nowhere. How can I be expected to bring up my children in such a place?'

'It looks like they are doing just fine,' said Owain.

'You know what I mean, Owain. Henry is the son of the king of England and William was fathered by one of Henry's strongest knights. Do you really think they will let us get away with this?'

Owain released his grip and walked back into the hut, closely followed by Nesta. He was barefoot and dressed only in a pair of leggings. The flesh on his chest was taut against the underlying muscle and his fair hair framed his face as pretty as any picture.

'Owain,' she continued, ignoring the surge of attraction, 'we have to talk about this sooner or later.'

'Why?' asked Owain, sitting on the edge of the bed and pulling on his leather boots. 'Why can we not just enjoy the moment and worry about the rest as it happens?'

'Because when Gerald rides in here, as he will, then who is to say one of my boys will not be cut down by a stray arrow?'

'That is highly unlikely,' said Owain.

'Really? I have already seen my mother cut down by an arrow meant for another and I have no desire to see a similar tragedy. We have had our fun, Owain, just take me back and I will beg Gerald to let you live.'

Owain sighed deeply and got to his feet. 'My dearest Nesta, I promise I will never let anything like that happen to you or the boys. I swear it upon my life, your safety will always be at the forefront of my mind.'

'How can you promise that, Owain? You don't know what Gerald is capable of.'

'I promise because I control the Cantref Mawr,' replied Owain. 'My men occupy vantage points from here as far down as Dinefwr and any movement not authorised by me will be reported by the time night falls.

If Gerald is stupid enough to ride against me, I can have you a hundred leagues away before the sun next sets.'

'I'm sure you can,' said Nesta, 'but that is no way for my boys to live. Let us go, Owain, I beg you.'

Owain lifted his hands and drew her face close to his, kissing her gently.

'Tell me,' he said eventually, 'does Gerald treat you as well as I?'

'He is a good man, Owain,' she whispered.

'There are men over in the whorehouse that I class as good, Nesta. It is not a measure of love, or desire or even caring. Does he make you feel the way I make you feel?'

'No,' she said, looking down at the floor.

'And don't you reckon you have suffered enough in this life? Don't you think that you deserve to feel like the princess that you are?'

'Yes but . . .'

'But nothing, Nesta. You are a very special person and deserve to be treated as such. Stay with me and I promise every day will be like the first.'

'Your words are like honey, Owain, and your touch burns me like the hottest fire, but we have to put the safety of others before our passion.'

'You leave the safety to me,' said Owain with a smile, as he pushed a wisp of her hair to the side of her head. 'All I need you to do is be the person you were meant to be.'

'Oh, Owain,' sighed Nesta. 'Your sweet words could charm the dead from their graves.'

'I don't know about that, Nesta, but I do know our own graves will welcome us all too soon. Therefore, we must grasp life while we can.' He pulled her closer to him and kissed her again, but this time she surrendered totally, wrapping her arms around his neck. Owain started leading her back to the bed but a call from outside made him look up in alarm.

'Owain, one of our scouts has arrived and begs audience.'

Owain smiled ironically at Nesta and gently loosened himself from the embrace.

'Wait here,' he said, 'I will be but moments.' He walked out of the hut, pulling on a shirt as he went. Outside, Bedwyr stood the other side of the stream, spear in hand and clad in leather armour.

'Who is it?' asked Owain as he walked.

'Jonas,' replied Bedwyr. 'He is down with the horses.'

Owain walked down the slope to the paddock. Several horses chewed nonchalantly on their feed, while another drank deeply from a leather bucket. Four men stood in a circle sharing a goatskin of ale, obviously thirsty from a long ride.

'Jonas Betterman,' said Owain, 'what brings you from your post before you are relieved?'

'My lord,' said Jonas, 'I come bearing grave news. Gerald has led a column from Carew to Dinefwr Castle and has been there for several days. They are camped on the plain below its walls and engage in war-like pastimes.'

'Such as?'

'They train every day with archers and swordsmen. They also prac-tise shield walls and the commands used for advances under the pike. It looks like they are gathering supplies from the area to support a campaign into the Cantref Mawr.'

'I suppose any knight that maintains an army has to keep them trained. This may be nothing more than good leadership.'

'My lord, our spies tell us that Gerald's stewards are procuring salted meats and sacks of oats, loading them onto carts. He has also bought over a hundred chickens and six milk cows.'

'I see,' said Owain, realising that such activity could only mean the column was about to embark on a campaign. 'What is his strength?'

'About a hundred horsemen and double that men-at-arms.'

'Archers?'

'Another fifty. The tale they tell in the village is that they are travelling east to Brycheniog, but one of the whores in our pay heard off one of the lancers that their real target lies northward. She couldn't get him to say more but it seems obvious that they intend to march on us here.'

'What is our strength in the south?'

'About fifty men in total,' said Jonas. 'We can slow them up from the cover of the trees but I fear we will be an annoyance only.'

Owain thought quickly. The Cantref Mawr was a notoriously difficult place to campaign in but the recent years of peace had seen the routes made easier, a situation he needed to change.

'Right,' he said. 'Get back to Dinefwr as quickly as you can. Rally every man still loyal to us and recruit them into your command. In addition, find all the foresters and carpenters from the villages and have them cut down any high trees along the sides of the main tracks into the cantref. Let's slow them up as much as we can. Work your way back here but as you go, burn every bridge over every stream and task the farmers with herding their cattle along the tracks. I want every route turned into a quagmire before the first Englishman sets foot beneath our trees.'

'Aye, my lord,' replied Jonas.

Owain turned to Bedwyr. 'My friend, to you I give the most important task. I want you to muster our archers, split them into two groups and worry the column at every opportunity. Whenever Gerald stops to negotiate an obstacle or slows down due to the heavy going, I want a storm of arrows to fall amongst them like autumn rain. I also want you to launch hit-and-run attacks throughout the night. Deny them any sleep for the entire time they are within our lands.'

'Aye, my lord,' replied Bedwyr.

'Good. Set to your tasks immediately. If that still doesn't turn them back, we will strike from their flanks but disappear before they have time to draw a blade. By the time they reach this place, any not dead by willow and steel will be exhausted and in no condition to fight.'

As his men left to seek saddles and fresh horses, Owain walked over to the pond where Nesta's two boys were still sailing their boats. He knelt down beside them, joining in the fun for a few moments before straightening up and speaking in a calm but firm voice. 'Right, you two young knights, it is time to get back to your mother. Tomorrow we will be going on another journey so eat well tonight and if you are good, perhaps you can each have your own horse.'

'Are we going to see my father?' asked William.

'No,' said Owain, 'you are going to see mine.'

Hen Domen

April 21st, AD 1110

Sir Broadwick sat on a chair in the room usually used as quarters for visiting guests. Opposite him was a large bed, currently surrounded by several women, a priest and a physician. On the bed lay the severely injured figure of Sir Julian, the knight so cruelly mutilated by the monster who called himself Diafol. Patiently Broadwick waited, his fingers tapping out a rhythm on the table at his side as the group tended to the victim's terrible wounds. Finally, they each finished what they were doing and left the room, leaving only the physician behind.

Broadwick stood up and approached the bed, standing alongside the physician as he poured small amounts of poppy milk between the lips of the patient.

'How is he doing?' asked Broadwick.

'He is remarkably strong,' said the physician, 'and his wounds are healing well. There is an infection in his right leg that gives him a lot of pain but if he can beat that, then there is no reason why he cannot survive, though to live the life that would be available to him seems hardly worth it.'

Broadwick looked down at the bandaged man. His arms and legs were heavily wrapped, though the stumps of each limb were stained through the seepage of pus and blood. Another bandage covered his eyes and though his mouth was uncovered to allow easy breathing, Broadwick could see the jagged but healed remains of the torn tongue within.

'Is he conscious?' asked Broadwick.

'Yes, but communication is impossible.'

'Let me be the judge of that,' said Broadwick. 'If you are done, then leave us alone.'

The physician placed his tools in his leather pouch and put them in his bag before leaving the room. Broadwick waited until the door was closed before sitting on the edge of the bed and placing his hand on the shoulder of the patient.

'Sir Julian,' he said quietly. 'Can you hear me?'

For a second there was no response, but then the man's head turned slightly and he moaned in reply.

'Good,' said Broadwick. 'I know you are in pain, my friend, but I need to find out who did this thing to you. Perhaps if you grunt once for yes and twice for no, we may be able to get somewhere. Do you think you can help me with that?'

Again the man moaned and Broadwick sighed deeply. This was going to be very difficult, if not impossible, but he had to try.

'Good,' said Broadwick. 'First of all, can you tell me if you saw the man who was responsible for causing you these horrible injuries?'

The man moaned once and encouraged by the success, Broadwick continued the questioning, receiving simple noises in return.

'Right. Next question. Is he known to you?'

No.

'Did you hear him speak?'

Yes.

'Is he of Welsh descent?'

Yes.

'Did you hear a name mentioned?'

Yes.

'Was it a name you heard anywhere before?'

No.

'Was the name Diafol?'

Julian paused a while before answering but eventually the grunt came, this time sharp, conveying the anger within him.

'All right,' said Broadwick, 'we have at least confirmed the man responsible, but I have to be honest with you and say I know nothing of this man. Somehow we need to find out a little more, and if I can put a face to him or even find out where he crawls to at night, I swear I will have his head for you. Now, a few more questions. Was he a brigand?'

No.

'A military man then?'

No.

'A peasant?'

No.

'How many men did you see? Were there more than ten?'

Yes.

'More than a hundred?'

Yes.

Broadwick's brows knitted in confusion. What man could muster that sort of force without word reaching the castellan?

'Then perchance he was a noble?'

No response.

'Was he a noble, Sir Julian?'

Again no answer.

'You're not sure?'

One grunt.

'So he may have been a noble but you can't be sure?'

One grunt.

Broadwick sat back, his mind working overtime. The description led him to believe that the culprit was probably Cadwgan ap Bleddyn, but he was supposed to be in Ceredigion. Perhaps it was his son, Owain.

'Julian,' he said, sitting forward again, 'have you ever seen Owain ap Cadwgan?'

No.

'So you would not know if this was the rebel prince?'

No.

Broadwick started to ask further questions but Sir Julian started coughing, spraying blood over the recently changed covers. Broadwick leaned forward and lifted him into a sitting position, wiping the blood from his own face with a piece of linen from the table at the side of the bed. Sir Julian's shoulders began to shake and he started to cry, but instead of shying away, Broadwick held him tightly, showing the brotherhood that men who had not experienced battle could never understand. As the crying subsided, Broadwick heard Julian try to form words and he sat back, holding his friend at arm's length.

'I'm sorry, my friend,' he said gently, 'I can't understand you. Try again.'

'Keee meee,' said Julian, his tears running from beneath his blood-soaked bandages.

'Keee meee?' repeated Broadwick slowly. 'Sorry, Julian, I . . .'

'Keee meee,' said Julian again, but this time a lot louder. 'Keee meee . . . Keee meee!' He started shaking and screamed at the top of his voice as the tears started again. '*KEEE MEEE!*'

'Keee meee?' said Broadwick again in confusion, but as Julian's shouting died away to a whisper, the light of realisation dawned in his eyes.

'*Kill me,*' he whispered to himself.

He stood up and backed away, shocked at his friend's request, but before he reached the door, the physician returned, drawn by the shouting, and ran over to the bed with more milk of the poppy.

'What happened?' asked the physician.

'I think his mind has gone,' said Broadwick.

'You ask too much of him,' said the physician. 'Why can't you leave him alone?'

Ordinarily the knight would have admonished the physician for his tone but he was too shocked. He had seen many men die over the years and many more wounded but never had he seen a fellow knight reduced to such a state. Without answering he turned and stormed out of the room, making his way to the kitchens. If there was ale to be had, it would be there.

Several hours later, Broadwick stood atop the palisade, looking over the open space towards the distant village. The moon glinted from between fleeting clouds and there was a threat of rain in the air. Lights shone from unshuttered windows and when the wind blew in the right direction, he could hear the faint sound of laughter from the taverns in the village.

'It sounds like the commoners are enjoying themselves,' said Baldwin, appearing at his side.

'Sometimes I envy them,' said Broadwick, much to Baldwin's surprise.

'Really?' he asked. 'What part of a commoner's life could you possibly envy?'

'The lack of responsibility,' said Broadwick. 'All they need to do is till the field and pay the tithe. After that, all they need to worry about is eating, sleeping and death.'

'It still doesn't appeal to me,' said Baldwin with a sigh. 'I would rather the fires of the hall, the meat of the hunt and the blessings of the abbot before we are called to the grave. I see no burden in that.'

'My lord,' said Broadwick, 'I have a great boon to ask.'

'Name it,' said Baldwin.

'I beg consent to leave this place and go out on a quest of my own. One which could take me a long time or even cost me my life.'

'Can I ask what this quest is?'

'It is personal to me and my code, and I would prefer to keep it within my heart.'

'You do realise there is talk of an invasion?' said Baldwin. 'If that comes to pass and you are not back, who is to lead my forces in his name?'

'There are other knights just as worthy,' said Broadwick, 'and if I am successful, there may not be a need for war.'

Baldwin paused and gazed out over the palisade, considering the request. Finally, he turned to his favoured knight.

'I am of a mind to deny your request, Sir Broadwick, but I know you are a man of honour and once your heart is set on a task, then there will be no turning you away. So go on this quest with my blessing but come back a better man with a lightened heart. Is there anything you need – men, weapons, money?'

'I need none of those things, and must do this on my own.'

'So be it,' said Baldwin.

Broadwick turned away and walked towards the steps leading down into the bailey.

'Are you leaving now, at such short notice?' asked Baldwin.

'No, my lord,' said Broadwick over his shoulder. 'I will ride with the dawn but first there is something I must do.' He continued down the steps and disappeared into the shadows of the castle.

Sir Julian was sleeping fitfully when Broadwick entered his chamber. The knight walked across the room and sat on the chair by the bed staring at the man he had ridden alongside many times. All afternoon his mind had been in turmoil for he had lost count of how many men he had seen die, yet none had affected him as much as the man before him. He leaned forward and shook Julian gently by the shoulders.

'Sir Julian, wake up,' he said quietly.

The wounded knight responded by turning his head towards the unseen visitor.

'Can you hear me?' asked Broadwick.

Julian nodded his head.

'I have brought you some things,' said Broadwick. 'We are both about to go on a journey.' He bent down and picked up a bridle, placing it next to Julian's face. 'This is from your horse. The destrier scent is strong upon it. Do you recognise him?'

Julian nodded gently, breathing in the smell of the most important possession in his life.

'I have also brought you this,' said Broadwick, and he placed Julian's heavy broadsword across his chest. 'It was found in the back of the cart along with your chainmail. No man should be without his weapon, my friend, no matter how heavy the wound.'

Julian lifted his heavily bandaged stumps and cradled the weapon as if it was a baby, remembering all the battles in which it had seen him safe.

'Finally,' said Broadwick, 'I have brought some ale and want to share a drink in your name. Will you join me?'

Julian nodded and Broadwick lifted him up into a sitting position before pouring a tankard of ale.

'To you, my friend,' he said, 'and the comradeship that all knights share.' He lifted the tankard to his mouth and drank half the contents before leaning forward and placing it against the lips of his fellow knight. He poured the ale slowly, pulling it away when Sir Julian coughed.

'Do you know why I am here?' asked Broadwick quietly when the coughing stopped.

Julian nodded gently and despite his pain, managed to smile.

'And you are sure you want this?'

Again Julian nodded his head.

'Then so be it,' said Broadwick, and he lifted Julian back up to a sitting position. He placed his left arm around the patient's shoulder and whispered into his ear. 'My friend, before you go, know this. I will track down the man who did this to you and make him pay a hundredfold. This I swear upon my oath and before God.' As he felt Julian's body tense in anticipation, Broadwick drew the knife from his belt and thrust it firmly up under Julian's ribs. Julian gasped in pain, his arms clamping tight around his killer's shoulders. 'Travel safely, my friend,' said Broadwick, 'and may God go with you.' With a final effort he drove the blade home, forcing it to one side to cut Julian's heart in two. Julian's head flew back in agony but Broadwick held him tight, feeling the life leaving his body.

For over a minute he stayed there, embracing his fellow knight, and though he was sad to see the man die, his heart was lighter for he would have wanted the same done for him. Finally, he laid Julian back down and covered his body with a sheet before returning to his quarters.

The following morning, the sun was not yet over the horizon when a lone man led his horse across the bailey towards the palisade gate.

'Hold,' said the gatekeeper. 'Who is it that leaves at such an hour?'

Broadwick removed his hood and looked at the guard without speaking.

The guard hesitated for a moment, hardly recognising the garrison commander, dressed as he was in the heavy cloak of a monk.

'Well done,' said Broadwick quietly. 'Now let me through. There is work to be done.'

'Yes, my lord,' said the guard, and he pulled the gates open enough for the knight and his horse to walk through.

Broadwick paused as he passed the soldier.

'You are new here, boy. What is your name?'

'Phillip, my lord, and I hail from Oxford.'

'Well, Phillip of Oxford, you will keep this moment between you and I.'

'My lord?'

'If anyone asks, just say that I rode out in full armour. Say nothing about my appearance. Do you understand?'

'Yes, my lord,' said Phillip.

'Good. When I return, if I find you were good to your word, then perhaps I can find you a place in my personal guard but if not, you will feed the crows before that day is out. Do I make myself clear?'

'Yes, my lord,' said Phillip.

'Good. In that case, I'll be on my way. Lock the gate behind me, Phillip, these are dangerous times.'

The guard watched the knight walk through the gates before sliding the bar closed and running up the steps to the palisade. Down below, Broadwick paused and mounted his horse before urging him forward onto the road.

'Who's that?' asked another guard walking over.

'I don't know,' lied Phillip. 'He didn't say.'

Tregaron

May 2nd, AD 1110

Cadwgan stood at the gates of his manor courtyard, peering down the long road leading south. A covered cart lumbered its way along the muddy path towards him, escorted by five heavily armed horsemen, each draped in leather capes against the worst of the Welsh weather. Cadwgan turned to the squire by his side.

'Jonathan, go to the great hall and ensure the fires are banked up.'

'Yes, my lord,' said the squire.

'And tell the kitchens to heat some potage. I have a feeling our guests are going to be both cold and hungry.'

'Yes, my lord,' said the squire, and he ran across the courtyard towards the two-storey manor house at the far end of the stockade.

Cadwgan returned his attention to the approaching caravan, wiping the rain from his face as one of the riders spurred his horse forward to approach the prince.

'My lord,' said the rider, 'it is good to see you again.'

'And you, Bedwyr,' said Cadwgan. 'I assume you have been sent from the Cantref Mawr.'

'I have, my lord. Owain tasked me to deliver this cart safely into your care.'

Cadwgan looked over at the cart, now only a few minutes away. 'And where is my son?'

'He had to stay back, my lord. Gerald has pushed into the forests and, despite our resistance, makes good headway. Owain has mustered his men to lead a counter-offensive.'

'How strong is Gerald's force?'

'Over five hundred, my lord, including cavalry.'

'Horsemen are of little use within the forests,' said Cadwgan. 'But enough talk, there is business to attend. Take your men to the stables and see to your horses. There will be food available in a short while and I will see you get a place to sleep.'

'You have my thanks, my lord, but I promised your son that as soon as the caravan was delivered, we would turn around and head back. Owain will need every man he can get.'

'Bedwyr,' said Cadwgan, 'your loyalty and courage are to be admired but you will be no use to my son after such a hard ride on the same horses. Stay this night and ride back on the morrow, well rested, well fed and much more able to offer a strong sword arm. Besides, it will soon be dark and you will have to camp anyway. It may as well be behind sturdy wooden walls.'

Bedwyr nodded, knowing the prince was right. They were already exhausted and another night under sodden canvas did not appeal to him.

'One night, my lord,' he said.

'Excellent. See to your men and get some dry clothes. When you are done, seek me out in the big house. I would have news about the troubles in the Cantref Mawr.'

'Yes, my lord,' said Bedwyr, and he turned aside as the cart finally lumbered through the gates, drawn by two exhausted horses. Cadwgan walked around the back and unhitched the tailgate, letting it drop down. He undid the ties on the flaps and pulled them to one side, peering into the gloomy interior. At the far end a beautiful young woman sat amongst a pile of dirty furs. Her eyes were swollen and tearful and under each arm huddled a tired young boy.

'Princess Nesta,' he said eventually. 'Welcome to Tregaron.'

Several hours later, Nesta came down into the great hall from her allocated rooms. Cadwgan sat next to the fire and he stood as she entered, before inviting her to take the seat opposite him.

'Princess,' he said with a smile, 'may I call you Nesta?'

'Of course,' came the reply.

'Good, and you will call me Cadwgan. There is no need for formality between the Welsh houses. Don't you agree?'

Nesta smiled but it was obvious she was still tired after the journey. 'Are the boys well?'

'Both are fast asleep,' said Nesta, 'aided by full bellies and a warm fire.'

'Good,' said Cadwgan. 'That means we can talk without interruption.'

'Perhaps for a little while,' said Nesta, 'but truth be told, I too am very tired.'

'Of course,' said Cadwgan, 'and it is very rude of me to keep you from your bed but I beg patience for just a little longer. Can I get you a drink?'

'A little warmed wine might be nice.'

Cadwgan raised his hand and summoned a nearby servant before dispatching her to the kitchens.

'So,' said Cadwgan, 'I heard that the journey was very taxing.'

'Indeed it was. This rain has turned the tracks into mud and the men had to dig the cart out on several occasions. On top of that, the canopy leaks and our bedding was constantly damp.'

'I am so sorry, Nesta,' said Cadwgan. 'No one royal-born should be subjected to such a torture.'

'Royal-born or not,' said Nesta, 'this whole thing is getting tiresome. My boys should be asleep in their own rooms, safe behind the walls of Pembroke instead of spending days on end soaked to the skin while avoiding an imminent war.'

'I agree,' said Cadwgan. 'And I am surprised at the actions my son took. It has placed us all in great danger and I can only assume it was a moment's whim without thought of consequence.'

Nesta sighed. 'I agree,' she said, 'but I have to say I am no less guilty in this regard. Owain's actions were ill-considered and dangerous but even so, when he entered my chambers at Cenarth Bychan, I should have insisted he release us, or at least ransom us back to Gerald. Instead, I acted like a foolish lovelorn child and fell for his charms.' She looked up at the prince. 'I deserve whatever fate throws at me, Cadwgan, but the consequences of my mistakes should not be inflicted upon my children.'

'Yes,' said Cadwgan, 'and perhaps there is something we can do about that.'

'Really?'

'I can't promise anything, Nesta, but I will say this. I expect Owain to come here in the next few weeks. When he does, I will press him to release you. Now, he can be as stubborn as a mule and I don't think he will agree. However, he is not stupid and I truly believe that between us we can persuade him to release the boys. It may not be perfect but at least they will be safe.'

'That would be the greatest of blessings,' said Nesta, reaching out and placing her hand on his arm.

Cadwgan smiled and looked over as the servant returned with the drinks. 'Thank you,' he said as she placed the two goblets on the table. He waited until the servant had left the room.

Nesta sipped her wine and they both stared into the fire for a few moments.

'Nesta,' said Cadwgan eventually, 'there is a question I am obliged to ask and I want you to be truthful, even though it may offend you.'

'Ask your question, Cadwgan,' said Nesta. 'The least I can do in return for your hospitality is repay you with an honest answer.'

'Do you love him?'

Nesta sighed deeply and looked into the flames for a while, seeking the answer deep in her heart. Finally, she turned back to Cadwgan. 'Your son is a handsome prince, my lord, with a silver tongue that could charm the birds from the trees. He is loving, attentive and seeks an ideal close to my heart: a free country for our people. He is passionate yet tender, fearless yet a charming rogue. His name is spoken in awe from coast to coast and men would gladly lay their lives down for him. Such men are rarely found, so how can any woman not fall in love with him? But in the cold light of day, if you seek a truthful answer before God, then the answer must be no, I do not love him, I don't think I ever have. I loved the *idea* of him.'

Cadwgan looked at her for a while before smiling gently. 'Thank you for being honest with me, Nesta, and I promise I will do everything I can to see you and your children released. Now, why don't you take that wine up to your quarters and get some sleep? We can talk again in the morning.'

'Thank you, my lord,' said Nesta, 'I think I will.'

She stood up and left the room, leaving Cadwgan alone before the fire.

'Oh, Owain,' he sighed to himself, 'what mess have you got us into this time?'

Ceredigion

For the past two months Broadwick had made his way slowly from Hen Domen, stopping off in remote villages or sleeping under canvas in secluded forests, keen not to draw attention to himself. His initial clothing had been changed for peasants' attire and the warm monk's cloak discarded in favour of a poorer version he found on sale in a market in Builth. Though of poorer quality than the previous one, it was much more representative of those worn by the traders who frequented the roads between the many Welsh towns. His hair and beard had been allowed to grow unhindered and though it went against his usual routine, he remained unwashed for days on end, adding to the guise of a well-travelled trader.

During the journey across Powys, he had been careful not to draw attention to himself and sometimes went unnoticed in the darker corners of raucous taverns, sipping his ale quietly while listening to those unable to manage their drink boasting of battles long gone or conquests still sought.

On other nights, when lucky enough to be offered shelter by poor farmers, he played his part of the trader to the maximum, telling made-up tales of his travels through Wales and the adventures he had shared with pauper and prince alike. Many of his hosts were enthralled and he often found that once they were comfortable in his presence, they were more likely to share tales of their own, especially those in the local area which affected their own lives. On such occasions, Broadwick often managed to subtly bring the subject around to the wave of attacks occurring throughout Powys, and though most of the time the farmers knew little or nothing about such things, occasionally tiny nuggets of information slipped through that gave him an idea as to the direction in which he should focus his endeavours.

Tonight was such a night. The poor weather made him seek shelter against the driving rain, and seeing the enticing sight of smoke bellowing from the chimney of a remote farmhouse, he knocked on the thick wooden doors. The farmer, Tomos ap Edwin, was used to offering shelter to passing travellers and welcomed him in. The farmer's son took Broadwick's horse to the stable and the English knight soon sat at the large table to one side of the room. A fire roared in the stone fireplace and two piles of wood stood higher than a man's head against the wall. Over the flames hung a cauldron of cawl and Broadwick's stomach grumbled in anticipation as the farmer's wife ladled heaps of the steaming stew into a bowl.

'Are you not joining me?' he asked the farmer sat opposite him.

'We have already eaten,' said Tomos, 'so please, don't stand on ceremony. It looks like you haven't had a decent meal in days.'

'Life on the road is tough,' said Broadwick, breaking a hand of bread from a loaf, 'and there is seldom the opportunity to eat well, especially between towns. To linger in one place too long invites the attention of brigands.' He paused and dipped the bread into the cawl, making a show of slurping on the juice as he pushed it into his mouth.

'Do you travel much?' asked the farmer's wife, ignoring the man's lack of basic manners and pouring ale into the wooden mugs in front of the three men.

'Indeed,' said Broadwick. 'I trade in cattle and am on my way to Gwent to secure a dozen milk cows for a client in Montgomery. It is a dangerous trade these days, but alas, it is all I know and the payment is good.' He picked up his mug and greedily gulped the poor-quality ale.

'Have you ever been attacked?' asked the farmer's son, Geraint, staring at the scar on Broadwick's cheek.

'This?' asked Broadwick, pointing at the long-healed wound received in a battle years earlier. 'Nothing so exciting, I'm afraid. It was received during a tavern brawl over the services of a two-penny whore. Alas, I was the loser on that occasion but you will be glad to know I acquitted myself well.'

The three men around the table all laughed but the farmer's wife gave only a polite smile.

'Master Ferrell,' she said, using the false name he had assumed, 'I hope you enjoy the cawl and the ale. Tomos will see you have a warm bed in the stables but if you don't mind, I will give my apologies and retire to my bed. I fear such stories are for the ears of men only.'

'Of course,' said Broadwick and he was about to stand up, but quickly remembered his cover. To show such grace would reveal his breeding and he couldn't afford to raise any suspicions. Instead, he bid her a good night before letting out a giant belch, complete with spittle.

The wife disappeared to the only other room in the longhouse and the men returned to their ale.

'So,' said the farmer, 'you are from Montgomery?'

'I am,' said Broadwick. 'I grew up on a farm similar to this. Alas, my family are long dead and the farm was burned by the English many years ago. I had to flee westward but found village life was not for me. Too many people in too small a place.'

'I know what you mean,' said the farmer's son. 'A village is all right for ale and women but I prefer the space of the open and the company of animals.'

'Then we are truly kindred spirits,' laughed Broadwick, and he raised his mug in a toast.

'Yes,' said Tomos, picking up the jug to refill the mugs, 'but a man cannot live on the road indefinitely. What do you intend to do as the hair on your head grows grey?'

'I haven't thought that far ahead,' said Broadwick, 'and truly suspect I will be in my grave before that decision has to be made.'

'Why?'

'Tomos,' said Broadwick, 'I see and hear a lot of things on my travels and I know the English are angry over the continued attacks on their supply columns. Especially by the brigand Diafol.'

'Diafol is no brigand,' interrupted the farmer's son, 'he is a rebel fighting for our freedom, nothing less.'

Broadwick's heart missed a beat as he dipped his bread back into the cawl. For the first time since he had left Hen Domen, he had found someone who not only knew of the mysterious rebel but also actually defended him.

'Of course,' he said calmly, desperate not to show his increased interest, 'and I only wish he had been around when my family farm was destroyed, but what I mean is this. Eventually they will hunt him down and to do that, they will need to send columns of soldiers into Powys.'

'They can search Powys as much as they want,' said the boy, 'but will find nothing except hills and sheep. Just last night I shared a tankard with a man who served under his command and he said Diafol is far away from here.'

'Really?' said Broadwick, hiding his excitement. 'I thought such men were sworn to secrecy?'

'They are,' interrupted Tomos, 'and unfortunately, allegiance to Diafol is a boast made by many ale-filled men, especially the young.'

Broadwick returned his attention to his cawl, painfully aware that the farmer's intervention was intentional and designed to stop his son revealing anything more than he should. After all, despite the friendly circumstances, Broadwick was still an unknown stranger.

'He was a bit drunk, to be fair,' said Geraint, seeing the warning look in his father's eyes.

'Anyway,' said Broadwick, wiping the juice from the bowl with the last piece of bread, 'this has been very pleasant but if you don't mind, I am exhausted after my journey and that haystack in your barn looks very inviting.'

'Of course,' said Tomos. 'I will have Geraint bring you a blanket.'

'That sounds very agreeable,' said Broadwick, and after bidding the farmer goodnight, he ran through the rain to the barn, realising that for the first time in months, he was a little closer to his quarry. A few moments later Geraint appeared and dropped a pile of fleeces on the hay.

'They smell,' he said, 'but will keep you warmer than a whore's curse.'

'You have my gratitude,' said Broadwick, 'and perhaps one day I can repay you and your father with a few drinks. Do you frequent any taverns around here?'

'Aye,' replied the boy, 'the Black Boar in Brycheniog serves fine ale and even finer women.'

'I will be sure to check out both,' laughed Broadwick. 'Thank you, Geraint. I will see you before I leave in the morning.'

'Have a good night, Master Ferrell,' said Geraint, 'and I hope you get those milk cows for the price you want.'

'Me too,' laughed Broadwick as he closed the barn door behind the farmer's son. He returned to the hay pile knowing that without realising it, the boy had just given him the location of known associates of Diafol and at last he had something solid to go on.

Ceredigion

June 27th, AD 1110

Two men armed only with knives, their faces blackened with mud, crawled slowly through the undergrowth, careful not to make a sound. The cover was sparse but as the moon was quartered and the cloud cover heavy, there was little light to give away their presence. Despite this, their movements were painfully slow, for they knew the success of their mission depended on what happened in the next few moments.

Gradually they neared the top of the hill, crawling amongst the rocks, their hearts beating faster than they had ever done before. One of the men tapped the other lightly on the shoulder and pointed to another rock a few paces away. To their dismay they could see an enemy guard peering out over the wooded valley they had recently left. Though they hadn't been discovered, they knew they had been lucky and any further movement would see the alarm being raised. For what seemed an age they watched the motionless guard, before realising that he was more than leaning on the rock before him, he was actually asleep. Hardly believing their luck, the two men continued up to the guard's position and rising from the ground as silent as smoke, one of the men clamped his hand over the guard's mouth while slicing deep into his throat with his blade. The guard panicked but it was too late and the assassin's hand stayed locked onto the Welshman's mouth. After a few moments, the man slipped lifelessly to the ground, carefully lowered by his attacker.

The killer wiped his blade on his victim's leggings before getting back down onto his belly and continuing along the enemy's forward line of sentries. One by one, more men fell to the slow but lethal assault and when the two attackers could find no more, they returned to the top of the hill where they had killed the first man.

One of the men produced a small pile of sheep's wool from his pouch, and using a flint, set it alight in the shelter of two rocks. As soon as the flames took hold, they signalled the valley below, covering and uncovering the small fire with a piece of linen. Sheltered as it was, the fire was only visible in the valley they had left and though they kept the flames small, to those awaiting the signal in the darkness of the night it was like the biggest bonfire.

Down in the forest, many pairs of eyes saw the signal and without waiting for the command, the army moved forward quickly. Horses were left under the trees far behind and any exposed metal was wrapped in sacking to avoid reflecting the moonlight and to limit any sound that may carry through the night air. Soldiers swarmed through the scrub and up amongst the rocks, passing the dead guards as they went. Soon hundreds of men had crawled forward to the ridgeline, keeping low to avoid their silhouettes being seen against the lighter night sky. The commanders and sergeants crawled forward to see the target. Down in the valley, the shapes of many huts and tents could be seen, their outlines made visible by the dozens of fires throughout the enemy camp. For many weeks the rebels had made this place their home, safe in the knowledge that Gerald's forces were under constant observation and also many days' ride away to the west. The first sign of danger and the rebels could uproot within minutes and be lost amongst the trees before the enemy could get anywhere near, but they hadn't counted on two separate columns, one of which was about to catch them completely unawares.

Fitzhamon peered down into the enemy camp, knowing that against all the odds, his luck had held out, and by moving only at night, while keeping complete discipline in the densest undergrowth during the day, he had managed what no other campaign had ever managed to achieve: to reach a rebel camp, deep in the heart of the Cantref Mawr.

Without speaking, he signalled to his officers either side and being fully aware of what was expected of them, the army spilled silently over the ridge and onto the slope leading down to the enemy camp. Keeping low, they picked their way carefully through the scrub, ready to commit to the charge should the command come.

At their forefront was Fitzhamon, and still astonished the alarm had not been raised he came to a stop at the edge of the camp, laying down amongst the bracken. The army followed suit and over two hundred men disappeared from sight.

Back up on the ridge, the sergeant of the archers peered down, trying to see the approach of the foot soldiers, but it was too dark and they were too far away. Still, he watched intently, waiting for the first sign of alarm to set his archers on their task. Finally, he knew he could wait no longer and realised that against all odds, Fitzhamon had actually managed to reach the camp edge undetected. With that knowledge in mind, he turned to his archers and hissed the command they had all been waiting for.

'*Prepare fire pots.*'

In one of the tents at the centre of the valley, Owain ap Cadwgan slept fitfully. For the past few weeks he had led the campaign of attrition against Gerald, hitting him hard before disappearing into the trees like a startled deer. Over and over again they had assaulted the English column, sometimes from the trees, sometimes from the high ground, both by day and by night. Casualties were suffered by both sides, though not as many as Owain had expected. Despite his constant attacks, the English still came, pursuing the rebels around the Cantref Mawr with relentless determination. Despite having the upper hand, the pressure of the chase had started to tell on Owain's men and when Gerald had set up a temporary but well-protected camp in the west of the Cantref Mawr, Owain had secretly welcomed the opportunity to withdraw his men and let them get some well-needed rest. Subsequently, they had made their way to their permanent camp, totally unaware that scouts from a second enemy column had been watching the camp for many weeks.

Owain woke and gazed up at the canvas above his head. Despite living the life of a rebel from a very early age, he was growing tired of the constant moving around from camp to camp and yearned for a return to those few precious weeks he had enjoyed with Nesta at his side.

He pushed the wolf-skin cover aside before ducking out of his tent and relieving himself onto the grass. Bedwyr sat at the campfire, hunched under his cloak and stirring the embers with a branch. Owain walked over.

'Can't sleep?' asked Owain.

'I did for a while but the pain in my shoulder keeps me awake most nights.'

'We'll see if we can get some poppy milk the next time we are in any of the villages.'

'I wouldn't bother,' replied Bedwyr. 'I was drinking so much of that stuff, I didn't know what season it was. I think it's just age catching up with me, Owain. I'm getting too old for this sort of campaign.'

'A few months more,' said Owain, 'and they will return to their warm castles and cold women. When they do, my friend, we'll find you a nice tavern and you can sit next to the fire, quaffing ale and regaling the whores with your exaggerated tales of bravery until the day you keel over.'

'That sounds like a good old age,' smiled Bedwyr. 'Perchance you will be sat beside me?'

'I think not, old friend,' replied Owain with a sigh, taking a seat on another rock near the fire.

'No, I suppose not,' replied Bedwyr. 'Your future includes living in a castle, or at least a manor house, your princess at your side and your many sons playing amongst the mountains of gold coins in your treasury.'

Owain smiled at the gentle dig.

'Perhaps, but if truth be told, I see no future further than the next few days. Each dawn extends that deadline, but more than that is beyond my hope.'

'Do you think we are doomed to fail?' asked Bedwyr soberly.

'I do. This fight has been caused by my love for Nesta and ultimately there are few that understand that cause. You and those who have grown up alongside me understand that passion, but the rest of them' – he waved his hand towards the sea of tents in the camp – 'fight only because they have no other option. Gerald wants me, and in the pursuit of that cause, he has forced these men to take arms.'

'Is that not a good enough cause?'

'If the whole of Wales took up arms, then yes, but I fear in isolation we are no more than an inconvenience to the English. A fly to be swatted aside.'

Bedwyr stared in surprise. 'I have never heard you speak like this before,' he said.

'I am not a stupid man, Bedwyr,' said Owain. 'I am fully aware that Henry can field an army a hundred times the size of ours and it is only a matter of time before he runs us down.'

'You talk as if we are already defeated, Owain. If you feel this way, why do we still fight?'

'What other choice do we have?' asked Owain. 'At least this way we are free until the day we die. Better to live one day as a wolf than a lifetime as a sheep.'

'We could just end this. Give them what they want and go home to our farms.'

'It's not as simple as that,' said Owain. 'Henry's anger still burns within him at the abduction of his son and even if it was possible, I could never let Nesta go.'

'Why not? Have you not quenched your thirst for her? Let her go, Owain, and bring this thing to an end.'

'I can't do that, Bedwyr. We have gone through too much together. All I can do now is hope Gerald tires of the chase and allows us to live our lives.'

'What do you mean?'

'I mean that I too tire of all this, and would exchange it all for a small farmstead with Nesta at my side.'

'You contradict yourself, Owain. First you preach the importance of fighting for freedom, yet moments later say you hope for peace. Which is it, Owain, for I have been at your side since childhood and deserve to know the leanings of your heart?'

'It is both, Bedwyr. My heart says it is better to die a death in the cause of freedom, yet my head says there has to be another way.'

'Perhaps there is another path.'

'What path?'

'Leave this country and go where they cannot reach you. Go to Ireland with your woman and seek refuge with those who have no love for Henry.'

'I can't do that, Bedwyr.'

'Why not? Most of us do not have that option, but you do. Take her, Owain, and live the life we would all sell our souls to live. You and your father have done more for this country than any other, so there are no debts to pay.'

Owain smiled and stared into the flames. For a few moments there was silence as both men dreamed about freedom. Finally, Owain turned to Bedwyr. 'Do you actually think that is an option?' he asked.

'Yes, I do,' said Bedwyr. 'I am tired, Owain, we all are. Take your princess and grow old in safety. The rest of us, well, we'll just go home.'

Again there was silence as the thought grew on Owain. Bedwyr was right. This game of cat and mouse had gone on long enough. It was time to think about bringing it to an end. He got to his feet to return to his tent.

'Your words may have some merit, old friend,' he said. 'I will sleep on them and we will speak again on the morrow.' He turned away, but stopped suddenly, his eyes wide with horror. Above the valley before him the night sky lit up with the flaming trails of a hundred fire arrows.

For a few seconds he watched the arrows climb into the sky, his mind not fully comprehending the danger, but he was torn from his trancelike state by the roar of his friend.

'*Alarm*,' roared Bedwyr, jumping to his feet. '*We are under attack!*'

A few voices responded in the darkness but before anyone could do a thing, the rain of deadly fire smashed into the camp, sending terror and panic throughout the makeshift army. Men and horses screamed in pain and tents burst into flame as the tar-fuelled fire spread instantly across dry canvas.

People rushed from their tents in confusion, desperate to escape the rain of death. Owain ran to get his sword but already the second volley was falling and though his men were now running to arms, many fell with burning arrows piercing their bodies. Screams echoed around the valley and panic ensued as volley after volley filled the air. Owain grabbed his chainmail and his sword before his tent burst into flames, hit by three arrows simultaneously.

'*Bedwyr*,' he shouted, 'muster the men at the river. Whoever is responsible for this will probably follow it up with men-at-arms, and we have to be ready.'

'*Aye, my lord*,' shouted Bedwyr, and he ran through the camp, dodging arrows as he went. Anything combustible was ablaze but still the arrows came, striking men and horses alike. Men strapped on their sword belts dressed in nothing more than their leggings and linen shirts, while others dragged pikes and clubs from burning tents.

'*Grab what you can*,' bellowed Bedwyr, 'but leave the wounded, we will see to them later.' Behind him, Owain pulled on his boots and his hauberk before drawing his sword and discarding the scabbard.

'You men,' he shouted, as a group ran past, 'four of you help secure the horses, the rest, follow me.' They ran towards another cart knowing it was full of shields, an essential defence against arrows, but before they could do anything, the cart was hit and the linen canopy burst into flames.

'*Get it off*,' roared Owain, 'or this battle will be lost before it begins.'

The men hacked at the straps and hauled the cover away before tipping the cart over to discard its load onto the floor.

'Make sure every man left standing gets a shield,' shouted Owain. 'I fear this is only the beginning.'

Across the valley, one of the sergeants spoke to Fitzhamon, his voice no longer a whisper. 'My lord, we await your command. The longer we delay, the better organised they will be. Best to strike now while there is confusion in their minds.'

Fitzhamon looked up at the sky. He had counted the volleys and knew there were another six to go.

'Any moment now, sergeant,' he said as another flew over his head. 'Prepare to move.'

'Pass the word,' hissed the sergeant, 'prepare to attack.'

All along the line hundreds of men got to their knees, each brandishing the weapon of their choice. With every face smeared with mud and ash they looked like demons, and Fitzhamon knew they would strike fear into any enemy. The last but one volley lit up the sky and Fitzhamon got to his feet.

'You know what to do,' he shouted, the need for silence gone. 'We are here to end this rebellion once and for all. A purse of silver to any man who rescues the wife of Gerald of Windsor but let not her safety interfere with the chances of victory. Don't forget the woman is Welshborn and as such her loyalties may lie with the enemy.' He drew his sword and held it high. '*Men of England*,' he roared, 'in Henry's name, take no prisoners, *advaaance*.'

***

The fat cook responsible for the vast amounts of food consumed in the rebel camp stumbled between the burning tents, desperate to escape the hail of arrows. In his arms he held the few items of value he possessed, knowing he had to reach the forest edge if he was to have any chance of escaping the fighting. All around him men lay dying, their screams ripping through the night air as their innards were burned by flaming tar.

Desperately he stumbled on, away from all the noise of the rebel army now re-forming on the banks of the river. He looked back, hoping he wasn't seen. Let them fight if they wished, he was a cook and war was no place for people like him. He left the camp behind him, his chest heaving through the exertion. The forest was only a few hundred paces away and if he could reach that, he could hide amongst the bushes and wait until it was over. He took another few paces but then stopped dead in his tracks, staring in fear at his worst nightmare come true.

'Oh, dear God,' he sobbed, dropping his precious bundle of items, 'please, not now.'

In desperation, he held up his arms in a gesture of surrender but as the first of Fitzhamon's men raced past, the blade of a pike severed his arm at the elbow and smashed into his skull.

The cook fell to the ground and the English pike man stamped on his victim's chest, levering his weapon free. All around him, armed men raced screaming into the rebel camp, their fear dominated by rage, and as the fighting commenced, the pike man caved in the head of the cook before roaring his battle cry and racing after his comrades.

'*Here they come,*' shouted Bedwyr. 'Form a line, shield wall.'

The panicked men dropped into the well-rehearsed formation and braced for the impact. Despite most of them now possessing a shield, they were still disorganised and ill-prepared for the assault. The English, on the other hand, had both momentum and surprise on their side and smashed into the shield wall with overwhelming force.

Almost immediately the Welsh line was breached in several places and the attackers poured through the gaps to engage those Welsh still running to reinforce the wall. Such was the speed of the attack that many of the rebels were still without chainmail or leather armour, and the English set about them with a fierce rage.

'*Keep going,*' shouted Fitzhamon. 'Destroy the camp. No quarter.'

Everywhere, men fell like wheat to the scythe, and despite their greater numbers, it was soon clear the untrained Welsh were no match for the disciplined English. Steel hacked through flesh with ease and skulls were caved in by heavy pikes as the enemy ran amok. Any rebels turning to run or begging for mercy were cruelly hacked down by the unrelenting attackers, and it was inevitable that the Welsh would not hold on much longer.

Owain looked frantically along the shield wall, seeing more and more breaches appear, and he knew it was only a matter of moments before the attackers turned on the rear of his defences. If they waited any longer, no matter how brave his warriors, they would be slaughtered to a man.

'*We have to retreat*,' he shouted to Bedwyr at his side.

'They are behind us,' shouted Bedwyr, 'and if we break the line now, we will be surrounded. There is only one way to survive this and that is to go forward.'

'Through their lines?' gasped Owain. 'But that is where they are strongest.'

'It is also the option they will least expect us to take,' shouted Bedwyr. 'Many may fall but some should get through to the trees. After that, every man must take his fate in his own hands.'

Owain hesitated, but Bedwyr grabbed his shoulder and screamed into his face, 'Wake up, man! Give the order or we will die where we stand.'

Owain nodded and turned away, his face ashen.

'*Men of Wales*,' he roared, 'prepare to advance!'

Those not engaged in mortal combat turned to stare in surprise.

'You heard him,' bellowed Bedwyr. 'We will head for the trees. Do not hold back, do not pause, do not give nor expect quarter.'

'Ready,' shouted Owain, '*advaaance*.'

With renewed vigour, the Welsh line surged forward and where previously the breaches in the shield wall had been a threat, they now helped their cause and those near the gaps found themselves in clear space, running as hard as they could for the distant trees.

The English were caught off-guard by the unexpected offensive and many turned, afraid they were to be attacked from the rear. The sudden change of focus was all the Welsh needed and suddenly they forged breaches of their own. Men poured through, striking left and right as they ran. More English broke off and within moments both offensive lines disintegrated, leaving hundreds fighting man to man in a life-or-death struggle.

Back in the camp, Fitzhamon raced amongst the burning tents looking for Owain, completely unaware he was in the fighting line. His men-at-arms killed anyone left in the tents before turning on those who lay wounded on the floor. Spear points pierced chests and pike heads cleaved skulls wide apart. No quarter was shown, with even the frightened young boys guarding the horses given short shrift, their spines shattered by the force of double-headed axes.

'*Where is he?*' screamed Fitzhamon when it became clear his quarry was not in the camp.

'Look, my lord,' replied a voice from a group of men at the edge of the camp.

Fitzhamon stared over at the main battle and his face fell when he saw the way it was unfolding. Rather than being forced back, the Welsh had struck forward and were now making for the safety of the far treeline.

'*Don't let them escape,*' screamed Fitzhamon. 'After them.'

As one the remainder of the English army turned and ran back the way they had come, close on the heels of Owain's routed men, who were now running for their lives.

'*Keep going,*' roared Bedwyr to a group of men paused before the treeline, 'save yourselves.'

By now, the whole of the rebel army were on the run, many of their heavy weapons discarded. Behind them the English pursued, dispatching any stragglers as they went, but unlike their quarry, they were still weighed down with armour and weapons. Subsequently, the lighter-burdened enemy pulled away and within minutes were crashing through the willow branches into the greater forest. Men ran blindly onward, desperate to escape the carnage, each unsure where to run, just aware that they had to keep going or die. Behind them the trees echoed with the screams of those not so fleet of foot, their dying cries urging them on to greater efforts.

Owain was amongst them and though he had lost sight of most of his men, Bedwyr stayed close at his side, pledged to protect the prince's life even if it cost him his own. Onward they ploughed through streams and thickets, shattered from the flight, and eventually Owain slowed down and fell to his knees, exhausted. Bedwyr leaned against a tree, gasping for breath. For a few moments, neither spoke, until eventually Bedwyr turned around and looked down at his comrade.

'We have to keep going,' he said. 'They will probably reorganise and spread out, searching for the weak and the wounded.'

'I don't understand,' said Owain. 'Our spies told us Gerald was in the east. Who are these men?'

'Whoever they are, it matters not. We have been routed, Owain. Our forces are decimated and we will be lucky to get out of this alive. Their speech suggested English and Flemish but there were certainly a fair few Welshmen amongst them.'

'It makes no sense,' said Owain. 'Who would bear arms against a fellow countryman? Are people so desperate that they would risk their lives and their souls for the shine of an English coin?'

'There are no answers yet,' said Bedwyr, 'but if you would learn the truth, first you have to live.' He extended his hand down to Owain. 'Come, it is time to go.'

Owain grasped his friend's hand and got to his feet.

'Where do you suggest?' he asked with a sneer. 'I am a defeated rebel without an army or a home. Either direction may lead to treachery or defeat.'

'There is only one place to go,' said Bedwyr, 'and that is north. If ever you needed the help of your father, now is such a time.'

Owain nodded silently and both men ploughed further into the forest. The situation may be a mess, but deep down Owain realised Cadwgan would have the answer.

Brycheniog

June 29th, AD 1110

Broadwick paid a boy a penny to find his horse suitable stabling near the river before heading along the back streets towards the town centre. Ordinarily he would have sought shelter in the castle overlooking the valley but tonight was different. He was not there representing the king and certainly did not want to be recognised as a knight, for despite the English presence in the castle, Brycheniog was still a hotbed of nationalistic fervour and an English soldier risked a slit throat if caught wandering alone through the dark and narrow alleys.

He made his way to the one main street of the town, knowing exactly where the tavern lay. He had visited Brycheniog Castle several times on behalf of his masters, and on one occasion had actually visited the tavern where he was now headed, to arrest a known criminal. The fact that the same premises were now implicated in the actions of Diafol didn't surprise him for it had always been a den of thieves and brigands.

Nervously he passed the drunkards and whores gathered outside the doors, not responding to the cat calls and invitations to fornication. He made his way inside, fully aware that a stranger would always draw unwelcome attention, but there was nothing he could do about it; he needed certain information and the Black Boar was the place to get it.

The room was hot and noisy. The floor was soaking with spilled ale and piss, and a girl of no more than eight years weaved her way amongst the customers before sweeping a pile of puke into a piss trough built into the floor. Two men carried a third out through the door before casting him at the feet of the whores, much to their amusement. The noise was deafening as poor men wagered the last of what they owned on games of chance. Others cheered their champions as arm wrestling threatened to break out into full-blown fist fights. Hungry dogs skulked between the trestle legs, hoping to find discarded crumbs from the trenchers of foolish men, but food was sparse in this tavern; it was all about the ale and the attitude of testosterone-fuelled men.

Broadwick took a seat at the end of a trestle table, nodding an acknowledgement to the bald brute of a man sat next to him. In front of him, a boy sat on a bench, his head resting on his folded arms as he slept off too much ale.

Broadwick's heart raced, knowing he was in a nest of vipers; and should his cover slip for even the briefest of moments, he would have a knife between his ribs before he could blink an eye. Even if it didn't, as a traveller in a place such as this the outcome could well be the same. One less stranger in the town made no difference to brigands such as these.

The two men responsible for throwing out the drunk came back into the tavern and while one went over to break up a fight between two whores, the other approached Broadwick, wiping his hands on his leather apron.

'Greetings, stranger,' he said, pushing the sleeping boy to the floor. 'Do you want ale or wine?'

'Ale,' said Broadwick with a nod.

'Do you have coin?'

Broadwick dug into a pocket under his cape, seeking the copper penny he had placed there ready, knowing that to have produced his leather purse would have invited trouble.

'Is this enough?'

'Enough for two drinks,' said the landlord, sweeping the coin into his fist. 'After that, get out unless you have more.'

Broadwick didn't answer but nodded his understanding.

'Where's your jack?' asked the landlord.

Broadwick silently cursed, realising his basic mistake. In places such as these, commoners brought their own jacks or tankards.

'Alas, it was stolen from me not two days since,' he replied, 'and I haven't had chance to make a new one.'

The landlord looked around before peering under the table and retrieving the drunk boy's leather cup. 'Here,' he said wiping the piss onto his apron, 'he won't be needing it for a while.' He turned and summoned a wench carrying a yoke across her shoulders, each bucket half full of ale.

'This one gets two drinks,' he said. 'After that, he's leaving. If he asks for credit, get someone to bust his teeth.'

The girl nodded and ladled scum-topped ale into the open-necked jack. Broadwick nodded his gratitude and drank half before placing it back on the table before him. The landlord stared at Broadwick, his eyes piercing as if searching the inside of his head.

'So,' he said eventually, 'who are you and where are you going?'

'My name is Ferrell,' said Broadwick, 'and I hail from Montgomery. I'm a trader in cattle and am making my way to Gwent to collect some milk cows for a client.'

'A cattle trader?' said the landlord, looking across at the bald man sitting next to Broadwick. 'In that case, you'll know my friend. This here is Heavy-hand. His family have driven cattle since before he was born.'

'No,' said Broadwick, thinking furiously, 'I can't say I do, but that may be because my usual territory is the north coast of Gwynedd. I am only down this way because my client won the cows in a wager.'

'Really?' said the landlord. 'And you expect to drive them the length of Wales without any trouble?'

'I know I ask a lot,' said Broadwick, 'but times are hard and a man needs to earn his way wherever he can. I was paid half up front so at least if I fail, I will not lose out.'

'There are greater things to lose than money, my friend,' said the landlord, standing up. 'This is a busy place, so drink up and either find some more coin or be on your way.'

'I will,' said Broadwick, and he sipped on his ale. He glanced sideways at the bald man, noticing he was still staring and had been since Broadwick had entered the tavern.

'Is there a problem?' he asked.

The man known as Heavy-hand didn't answer.

Despite every bone in Broadwick's body crying out for him to smash this man in the face, he turned away and summoned the ale girl. 'I'll have that second drink,' he said.

'You haven't finished that one yet.'

'It's not for me, it's for my talkative friend here.' He jerked his thumb over his shoulder.

The girl shrugged her shoulders and leaned over with the ladle. Heavy-hand's eyes narrowed with suspicion but he held up his tankard anyway, ensuring the girl filled it right to the top.

'So,' said Broadwick, lifting up his drink. 'A toast to having no problems.' He downed what was left of his drink before placing the jack on the table. Heavy-hand paused for a moment before downing his own drink in one and slamming his tankard onto the table.

Broadwick stood up, realising things weren't going to plan and it would be better to return when it wasn't so busy, but before he could turn away, Heavy-hand reached over and grabbed his arm, pulling him back into his seat.

'You bought me a drink,' said Heavy-hand, his voice deep and rough. 'To leave now would place me in your debt and I owe dues to no man.'

'Don't worry about it,' said Broadwick standing up again, but this time two hands hit his shoulders from behind, forcing him back onto the bench.

'You heard my friend,' said another voice, 'sit down and have another drink.'

The ale wench appeared as if from thin air to refill his jack as well as the tankard in front of Heavy-hand. Broadwick was painfully aware of the man still behind him and was careful not to do anything out of place. To do so could mean a knife in his back.

Heavy-hand lifted his tankard and drained it again without taking his eyes off Broadwick. The knight shrugged and did the same before replacing the jack on the table.

'So,' he said with a smile. 'Are we done here?'

'Not so fast, my friend,' came the reply. 'It's not often we get north-erners down this far south and don't give me that crap you fed the landlord. If you knew anything about cattle you would know that to walk a milk cow from one end of the country is almost impossible and anyway, the value is so small your client would be better off just asking for the money instead.'

'I don't know the reasons why,' said Broadwick, 'all I know is I was well paid to fetch them and money is money.'

'Naah,' said the bald man again, 'something just doesn't add up here. You may be who you say you are, but somehow I don't think so.'

'Listen—' said Broadwick, but before he could continue, Heavy-hand slammed a dagger into the table between them.

'No, you listen,' he snarled. 'This is my town, my tavern and my rules. We don't like strangers coming down here and snooping around, especially those who lie through their teeth. Now, usually you'd be fed to the pigs, but you bought me a drink and I respect that.' He leaned back and withdrew the knife to pick at some stale meat between his teeth. 'I am going to give you the benefit of the doubt, stranger. However, if any of us see your ugly mug around here again, let's just say you won't find our hospitality so welcoming. Understand?'

'Understood,' said Broadwick quietly.

'Good, now get out and don't come back.'

Heavy-hand nodded at the man behind Broadwick and the knight felt a blade under his chin, encouraging him gently from his seat. Without a word he walked over to the door, and as he stepped out, received a boot to the small of his back, sending him sprawling in the filth of the street. Again there were the accompanying hoots of laughter from the dross hanging around outside but ignoring their catcalls, he stumbled away through the mud, confident he had achieved what he came to do.

Hours later, the last of the men staggered from the tavern, most the worse for wear. Heavy-hand's comrade was already outside, a skin of ale in one hand while his other was up the skirts of a whore. The girl laughed and dragged him back inside, seeking a more suitable location for the transaction to take place. As they disappeared from sight, Heavy-hand emerged on his own and headed for his shack in the back street, where his beaten wife lay dreading his arrival.

As he walked, he slipped in the mud and fell against the door of a house, causing a dog inside to bark wildly.

'Shut up, you mangy mutt,' he shouted, banging on the door, 'or I'll break this poxy door down and kill you with my bare hands.'

He heard the squeal of the dog as it was silenced by the terrified owner inside and stumbled on, guzzling ale from a flask of his own. As he neared his house, he paused in front of the town's smithy and laughed as he relieved himself into the horse trough. People peered from behind closed shutters but they knew better than to challenge him when he was in this sort of mood. Many had done so, none had survived.

Heavy-hand took a few more steps and paused outside his house before draining his flask and throwing it to one side. Finally, he let out a satisfying belch, but before he could stagger the last few steps a solid fencepost smashed into the side of his head and he collapsed into the mud. The attacker quickly tied his victim's hands and rammed a rag into his mouth, before hauling him to his feet and pressing a blade against his throat.

'We meet again, my friend,' snarled the attacker. 'Now start walking.'

Within the hour both men were astride a pair of horses riding into the surrounding hills. Heavy-hand was tied securely and still groggy from his wound, while the other rode behind with his sword lying across his lap. Broadwick had got his man.

The mixture of the heavy drink and the blow to the head meant the sun was already high when Heavy-hand returned to any sensible level of consciousness. He groaned heavily and forced his eyes to open, not knowing where he was, only that he was in a lot of pain and his vision was blurred. He tried to move but found he was on his back, his arms and legs spread-eagled and tied to four nearby tree trunks. Above him he could see the canopy of the trees and he guessed he was somewhere deep in the forests surrounding Brycheniog.

He groaned again and turned his head, only to gasp aloud at the searing pain in his smashed cheekbone. His vision cleared and he could see a man kneeling by a fire, grilling something over the open flames. The cloak looked familiar and as the man stood up, Heavy-hand recognised him as the stranger from the tavern the night before.

'Ah, you're awake,' said Broadwick, turning around to see his prisoner. He slid a piece of hot rabbit from his knife and chewed quickly, trying not to burn his mouth. 'Excuse me,' he said, 'but I haven't eaten since yesterday and a man has to eat. Don't you agree?'

Heavy-hand tried to speak but his tongue was dry and swollen.

'What's that?' asked Broadwick. 'You want some water? But of course, please excuse my poor hospitality.' He walked over and knelt on the ground before holding a skin of water to the prisoner's mouth.

'Who are you?' gasped Heavy-hand eventually.

'I told you,' said Broadwick, taking another piece of meat from his knife, 'just a trader passing through, and to be honest, I expected a slightly better welcome than the one I received last night.'

'You are no trader,' spat Heavy-hand, 'and I knew it the moment I set eyes on you. I should have killed you while I had the chance.'

'Yes, you should have,' said Broadwick, 'and you are right, of course, I have been somewhat untruthful regarding my name and indeed my trade.' He swallowed the piece of meat in his mouth and stared at the man on the floor. 'I suppose you have the right to know,' he continued. 'My name is Sir Broadwick of Shrewsbury and I am a knight of Henry.'

Heavy-hand's face folded into a look of hatred.

'Oh, don't look so shocked,' said Broadwick. 'I'm as unhappy about my appearance as you seem to be, but it was necessary to get near the man I am looking for.'

'And who would that be?'

'Diafol, of course, who else?'

Heavy-hand's eyes opened wide and his face broke into a semblance of a smile. Within seconds he was openly laughing.

'And what is so funny?' asked Broadwick.

'You,' said Heavy-hand, 'you've gone to all this trouble and yet you managed to get the wrong man.'

'I've got exactly the man I need,' said Broadwick.

'Let me tell you, my friend,' said Heavy-hand, 'you may have the upper hand at the moment but I can tell you right now, I am not Diafol.'

'I know,' said Broadwick, nonchalantly picking some more meat from his knife.

'But I thought you said . . .'

'I said I have the man I need. I never thought for a second I had actually captured Diafol. You are far too stupid.'

'I don't understand,' said Heavy-hand. 'If you knew I was not he, why go to all this trouble to bring me here? Did my manner in the tavern offend your precious English sensibilities that much?'

'No,' said Broadwick. 'I brought you here because you are going to tell me who Diafol is.'

For a few seconds there was silence, until Heavy-hand started to laugh again. 'You are still drunk on that piss-poor ale,' he said eventually. 'Even if I knew what you want to know, what makes you think I would ever tell you?'

'Because,' said Broadwick, 'you will not have any other choice.'

The man struggled against his bonds before tilting his head up to spit in Broadwick's face. 'Do what you like, Englishman,' he snarled, 'I will never talk, even if you take me unto the gates of hell itself.'

The knight's eyes shut and he used the back of his shirt sleeve to wipe away the spittle from his face. 'I was afraid you were going to say that,' he sighed, his brow furrowing as he saw spittle on his last remaining piece of rabbit. 'It's always the same in these circumstances. I make a threat, the prisoner declares defiance, but it always turns out the same in the end. The victim talks.'

'Not this time,' snarled Heavy-hand, 'and I swear if I get out of these bonds I will chew your face off.'

'I have no doubt you will,' said Broadwick, pulling the soiled rabbit meat from his knife and casting it away, 'but that is not going to happen. Now, I have to go and feed my horse, so I want you to be a good man and stay where you are, but just in case you have any different ideas, here's something to convince you otherwise.' With astonishing speed, the knight leaned forward and drove his knife through his captive's kneecap, pinning it to the ground beneath.

Heavy-hand's head tilted back and he screamed in pain, his cries echoing amongst the densely packed trees around them.

'Scream as much as you want,' said Broadwick calmly, 'we are miles from anywhere and there is no one to hear your cries except me and the birds. Now, don't you go anywhere, I'll be back in just a moment.'

Half an hour later, Broadwick sat on his haunches, staring at his prisoner. Heavy-hand stared back defiantly, even though his face was awash with sweat from the agony of the knife still lodged in his knee.

'I don't know why you are putting yourself through this,' said Broadwick calmly. 'It's obvious you are the main man in the village and nothing happens around there without your say. Isn't that right?'

'I have no idea what you are talking about,' gasped Heavy-hand.

'Then let me explain. I think it's fair to say most of the men in that tavern of yours have wielded a weapon or two against their enemies in their time. Nothing wrong with that, for it is no more than I have done myself. However, though that is a fine trade during times of war, such skills are in poor demand during times of peace, unless of course they are sought by someone who doesn't pay much credence to treaties. So, bearing this in mind, and the fact that you seem to be a man of influence, I have every reason to believe that not only have many of your friends in the tavern ridden alongside Diafol, I suspect that you would have been instrumental in their recruitment. How much did he pay you, Heavy-hand? Five silver pennies for each man recruited, perhaps ten? Whatever it was, I hope it was worth all this pain.'

'Kill me if you will,' said Heavy-hand. 'I am not afraid to die.'

'Oh, I'm not a murderer, my friend. I have codes by which I live my life.'

'You're not going to kill me?'

'Not in the short term,' said Broadwick, 'and there is even a way you can get out of this alive to return to that rats' nest you call a town.'

'What do you mean, not in the short term?'

'It's like this,' said Broadwick. 'I could easily kill you here. I could torture you, get what I need to know and then cut your throat. But therein lies no fear for men such as you or I, and I suspect it could take time, so there has to be a more subtle way to make you talk.'

'Hah,' sneered Heavy-hand. 'You talk pretty words but make no sense.'

'Then let me be blunt. If you tell me what I want to know, I will let you go. Your knee will probably heal in time and though you will no doubt need a crutch to walk, it's not such a great price to pay in return for your life.'

'And if I don't talk?'

Broadwick leaned forward and tugged his dagger free from Heavy-hand's knee, causing his prisoner to scream in agony once more. The knight waited until there was silence.

'Finished?' he asked. 'Good. In that case I will continue. If you don't talk, I will still let you live. In fact, I will take you on my horse to the nearest farm and dump you on their threshold. However, before we leave here, I will administer several small wounds upon your body, none of which will kill you.'

'What sort of wounds?'

'Oh, nothing major,' said Broadwick, 'just a few nicks of my blade here and there.'

'What sort of wounds?' asked Heavy-hand again.

'Oh, you want detail? Well, before we leave I will cut both the tendons in your heels. I will also cut the backs of your knees, the backs of your hands and inside your elbows. If I'm enjoying myself, I may also do your shoulders. By doing so, you will never be able to stand or walk, feed yourself or even hold a tankard. Your enemies, and I would have thought you have made a few, will mock you as they pass, beggars will spit on you as you plead for food and children will see you as a thing of ridicule as you sit in your own filth, fit only for their taunts as they poke you with sharpened sticks. For that is what you will become, Heavy-hand, the lowest of the low trapped inside a useless body, yet unable even to take your own life. The best you could hope for is that someone may kill you out of pity.'

'Do whatever you want, Englishman,' snarled Heavy-hand in defiance, 'you'll get nothing out of me.'

'We'll see,' said Broadwick. 'I'll just leave those thoughts with you for a while and then return to ask again. After that, there will be no renegotiation.' He walked back over to the fire and sat against a tree, using a peeled stick to pick fragments of meat from between his teeth.

Heavy-hand collapsed back onto the grass and closed his eyes, though more from pain than tiredness. Despite his defiance, the future that Broadwick had so graphically explained played on his mind, so when the knight returned to stand over him an hour or so later, his thoughts were awash with both fear and defiance.

'So,' said Broadwick, deliberately turning his blade over and over in his hand for Heavy-hand to see, 'have you had a change of mind?'

'How do I know you will keep your word?'

'Because I am an English knight,' replied Broadwick.

'That's not enough.'

'It's all you get. Now make your choice for I am growing impatient.'

After a few moments' silence, Heavy-hand sighed and his head fell back. 'I'll tell you what you want to know,' he said.

'I did say you would,' said Broadwick, 'but be warned, if I even suspect you are lying to me, I will carry out my threat. Now, who is this Diafol?'

'I have never met the man,' said Heavy-hand, 'nobody I know has, but there is a name that comes up every time Diafol is mentioned.'

'And that is?'

Heavy-hand paused for a moment and stared into Broadwick's eyes before spitting out a name.

Broadwick's eyes narrowed in confusion but soon widened as he realised who Heavy-hand had just implicated.

'Oh, that's good,' he said, his mind racing, 'and it all makes so much sense.' He turned to Heavy-hand. 'Thank you, my friend, you will be glad to know that I believe you.'

'So are you going to release me?'

'I am a man of my word,' said Broadwick, and he bent down to cut Heavy-hand's bindings. He looked around and found a suitable branch on the forest floor before throwing it towards the wounded man. 'Here, use this as a crutch and head downhill until you reach the river. There is a farm a few hours' walk upstream.'

'You said you would take me,' snarled Heavy-hand.

'If you recall, I said I would take you if your legs and arms were useless. As far as I can see, you have three perfectly usable limbs.' He looked up at the sky. 'It will be dark soon,' he continued, 'and I'm sure I heard forest pigs around here earlier, so if I was you, I'd start out as soon as possible. Those pigs are partial to a bit of red meat.'

He turned and walked away, ignoring the shouts and insults from the freed prisoner behind him.

Tregaron

August 22nd, AD 1111

Nesta and her sons had been at Tregaron for over a year and had settled in well with Cadwgan. At first, Owain had been a frequent visitor but as the pressures from the English columns had grown greater, his visits became less frequent and she had started to yearn for the security she and her family had once enjoyed. As was usual at this time of the evening, she sat at a table in the lesser hall, enjoying a bowl of cawl, but she looked up with surprise as her youngest son came running in, his face flushed from the exertion of a long run.

'Mother, come quickly!' shouted William, and he ran back out of the hall. She put down her bowl and got to her feet, following him into the courtyard. Outside, people were running to the palisade gates, keen to see the awful sight before them. Nesta pushed her way through, finding herself next to Cadwgan as they looked across the fields to the treeline.

In front of them she could see dozens of men spread out across the open ground. Some leaned on each other, while others used makeshift crutches made from branches. More and more emerged from the treeline and as they got closer, everyone realised exactly what they were seeing. The remnants of a defeated army.

'Oh, sweet Jesus,' said Nesta, watching the tired and wounded men stumble towards the manor. 'Who are they?'

'They must be the remains of Owain's army,' said Cadwgan quietly, 'and I can only pray my son is amongst them.'

As more wounded emerged from the trees, the servants and staff of the manor ran forward to help. Nesta followed them, determined to do what she could. Cadwgan turned to those still standing within the manor courtyard.

'*Don't just stand there,*' he shouted. 'Empty the main hall. I want blankets, fresh water and food as quickly as you can get it. Someone ride for the physician and tell him to get here as quickly as he can. The rest of you, go and help bring them in. They are our fellows out there and it looks like they have suffered a hell of a defeat.'

People ran everywhere as the manor burst into activity. Out in the fields, Nesta ran to help a woman struggling to support a young man leaning on a stick. The broken shaft of an arrow stuck out of his thigh and the smell of putrefaction had already set in.

'Come,' said Nesta, 'let us help you.'

'Thank you, my lady,' said the young man. 'The physician will be able to help me, right? I mean, I know it smells really bad but if he can pull the rest of the arrow out, with some of his powders he can clean this up real quick.'

The two women made eye contact but both knew it was rare that anyone survived such a bad infection.

'Of course he can,' said Nesta. 'Why, it is little more than a flesh wound. Now let's get you back.'

They took the boy to the hall and left him lying on a bed of furs before returning to the fields. For the rest of the day they went back and forth, helping anyone they could. The men were in a terrible state, having walked for days. Most carried wounds from the battle and all were starving from lack of food. Back in the manor, people did what they could to make the wounded comfortable and while some just needed rest and a plate of good food, others were horribly injured and even though they had managed to get this far, it was obvious they wouldn't last much longer.

Cadwgan approached his steward.

'Master Rogers, I want you to work with the physician and separate these men into three groups. Those with minor wounds you can move into the barracks along with our other men. If room is limited, break out the campaign tents and set them up in the courtyard. Any who are wounded but have a chance of survival are to be kept here in the hall. Ensure they get the very best of attention. They have fought on our behalf and now need us to return the favour.'

'And the third group, my lord?'

'It hurts me to give this instruction,' said Cadwgan, 'but in my experience, the sight of comrades dying at your side tends to drag down those who have a chance to live. Make room in the stables and move anyone who's not going to make it out there. Make them comfortable and give them everything they need. Send to the nearest villages and collect all the poppy milk you can find, at sword point if necessary. The priority must be our wounded but any surplus will be used to help the passing of those too injured to survive.'

'Yes, my lord,' replied the steward as he turned away to seek the physician.

─── ───

Later that night, Nesta made her way to the stables to comfort those they knew had little hope of survival. Dozens of men lay on improvised beds of straw and the place reeked of infection. Occasionally voices cried out in the candlelit gloom, some calling on God for a miracle, while others stayed silent, too weak as they waited for release. Servants did what they could but poppy milk was in short supply and reserved for those who might yet live. Slowly and quietly

Nesta made her way along the rows of men, offering gentle words of scant comfort, holding their hands and wiping their brows wherever it was needed. Her heart ached at such suffering and when she reached the last man, a feeling of pointlessness swept over her like a heavy wave.

On the straw before her lay the young man with the leg wound she had helped earlier in the day. Even in the poor light she could see his ashen face was awash with sweat. At first she thought he was asleep and, careful not to wake him, she turned away but stopped as he called after her.

'My lady,' he whispered, 'please don't go.'

Nesta paused and, taking a deep breath, turned to face the wounded man.

'I thought you were asleep,' she said with a false smile.

'I can't sleep, my lady,' he said, 'the pain is real bad.'

'Have they given you anything?'

'The physician gave me some bark of the willow to chew but it makes no difference.'

Nesta knelt beside the man and used a piece of linen to wipe his brow. 'What's your name?' she asked gently.

'Cotter, my lady.'

'How old are you, Cotter?'

'Almost sixteen, my lady.'

Nesta hid her sadness and took his hand. 'Do you have a family?'

'Yes, my lady, my mother and sister. They are in service to a lord in Carmarthen.'

'What about your father?'

'Dead, my lady. Hung for stealing bread from the master's house.'

Nesta squeezed his hand, unsure what to say.

'Am I going to die, my lady?' he asked eventually.

Nesta hesitated, not sure whether to tell him the truth.

'I'm afraid, my lady,' said the boy before she could answer, his voice breaking. 'What if I don't go to heaven? What if the devil himself awaits me?'

'That's not going to happen,' said Nesta.

'But you don't know that. I never went to church. I am a bad man, my lady. I am going to hell.'

'No, you are not,' said Nesta.

'But I don't even pray any more.'

'Then let's do that now,' said Nesta. 'We'll pray together.'

The boy nodded weakly and held up his other hand. Nesta held his hands in hers and recited a prayer, beseeching God for forgiveness for all the boy's sins and begging for his acceptance into heaven. As she did she felt the boy tighten his grip and looking down, could see two rivulets of tears flowing down his cheeks. She finished her prayer and, after a moment's pause, leaned forward to embrace him, squeezing him tightly as he sobbed.

'Don't you worry, Cotter,' she said, 'everything is going to be all right.'

Eventually the tears subsided and she laid him gently back down on the straw bed. He looked at her weakly and tried to smile. 'Thank you, my lady,' he said eventually. 'My heart is lighter.'

'You just get some rest, Cotter,' she said, brushing his wet hair back from his eyes. 'I'll come back tomorrow.'

She stood and turned to walk away but as she was about to leave, an older, gruffer voice called out from the shadows. 'Well, is it worth it?'

She turned and peered into the stall, seeing an old man leaning back against the wall. His chest was bare, though his stomach was wrapped with bloodstained bandages. In his hand he held a flask of wine.

'Sorry,' she said, 'what did you say?'

'I said,' replied the man slowly, 'is it worth it?'

'Is what worth it?'

'All this,' said the man, waving his arm vaguely towards the rest of the stable. 'All these men, dying in pain just so Owain can bed you like a common whore.'

'*What?*' gasped Nesta.

'You heard me,' said the man as he took a swig of wine from his flask. 'The only difference between you and the whores of the docks is that they get paid in coin while you get paid in blood.'

'You can't speak to me like that,' Nesta choked. 'I will have you punished.'

'Really?' said the man. 'Go ahead. I will be dead by the morrow anyway, so a blade will be better than the slow death your lust has inflicted upon me.'

'No,' said Nesta. 'It's not like that.'

'Then explain to me,' said the man, 'why is it that hundreds of men died back there in the forests and why are we lying here in agony, waiting to join our comrades with nothing more than wine as our confessor? Is it for freedom? Is it for justice? Or is it because you can't keep your legs closed?'

Nesta gasped and her hand flew to her mouth in shock. One of the servants had heard the exchange and ran over to intervene.

'You shut your mouth!' she shouted at the dying man. 'Lady Nesta has done more to help the wounded than any other person here.'

'And so she should,' growled the man, 'for it is she that caused this mess.'

Nesta turned and fled out into the night, closely followed by the servant. She ran across the courtyard, stopping only as she reached the gateway. Gasping for breath, she placed her hand on the wall and stared out at the forest in the distance.

'My lady,' said the servant, arriving at her side. 'Take no notice of that man. His heart is bitter and he will soon rot in hell for what he said. I will tell the master and see he is punished.'

'No,' said Nesta eventually, 'for as hurtful as his words were, no man should be punished for telling the truth.'

'My lady?'

'He is right,' said Nesta, wiping away her tears. 'All this death and all this pain is down to our foolishness and failure to see what is becoming more obvious by the day, but the desperate thing is, I don't know how to end it.'

The next few days were horrendous for the household of Cadwgan, and Nesta lost count of the number of trips she had made into the fields. Behind the manor, Cadwgan's men dug a large pit for those who died, covering them with quicklime and a thin layer of dirt. The mass grave was left open to accommodate the many still expected to succumb to their wounds, so the smell around the manor was one of putrefaction and the mood was subdued.

For a moment Nesta rested on a log, taking advantage of the reduced trickle of men from the trees. All status had been put aside as the princess worked alongside the staff to help those still returning from the battle. Several other women sat nearby sharing a basket of apples and a tray of bread brought from the ever-busy kitchens. She stared into the distance, hoping against hope that Owain would appear, but so far not one warrior she had spoken to knew where he was or indeed if he had actually survived.

'My lady,' said the woman at her side, 'you look exhausted. Perhaps you should retire to your rooms, even if only for a few hours.'

'My place is here alongside you,' said Nesta. 'Besides, it seems the flow is becoming a trickle.'

'I'm sure Master Owain will be all right, my lady.'

'I hope so,' replied Nesta. 'These past days have been hard but it stops me thinking about what may have happened to him. Now we are down to the final few, I find my thoughts wandering even more and I fear the worst.'

'He will be fine, my lady,' said the girl with an encouraging smile.

'Here we go again,' said another voice, and they all looked up to see a group of ten men emerge from the trees at the far right of the forest. The women picked up their water flasks and baskets of bloodstained bandages before running across to meet them.

Nesta stayed where she was, staring away from the forest. On a single track leading over the brow of a hill, two men limped towards the manor. Nesta recognised the unkempt fair hair of one and raced up the path before throwing herself into Owain's arms. The young prince winced in pain as she hit the bruises he had received in the battle but said nothing, just returning her embrace as tightly as he was able.

'Owain,' she managed eventually, 'I thought you were surely dead. Are you wounded?'

'No,' he said, pushing her away to arm's length. 'Just a few bumps and scrapes but nothing worth worrying over. I survived, though many of my men did not. We were caught unprepared and I fear most lie rotting in the forests of the Cantref Mawr.'

'Perhaps not as many as you think,' said Nesta. 'We already care for many within the manor, though I suspect their fighting days may be over.' She turned to Bedwyr. 'And what of you, Master Bedwyr, do you carry wounds that need attention?'

'If you have a salve that can ease a wounded pride, then it will be gratefully received,' replied Bedwyr, 'but apart from that, my flesh and bones are intact.'

'Good,' said Nesta. She turned back to face Owain. 'I know you are hurting inside but now is not the time for soul-searching. We need to let your father know you are alive and get you rested. There will be time enough for recriminations on the morrow, but for now put such things out of your mind.'

Owain nodded and together they made their way back down to the manor.

Days later Owain, Cadwgan and Nesta sat at the small table in an ante-chamber to the kitchens, having just finished their sparse but perfectly adequate meal.

The main hall was still full of wounded but those left were likely to survive. The stables were now empty of men and the dead buried under the soil of the communal grave. Cadwgan sipped on his warmed wine and looked over at his son sitting next to the princess.

'Owain,' he said eventually, 'now we have this situation under control there is business to speak of.'

'Father,' replied Owain, 'I know what you are about to say but I assure you this will not happen again. We were betrayed by men who should have known better and when my men are fit again, I will take my revenge on all the English interests within a hundred leagues.'

'Owain—' said Cadwgan, but he was cut short.

'I know we are short on men,' Owain continued, 'but if you can loan me some money, I can make up the numbers from the streets of Brycheniog.'

'Owain,' said Cadwgan again.

'I know I ask a lot but I reckon I can repay you within a month, especially if we come across some Flemish traders.'

'*Owain*,' shouted Cadwgan, banging his fist on the table and making Nesta jump in fright, '*enough*! Your talk and bravado has already caused us too much in money and heartache, not to mention all those lives that were so needlessly wasted.'

'How can you say that?' gasped Owain. 'You were once in my shoes and just as many men died under your command.'

'Not in one battle,' snapped Cadwgan, 'and never as a result of a whim.'

'A whim? What do you mean?'

'You know what I mean,' said Cadwgan. 'This whole thing is the result of your unnatural obsession with this woman here.' He waved his hand towards Nesta, who lowered her head in shame.

Owain's face dropped and his voice lowered dangerously 'Be careful with your words, Father,' he replied, 'for I will suffer no insult to the Lady Nesta.'

'I offered no insult,' said Cadwgan. 'Is she not a woman and are you not obsessed?'

'She is a princess, and will be treated as one.'

Nesta placed her hand on Owain's arm. 'Owain, your father means no offence. Hear him out.'

'Thank you, Nesta,' said Cadwgan. 'It is time for plain speaking. As we ate our food today, many men still groaned from their wounds and families grieved for their fallen. Our back paddock has been planted with dozens of our men and heaven only knows how many rot in the forests or hang from the trees, victims of English retribution.'

'I told you—' started Owain.

'Shut up,' said Cadwgan. 'I am speaking. Your abduction of this woman has already cost the lives of many, yet it will be a drop in the ocean if we allow this foolishness to go on. If you are correct about this defeat, it was not even at the hands of Gerald but a different column, one of which we had no prior knowledge, and if this is the case, how many more seek you as we speak? I have already had to attend King Gruffydd in Gwynedd and explain your actions, and let me tell you, he is not a happy man.'

'Gruffydd is no more than Henry's lapdog,' said Owain. 'He supports the treaty only because it favours him and his lands.'

'Then it is no more than I would do in his position,' said Cadwgan. 'However, his concern is greater than that of his own kingdom. Gruffydd has told me that my brother Iorwedd has been released from Hen Domen Castle and currently leads a column from the east. Iorwedd has accepted the English coin and has sworn to face us across the field of battle unless this situation is resolved.'

'Your brother has sold us out?'

'Apparently so. I am no more happy about this situation than you but the point is, he currently fights for the English barons.'

'He worries me not,' said Owain. 'With your forces and mine combined we are more than a match for anything Iorwedd can bring.'

'Think not quantity, Owain. Think nationality. I would lay down my life and the lives of every man under my command to keep you alive, but to face our own people from Powys is a disaster that must not happen. Brother will be fighting brother and father fighting son. It cannot happen, Owain, and I would rather see an English banner fly above Powys than take part in such a war.'

'Can't you send dispatches explaining the situation?'

'What explanations could I possibly send? That you still hold Nesta and her children captive and would rather see men die than give her up? How do you think that will be received, Owain?'

'Then what do you suggest?' asked Owain.

'You have to let her go. Allow Nesta to return to Gerald and perhaps this disaster can be averted.'

'Never,' said Owain quietly.

Silence fell for a few moments, before Cadwgan spoke again. 'I don't think you understand the seriousness of the situation.'

'*I said no!*' shouted Owain, his own fist banging on the table. 'I love Nesta and will fight to the last man to defend her.'

'*Defend her from what?*' roared Cadwgan. 'From her place in front of a warm hearth where she belongs? For that is what this is all about. Nesta is your prisoner and Gerald will stop at nothing to get her back.'

Silence fell again and Owain looked at Nesta. 'What do you think?' he asked.

'Your father is right,' said Nesta. 'This has gone on long enough. Let me go and I will do all I can to persuade Gerald to withdraw his forces. If I am no longer here, then there is no reason for Iorwedd to continue his campaign.'

'I can't do it,' said Owain eventually. 'If I do, then all this has been for nothing. I love you, Nesta, and cannot see a life without you. If that means I must die in the pursuit of that dream, then so be it.'

'But what about everyone else?' asked Nesta. 'Why should they suffer just because of the mistakes of us two?'

'Bigger wars have been fought for love before now, Nesta,' said Owain gently. 'If we just fight a little bit longer, I know we can get through this. Rumours abound that Henry will soon be fighting a war in France, and when that day comes he will have to recall many of those now seeking us out across Wales. He can ill afford to run one campaign, let alone two. I know I have left you alone these past few months but I promise I will never leave your side again. I know I am not wrong in this but if I am, then I will be judged before God himself.'

'And is this your last word on the subject?' asked Cadwgan.

'It is,' said Owain.

Cadwgan glanced at Nesta before continuing. 'In that case, there is perhaps something else you can do to lessen the effects of your stubbornness.'

'Which is?'

'Let the children go.'

'And how is that supposed to help?' asked Owain.

'He means the children have nothing to do with this,' interrupted Nesta. 'I can understand you want me by your side and to a certain extent I am just as complicit in this mess as you. But please, I beg of you, don't let my children suffer any more than they already have. You have to let them go, Owain. Take them to the Cathedral of Saint David. My brother Hywel is there convalescing from his time in captivity. He will ensure they are safe within the sanctuary and when all this is over, whatever the outcome, he will see them safely to Gerald.'

Owain glanced at Cadwgan. 'Is this your idea?' he asked.

'It matters not whose idea it was, Owain,' interrupted Nesta, 'it is the only way we can now proceed. I have no desire to see you humiliated but if you want me by your side, it has to be without my children. Let them go and I am yours.'

Owain sat back and looked up at the smoke-blackened ceiling. He knew he had been cornered and despite not wanting to separate Nesta from her children, he realised it was probably the right thing to do.

'Very well,' he said eventually, 'we will make the arrangements but when this is over, I promise you will be reunited with them as soon as possible.'

'We'll worry about that later,' said Nesta, her hand reaching out to cover his on the table. 'For now, just know that you have made me very happy.'

'So be it,' said Cadwgan, standing up. 'I need to see how the injured are getting on. Tomorrow we will arrange transport to the cathedral.'

'Thank you, Prince Cadwgan,' said Nesta. 'You will never know how grateful I am.'

'Don't thank me, Nesta,' he said, 'for if I had my way you too would be on that cart. I have failed in my argument but at least the consequences may be reduced.'

'Whatever the outcome, my lord, I will always know you tried your best.' She tiptoed up and kissed him on his cheek before watching him walk from the kitchens.

The following morning, Nesta kissed the children goodbye before watching their cart rumble out of the gates of Tregaron, escorted by a hundred of Cadwgan's men under a white flag of truce. They were under strict instructions that should they encounter the enemy in any way, shape or form, they would avoid conflict at all costs and leave the children in the care of the English. If, however, they managed to avoid all contact, then they would be delivered into the hands of Hywel ap Rhys at Saint David's Cathedral.

'Look after them, Bedwyr,' said Nesta as the warrior reined in his horse before her. 'If anything should happen to them, my life would be over.'

'I swear I will defend them with my life, my lady,' he said, and with a kick of his heels urged his horse on in the wake of the wagon.

'They'll be fine,' said Owain, putting his arms around her from behind. 'Bedwyr is the best warrior we have.'

Nesta placed her hand over her mouth to stifle the heartfelt cries threatening to burst from her very soul.

'This will be over soon enough, Nesta,' continued Owain, 'and then perhaps we can get back to normal.'

'Can we?' asked Nesta, wiping the tears from her eyes with the heel of her hand. 'Because as far as I can see, there is no end in sight.'

'Don't say that, Nesta. We have come too far to turn back now. Just be patient and I promise I will make all this better.'

'No, Owain. My children are leaving and I know not if I will ever see them again. Not even your honeyed words can ease the despair of that thought.' As the wagon disappeared from sight, Nesta waved for the last time before turning to walk back to the manor house.

'Nesta,' said Owain as she walked away, 'wait', but Nesta didn't answer. All she could comprehend was the pain in her heart as the tears finally burst forth.

Later that night, Nesta lay sleeping in her chambers as Owain and Cadwgan walked around the courtyard with some of the manor dogs.

The night was warm and up on top of the walls the extra guards could be seen talking quietly in groups, nervously watching for signs of any follow-up by those responsible for the slaughter.

'So,' said Cadwgan, 'what next for you and Nesta?'

'I'm not sure,' said Owain. 'I need time to gather my thoughts. Before the battle, Bedwyr suggested I take Nesta to Ireland and leave all this behind me.'

'Your comrade is an astute man, Owain, and his thoughts have merit.'

'Perhaps it would have been possible before,' said Owain, 'but not now.'

'Why not?'

'How can I leave now, Father, after so many were killed? If I was to run like a frightened child, my name would be laughed at from Deheubarth to Gwynedd.'

'Why does that worry you so, Owain? You won't be the first to have lost a battle. Indeed, I myself came off second best many times.'

'Yes, but you always regrouped and came back stronger.'

'The times were different then. Our men had more fervour about them and independence was always a possibility. These days, our numbers are fewer and age adds weariness to those that still dream. Cut your losses, Owain, and seek a place of safety. Go to Ireland, and when this has all blown over, perhaps you can both return.'

'Even if I did,' said Owain eventually, 'the English spies will have every dock watched.'

'At the moment, perhaps,' said Cadwgan, 'but even Henry will tire of the chase eventually.'

Both men stared over the parapet towards the distant trees in silence.

'You can't stay here, Owain,' said Cadwgan eventually. 'Word is already out about what happened and it is only a matter of time before the English columns appear upon the road. You have to move on.'

'And what about you?'

'I intend to confront my brother in Powys. He is no traitor, Owain, and I suspect he has been the recipient of lies and trickery. Perhaps I can talk some sense into him before it is too late, but you and Nesta must move on, if only for her sake. The sooner you go, the better chance you will have.'

Owain sighed. 'I understand,' he said, 'and will make arrangements as soon as I can.'

'I will furnish you with the names of those still loyal to our family name,' said Cadwgan. 'They will give you shelter and when Gerald turns his attention elsewhere, make a run for Ireland.'

'That man is obsessed,' said Owain, 'and will stop at nothing to catch me.'

'He just wants his wife back, and until you realise that, then there will be no peace upon you.'

'No,' said Owain, 'it's more than that, and he would surely have sent men in his name if it was only about her rescue. I suspect Henry's hand is in this.'

'If that is indeed the case, then there will be no let-up. Make your plans, Owain, and be gone before it is too late.'

Back in Pembroke, word had reached Gerald about Fitzhamon's successful attack in the Cantref Mawr and he paced the floor of the lesser hall, his mind racing. A knock came on the door and John of Salisbury walked into the room without waiting for a reply.

'My lord, you summoned me?'

'Indeed,' said Gerald. 'This messenger from Fitzhamon, what did he say exactly?'

'Only that Owain had been routed and was in full flight before our own forces.'

'Was there any news about my wife?'

'No, my lord, though we have had word that your sons are being returned to you under a flag of truce.'

'That's not good enough,' said Gerald. 'I need to know that Nesta is safe.'

'You have your sons back, my lord, is that not enough for now?'

'*No, it's not!*' shouted Gerald. 'I need to know if she is alive, Salisbury. What is it about that desire that is so difficult for you to understand?'

'I would suggest she is safe, my lord, and even if her whereabouts are not known at the moment, we still have another three months until the winter sets in.'

'We must find her before then,' said Gerald, 'and if we do not, we will continue the search throughout the winter months. This farce has dragged on long enough and needs to come to an end.'

'Through the winter, my lord. Is that wise in territory controlled by the rebels?'

'I care not about the weather, the rebels or anything else you have to say on this matter,' snarled Gerald. 'I want her found, and henceforth no stone will be left unturned, no matter what the circumstances. Understood?'

'Yes, my lord.'

'Good. Now send a messenger to Fitzhamon and ask him for more detail about the battle.'

'Yes, my lord,' said Salisbury, and he left the room.

Gerald sat down and retrieved the letter he had received from King Henry a few days earlier. With gritted teeth he read the king's message again, fully aware that the carefully crafted words therein were nothing more than threats that if Nesta was harmed or not recovered in the very near future, Gerald would be held personally responsible. Slowly he crumpled up the note, knowing full well there were already whispers that Nesta was not taken against her will but left of her own accord and unless he could prove that to be false, his reputation would lie in tatters and ruination would soon follow. With the return of the boys, the capture of Owain and rescue of Nesta were never of prime importance compared to the infiltration of the Crown's influence throughout west Wales, but now Henry was becoming impatient, Gerald's priorities had changed and there was no turning back.

Outside the hall, Salisbury made his way back across the bailey, deep in thought. Despite his loyalty to Gerald, his private audience with the king had made him consider his own future, and it was obvious that Gerald no longer enjoyed Henry's favour. However, Salisbury also knew that the castellan was still a respected knight and he could not risk doing anything to hasten his demise.

However, he was also aware that the political winds were changing and if he bided his time yet remained prepared to make his move when the time was right, there was a possibility that his anticipated rise to prominence could be sooner rather than later.

Ceredigion

March 24th, AD 1113

For the next eighteen months or so, life was difficult for Owain and Nesta. With the children gone, they sought refuge in the homes of men still loyal to Owain's father. However, the constant pressure from Gerald and Fitzhamon meant they had to keep on the move throughout the west of the country, seeking shelter and support wherever they could. Nesta's manner had become unhappy as the pressure of missing her children intensified, and for the first time hardly a day passed without the two fugitives arguing over something trivial.

Bedwyr had re-joined them after delivering the children safely into the custody of Gerald, but the rest of the men had dispersed, seeking payment as mercenaries rather than chasing around the country with a smitten prince.

Cadwgan and his army had moved east to confront his brother's forces on the border with Powys, while in the north Gruffydd refused to become embroiled in the argument and while he refused any English column the right to cross his kingdom to seek the wayward prince, he also refused to give Owain sanctuary.

For the past two summers Gerald had continued his unrelenting search for his wife, and each year, as soon as the weather broke, his men rode from village to village seeking information. Sometimes the weather meant they had to stay in stables and farmhouses until conditions allowed them to move on, but move on they always did, determined to track the fugitives down. On several occasions they missed their quarry by only days and despite the hardship, each near miss brought them closer to their goal. As often as his position allowed, Gerald joined his men on the search, and it was on one such occasion in a village near the coast that their luck changed. After bribing one of the tradesmen, Gerald discovered they had missed Owain and Nesta by only hours. With the tracks of the horses still visible on the ground, Gerald rode hard along the coast along with his fifty loyal men. The better weather meant the going was easier and by the time the sun was at its highest, Gerald's scout came galloping back along the cliff edge towards him.

'My lord,' he shouted, 'we are in luck. There is a fishing village not a few leagues hence and our quarry seek shelter in the tavern upon the dock.'

'Did they see you?' asked Gerald, his heart racing at the news.

'No, my lord.'

'Good.' He turned to his second-in-command. 'Sir Godwin, take half the men and circle around the far side of this fishing village. Cut off any escape routes. The rest of you, come with me. Before this day is done I will have that rebel's head on a spike and my wife at my side.'

The column split into two and within the hour Gerald stood atop a hill looking down into the village. On the hill opposite he could see the other half of the column spreading out. His plan had worked. Owain and Nesta were still in the village and as far as Gerald could see, this time there was no escape.

Bedwyr stood outside the tavern, putting extra feed in a nosebag for his horse. The morning's ride had been hard and Nesta had complained of stomach cramps almost the entire journey. As his horse ate, Bedwyr rubbed him down with a fur glove, working his way from front to back, but as he reached the hindquarters a glint of light caught his eye, high up on the hill. Bedwyr squinted into the sun, hoping he was mistaken, but when he saw a line of twenty armed warriors riding carefully down the path, his heart sank. They had been found.

Inside the tavern, Nesta sat opposite Owain, watching him wolf down the steaming cawl. He looked up and smiled before pausing and looking at her still-full bowl.

'Not hungry?' he asked.

'Not much,' she said with a weak smile, 'just tired.'

'Perhaps you are sickening from something,' he said, 'and need some quality rest. We can stay here for a few days and after that strike out to meet my father in the east.'

'I'm not sick, Owain, just exhausted from the constant travelling. It needs to end.'

Owain paused and put his spoon back into the bowl before looking up at the woman he once loved.

'Nesta, we have talked about this. It will end soon enough. There is talk of war in France and when that day comes, I have no doubt Henry will recall Gerald.'

'I don't care about wars or Gerald,' said Nesta, 'I just want this whole thing to be over. My children are growing up without me, Owain. I need to be with them.'

'And you will be,' said Owain. 'Just be patient.' He reached out and touched her hand, but she pulled it away.

'Owain, you are not listening to me. I want this to end now. I can go on no longer.'

K. M. Ashman

'I too am tired, Nesta,' he replied, 'but we can't give up now after coming so far.'

'Why not, Owain?' asked Nesta. 'Surely even you can see that we are living a lie?'

'What do you mean?' asked Owain. 'You must know I still care for you.'

'I know,' said Nesta. 'But therein lies the problem. Caring isn't enough. In the beginning there was passion and fire, now there is only fear and caring. We were going to free our country, Owain. Instead we flee from hiding place to hiding place like common criminals. Tell me this breaks your heart, as much as it does mine.'

For a few moments there was silence as her words sunk in. This time it was Nesta's hands that reached out across the table to take his.

'Owain, our journey is over but yours can continue. Let me go back and Gerald will soon let this whole thing end. You can rebuild your life and become the man you want to be, but it has to be without me at your side.'

'I don't know, Nesta,' he began, but before he could continue the door burst open and Bedwyr called across the room.

'*Owain, Nesta, we have to go. Gerald is here.*'

'By the devil's teeth,' snarled Owain, pushing the table away from him, 'does that man never rest?'

'Please, God,' said Nesta, getting up from the bench, 'will this torment never end?'

'Come, Nesta,' shouted Owain. 'We have to go.' He grabbed her arm and pulled her out of the tavern. Bedwyr stood outside staring at the approaching men.

'The cliff path is tricky,' said Owain, looking up, 'and it will take a while for them to get down here. If we hurry, we can be gone before he knows we are here.'

'He already knows,' said Bedwyr, and he pointed up to the hill to their rear.

Another twenty men were lined up across the slopes behind them, each astride a horse and bearing a lance. Owain gasped in shock and looked around, seeking another escape route.

'It's over, Owain,' said Bedwyr. 'We are trapped.'

'It's never over,' said Owain, and he ran along the dock looking down at the boats below. One of them had already cast loose its moorings and looked ready to set sail. 'You there,' he shouted, 'where are you going?'

'Out to the fishing grounds,' came the reply. 'Who wants to know?'

Owain thought furiously and dug into his pocket, retrieving his purse. 'Listen,' he shouted, 'my name is irrelevant but I am in dire need of your aid. If you help me get her away from here, I'll give you ten silver pennies.'

'Ten pennies,' said the fisherman, looking over to his partner on the boat. 'Where do you want us to go?'

'Anywhere,' said Owain, 'just get us as far away from here as you can.'

'The weather is good,' said the fisherman, 'so I suppose I could take you to Ireland, but the price would be steeper.'

'Get us to Ireland and I will double the price,' said Owain. 'Do we have an agreement?'

'Aye, we do,' said the fisherman.

Owain turned and looked over towards the approaching column. They were just reaching the bottom of the track and would be galloping along the shore any second.

'Bedwyr,' he shouted, 'Nesta, come quickly.'

Bedwyr led Nesta over.

'Listen,' said Owain, 'this boat is going to take us to Ireland. Get down the ladder. Bedwyr, you first and then Nesta. I'll come last.'

Bedwyr climbed down the ladder and waited, but up above Nesta stared at Owain.

'I can't,' she said.

'Of course you can. We'll help you.'

'No,' said Nesta, 'you don't understand. I'm not going.'

'Nesta, in the name of God get down that ladder or we will both die where we stand.'

'I can't,' shouted Nesta again, tears coming to her eyes. 'Did you not listen to me in the tavern? I have had enough of running, Owain. I need to see my children and if I go to Ireland, then heaven only knows when that will be.'

Owain stared at Nesta in shock. He swallowed heavily and then spoke. 'It will probably be for a few months only, a year at most.'

'It has already been too long,' sobbed Nesta, 'and I should have made this decision a long time ago. I need to go home, Owain. I need to see my children.'

'Then I will stay here with you,' said Owain eventually. 'Perhaps Gerald will show us mercy.'

'*No*,' gasped Nesta, 'he has sought you for almost four years. Do you really think he will let you live after all this?'

'Nesta, I can't leave you here after everything we have been through.'

'Our time is over, Owain. What we once had has long gone, you have to see that.'

'Nesta . . .' said Owain, looking up at the horses now galloping along the shore.

'*Owain, be gone*,' shouted Nesta. 'Before it is too late.'

'I loved you, Nesta,' said Owain, 'I really did.'

'And I loved you,' said Nesta through her tears. 'Now please, I can't bear it any longer. If you die upon this dock, then it will all have been in vain. You have to go.'

Again he hesitated, his heart breaking at the thought of leaving her.

'*Owain!*' screamed Nesta. '*In the name of God, leave me.*'

Owain stared in silence. Deep inside he knew she was right. 'We could have done it, Nesta,' he whispered, his voice breaking. 'If only a few things had been different, we could have been majestic.' He reached up and wiped a tear from her cheek before turning away and leaping from the dock onto the folded nets of the boat below.

Nesta heard the horse's hooves pounding along the dock behind her and she turned to see Gerald bearing down on her. Before the horse had the chance to fully stop, Gerald jumped from the saddle and ran across to his wife.

'Nesta,' he gasped, 'at last!' He held her tightly and Nesta returned the embrace, albeit with slightly less enthusiasm.

'Are you well?' asked Gerald as his men lined up on the dock. 'Are you hurt?'

'I am fine,' said Nesta. 'How are the boys?'

'The boys are well,' said Gerald, 'and miss you terribly, but we will talk of this later. There is still work to be done.' He released Nesta and drew his sword. 'Now where is this brigand, for there is settlement to be had?' He looked out at the boat being rowed away from the dock.

'Archers,' he ordered, 'prepare your bows quickly, and somebody get me a flame.'

One man dropped to his knees and after producing a pile of sheep's wool from a pouch, struck a flint to kindle a small fire. The flames rose within seconds and his comrades stepped forward, lighting their tar-coated arrows before running along the dock to bring the boat into range.

'Gerald, no,' gasped Nesta, realising the risk, 'you can't do this.'

'Oh yes, I can,' said Gerald. 'There is no way I am going to let that man get away with what he has done.'

'Gerald, listen to me,' said Nesta. 'There are things you don't understand.' She stepped forward and grabbed his arm. 'Let me explain.'

'*Get out of my way, Nesta,*' roared Gerald, pushing her to one side. 'That man is going to pay, whether you like it or not.' He turned to the archers. '*Ready.*'

The archers drew back their bowstrings and took aim at the ship, the ends of their arrows now ablaze, sending trails of black smoke into the air. Nesta looked around in desperation, knowing that unless she did something, Owain would be dead within the next few minutes. Suddenly she ran over and stood on the edge of the dock, looking down at the dirty black waters below.

'*Gerald,*' she shouted, 'if you release a single arrow at that boat, I swear I will throw myself from this dock.'

'What? Don't be stupid, Nesta.'

'*I mean it, Gerald,*' she screamed. 'Enough men have died in my name and I swear I will follow them before I see one more soul perish.'

Gerald stared at her in frustration. Over the last few years his life had been dedicated to finding this woman, and though at first he had worried for her safety, over time any feelings he had once felt for her were now overwhelmed with anger and frustration. Yet despite this, something still stirred deep inside. The woman who had once took his breath away at the court of the king still lived, and despite the turmoil in his mind, she was still the mother of his son. He looked across at the boat, seeing the man who had caused him so much pain and embarrassment staring coldly back at him. The need to kill him burned like a fire but Nesta's words held him back from giving the order.

'Nesta,' he said eventually, 'you don't know what you are saying. This man has caused the deaths of hundreds on both sides. He has embarrassed me before the king, stolen my wife and held my son prisoner. I have a God-given right to kill him and if you protect him now, then you are just as responsible as he.'

'Then you will have to hang me from one of your gibbets because I swear, as God is my witness, if your men release those arrows, I will jump from this dock. My cloak will see me sink like a stone, Gerald, and all this will be for nought.'

Gerald glared in anger but he could tell she wasn't bluffing.

'My lord,' shouted one of the archers, 'he is getting out of range. What are your orders?'

Gerald looked at Owain in the boat and then back at his wife. If it hadn't been for Henry's warning, he might have called her bluff, but he knew it was a chance he could not take. There was too much at risk.

'Lower your bows,' he said, and as Owain sailed out of range, Gerald turned away from his wife.

Nesta breathed a sigh of relief and ran across to her husband. 'Gerald,' she said, grabbing his arm, 'wait.'

Gerald snatched his arm away and continued to walk.

'Gerald,' she cried, her shoulders shaking through her sobs, 'please, you don't understand.'

Gerald turned and looked at his wife. He hadn't seen her for almost four years and here she was, standing a few paces away, her heart breaking, yet inside he felt nothing.

'No, Nesta,' he said finally, 'I don't understand. And I doubt I ever will.'

Pembroke Castle

April 8th, AD 1113

A week later, Nesta sat in her chambers, once more safe behind the solid palisades of Pembroke Castle. Despite her joy at seeing the boys again, it couldn't lift her air of despondency, and though she and Gerald had talked on a daily basis, Nesta knew that things would never be the same between them.

She sat peering out through one of the very few windows in the tower, her mind still reliving the past few months. A knock came on her door and she looked up in resignation. Her peace and quiet had been short-lived.

'Come in,' she said.

The door opened and a face peered nervously around the door. 'My lady,' said Emma, 'I just heard you are back. God be praised.'

Nesta stood up and walked towards her much-missed maid, and halfway across the floor burst into tears. Emma walked quickly towards her and much to her surprise, Nesta threw her arms around her, hugging her tightly as she sobbed uncontrollably. Eventually the tears subsided and Nesta pushed herself away, wiping her eyes on a handkerchief.

'I'm sorry, Emma,' she said, 'I don't know what came over me. I guess it was just the emotion of seeing you again.'

'That's all right, my lady,' said Emma. 'I missed you more than you can ever know and prayed every night for your safe return.'

'Thank you,' said Nesta. 'You mean the world to me and you are the closest thing to a family that I have right now.'

'Nonsense,' said Emma. 'You have your boys, you have Gerald and don't forget your brothers.'

'My boys can't share my burden, Emma,' replied Nesta. 'Gerald is as cold as a corpse, and who can blame him? As for my brothers, I have seen neither for years, so despite you not enjoying the benefits of being royal-born, you are as good as a sister to me. Does that burden you unduly?'

'Of course not, my lady,' replied Emma. 'In fact, I am honoured. Truthfully you are just echoing my thoughts and before you were taken away, I looked forward to our talks with an eagerness unbounded.'

'Me too,' said Nesta. 'And now I am back, we should rekindle our friendship.'

'Where are the boys?' asked Emma, looking around. 'I haven't seen them today.'

'They are here somewhere,' laughed Nesta. 'Running around the battlements, I expect, and getting under the feet of the guards.'

'Everything is getting back to normal, then,' said Emma with a smile.

'The memories of the young are thankfully short,' said Nesta, 'and soon these past few years will be nought but an adventure to be recalled when they are headstrong young men.'

'And what about your memories, my lady?' asked Emma.

'What do you mean?'

'To be raped is bad enough but to then be held prisoner for all this time by that scoundrel must have made every day a hell on earth.'

'Emma, though Owain's attentions were not initially encouraged, he is actually a very kind and charming man. I suspect the stories of my rape were started by others desperate to protect my honour. I have to admit that over time I fell for his charm and apart from the past few months, my time with him was mostly happy.'

'I'm sorry, my lady,' said Emma, visibly shocked. 'I never knew.'

'There is no way you could have,' said Nesta, 'but the master must never know. His pride has been hurt badly, Emma, and it is going to take a long time for those wounds to heal.'

'Just show him you still care for him, my lady. In time, he will come around.'

'He is not the easiest man to love, but for my sons' sakes, I will try my best.'

'Anyway,' said Emma, 'I have to go, I have duties to attend. While you were gone I was allocated responsibilities in the kitchens. Now you are back, perhaps the master will allow me to return to your service as maid.'

'I will ask,' said Nesta, 'and thank you for coming, Emma, it means a lot.'

'I will see you soon, my lady,' said Emma, and she turned to leave the room. As she opened the door, she jumped in shock at the sight of a man standing outside. 'Master Salisbury!' she gasped. 'Please excuse me, you gave me a fright.'

'I'm sorry,' said Salisbury, 'I had no such intention. I just came to speak to Lady Nesta. Is she available?'

Emma looked over her shoulder and saw Nesta standing just behind her. Nesta's face wrinkled and she felt her skin crawl at the need to speak to the man she found so distasteful.

'Well,' continued Salisbury, when no answer was forthcoming, 'is she here or not?'

Emma looked over at Nesta again, and the princess cast her eyes up to the ceiling in frustration before composing herself and nodding at Emma.

'Of course,' said Emma, 'please, come in.'

The constable walked into the bedchamber and looked around the room as Emma closed the door behind her.

'Master Salisbury,' said Nesta, walking across the room, 'hardly a day has passed since I saw you last. How can I help you?'

'My lady,' he said, 'I have some worrying information that concerns you. I was going to tell you upon your arrival but thought it would wait until you were rested.'

'What information?' asked Nesta.

'It is with regard to your brother.'

'Hywel?' asked Nesta. 'Is he ill?'

'I talk not of Hywel, my lady, I am referring to your other brother. The one in Ireland.'

'Tarw! What of him?'

'Yes, Tarw. It seems that while you were away, your brother returned from Ireland and currently haunts the forests of Deheubarth gathering like-minded men about him.'

'Like-minded men?'

'There is no easy way to say this, my lady. Your brother has taken it upon himself to fight the Welsh cause, seeking freedom from the English Crown. He has already attacked several of the king's interests, including a column intended to bring supplies to this very castle. In short, it would seem that your brother has chosen the path of the brigand.'

Nesta gasped and sat down at the table. 'Are you sure?' she asked.

'There are too many witnesses to think otherwise. It seems at first he based himself in the castle of your father and satisfied himself with rebellious talk amongst the market places of Deheubarth, but it soon escalated to open defiance. Finally, he was challenged by the sheriff of Pembroke outside Kidwelly Castle, but your brother refused to leave quietly, instead upturning the carts of Flemish traders lawfully selling their wares. The following day the sheriff sent out a party of men to arrest your brother and had he just complied with their wishes, we probably could have overlooked his misdemeanours with a warning. Alas, he had other things in mind.'

'What did he do?'

'He killed the sheriff's men.'

Nesta's mouth dropped open in shock. 'No,' she said, 'he wouldn't. I know he possesses a fiery temper but he is no killer. He must have been defending himself.'

'Self-defence is no justification for murder, my lady. Those soldiers were simply carrying out their duty. Your brother must have heard they were coming and deliberately set a trap. Four men were killed that day, making your brother a murderer. Since then his crimes have escalated and he is now a wanted man across Deheubarth and Gwent.'

'I don't know what to say,' said Nesta.

'I'm sorry to be so blunt,' said Salisbury, 'but I thought you would prefer to hear this news as soon as possible.'

'Thank you, constable,' said Nesta. 'What happens now?'

'I'm afraid we will have to bring him to justice. I know he is your brother but many people know of his crimes, and if he is not dealt with appropriately, then it will send the wrong message to all who may think of challenging the Crown. I'm sorry, my lady, there is nothing I can do.'

'I appreciate your candour,' said Nesta, standing up, 'but if you don't mind, I would like to be alone with my thoughts.'

'Of course,' said the constable, and he turned to leave. Nesta followed him to close the door, but just as he reached the doorway he stopped and turned around.

'Nesta,' he said, 'there is something else.'

Nesta stopped, quite surprised at the lack of formality.

'Constable?'

'If there's ever anything I can do to help you, you know you can rely on me, yes?'

'I do,' said Nesta.

'I mean it,' said the constable, reaching out and touching her arm. 'I like to think we have become close friends in the past few years and your presence was missed when you were away. Anything I can do to help you in whatever situation you may find yourself, you only have to ask.'

'Thank you, constable,' she replied, 'I will.'

He took her hand and kissed it gently before turning and stepping through the door. Nesta locked it behind him and walked over to sit on the bed. The constable's actions were unusual and certainly outside the expectations of formality, but she put him to the back of her mind. Her brother had returned, and if Salisbury was speaking the truth, then Tarw was in mortal danger.

The Forests of Montgomery

June 9th, AD 1113

Broadwick stood hidden in the foliage of a dense bush, waiting for his target to emerge from amongst the trees. In his left hand he held a bow with an arrow already notched. His breathing slowed as he heard his quarry getting closer and he lifted his weapon to take aim on the area selected for the carefully constructed ambush. His target emerged, looking around nervously as if knowing he was in danger but unable to detect anything. He stepped into the clearing.

With a clear shot available, Broadwick's heart started racing. Holding his nerve he drew the bowstring back to its fullest extent, before sending the lethal bolt scything through the air to embed itself deep into the heart of his victim.

For a few seconds the target stumbled on but then fell forward into the mud, already dead from the magnificent shot.

With a sigh of relief Broadwick walked out of the bushes towards his victim. A bow was not his usual choice of weapon – such things were better off in the hands of experienced archers – but this was different. He had wanted to test the skills learned when he was a squire to a knight many years ago. To achieve such a result after such a long time was surprising and yet very satisfying.

He looked down at the corpse, kicking it hard to make sure it was already dead.

'Enough,' roared a voice, and Broadwick looked up to see Baldwin emerge from the trees. 'Can't you see the poor fellow is already dead?'

'I take no risks, my lord,' said Broadwick, 'and have seen more than one man injured after thinking his quarry had long since died.'

'I think we can safely say he is dead,' laughed Baldwin, 'but I will check closer when I see him on my trencher at our meal tomorrow.'

Broadwick looked down at his victim again. The hunt had been long but the outcome was worth it, and the magnificent boar at his feet would make a fine centrepiece in the main hall at Hen Domen.

'I look forward to it,' he replied, 'but just hope he isn't as tough as he looks.'

Several hours later, Broadwick and Baldwin rode back through the gates of Hen Domen Castle. Behind them came the beaters, the men tasked with scaring any prey out of the foliage and into the path of the hunt. A cart carried the results of the two-day expedition – three deer, three geese and, of course, the magnificent boar.

'That was a very satisfying few days,' said Baldwin, sliding from his horse. 'It has been a long time since I last enjoyed a hunt so much.'

'Indeed,' said Broadwick, 'and I had forgotten how much the blood rushes during the stalk. We must do it again soon.'

'I agree,' said Baldwin, 'and it is good to see you focused once more. Since you arrived back from whatever quest you set yourself, I have to say you seem distracted.'

'My apologies if my services are found wanting, my lord,' said Broadwick, 'but I was very close to concluding my quest when your order to return reached me. I would be dishonest if I did not say your command filled me with frustration.'

'I understand,' said Baldwin, 'but at the time it seemed Henry was poised for an all-out war against Gruffydd and I needed my best knight at my side. Subsequently, with the rescue of Nesta, it seems the tensions have eased and though we may not be riding into war, your presence here makes me much happier.'

Broadwick grunted his acknowledgement but did not reply. Since he had returned to Hen Domen several months earlier, his heart had not settled. The information extracted from Heavy-hand lay like a weight upon his soul and he knew that whatever happened, he could not rest until he had settled his conscience. The name in his possession could not be shared with Baldwin, or indeed any man, for two reasons. The first was that obviously Heavy-hand might have been lying and many men could die as a consequence, but though Broadwick traded in war and death, he was still a knight and subject to a code of honour that precluded the deaths of innocents. The second reason, and much more important, was if Diafol found out he had been unveiled, then he would be forever on his guard and probably impossible to reach, and that option Broadwick could not and would not contemplate. Subsequently, without the knowledge of Baldwin, he had paid for the services of spies in many of the towns and villages throughout the south to obtain information, and not a day went by without him hoping that some word would arrive as to Diafol's whereabouts. Consequently, when his squire told him he had a messenger waiting for him in the gatehouse, Broadwick's heart skipped a beat.

'My lord,' said Broadwick as Baldwin made his way up the keep steps, 'I will join you shortly. My squire informs me there is some business I have to attend.'

'Of course,' said Baldwin. 'I am going to retire to my bedchamber. My body is not as it used to be and craves some comfort after the past few days. Do what you have to do and we will share ale over the meal tonight.'

'Yes, my lord,' said Broadwick, and he turned away to stride over to the gatehouse accompanied by the squire. Inside, a wizened old man lay sleeping on one of the guards' cots.

'Is this he?' asked Broadwick.

'Yes, my lord. He arrived yesterday but would not leave a message. He insisted on seeing you in person. He has been fed and watered but I arranged for him to stay here as he smells like a pigsty.'

'You have done well,' said Broadwick, removing his leather riding gauntlets. 'Leave us and make sure nobody comes in without prior warning.'

'Yes, my lord.'

When the door was shut, Broadwick pulled up a stool next to the cot and sat down. He leaned over and shook the man, noting that his squire had indeed been correct, he stank to high heaven. 'You,' he said loudly, 'wake up.'

The sleeping man jumped and dragged himself hurriedly to the head of the bed.

'What do you want?' he asked nervously. 'I am allowed to be here, the boy said so.'

'I know,' replied the knight. 'My name is Sir Broadwick and I hear you have a message for me.'

The man stared for a moment before shuffling to the edge of the cot. 'Of course,' he said, 'please forgive me.' He looked around nervously. 'These places don't have good memories for me and for a few moments I thought I was back in the dungeons of Pembroke.'

'So I take it you are a criminal?'

'I was, my lord, but no longer. Now I work where I can for whatever I can.'

'So what is this message you have for me?'

'My lord, I was working for a pig farmer in Kidwelly when my master came to me with a task. He gave me a horse and food and said

I was to bring a message to you with all haste. He also said that if you received it, you would pay me with a silver penny.'

'Well, I haven't received it yet, my friend,' said Broadwick. 'So out with it before I have you beaten for wasting my time.'

'My lord, he said to tell you that the Welsh prince has returned from Ireland and currently ravages the lands of his birth.'

'Is that it?' asked Broadwick.

'Those very words,' said the man. 'Do I get the penny?'

'Aye, you will receive your payment,' said Broadwick, 'but I want you out from these walls by tomorrow.'

'Aye, my lord. I will be gone by dawn.'

Broadwick got up from the stool and walked out of the gatehouse, glad to be in the fresh air.

'Master Simms,' he said, addressing the squire, 'go to the steward and get a silver penny in my name. Pay the messenger and make sure he has a hot meal before he goes.'

'Yes, my lord.'

Broadwick continued across the bailey towards the motte, his mind racing furiously. The message had obviously been kept bland in case the messenger decided its value was too good not to share but if he understood it correctly, it meant that the chase was back on.

The Forests of Montgomery

July 11th, AD 1113

Fine rain fell from the sky, soaking the line of miserable captives kneeling in the mud. Behind them, what remained of their wagons lay burning on the trail, the result of an ambush by the Welsh rebels. Horses and men alike lay dead or dying amongst the carnage, and those few still alive knew their chances of living beyond this day were non-existent. Most of the survivors were traders, keen to do business with the English Crown, while others were the soldiers tasked with protecting them. Others still were prisoners being taken into slavery in one or more of the castles. The fight had been short and with the advantage of surprise, Diafol's makeshift army had overwhelmed the inexperienced guards at the cost of only a couple of men.

Two men stood a few paces away on a slight ridge, watching the prisoners as the rest of the attackers searched the carts for bounty. Alongside the two men squatted a third, a warrior known as Dog, chewing nonchalantly on a salted ham retrieved from one of the carts.

'So, where is he?' asked one of the men.

'Who?' asked the second.

'Diafol. We've done what was agreed, so he has a price to pay.'

'Have you ever seen him?'

'No. This is my third action and I still haven't had sight of him.'

'Perhaps he is a myth,' responded his comrade, 'and exists only in the minds of those who pay the purse.' He turned to the man squatting at his side, a strange character dressed in filthy clothes that stank to high heaven. His unkempt hair was long and a ragged beard hung from his face, yet despite his appearance, his eyes were sharp and he had a way about him that made the men wary of his wrath.

'What about you, Dog,' said the first man, 'have you ever seen this Diafol?'

Dog didn't answer for a few moments, still concentrating on the hambone in his fist, but eventually he let out a belch and threw the bone to one side before taking a long drink of ale from the goatskin flask on his belt. Finally, he stood up and turned to the guards.

'Aye, I have seen him,' he said, 'and am one of the few who yet still live, so if I was you, I'd be careful what you wish for.'

'I only meant . . .' started the guard.

'You will be paid,' said Dog. 'Diafol always pays his debts, so shut your mouth and do your job, unless of course you want to join them.' He nodded towards the prisoners.

The man fell quiet, not only because of Dog's reputation but also because he knew that any questions about Diafol's true identity often drew violence as an answer.

An hour later, a messenger emerged from the trees and approached Dog, whispering quietly into his ear. Dog nodded and stood up before turning to the two guards. 'Well, it looks like it is going to be your lucky day,' he said. 'Diafol is coming here in person so if I was you, I'd try to make myself as inconspicuous as possible.'

The two young men nodded, their nervousness already apparent. A few minutes later, several warriors emerged from the trees, followed by the man known as Diafol. If the two guards expected a warrior of immense presence, they were bitterly disappointed, for the man rapidly becoming the most feared brigand in the south-west was of average size and wrapped in a heavy grey cloak. The hood was raised, covering his features, and he carried no weapons they could see.

The two guards held their breath as Diafol approached, but he walked straight by, interested only in the half-dozen men who had been chained in one of the wagons. He approached the first man, staring him straight in the eye.

'Who are you?' he asked simply.

'My name is James, my lord,' said the man, 'and I'm from Gwent.'

'Why was you a prisoner aboard this caravan?'

'I was sentenced to hard labour in the quarries.'

'Your crime?'

'Striking a tax collector who wouldn't listen to reason.'

Diafol moved on to the next man. 'You?'

'Huw, my lord, and I am also enslaved, though for killing an Englishman.'

'He is a child killer,' said the other prisoner under his breath.

'He was no child,' said the second prisoner, 'he was almost nine years old and he stole my pie in the market.' He turned back to Diafol. 'Anyway, my lord, he was an Englishman's brat and one less of those is always good in my eyes.'

Diafol nodded silently before moving further down the line, asking the same questions to each man in turn. Finally, he turned to Dog, now sitting on a nearby rock. 'Where are the rest of the prisoners?'

'Back amongst the trees, a mixture of soldiers and treacherous merchants. Do you want me to slit their throats?'

'No. Free these men and task them with guarding them. They have my permission to inflict whatever pain they themselves have suffered at the hands of the English.'

'What about the child killer?' asked Dog.

'He remains manacled. Place him in one of the carts.'

'Aye,' said Dog again, but this time he looked up at his comrades.

'You heard him,' he said, 'release these men and issue them each with a blade. Get to it or you'll have me to deal with.'

———

A few hours later, Diafol once again walked up and down a line of prisoners, his hood still raised to protect his identity. Most of the captives had blackened eyes or nursed broken arms, while others had bloodstains around their mouths where their teeth had been broken with fists or boots. None had escaped the revenge of the freed slaves and all looked miserable as the rebel commander contemplated their fate.

'Which of you are conscripts,' asked Diafol, 'and which of you sought the king's coin?'

For a few moments nobody moved, but eventually one of the younger men stepped forward.

'My lord, I was a stable hand in Gloucester. My master sold me to the local castellan, where I was taught the use of pike and spear. There was no other option and I would fight on the other side given the chance.'

'Do you have a family?'

'A mother and two younger sisters.'

Diafol nodded silently and turned to the next man. 'You?'

'A trader, my lord. Let me live and I can ensure you have access to the finest goods. Spices, silk . . .' His voice trailed off as Diafol continued down the line, stopping before a strong-looking man.

'You look strong and well fed,' said Diafol. 'I smell castle life upon you.'

'My lord,' came the reply, 'I am indeed a soldier of the king and will command a fair ransom. We have done nothing wrong except obey our betters.'

'Who else here is worth a ransom?' asked Diafol, looking around. He waited silently as another ten men stepped forward. He turned back to the first man. 'Take your comrades and get into the cart. You will be going back to Hen Domen at dawn. The rest of you, pick up a handful of soil from the ground before you.'

The professional soldiers walked quickly over to the wagon, glad to have escaped whatever punishment Diafol had planned. With confused looks upon their faces the rest of the prisoners and the traders bent down to scoop the mud from the floor.

'Hold it out,' said Diafol. Each man extended his arm.

'By your own admissions,' said Diafol, 'you have all confessed to being guilty of aiding the enemy. Some of you are traders bringing succour and comforts, while others are of poor stock, men who would normally have to scrape a living from the very soil within your fists. Some have given representation that they had no choice in such matters. However, you have still supported the false king against your country-men and the fact is you ride under the enemy's flag. Unlike those other soldiers, who have trained hard and chosen the way of the warrior, you have no worth to me as prisoners. Under English law that would normally mean you would be killed or sold as slaves, but I realise you are of value to your families as working men. Therefore, you will be set free immediately.'

A murmur of shock rippled along the line.

'Thank you, my lord,' said one of the men.

'However,' continued Diafol, 'I can't ignore the fact that many of you are trained in the way of weaponry and that circumstances may once again turn you against your countrymen. To avoid this, your use as fighting men will henceforth be denied to the English.' He turned to the guard commander at his side. 'The soil in each fist indicates their favoured arms. Have one of your axemen take them off at the elbow.'

'No,' shouted one of the men again, 'please, show mercy, my lord!'

'The judgement is merciful enough,' said Diafol. 'The cut will be clean and the wound sealed with boiling tar. Those that survive will be released with a purse to fend for their families while they heal. With one arm you may be able to find work but never again will you bear arms against your fellows.'

'What about us?' asked one of the traders nervously. 'We bore no weapons.'

'Granted, but I suspect you profited by supporting those who did. Your crime is no less serious.' He turned to the guard commander again. 'The traders will have both arms removed. Take them away.'

As the prisoners shuffled away, their voices loud with protestation, Diafol turned to Dog. 'Where is the child killer?'

A soldier dragged the terrified man from the cart and threw him at Diafol's feet.

'Please,' gasped the man, grabbing at Diafol's feet. 'Show mercy. I have never raised a hand against any Welshman. My crime was the killing of an Englishman. Are we not brothers in such a thing?'

'I have never killed a child,' said Diafol. 'Don't compare yourself with me.'

'Of course,' whimpered the man. 'I meant no insult, but surely you can see, if he had lived, he could have grown to be an archer or even a knight with the blood of hundreds on his hands?' He got to his feet, clutching a handful of dirt. 'Look,' he said, his voice panicked and his eyes wide with fear. 'This is the hand that wielded the blade. Take it like the others. I will herd sheep for the rest of my life. I may even seek to be a priest and do penance for my sins but, please, don't kill me . . .'

His voice died away as he saw the cold stare in Diafol's eyes.

'Whether you be Welsh, English or any other,' said Diafol, 'there is no place in this world for child killers.' He nodded at the two soldiers behind the captive. Both men stepped forward and grabbed him, ready to take him away.

'What are you going to do?' sobbed the prisoner.

'That boy may have indeed become a knight or an archer,' said Diafol. 'Alternatively he could have become a priest or a physician. Thanks to you he will never have that choice.' He paused for a few moments before looking at the soldiers holding him captive. 'Take the skin from his flesh and cast him into the forest. Do not gag him, I want God to hear his screams.' As the soldiers dragged away the panicking prisoner, Diafol turned to his own men. 'The rest of you, muster here in the morning, when the contents of the caravan will be shared out as usual. Once you have your cut, return to your villages, but remember to keep your mouths shut. You will be contacted when next your services are needed but until then, any whisper of loose tongues and you'll find Dog waiting for you when you least expect it. Understood?'

'Aye!' shouted the men.

'Good. There's ale and meat back at the fires, so enjoy the fruits of your labour.'

The men dispersed and made their way back to the camp. The ambush had been perfectly executed and the loss of only two men was a price worth paying. In addition, the wagons were full of valuable items all destined for the castles of the English, so the share-out was highly anticipated.

Dog tied the flaps on the back of the cart containing the English prisoners before returning to stand alongside Diafol.

'What now?' he asked.

'You take those prisoners back to Hen Domen,' said Diafol, 'and make sure the castellan there gets the message. I have some business to attend but will meet you as usual in three weeks.'

'So be it,' said Dog, and he headed back towards the cart.

Hen Domen

July 12th, AD 1113

One of the castle guards stood atop a gate tower, his eyes heavy after a particularly long stint. Usually he would have been there only half the night but a brawl with one of his comrades had seen him punished with a double duty. His eyes closed for a few seconds and he leaned against the wall, taking shelter from the biting wind. Despite it being the height of summer, the weather had been bad and the winds in particular cut through his cloak like the sharpest knife.

The night was still dark, with dawn a long way off, and the guard hunkered down, knowing that the sergeants had enjoyed a night of ale and debauchery and were therefore unlikely to undertake any spot inspections.

Just a few minutes, he thought, closing his eyes, *nobody will ever know*, and for the next hour before dawn, with the front of Hen Domen unguarded, nobody saw the lone cart lumbering towards the castle gates.

⌣

'*Alarm!*' shouted a voice in the darkness. 'We are under attack.'

The sleeping guard woke with a start, momentarily confused as to where he was. With horror he realised the dawn was already lightening the sky and he had obviously slept for far longer than he intended. He jumped to his feet, running over to the palisade to see what was happening.

Down below a cart burned fiercely, its flames reaching high up the palisade wall.

'*Raise the garrison!*' someone shouted. 'All men to the walls.'

Within moments, the sound of horns echoed around Hen Domen and weary-eyed soldiers, some still drunk, emerged from the huts built along the inner palisade wall. Men ran everywhere but the first to the palisades were the archers, peering into the gloom to spot the threat.

'Can anyone see anything?' shouted a sergeant.

Nobody answered for sight was limited to the light provided by the roaring flames below. The archers were soon backed up by men-at-arms, some carrying long poles to push away any siege ladders that might be deployed.

Broadwick climbed the ladder to the tower and stood alongside the guard as he buckled on his sword belt.

'Brief me,' he ordered, leaning over to peer at the wagon.

'My lord,' stuttered the guard, 'the wagon must have been rolled into place in the dead of night before being fired.'

'And you heard nothing?'

'No, my lord.'

'And you were awake?'

'All night, my lord,' swore the boy, knowing full well that to fall asleep on duty was punishable with fifty lashes.

'Have you seen anything else?'

'No, my lord.'

Broadwick peered over again. The cart was now a raging inferno but it was no danger to the castle walls – it was too far away. Knowing it could be a trick, he held back from sending out any men to extinguish the flames, instead choosing to wait until the sun was up.

'My lord,' gasped the guard in horror, 'look.'

Broadwick stared as something fell off the cart before writhing on the floor as it burned.

'Oh, God's teeth,' swore the guard, 'it's a man!'

Another body fell from the cart and Broadwick turned to face the men in the bailey below.

'*Open the gates*,' he roared. 'There are men on that cart.'

Moments later, dozens of men-at-arms ran through the gates and formed a defensive line on the far side of the cart. Behind them, more came bearing buckets of water, throwing them onto the flames before passing the buckets back along the line. Others beat the flames with cloaks and blankets, desperate to extinguish the fire, but by the time it was out, only part of the cart remained and the air was filled with the stench of burning flesh. Broadwick climbed down from the tower and walked over to the scene of the carnage.

'My lord,' said one of the sergeants. 'It seems the back of the wagon was filled with men tied back to back.'

'I don't understand,' said Broadwick, 'why did they not cry out?'

'Because of this,' said the sergeant, pointing to a burned corpse on the ground. Broadwick stared at the gag in the body's mouth as the full horror of the tragedy dawned upon him.

'These men must have been alive when the cart was first torched,' gasped Broadwick, 'but their bonds ensured they couldn't escape or cry out. They were burned alive.'

'This is beyond heartless,' said the sergeant. 'To be burned alive should be a fate reserved only for the most criminal of villains.'

'It's worse than that,' said Broadwick. 'Whoever did this knew we would suspect an attack and hold back from opening the gates. When our guards first raised the alarm, these men were probably still alive, but we waited as they burned.'

'Oh, sweet Jesus,' said the soldier. 'Who would do such a thing?'

'I know exactly who it was,' said Broadwick, 'and it is time he was brought to summary justice.' He turned away and stormed back up to the keep, heading for his quarters.

———

'Sir Broadwick,' said Baldwin, walking into his room, 'what is the situation? Are we under attack?'

'No, my lord,' said Broadwick. 'The castle is safe but it looks like a group of men have been murdered outside the gates.'

'What men?'

'I don't know yet but I suspect they will be English men-at-arms.'

'Then why are you retrieving your armour?' asked Baldwin. 'Where do you think you are going?'

'My lord,' said Broadwick, turning to face the castellan, 'this has gone on long enough. The man responsible for these atrocities hides behind the shield of a false name and we have to do something to stop him. Killing him is not enough. We have to unmask him, parade him before the populace before subjecting him to some of the horrors he has inflicted on others. Only by doing that can we stop any other would-be rebels following his lead and carrying out similar repugnant acts in his name. To kill a man is one thing and I am no innocent in such matters, but what this man does goes beyond all reason.'

'My friend,' said Baldwin, 'I can see this has affected you deeply but I cannot allow you to leave. Your services are required right here at Hen Domen.'

'My lord,' said Broadwick, 'you have been a good sponsor to me and for that you have my eternal gratitude. In return, I hope I have displayed loyalty over and above your expectations but if I have fallen short, or leave you short-changed by my departure, then I will see you recompensed in full as soon as I am able.'

'This is not about coin, Broadwick,' said Baldwin. 'It is about friendship and recognising you are one of the best knights ever to have ridden for any master, be he baron or king. Let the capture of Diafol be another man's worry. Your place is here, carrying out the king's law and God's judgement.'

'I can't, my lord,' said Broadwick. 'I made a solemn oath on a comrade's deathbed and I must see out that promise, even if it takes me until the end of my life. These past few months have allowed my mind to stray from my vow but the deaths of those men out there brought it once more into my heart. Diafol must die, my lord, and I am the one to kill him.'

'But why you?' asked Baldwin. 'Help me to understand.'

'Because I believe Diafol holds a grudge against me and with every life he takes, innocent or otherwise, he believes he is making me pay.'

'Are you sure about this?'

'As sure as I can be.'

Baldwin sighed deeply, knowing the knight had made up his mind. 'So be it,' he said eventually. 'Take what men you need. Get this done, Broadwick, and return as soon as you can.'

Broadwick grasped the castellan's wrist. 'If God is with me,' he said, 'I'll see you before the year is out.'

An hour later the sun was fully up and the remains of the wagon dragged to one side. The charred bodies lay on the boards of a new cart, waiting to be taken to the graveyard, and Baldwin stood talking quietly to the castle steward near the gates. He looked up as Broadwick rode from the stables.

This time there was no subterfuge and Broadwick rode erect, wearing a coif pulled back around his neck and the tabard of his house over a chainmail hauberk. His sword was strapped to his belt and he carried a lance in his hand. Beside him rode his squire, leading another horse loaded with stores, while bringing up the rear were six heavily armed horsemen. Broadwick reined in his horse and looked down at the castellan.

'So this time you decline the habit of a monk,' said Baldwin with a smile.

'The time for such things is over,' said Broadwick. 'I will ride out and seek him as the man I am, a knight of Henry, nothing less. I now believe Diafol will not shrink from confrontation but will relish the opportunity to avenge his mother. If so, it will be the biggest mistake he has ever made.'

'Then may God be with you,' said Baldwin, and Broadwick urged his way towards the open gates. As he neared he shouted up at the sergeant on duty atop the gate tower.

'Guard commander.'

'Aye, my lord,' came the reply as the sergeant leaned over the parapet.

'Is the night sentry still on duty?'

'No, my lord, he has been relieved and now lies asleep in his bed.'

'Then drag him from it and set the lash about him. Last night he was asleep at his post.'

'Are you sure, my lord?'

'As sure as I am that if you ever question a command from your superior again, then we will have the hide from your back. Understood?'

'Yes, my lord,' replied the sergeant, and as men ran across the bailey to drag the guard from his cot, Broadwick and his men rode out of Hen Domen.

Deheubarth

July 15th, AD 1113

The drover and his son waded through the ankle-deep mud, their voices ringing through the warm morning air. The rain that had beset them since leaving Gwent had blown over and at last the warm July sun meant they hoped to get at least halfway to their destination at Kidwelly before night fell. In front of them walked a herd of twenty cows, along with two dozen sheep, all intended for the garrison at Kidwelly Castle.

To either side of the muddy path rode five well-armed horsemen, seasoned mercenaries who sold their services to the highest bidder and in this instance had received a hefty purse for protecting the much-needed meat herd from brigands.

Behind the drovers came the wagons, some loaded with wine and corn, while others held weapons and armour, all essential goods for the garrison. On the lead cart sat a man of enormous girth and he swore profusely at every heave of the cart as it lurched from pothole to rut, causing the goods in the back of the wagon to fly from side to side.

'Watch where you are going,' he shouted for the tenth time that morning, 'or I swear I'll have you hung for stupidity the moment we reach Kidwelly.'

'I'm sorry, Master Pollard,' said Samson, the stick-thin cart driver managing the mules. 'I have ridden these roads all my life and never have I seen them in such a state.'

'Stow your excuses,' growled Pollard. 'I paid you to get me and my carts to Kidwelly in one piece and if there is any damage whatsoever to my goods, I will see the sheriff and get the cost of their replacements refunded from your purse plus interest. I should never have paid you up front.' He adjusted his position on the cart, easing the rope securing him to the bench. 'And another thing,' he said, 'this rope is ridiculous. Do you not have a belt of leather in its stead?'

'Alas, no, my lord,' said Samson. He pulled on the reins, drawing his mules to a halt as the herd in front came to a stop.

'What now?' groaned Pollard, and he watched in frustration as the two drovers set off down the adjacent slope to retrieve a wayward bullock.

'They won't be long, my lord, the herd is just thirsty. Why don't you take the opportunity to stretch your legs?'

Pollard stared at the skinny driver, not sure if he was being sarcastic, but realising he needed to relieve himself, just grunted in response and set about untying the knotted rope around his ample belly. Samson climbed down from the cart and walked around the other side to help the merchant down.

'Get your hands off me,' growled Pollard as he climbed down the small ladder. 'I am not an imbecile, which is more than I can say for you.' He picked up a bag of water-softened hay from under the seat before making his way into the bushes at the side of the road, his stomach aching from his need to defecate. Samson retrieved a hunk of pork from a leather bag and walked over to watch the drovers chase the spirited bullock across the valley floor.

Mentally, Samson was exhausted. It was always a hard journey anyway but the constant moaning from the merchant was making this one almost unbearable. He sat on a fallen log, amused at the antics of the animal far below.

'Perhaps that's what I should do,' mused Samson to himself, 'just get up and leave the caravan. Let someone else worry about the merchant and his oft-mentioned precious wares.' He took another bite of the pork and washed it down with honeyed water. The next few minutes were enjoyable but the last piece of pork went uneaten as the situation took a drastic turn for the worse.

Down below the chase had been abandoned and Samson watched in growing horror as two unknown horsemen burst from the trees. Despite them being unarmed, both drovers were quickly speared by the riders and their cries echoed up the valley, alerting the caravan above to the threat.

'*Alarm!*' shouted one of the caravan guards. 'There are brigands amongst us.'

All the mercenaries remounted their horses and raced down the hill, each drawing his sword as he went, while all the remaining people from the caravan ran to the edge of the track to see the drama unfold.

The first of the mercenaries reached the flood plain and rode hard after the two men who had killed the drovers. Within seconds they were joined by their comrades, and all ten men were soon chasing the brigands, leaving the dead drovers far behind them.

'What's going on?' huffed a voice, and Samson turned to see the fat merchant returned from his toilet.

'I'm not sure,' said Samson. 'It seems our drovers have been killed and our guards are about to cut down the brigands responsible.'

'You make no sense,' said Pollard. 'Our drovers are fit and well.' He pointed back to the other side of the plain, where the two men who had seemingly been dead only moments earlier were now up and running towards the treeline. 'They must have escaped serious injury,' continued Pollard, 'and now make good their escape.'

'No,' said Samson, 'it can't be. I heard their screams echoing around the valley. Such sounds were the cries of mortally wounded men.'

'Obviously not,' said Pollard. 'You must be mistaken.'

Both men fell silent and watched the mercenaries close in on the brigands, but before they were within a hundred strides, the edge of the undergrowth came alive as dozens of horsemen burst from the trees.

'Oh, sweet Jesus,' the merchant sobbed. 'What's happening?'

'It's a trap,' gasped Samson, getting to his feet, 'and all this has been carefully staged.'

'I don't understand,' said Pollard. 'How did they know our men would chase them down?'

'Because they told them,' said Samson, pointing at the fleeing drovers, 'and if they were in on it, that can only mean one thing.'

'What?' asked Pollard, staring at the skinny man.

Samson stared back at the merchant, his mind racing furiously. 'Listen,' he said, 'we are in mortal danger. If you want to live, you have to do exactly as I say.'

'What are you saying?' asked the merchant. 'Why are we in danger? What do you want me to do?'

'We have to hide,' said Samson. 'This whole thing is obviously an ambush designed to separate us from the mercenaries and if I'm not mistaken, this place will soon be awash with foot soldiers.'

'*What?*' Pollard moaned. 'You are talking nonsense.'

'Listen to me,' hissed Samson, gripping the fat man's arm. 'I may be wrong but I don't think so. We could be overrun within moments, and I for one don't intend to be here when that happens.'

'But where will we go?'

'Not far,' said Samson. 'Just into the trees while all this gets settled. Now I am going whether you stay or not.'

'But what about my goods?'

'Your goods are no longer your own, Master Pollard. The only thing you have of any value is your life. Now let's go.'

On the hill above the carts, Dog watched the battle unfold down on the flood plain. The result was never in doubt and minutes later all the mercenary guards lay dead, the victims of overwhelming strength. Up on the hill above the caravan, the watchers got to their feet as one and with an almighty roar ran down the hill to fall upon the stranded caravan.

Cart drivers ran back to their horses, hoping to escape, but the remaining cattle on the road meant it wasn't an option and they died alongside their mules, their blood mingling with the cloying mud. With only a few foot soldiers left as guards, the remaining caravan was no match for the attackers and people died screaming as the brigands slaughtered everyone without quarter. Civilians and soldiers alike were brutally cut down, their cries for mercy still upon their lips, cruelly ignored by the men with bloodlust racing through their veins. Finally, the last of the cries died away, replaced with the occasional whimper of the wounded.

Dog walked amongst them, ankle-deep in pools of blood. 'The day is good,' he said simply. He turned to his second-in-command. 'Is everyone dead?'

'There were six whores in the last cart. The men have asked that we spare their lives.'

'What's in the other carts?'

'A goodly haul,' said the man. 'Sweetmeats, spices, cloth, that sort of thing.'

'Any money or valuables?'

'Not yet, though I saw a few pretty baubles around the necks of these lot.' He nodded to some of the women lying in the mud.

'Relieve them of anything of value,' said Dog, 'and throw their corpses down the bank.'

'What about the whores?'

'Give them to the men,' said Dog, 'but cut their throats before we leave. We want no one left alive to bear witness.'

'Aye, my lord.'

'My lord,' someone shouted suddenly, 'over here!'

Dog made his way over to one of the rebels, who was standing over a small but ornately decorated chest. 'What's in there?' he asked.

'I don't know,' said the other man. 'The chest is locked.'

Dog withdrew a bloodstained axe from his belt and hacked at the timber around the hasp. As soon as the wood splintered, he wedged the blade between two boards and prised them apart. Other men who had gathered around gasped in surprise as the contents were revealed. Nestled amongst a bed of red silk lay a golden cross inlaid with a dozen jewels. Some men crossed themselves as their leader lifted the cross up to the sunlight, admiring its beauty and undoubted value.

'Well, what do you know?' said Dog. 'Our spies were correct, this is indeed a rich caravan, and this little beauty will keep us in food and ale for many a month.' He placed the cross into a pocket inside his jerkin before turning to face his men.

'I suspect Diafol will show great interest in such a bauble,' said the other brigand.

'This is nothing to do with Diafol,' said Dog. 'Now get back to work. I want this caravan stripped of anything worth selling before dark and the livestock hidden amongst the trees. Instruct the drovers to take them into the Cantref Mawr and they will receive a penny for every animal that arrives safely.'

'What about the enemy bodies?' asked his comrade.

'Let them rot,' said Dog. 'Now, where are those whores?'

⌣

A few hundred paces away a very fat man and his skinny comrade lay still amongst the depths of the bushes, their hearts still racing from the exertion of the climb and the horrific death cries of those they had ridden alongside for many days. All around them the forest was alive with the comings and goings of the brigands as they made their way back from whence they came, each carrying whatever bounty they had stolen from the caravan.

The hidden men hardly dared to breathe in case they were overheard by anyone close by, until finally the skies darkened and the remaining brigands abused the whores by the light of the burning carts before killing them in cold blood.

Pollard and Samson remained hidden for several hours in case any brigands remained, but as dawn's light crept between the foliage of the bushes they finally emerged, carefully climbing down the slope towards the carnage on the path.

'Oh, dear God,' said Pollard as they walked slowly between the bodies. 'What sort of devil takes pleasure in this?'

'Just be thankful you remain alive,' said Samson.

'Shouldn't they be buried?' asked Pollard, pointing at a mound of corpses.

'There's a shovel over there,' said Samson. 'Feel free to dig the graves.'

Pollard scowled at the cart driver but realised he talked sense. It was too much for two men and besides, they had to reach safety as soon as possible. 'What now?' he asked.

'Now,' said Samson, 'we walk.'

Pembroke Castle

July 17th, AD 1113

Nesta sat on a bench within the bailey taking in the evening air. Gerald had ridden to London again at the behest of Henry, while she had remained at home, confined to the boundaries of the castle. The outer palisades were well manned with guards for though Owain had fled to Ireland, the new threat from Tarw meant Gerald was nervous and was not about to take any chances.

Emma stood to one side, reappointed as Nesta's personal maid, and despite the years apart, she had become even closer to the princess than she had been before the abduction. Despite her lowly position, she had rapidly become Nesta's confidante, but more than this, was seen by Nesta as more of a close friend than a maid.

One of the other servants walked across the bailey to whisper in Emma's ear, and the maid's eyes narrowed in confusion before she turned to follow the girl towards the kitchens.

Back in the bailey, Nesta was oblivious to anything else happening around her, just happy to see her boys playing safely within the castle, so when an unexpected voice spoke behind her, she jumped up and spun around, surprised to see John Salisbury.

'Master Salisbury,' she said, standing up, 'you gave me a shock.'

'My apologies, Lady Nesta,' said the constable with a smile that didn't reach his eyes, 'it seems to have become a trait of mine recently. Quite unintentional, I assure you, so perhaps I should sing a bawdy song whenever I approach.'

'I'm sure that isn't necessary,' said Nesta, hoping the distaste she felt for the constable wasn't evident on her face. 'What can I do for you?'

'On the contrary,' said Salisbury, stepping closer, 'I thought I may be able to offer you something.'

Nesta took a step back, offended by his presence and the lecherous look upon his face.

'Before your husband left,' continued Salisbury, making no effort to disguise the way his eyes ran up and down her body, 'he made me swear I would look after you, and it is an oath I gladly accepted.'

'I think my safety goes without saying,' said Nesta, looking around the castle walls. 'If I didn't know differently, this could almost be mistaken for a prison.'

'Oh no,' said Salisbury, his brows raised in mild shock, 'perish the thought, my lady. This castle is your home and it is important you see it as such.'

'Really?' asked Nesta. 'What would happen if I walked over to those gates right now? Would the guards let me through to wander by the river or stroll through the town to throw pebbles into the dock? Could I walk to the coast and gaze on the majesty of the sea or watch the hawks fly high above the cliffs as I did in my youth? Could I do that, Master Salisbury? Could I run barefoot through the fields or wander through the woodlands, seeking out the faeries and creatures of my childhood stories?'

'Alas not, my lady, as you well know. Times have changed and the creatures that haunt the forests these days are the sort who only wish you harm.'

'Then what sort of home could it possibly be?' asked Nesta. 'For that is what I yearn for, Master Salisbury, the same freedom for my children that my own upbringing gifted me and my brothers.'

'Hmmm,' said Salisbury, 'am I not correct in recalling that you were dragged into the politics surrounding the battle of Mynydd Carn?'

'I was, yet it was but a moment in time surrounded by the most wonderful memories. Memories that cannot be made when kept locked like a prisoner behind my husband's walls.'

'I'm sorry you feel like that,' came the reply, 'but perhaps I can ease the pain, even if only a little.'

'And how can you do that, may I ask?'

'My lady, I thought it may be good for you to host an evening in the lesser hall. Perhaps we could have minstrels, poetry, even perchance some dancing?'

'Dancing,' laughed Nesta. 'It has been a long time since I danced, Master Salisbury.'

'Then what more reason do we need? You could invite the castellans from Kidwelly and Carew, along with their wives and daughters. In addition, I'm sure all the local lords and sheriffs would jump at the chance to bring their wives to the most prestigious castle in Wales.'

'I don't know,' said Nesta. 'What would Gerald say?'

'It was his idea,' said the constable. 'He cares for you, my lady.'

'Thank you,' said Nesta, 'but I don't think I am in the right mood for any sort of celebration. My apologies, but I have to decline.'

The constable stared at Nesta and for a moment she saw something in his eyes that scared her.

'My lady,' he said, his voice much colder. 'I don't think you understand the situation. It was not an invitation; it was an instruction. The event will be held ten days hence and you will play the charming hostess in Gerald's name. I hope you understand.'

'Master Salisbury,' said Nesta as he turned to walk away. 'You may be my husband's constable but don't deem to think you can command me in his name.'

'Oh, I don't,' said Salisbury, turning around to face her, 'but in the circumstances, I think it is in your best interests not to upset him, don't you agree?'

'What circumstances?'

Salisbury just stared at Nesta, his eyes cold and uncaring. 'I think you know what I mean,' he said as he strode away.

Nesta sat back down and she suddenly realised what she had momentarily seen in the constable's eyes. Cruelty.

'William, Henry,' called Nesta half an hour later, 'come on, it is getting dark.'

The two boys ran over but not before running several circles around the maid who was approaching across the bailey.

'Come on, you two,' laughed Emma, 'you heard your mother. It's time for your bed.'

'But I'm hungry,' said Henry.

'Me too,' said William.

'Well, if you go straight up, perhaps I'll bring something on a trencher.'

'Can we have boar?' said Henry. 'I like boar.'

'Perhaps a little chicken. Too much boar before you sleep will bring the night terrors. Now off with you or I'll have you hung from the castle walls by your thumbs.'

The two boys ran laughing across the bailey and up the steps of the motte, leaving Emma and their mother behind them.

'Thank you, Emma,' said Nesta. 'They are getting quite hard work.'

'Just in a rush to grow up,' said Emma, 'as are all boys of such an age.' She paused and looked at Nesta. 'My lady, does something ail you?'

'No, it's just that constable again. He makes me more uncomfortable every time I speak to him. Do you know, he has come to my chambers three times in the past two days? The last time he brought ale and cheese and said it is nice to share time with friends. I don't trust him, Emma, and now Gerald is away I fear him even more.'

'Then you must lock your door, my lady. If I come to your room, I will knock five times so you know it is me.'

'I think I will,' said Nesta. 'Come, let us head back.'

'Wait,' said Emma, and she sat down alongside the princess.

'Emma, what is it?' asked Nesta.

'My lady,' said Emma, looking around the bailey, 'a few moments ago I was approached by one of the girls from the kitchens. She lives down in the town and comes up each day to work.'

'What about her?'

'She asked me to give you a message but begged that it be given directly to you.'

'What does it say?'

'I don't know,' said Emma, 'for it is sealed.'

'Do you know this girl?'

'I became her friend when I was in the kitchens.'

'And she can write?'

'I don't think it is from her, my lady. She says she was approached by a handsome man in the village. It could be Owain or one of his messengers.'

Nesta gasped and looked down as Emma placed the small document in her hand. She closed her fist around it immediately, concealing it from any prying eyes.

'Thank you, Emma. Now come, we should return before John Salisbury has us horsewhipped.'

'I'd like to see him try,' said Emma, and both women laughed as they made their way back up the motte.

———————

Despite her desperation to read the letter it was several hours before Nesta managed to lock her bedroom door behind her and sit on the edge of the bed. Nervously she broke the seal on the letter and placed it in the pool of light given off by the candle on the table.

Meet me outside the postern when the moon is at its fullest.

She read the simple message several times, her brow creased with puzzlement. The note was unsigned but that was understandable, for if the kitchen girl had been caught or had betrayed the message sender, then it was probably important his identity was kept secret. What she couldn't fathom was why Owain would return so soon after fleeing for Ireland. She knew he was headstrong but such an action was surely foolish beyond comprehension. Even with Gerald away, the castle security was heavy and he risked discovery.

She read the message again before holding the parchment in the candle flame, watching it turn to black ash. Finally, she crushed the remains between her palms and dusted them onto the floor, before washing her hands in the water bowl on the table against the wall. She sat on the bed in silence, her mind racing, calculating the date. Five knocks came on the door and she opened it cautiously to reveal Emma standing outside holding a tray.

'Ah, you remembered,' said Emma with a smile.

'I did,' said Nesta.

'I've brought you some supper. Warm milk and spiced goat.'

'It sounds lovely,' said Nesta as Emma put the tray on the table.

'Do you need me for anything more, my lady?'

'No, you go to your bed.'

'Have a good night, my lady,' said Emma, and she turned to leave.

'Emma, when did you get the note from the kitchen girl?' said Nesta.

'Today, my lady.'

'And when did she get it?'

'A few days ago, but she has been busy in the kitchens. Is there a problem?'

'Not at all.' Nesta reached under the table and retrieved a leather drawstring purse. 'Give her this,' she said, producing a penny, 'and ask her to say nothing of the note to anyone.'

'I'm sure she will be very grateful, my lady. Anything else?'

'Yes. When is the next full moon?'

'I believe it is tonight, my lady.'

'I thought so,' said Nesta. 'Just checking.'

'Good night, my lady.'

'Good night, Emma.'

Nesta locked the door behind her maid and ran over to the window, peering upward into the night sky. Sure enough, the bright moon flashed between the fleeting clouds and Nesta realised she may already be too late. Hurriedly she donned her cloak, securing it tight around her body before opening the door to peer outside. As soon as the corridor was empty, she made her way to her husband's chambers. She ducked inside, closing the door behind her before holding up the candle to see in the darkness and making her way over to the table beside the bed. Beneath the table was a small chest, and she smiled with relief when she found it was unlocked. Her hands delved into the contents, moving aside some letters to find the object she had seen only once before. For a few seconds she was unsuccessful but finally she retrieved a heavy ring holding the keys to the postern gates.

Nesta closed the chest and made her way quickly back out of the room, before making her way to the door of the keep. The duty guard turned to face her as she approached.

'Lady Nesta,' he said, 'can I help you?'

'Yes,' she said with a smile. 'I cannot sleep, so I thought I would go out for a walk around the bailey.'

'At this hour?'

'It's perfectly safe,' said Nesta. 'I have never seen so many guards atop the palisade.'

'As you wish,' said the guard, 'though I am bound to say, you will not be allowed beyond the castle gates without the permission of the constable.'

'I have no intention of doing so,' said Nesta with a smile. 'In fact, I may just pay a visit to that beautiful foal that was born yesterday. Have you ever seen a thing so pretty?'

'It will surely become a magnificent destrier one day,' said the guard. He stood to one side. 'Be careful descending the motte.'

Nesta nodded and left the tower before walking down to the bailey. She felt the eyes of the guard upon her back and wondered if he would send word to the constable, but it was a risk she had to take. She made her way over to the stables and walked inside, listening to the hushed breathing of the many horses in the dark. After a few moments she peered back out of the door and seeing the guard had closed the door up on the tower, slipped out into the shadows, making her way to the palisade tower furthest from the main gates. Up above she knew there would be a guard, possibly two, but she also knew that the door to this tower would be locked . . . and she had the key.

Silently she crept inside, locking the door behind her. The darkness was overwhelming and she cursed herself for not bringing a candle or a lamp. Carefully she walked around the walls, using her outstretched hands to find her way. As she reached the outer wall, her fingers touched the hinges of a door and she quickly felt for the lock. Her hands shook as she separated the two keys and she was relieved when the first one she tried slipped easily into the lock. After a few seconds' resistance, the lock turned with a clang and Nesta grimaced in the dark, hoping the sound hadn't reached the guards atop the palisade. She waited a few moments more before carefully opening the postern door and peering outside the castle walls.

Outside the darkness of the room the night sky seemed almost light and as the full moon appeared from behind a cloud, she could see across the defensive ditch as far as the treeline several hundred paces away.

'Hello,' she whispered, taking a few steps forward, 'are you there?'

When there was no answer she walked a few paces along the wall, careful not to step out of the shadows.

With guards no further than a few feet above her head she was reluctant to call out again but waited as long as she dared, her heart racing at the possibility of being found out. After a while she began to shiver in the cold night air and with a heavy heart returned to the postern, realising she must have been too late. She peered one more time over to the treeline before closing the door and turning the key, this time remembering to do it slowly to avoid making a noise. Finally, she turned and made her way to the inner door, but froze in fright as a hand clamped over her mouth from behind.

'Shhh,' someone whispered quietly, 'there's a guard just outside the door.'

Nesta remained still, her eyes wide with fright as the voices outside the door drifted away.

'Keep quiet,' whispered the voice as the man released her from his grasp. 'I will light a candle.'

Nesta watched as the sparks from a flint illuminated the man now kneeling on the floor and a small flame caught in a fist-sized ball of dried wool. The man held a candle to the flame before blowing out the wool and getting to his feet. He turned around and allowed the candle flame to gather strength before holding it up high to shine between him and Nesta.

'Hello, Nesta,' he said with a smile. 'It's been a while.'

For a few seconds, Nesta was speechless, but she finally grinned in recognition. 'Tarw!' she gasped, and she threw herself into her brother's arms.

Pembroke Castle

July 17th, AD 1113

For the next half-hour the siblings exchanged news about what had happened to each other since they had last met a few years earlier, but finally Nesta reached out in the candlelit gloom and touched her brother's arm.

'Tarw,' she said, 'I could stay here until dawn listening to you speak. In fact, I would gladly see you under the same roof for the rest of our lives, but alas, the guards know I am down here in the bailey and it won't be long before they grow concerned. As much as I love your company, I am guessing there is a purpose to your visit other than to catch up with childhood memories.'

Tarw glanced towards the inner door, knowing she was right. He had already risked everything to be here and it would be foolish to risk discovery at this late stage.

'You are as astute as you are beautiful,' said Tarw, 'and yes, there is a reason I have come. The truth is, I came from Ireland intending to revive the sleeping heart of Deheubarth and rise against the English. For many years I have dreamed of rallying our father's loyal servants around us and accompanied by their sons leading the fight against the invaders, but alas, I have found the dragon sleeping and those few men who still bleed the blood of Deheubarth are few and old.'

'It has been a long time since any man rode under the flag of the Tewdwrs,' said Nesta, 'and many have moved on with their lives.'

'But how can that be?' asked Tarw, walking around the room in frustration. 'They pay taxes to a false king, are punished for seeking justice and are having the lands of their fathers ripped from beneath their very feet. Surely they can see this. Even the Flemish and the French are given sovereignty over our countrymen and unless our people wake up soon, it will be too late.'

'You have been gone a long time, Tarw,' said Nesta, walking over to him and taking his arm. 'The English reach is everywhere and there's not a village square from here to Montgomery that hasn't seen a father or son hanged for uttering even a hint of treason.' She paused for a moment before continuing. 'Tarw, you do know there is a price on your head?'

'Of course I do, but it worries me not. Although my men are few in number, they are loyal and true. We hit the English columns wherever we can, but my purse grows lighter by the day. I need help, Nesta, the sort of help only you can bring.'

'I have some money of my own and there are my precious stones, but I do not have enough to fund an army.'

'I do not need your money, Nesta. What I crave is information.'

'What sort of information?' asked Nesta, releasing his arm and taking a step backward.

Tarw stepped forward and took her two hands in his own. 'Nesta,' he said gently, 'God knows you shouldn't be here. You should be in a castle of your own as the wife of a Welsh king, not a pawn in a political game. By marrying you off to Gerald, Henry thinks that the people of Deheubarth will see the union as one sanctioned by those who should be ruling these lands. People like me and Hywel. By sitting at his side as Gerald passes judgements in the king's name, you are unwittingly adding the compliance of our family name to his rule, and anyone with the slightest spark of defiance will see his reign as justified.'

'I don't know what you want, Tarw. What is done is done and I can no more leave Gerald than I can fly from the nearest tower.'

'I realise that, Nesta,' replied Tarw, 'and though that would have been the ideal, the time for such things has long gone. However, there is another way you can help. By being inside the circle of Gerald and his garrison you have access to information that we could use. The routes and timings of caravans or important visitors. The movement of men-at-arms or if the English decide to mount an assault on any of our positions. All this information can keep us one step in front of Henry, and while he chases shadows, I can build an army to challenge his rule in Deheubarth.'

'I don't know, Tarw,' said Nesta. 'It is seldom that Gerald discusses such things in my presence.'

'But he does sometimes?'

'On occasion.'

'Then that is all I can ask of you.'

'But what if I am caught?'

'Don't be caught, Nesta,' said Tarw, grabbing his shoulders. 'Take no chances and should you think there is a chance of being found out, then step back. I will understand.'

'So how do I get this information to you? I can't come here very often for Gerald has the only keys.'

'We will have two more sets made: one for you and one for me. The next time I come I will bring a wax tablet and take impressions. Each month when the moon is full, I will return and pick up any messages.' He glanced around the room. 'Look, there is a loose stone against the wall. Leave any messages behind the stone and I will pick them up the next time I come.'

Nesta looked thoughtfully at her brother for a few moments. 'No,' she said, 'I will not do it.'

Tarw took a step back and stared at Nesta. 'You won't?'

'I will find out what I can, when I can. I will also leave your messages behind that stone but what I will not do, Tarw, is allow you to have keys to both postern gates.'

'But . . .' started Tarw.

'Tarw,' interrupted Nesta, 'I love you dearly, but you are a wanted rebel who has sworn to kill as many Englishmen as you can. By giving you the keys to the castle what is to stop you bringing your men in the dead of night and slaughtering everyone in their beds?'

'I would never do that to you,' gasped Tarw.

'Perhaps not, but in the heat of battle it is possible for many innocents to fall, and I will not risk my children again.'

'Again?'

'They have already suffered enough trauma and they need to grow up in a safe place.'

'Nowhere is safe, Nesta, not even Pembroke Castle.'

'Maybe not, but I will not make it worse by handing over the keys. Besides, though I trust your word, what if you were to get injured or worse? Your men may not be so trustworthy when keeping your promises.'

'So what do you suggest?'

'I will give you a key, Tarw, but it will be the one for the outer door only, and you must swear upon God's name that you will not share knowledge of its existence with any other soul. Promise me this one thing and I will gladly get whatever information I can. You will have access to this room but no further. More than that I cannot offer.'

Tarw stared at the key in his sister's hand before finally looking back up at her. 'Agreed,' he said.

'Good. I will arrange for the copies to be made. After that I will come whenever I can and leave anything of importance behind the stone. Now, we have already been here too long.'

Tarw hugged his sister. 'Thank you, Nesta. History will show you were ever true to Deheubarth.'

'Just be careful,' said Nesta. 'Now be gone.'

Tarw ducked out of the external door and into the night. Nesta locked the door behind him and after leaving the tower, locked the inner door before heading back up the motte.

'Ah, there you are,' said a voice as she climbed the steps. She looked up to see John Salisbury standing at the tower door alongside the guard.

'Master Salisbury,' she said. 'You are up late.'

'Not as late as you, it seems. Where have you been?'

'Were you not told?' said Nesta, glancing at the guard. 'I went for a walk and became enamoured with the new foal.'

'Indeed,' said Salisbury, 'but you were gone so long we thought you must have got lost or fallen asleep.'

'The time ran away from me,' said Nesta, 'but I am back now, so if you don't mind, I will return to my quarters.'

'Of course,' said Salisbury. 'Perhaps you will allow me to accompany you?'

'That won't be necessary,' said Nesta, a little too harshly. 'I am very tired and need my bed.' She pushed past him and made her way up the stairs, her heart racing as she realised how close she had come to discovery.

'As you wish,' said the constable quietly. He turned to the guard. 'You were right to wake me,' he said. 'She is up to something.'

'My lord,' said the guard, 'there is one more thing. When she didn't return, I became worried for her safety so went down to find her. She was nowhere to be found.'

'Was she not with the horses?'

'No, my lord. Wherever she went, it wasn't the stables.'

Pembroke Castle

July 18th, AD 1113

Nesta sat at the table in her quarters, her mind churning over what she was about to do. Her meeting with Tarw had left her in a quandary and though there was an obvious solution, it involved great risk on her part and the only way to proceed was to trust a third party, an action that was never a good thing when involved in the business of deceit. Discovery meant certain punishment from Gerald and perhaps even the king, but there was no other option, she had to help her brother and to do so meant she had to involve the one person she was close to – Emma. There was a knock on the door and Emma walked in, giving the princess her usual pretty smile.

'My lady, you summoned me?'

'I did,' said Nesta, standing up. 'Please, come in and join me. Do you want some wine?'

'No, thank you, my lady,' said Emma. 'I still have work to do in the master's quarters. I am told he is due back in a day or so.'

'Yes, he is,' said Nesta. 'It seems his business took less time than we thought.'

'It will be good to see him again, will it not?'

Nesta smiled but did not answer.

'My lady, does something bother you?'

'I have to admit there is something on my mind,' said Nesta, 'but I hesitate to share it with you for to do so puts us both at risk.'

'At risk of what?'

'Punishment, trial, even possible execution, and you of all people do not deserve that.'

'My lady,' said Emma, 'I have been with you for many years, and your mother before that. If there is anything I can do for you, then please share it for I swear I will carry out your whim without question.'

Nesta thought for a while, wondering whether it was worth the risk. Finally, realising she had no choice, she took Emma into her confidence. 'Emma,' she said, 'there is something I need doing. Something I cannot do myself.'

'Name it,' said Emma, returning Nesta's stare.

'I have two keys in my possession that I need copied,' said Nesta. 'Please don't ask what they unlock for their purpose must remain secret but suffice to say, it may save our lives one day.'

'Cannot the blacksmith make copies?'

'No, for their existence must forever remain a secret between you and me. To that end, I need someone to obtain copies from outside of these walls. You are the only person I can trust, so I am bound to ask, do you know such a person?'

Emma smiled. 'Is that it?' she asked. 'Is this the task that brings so much worry to your face?'

'It is.'

'Then worry no more, my lady. As it happens, I believe I have attracted the eye of a young blacksmith near the docks and he always walks with me when I get chance to go to the market. If you were to send me out of the castle on the pretence of bringing you something, I can take the opportunity to ask my suitor to make what you need.'

'A suitor?' said Nesta with a smile. 'You never told me about this before.'

'Unfortunately, it's an attraction not shared. He is nice enough but he is a bit simple in the head. I am holding out for someone with a better future.'

'Like the steward's groom perchance?' asked Nesta with a knowing smile.

'My lady, I'm sure I don't know what you mean,' said Emma, but the glow on her cheeks told Nesta differently.

'So,' continued Nesta, 'do you think you can get this blacksmith to make the keys without too many questions?'

'I'm sure of it,' said Emma. 'I will say I lost the keys to the kitchens and will be in trouble if anyone finds out.'

'Excellent,' said Nesta. She lifted a chain from around her neck. 'These are the keys in question. If you could get them back to me before the master returns, I would be very grateful. You are a true friend, Emma, probably the only one I have right now.'

'My lady, you are more than a friend, you are my princess and always will be,' said Emma. Without a word more, she turned and left the chambers, leaving Nesta smiling behind her.

'Oh, if only there were more like you, Emma,' she said quietly to herself, 'this life would be so much easier.'

The following day, the castle was busy preparing for the return of the castellan. Gerald's column was less than five leagues away and Nesta was overseeing the preparation of a feast in honour of his return. Salisbury drilled the men-at-arms within the bailey, determined to impress the castellan, while servants ran everywhere, sweeping and cleaning as if their lives depended on it.

'Master cook,' said Nesta, down in the kitchens, 'you are new to Pembroke yet come highly recommended. Please regale me with what delights you have prepared for the master.'

'There is a selection of game, my lady,' replied the cook, 'as well as the choicest of beef cuts, but the centrepiece will be a whole boar stuffed with apples, figs and spices. There is also a selection of flavoured bread, something I have developed over the years of serving many masters.'

'My husband is not known for his sense of adventure when it comes to food,' smiled Nesta, 'but I'm sure it will be fine.'

'I will ensure there are also adequate plain loaves, my lady. The last thing I want to do is upset Sir Gerald.'

Nesta smiled but over the cook's shoulder she could see Emma standing in the doorway, trying to catch her attention.

'Master cook,' said Nesta, 'I have some business to attend for a few moments, but perhaps when I return I could taste whatever sauces you have prepared.'

'It will be my pleasure, my lady,' said the cook, and he stepped aside to let her leave the kitchen.

'Emma,' whispered Nesta as she exited into the corridor, 'did you get them?'

'I did, my lady,' said Emma, handing over two sets of keys, 'though it cost me an unpleasant kiss in return.'

Nesta laughed out loud. 'In my experience, Emma, such a thing does not exist.'

'You do not know the blacksmith, my lady. Trust me, it is not something I wish to repeat.'

'Emma,' said Nesta, 'I have already asked a lot of you, but there is one more boon I would ask.'

'Anything, my lady.'

'Come with me.'

The two women climbed the stairs until they were outside Gerald's private quarters.

'I have business inside,' said Nesta, 'but worry in case I am discovered by Salisbury. I will be but a moment but need you to act as a guard. Can you do that?'

'Of course,' said Emma. 'Should he appear I shall feign a faint and throw myself into his arms.'

'Quite a sacrifice,' replied Nesta with a grimace, 'but it will definitely detain him for the few moments I need.'

'Then go quickly, my lady, before my taste in men returns.'

Nesta smiled and walked through the door. Quickly she went to the chest and replaced the original keys where she had found them two days earlier, before returning to the corridor where Emma was waiting.

'You were as quick as a flash,' said Emma. 'Is the task complete?'

'It is, and you have my gratitude, but tell me, are you not curious as to the nature of this subterfuge?'

'It is none of my business,' said Emma. 'If you want to tell me, you will, but in the meantime, I will forget what has taken place here.'

'Thank you, Emma,' said Nesta, 'and just trust me when I say, I act for the greater good.'

'Your explanation is welcome, my lady, though unnecessary.'

'Come,' said Nesta, taking her arm, 'let's go and taste the cook's gravy. I heard it is the most sublime thing to come out of England.'

Pembroke Castle

July 20th, AD 1113

Tarw moved slowly, painfully aware that the palisades above were patrolled by English sentries. He neared the postern gate and leaned against the door, waiting for Nesta to open it from the inside. For an age he waited, and was about to leave when the sound of a key in the lock made him turn back. He moved his hand to his sword, always wary of any situation that may be a trap.

The door opened slightly, and in the moonlight he could see his sister's face peering out, framed by the flickering light of a candle behind her.

'Nesta,' he whispered with relief, 'I thought you would never come.'

'I had to wait until Gerald was asleep,' she explained as he entered the room. 'Luckily he is now blind drunk, as is most of the garrison. If we are attacked tonight, I suspect they would all be killed in their beds.'

'Don't tempt me,' said Tarw with a smile, and he hugged his sister tightly. 'So how are you?'

'Much the same,' said Nesta. 'Gerald treats me well, yet it seems I am no more than a prisoner in my own home.'

'He is an English knight with the blood of our countrymen on his hands,' said Tarw. 'Never forget that fact.'

'He is as loyal as you or I, Tarw, just to a different master. Judge him on his heart, not his banner.'

'I feel we should change the conversation lest we argue,' said Tarw. 'Do you have the key?'

Nesta removed a leather tie from around her neck and handed it over. On the end was the key to the outer door.

'Where is the other?' he asked.

'I have already told you, I will not entrust the key of the inner door to your possession. However, I now have my own copy so I can come and go as I please.'

'So be it,' said Tarw, placing the necklace around his own neck.

'Tarw,' said Nesta, 'there is something we need to discuss, news that may be welcome to you.'

'And what news is this?'

'I was in the hall today when Gerald gave the garrison some news straight from London. It seems that Henry has promised an amnesty to all rebels who have wronged the Crown in the past, in return for a pledge of servitude. Your name was mentioned.'

'In what manner?' asked Tarw warily.

'He needs soldiers to fight alongside him in France, and Henry told Gerald that should you accept the offer, not only will you serve as an officer as becomes your station but if victorious, upon your return he will grant you lands and a modest income.'

'There was no mention of Dinefwr?'

'Unfortunately not. It seems he sees you as a potential threat and wants you distanced from those still loyal to the Tewdwr name.'

'I don't understand. Why does he want me? One man does not an army make.'

'Granted, but he also wants you to supply fifty men-at-arms to his cause. They will serve under you and be paid the same as the English.'

'And you think this is a good thing?'

'It may not be what you see as a long-term resolution but surely it betters living in the woods no better than a common brigand?' She paused before touching her brother's arm. 'Tarw,' she continued, 'don't you see? This is a fantastic chance of returning your life to normality. Ordinarily I would never suggest you ride to war, but as an officer you would be close to the king and unlikely to fall in battle. In a few months you could be safe within the walls of your own manor and raising a family of your own. Does that not appeal?'

Tarw looked at Nesta in the candlelight before taking a step backward. 'No, Nesta,' he said quietly, 'it certainly does not appeal, and the fact that you ever thought I would give such an idea consideration shows we are far removed from the brother and sister that played together all those years ago.'

'What do you mean?' asked Nesta stepping towards him. 'I worry only for your safety. You must know that?'

'Granted, but my safety comes second to the main purpose of my life, and that is to drive the invaders from my father's lands. I have trained too hard and waited too long to change my colours now, Nesta, and I am surprised you thought my mettle so weak. I would never ride under the flag of Henry – or any other English king for that matter. In my veins runs the blood of Rhodri Mawr and to deny that heritage would be akin to denying my own name. I cannot do it, Nesta. The answer is no.'

For a few moments there was silence, until eventually Nesta sighed deeply and stepped forward to take his hand.

'I already knew what your answer would be, Tarw, but I had to try. You and Hywel are all I have left and I would sell my very soul to keep you safe.'

'I understand, Nesta, and you have my gratitude, but let this be the last of it. I am avowed to making this land free again, and as God is my witness, I will achieve that aim or die trying.'

Nesta smiled and stepped back. 'You should leave,' she said, 'but there is one more question before you go. Please forgive me for asking but I have to know the truth, no matter how painful the answer.'

'Ask your question, dear sister, and I swear to answer as truthfully as I am able.'

'It is said that the attacks from rebels across the south are increasing. It is also said that the brutality knows no bounds and even women and children are shown no quarter.' She paused. 'Tarw,' she continued, 'some say that it is you who is to blame.'

'Is that what you believe?' asked Tarw gently.

'Of course not,' said Nesta, 'and even if you are the devil that they say you are, I will love you no less, but I have to know the truth. Are you responsible for so much bloodshed?'

Tarw looked up at the ceiling in the dark and took a deep breath before returning his gaze to his sister.

'Nesta,' he said, 'I am a rebel in an occupied land. Not a day goes by without the lives of me or my men being threatened. On occasion I have to do things of which I am not proud and, yes, that often extends to attacking the supply lines of the English. I make no apology for doing so for it is either that or starve and, yes, that sometimes includes taking the lives of men in the pay of the English Crown, but as God is my witness, I have never killed or arranged to be killed any innocent woman or child. I am aware of the incidents you speak of and there is talk that they are the responsibility of a band of mercenaries under the command of someone called Diafol, but I swear before you now on the memory of our mother and father, I am not responsible.'

Nesta smiled and threw herself into his arms. 'Thank God above,' she whispered, and they held each other for several moments before Tarw pushed her gently away.

'Enough,' he said. 'You should go back before you are missed. Let us not meet like this again for a while. It's far too risky. I will check for notes once a month, but if there is an urgent message, leave a plaid cover hanging from the tower. My spies will see the signal and I will seek your note as soon as I can. Is that possible?'

'It is,' said Nesta. 'Be careful, Tarw. When the king finds out you have refused his offer, I suspect he will direct Gerald against you, and that can only end in tragedy.'

'I can look after myself, dear sister,' said Tarw. 'Fret not a moment longer.' He turned to open the postern outer door before glancing back. 'Goodbye, Nesta. We will speak again soon.'

The door closed behind him before Nesta could respond and in the flickering candlelight she simply held up her hand. 'Goodbye, dear brother, fare ye well.'

Pembroke Castle

July 3rd, AD 1115

Almost two years had passed since Nesta was reunited with her brother and in the intervening time they communicated often, sometimes meeting in the postern tower but more often via secret notes, passed to Tarw's representative by Emma amongst the stalls of the market in the town. Though Nesta worried about everyone's safety in the subterfuge, there was little guilt, for the suffering caused by Tarw was nothing compared to that of the people of Deheubarth at the hands of the English, and Salisbury in particular.

The constable had steadily grown in power and influence, and though he was still second to Gerald in importance, his reach and particular fondness for cruelty was felt far and wide. In addition, his increasing attraction to Nesta became more pronounced, though always expressed beyond the sight of anyone who might have relayed their concerns to Gerald.

Nesta and Gerald's relationship had got better over that time and though it was never mentioned, it was obvious to the castellan that Nesta's abduction was not entirely against her will. Still, with his pride and honour at stake, the subject was avoided and the story of rape and kidnap was the favoured version in and around the castle.

Tarw had also increased in influence over the period and now operated out of the Cantref Mawr with a growing band of rebels unhappy about the situation developing in the south. With carefully selected targets, Tarw harried the English supply caravans at every opportunity, until the Crown was forced to protect them with heavily armed guards, a commitment the English could ill afford with Henry on campaign in France.

The past two years had been difficult for Sir Gerald as castellan at Pembroke Castle. Many of his men had been sequestrated by Henry for his campaign to Normandy. Upon the king's return many months later, those men not required for the king's standing army had been released from service and allowed to go home. This meant that many of the castles in Deheubarth, despite being fully controlled by the English, were actually very poorly manned, and as a result the rising banditry was becoming increasingly worrying. No man English-born ventured far from the many castles or fortified manors these days, and those who did were always under the protection of an armed guard.

Today was no exception for though Sir Gerald was out on a hunting trip, the armed knights lining a nearby ridge encouraged any man with ill intent to stay far away.

Gerald sat astride his hunter, waiting for the hounds to be released. The hunt had gone well and a stag had been cornered in a thicket close to a bend in the river. For the last two days, he and his men had enjoyed the chase and though it was now coming to an end, the change of pace had done wonders for his troubled mind.

The increased numbers of rebels meant the chances to hunt came few and far between these days but though the perpetrators were mainly Welsh-born, local farms and manors were just as likely to be attacked as English interests. Even the poor hated the rebels for they were indiscriminate in their attacks, but there was, however, one exception: the brother of the castellan's wife, Tarw.

Tarw was different to the others. He was careful to only attack the assets of the English Crown, and even then violence was kept to a minimum. Merchants were returned unharmed and though any men-at-arms had their thumbs removed with a sharp blade, seldom were any killed unless in the act of warfare.

This was a problem for Gerald as Tarw was slowly building a reputation for bravery and kindness, a potent mixture when you were a rebel prince, and Gerald knew that left unchecked, he could soon have disaffected commoners flocking to his banner. For two years the prince had gradually built his force and though Gerald had made it his mission to pursue the rebel prince, his quarry always seemed to be one step ahead. However, with Tarw's influence seemingly increasing by the day, the time was fast approaching when his threat would have to be addressed.

'My lord,' said Godwin, the castellan's comrade, at his side. 'The stag is cornered. Do you want the kill?'

Gerald looked around and saw one of the squires nearby. 'No,' he said. 'See if Master Cleveland there is up to the task.'

'My lord, the stag has seventeen points. Surely you would want this one yourself?'

'I have killed many a stag, Godwin,' said Gerald, 'but today my mind is on other things. Prizes such as these are getting harder to find, so let's give the young man a chance to do something he will remember for the rest of his life.'

Godwin nodded and called the squire over. 'Master Cleveland,' he said, 'this is your lucky day.'

———————

Several hours later, Gerald and his men were all back in the great hall, enjoying the festivities after two hard days on the hunt. A lone musician played boisterous tunes at the far end, while a group of servants kept the central table groaning with ale and mead.

Sir Gerald and his men sat at their own table, enjoying the rowdy antics of the squires on the opposite side of the hall. They too had once been squires and remembered fondly the making of friendships that would stay with them for the rest of their lives.

Master Cleveland had been successful in the kill and after having his face smeared with the stag's blood by the castellan, had been allowed to host his own table at the hunt celebration as a reward. At the centre of the table was the stag's head, a trophy that elevated the killer to god-like status amongst his peers. This was a rare event and unleashed from the strict codes by which they lived, the squires drank copious amounts of ale straight from the flagons, determined to get as drunk as they could in the quickest possible time.

'Master Cleveland has come on well this last year,' said Godwin.

'He has,' said Gerald, 'and I think another twelve months will see him ready for knighthood. What funds has his family deposited with us?'

Before Godwin could answer, the far door crashed open and one of Gerald's officers burst into the hall. He looked around quickly and spying Gerald walked quickly over to the castellan.

'Sir Thomas,' said Gerald, 'calm yourself, unless of course the castle is under attack.' The comment was meant as a joke but the look on the officer's face cancelled out any air of joviality.

'My lord,' said Thomas, 'I bring news that you may want to hear most urgently.'

'Then spit it out, man,' said Gerald, leaning forward in his seat.

'My lord, my spies have reported an armed group assembling in the Cantref Mawr.'

'Rebels?' asked Gerald, his interest piqued.

'Aye. It seems they have their sights set on the supply routes from Hen Domen to Raglan and intend to ride at the end of the month.'

'Interesting,' said Gerald, 'but it is far out of my jurisdiction. I will send word to the castellan at Hen Domen.'

'My lord,' said the officer, 'I would not normally bother you with such things but there is more. I have a spy who has managed to infiltrate the rebels and he tells me this offensive is going to be the largest in years. Almost every wanted man from Shrewsbury to Ceredigion will be amongst them. Surely this is an opportunity too good to miss?'

'Perhaps, but our garrison is the weakest it has been for many a year. I appreciate your enthusiasm, Thomas, but alas, all we can do is forewarn those closer to the threat.'

'Can we not petition the king for extra men?'

'Henry has just disbanded half his army so I doubt he would deem it fit to send a column after some rebels.'

'He might on this occasion, my lord.'

'And why is that?'

'Because the rebel commander is Gruffydd ap Rhys.'

'*Tarw*,' gasped Gerald, getting to his feet. 'Are you sure about this?'

'My source is as reliable as they get, my lord, and he hasn't failed me yet. I would bet my life he tells the truth.'

Gerald walked from behind the table and paced the floor of the hall, his mind racing. For the first time in years, he actually knew what Tarw was going to do, and though the location wasn't known as yet, the fact that Thomas had a spy amongst the rebels gave him every confidence that the situation could change. It was an opportunity almost too good to be true.

'Godwin,' he said, turning to his second-in-command, 'how quickly can we get a rider to London?'

'To what end, my lord?'

'To petition the king for extra men.'

'There is no need to go to London, my lord, the king is currently stationed at Bristol Castle.'

'He is?' said Gerald. 'How did I not know this?'

Godwin shrugged his shoulders. 'I assumed you did, my lord. He is attending a tournament there and intends to knight those who fought well in the Normandy war.'

'There was no war in Normandy,' scoffed Gerald, 'they were skirmishes, nothing more. To award knighthoods for such trivial events diminishes the station.'

'Perhaps, but nevertheless he is at Bristol and no doubt has a strong force at his disposal. With good weather and fresh horses from our castles along the way, we could have a message in Henry's hands within four days.'

'Do you think he would see this as a worthy cause?'

'You would know better than anyone, my lord, but I would suggest that an opportunity to catch or kill Tarw would whet even the king's appetite. The fact that the Welsh prince refused his offer of amnesty lies sore upon him, and I suspect he would like to send any of similar ilk a message they won't forget in a hurry.'

Gerald turned to Thomas. 'You say this rebel column will march out at the end of the month?'

'Aye, so I have been told.'

'Then that gives us enough time. Do you know where their attention will fall?'

'No, but I would suggest that any caravan heavy upon its axles will warrant their attention.'

Gerald smiled. 'I like the way you think, Thomas.'

He turned back to Godwin. 'This is an opportunity too good to miss. We will send a message to Henry immediately requesting cavalry and men-at-arms. Ask that they meet us in Builth no later than fourteen days from now, which will give us time to deploy. In the meantime, assemble the rest of our men and prepare to ride by dawn the day after tomorrow.'

'Aye, my lord,' said Godwin, and he turned to leave the chamber.

'Thomas,' said Gerald, 'get a message to your spy and tell him to keep you informed. If we manage to catch Tarw as a result of his information, I will make him a very rich man.'

'Of course, my lord,' said Thomas, and he followed Godwin from the hall.

As the knights dispersed, the drunken squires watched in bemusement, not party to the arrangements. Master Cleveland left his chair and walked over to the castellan. Despite his drunkenness, he had a look of concern upon his face.

'My lord, forgive me,' he said, 'but it seems you are about to embark on a campaign. Should I instruct the squires to make ready their mounts?'

'Not this time, Cleveland,' said Gerald. 'We have hard riding before us and can't afford to wait for stragglers.'

'My lord, it is true I am heavy with ale but I swear you will not find me wanting. Please take me with you.'

'Master Cleveland,' said Gerald, 'I respect your loyalty but you are needed here. I am taking the rest of the knights with me, so the garrison will be without a mounted force. Take your peers to the well and sober them up with cold water. John Salisbury will command the castle in my stead but you and your peers will man the palisades. Are you up to this task?'

'Aye, my lord. We will not fail you.'

'Good, for my wife and children abide within these walls and I am relying on you to look after them.'

Cleveland seemed to grow where he stood and his chest puffed out proudly. 'Leave it to me, my lord,' he said, and as Gerald strode away, Cleveland turned to the rest of the squires still drinking at the far end of the hall. 'Stow the flagons, comrades,' he shouted, 'a call to arms is upon us and heaven help any man who fails in his duty.'

Builth Castle

July 18th, AD 1115

Gerald stood atop one of the wooden towers of Builth Castle, staring out across the cleared scrubland towards the village. The night was dark and a heavy rain drove hard against his cloaked body. Despite the discomfort he welcomed the weather, for it eased his troubled mind. He and his men had been at Builth for seven days and though the local constable had allocated him another thirty men-at-arms, he knew it wouldn't be enough. If Tarw had even half the numbers he was credited with, Gerald needed the extra men from Henry, and they were already a day overdue. Someone climbed up the ladder and joined him on the parapet.

'Godwin,' he said, turning to meet his second-in-command. 'You should be taking advantage of warm ale and a warmer hearth while you have the chance.'

'As should you, my lord,' said Godwin, pulling his cloak tighter against the rain. 'If this weather holds, it could be a miserable few days in the saddle.'

'Unless Henry's men turn up soon,' said Gerald, 'the only riding we will be doing is back towards Pembroke. As much as I want Tarw's hide, I will not commit our men to a battle they cannot win.'

'They will be here, my lord,' said Godwin. 'Our messenger said the king was very enamoured at the thought of killing or capturing the Welsh prince and promised his full support.'

'Then where are they?' asked Gerald, looking back out over the village. 'They should have been here by now.'

'This rain makes life difficult for any rider, my lord, but the weather takes no sides, so rest assured that Tarw will be finding it just as hard as us.'

'Do you know who will be commanding the king's column?'

'I have no names but it is rumoured the honour has been allocated to one newly knighted on the fields of Normandy.'

'Why doesn't that fill me with confidence?' sighed Gerald.

'Come inside, my lord,' said Godwin, ignoring the question. 'The sentries will inform us of any approach and we need to talk tactics.'

'Go ahead, Godwin,' said Gerald. 'I will join you momentarily.'

Godwin retreated from the palisade and returned to the troop hall down in the bailey.

Several hours later, a column of over a hundred riders rode along a muddy track, every man weary from the hard ride from Bristol. At their head rode two knights, each a trusted man of King Henry. The trees around them thinned out and as they left the relative protection of the forest, one of them called a halt and looked over to the castle on the opposite side of the valley.

'There it is, at last,' he said.

'And a more welcome sight no man ever set eyes upon,' said the other. 'Our men are in dire need of warm quarters.'

'They will have little time to rest, I feel,' said the first knight, 'for I understand Tarw's attack is imminent, and I suspect that Sir Gerald will seek immediate deployment.'

'Half a day is all I need,' said the second man. 'Just some time for my men to get a hot meal, dry their breeches and rest the horses. After that I would pitch them against any foe.'

'Then the quicker we get there, the more time they will have.' He spurred his horse and headed for Builth Castle, his column of English lancers close behind.

'My lord,' whispered the page, shaking Gerald's shoulder gently. 'I have been instructed to inform you there is a column nearing the gate.'

Gerald sat upright, blinking the sleep from his eyes. He had been sleeping on a pile of deerskins on the floor of the lesser hall amongst his men, keen as always to share both their victories and their trials.

'Bring me my cloak,' he responded, rubbing his face vigorously. The page ran to the far side of the hall, while Gerald pulled on his boots.

'What's happening?' asked Godwin, sitting nearby.

'Go back to sleep, my friend,' said Gerald. 'It seems the reinforcements have arrived at last. I will see them in and greet their commander.'

'I cannot sleep anyway,' said Godwin, 'so I will join you.' He reached for his own boots and as soon as he was suitably dressed, picked up a tankard from a nearby table, downing the stale ale in one draught.

'That's better,' he said, wiping the liquid from his heavy moustache, 'now we can talk business.'

The two knights walked from the hall and into the bailey. The rain was falling lighter now, and the wind had died away completely. The column had already entered the castle and the night air was full of steam and noise as exhausted men tended their equally exhausted horses.

'There are empty stables at the north wall,' shouted the steward above the noise, 'as well as dry hay and oats. As soon as your mounts are stabled, assemble back here at the lesser hall. We have fires banked high and plenty of hot cawl.'

A half-hearted cheer rose from the soaked riders and as many headed towards the stables, Gerald and Godwin made their way against the flow, looking for the knight in charge.

'Master Elliot,' said Gerald, seeing the steward at the base of the motte. 'Where is the commander of these men?'

'Sir Gerald, they have already been welcomed into the keep by my master. He said to join them as soon as you could.'

Gerald nodded and ran up the steps of the motte towards the timber keep, closely followed by Godwin.

'The constable is expecting me,' he said to the guard on the door.

'Of course, my lord,' said the guard, stepping aside, 'you will find him in his chambers on the top floor.'

Gerald and Godwin climbed the stairs and waited as another guard went to inform the constable of their arrival.

'This fool has ideas above his station,' grumbled Godwin.

'Be courteous, my friend,' said Gerald. 'This is his castle, not ours, and as such his responsibilities match mine in the eyes of the king.'

'An unknighted constable matches the lowliest beggar, in my eyes,' said Godwin, 'for usually they have gained their position by using nothing more than honeyed words and heavy purses. If I was king, I would make every one of them earn their title on the battlefield.'

'And a fine king you would make, my friend, but that is a dream for another day. Now hush, for his man returns.'

The guard reappeared and led them down a short corridor to another door. 'You may enter,' said the guard. 'They are waiting.'

Gerald and Godwin walked in and saw three men stood around a table near a roaring fire. Each held a goblet of wine and was laughing heartily at some unheard joke.

'Sir Gerald,' said the constable as they walked in. 'Please, remove your cloaks and make yourselves at home.'

A manservant took their cloaks, while a maid brought them each a goblet of wine.

'Join us,' said the constable. 'I'm sure you are keen to make the acquaintance of the men you will be fighting alongside.'

The constable's two guests nodded slightly towards Gerald, conscious that he enjoyed the king's favour. Gerald looked at the second man, his eyes narrowing slightly as he struggled to recall where he had seen him before.

'This is Sir Gerald of Windsor,' said the constable to the newly arrived riders, 'castellan of Pembroke, and this is his right-hand man, Sir Godwin.'

'Greetings, Sir Gerald,' said one of the men. 'My name is Harry of Worcester, baron of the western Marches, and my comrade here is the Welshman tasked with aiding you against his wayward countryman.'

'I know you,' said Gerald, staring at the second man. 'We have met before.'

'We have,' came the reply, 'and it has to be said, in less than friendly circumstances. However, things have changed and my allegiance is now to the king of England.'

'Introduce yourself,' said the baron to his comrade, 'for you are now the king's man and I'm sure Sir Gerald here will see the merit in this alliance.'

'I think introductions are unnecessary,' said the second man slowly, 'for I see the light of recognition in Sir Gerald's eyes.'

'That you do,' growled Gerald, crushing the goblet within his fist. 'The last time I saw your treacherous face it was fleeing to Ireland in a fishing boat. You are Owain ap Cadwgan, the man who raped my wife.'

For a few seconds there was an awkward silence, broken suddenly as Godwin drew his sword.

'*Hold your arm,*' shouted the constable as Owain stepped backward to unsheathe his own weapon. 'There will be no bloodshed within these walls.'

'Spare me your words,' spat Godwin, 'and stand aside. This man has the blood of many Englishmen on his hands, including those I called comrade. The fact that he now pretends to be an ally makes a mockery of the Crown. Now get out of my way.'

'If you attack him, you attack me,' said Harry of Worcester dangerously, 'and win or lose, you will have the weight of my men fall upon you within minutes.'

'That's a risk I am willing to take,' said Godwin. 'Now step aside.'

Gerald lifted his hand and grabbed Godwin's arm. 'Sheathe your sword, my friend,' he said quietly. 'This is not the time nor the place.'

'It is exactly the time and the place,' said Godwin. 'This man kidnapped your son and raped your wife. It should be you wielding this blade, not I.'

'Perhaps, and that day may yet come,' said Gerald, still glaring at Owain, 'but today is not that day.'

Godwin turned and stared at his comrade. 'Gerald, this man has spilled the blood of many I called friend. Forget not the years we sought him out, swearing to kill him or die trying. Well, here he is, trapped within these four walls as you once were at Cenarth Bychan. Surely that in itself is a justice granted by God himself.'

'I have no knowledge of the ways of the Almighty,' said Gerald, 'but I am a knight and as such have made vows of honour and chivalry. What this man has done to me and my family deserves revenge but while we all accept the hospitality of the constable, my sword will remain sheathed.'

For a few moments, Godwin stared at Gerald before finally lowering his sword.

Owain and Sir Harry followed suit and the constable breathed a huge sigh of relief.

'Thank you, Sir Gerald,' he said, 'your manner does you and your position proud. Let me get your goblet replaced.'

'There is no need,' said Gerald, 'we are leaving.'

'But I thought . . .'

'I don't care what you thought,' said Gerald, 'all I said is that I will not take this man's life while I am your guest. I did not say I would share ale with him.'

'Sir Gerald,' said Worcester, 'you have every right to be alarmed, but Owain is now a trusted man of Henry and indeed, he was the king's first choice to lead our column in your struggle to capture Tarw. Who else has the experience required to fight a rebel Welsh prince other than one who also once bore that mantle himself?'

'I need the arrows and swords of men who kneel to the same king as I,' said Gerald. 'This man is a murderer and a rapist, nothing more, nothing less, and the fact that he has somehow managed to gain amnesty from the Crown and rides under our banners now makes him a traitor to his own people. I would sup with the devil himself before I share wine with this filth.'

'Gerald,' said Owain, entering the argument for the first time. 'I know you hold a grudge and that is to be expected. I cannot undo what was done and must carry that burden for the rest of my life but there are two things that you must know. First of all, I did not seek out the king's amnesty, it was he who came calling. His messengers sought me out and offered recognition of my claim in return for my sword arm in Normandy. I have not denounced my parentage or my country and carried my own colours alongside his, a fact welcomed by every Welshman on the campaign. My countrymen were so gladdened by our banners they fought like demons and Henry was so impressed by our collective strength in battle, he knighted me in front of my fellows. I carry the same title as you, Sir Gerald, earned in the furnace of war. At the very least, that should earn some merit in your eyes.'

'And the second thing?' asked Gerald.

'The second matter regards your wife,' smirked Owain, 'and is a touch more delicate, but as we are now equals in the eyes of the king, I will talk straight. I did not rape Nesta, she lay with me of her own free will.'

For a few moments there was silence again as the two men glared at each other.

'She may have lain with you,' said Gerald eventually, 'but it was a price she paid to ensure we all survived your murderous intent. By succumbing to your animal lusts she gained time for me to escape and ultimately track you down. In my eyes, whether violence was employed or not, that is still rape.'

'Then I will argue that point no more,' said Owain, 'for to give the details of our liaison will only discredit the lady further and raise your ire.'

'Be careful what you say,' warned Godwin, 'for though he be my master, Sir Gerald may not so readily stop my sword should you continue in this vein.'

'Then of course I will desist,' said Owain. 'But know this – if you should draw your sword again, I will be forced to defend myself and it may not go all your own way.'

Godwin's hand went to the hilt of his sword but it remained sheathed.

'Have you finished?' asked Gerald.

'I have,' replied Owain, 'though there is the small matter of the task before us to be discussed. No matter what your thoughts are of me, the king has gone to great expense to furnish the column currently in the bailey. I would propose we shelve our differences and concentrate on the job before us.'

'We will talk of warfare tomorrow morning,' said Gerald, 'for I will remain here not a moment longer, but know this – one, you are not and never will be my equal; and two, when this is over, there will be a reckoning.'

'So be it,' said Owain, and he watched as Gerald and Godwin left the constable's chambers.

———

The following morning all four men sat at a table in a side chamber off the lesser hall. The officers of both sides were also present and though the atmosphere was tense, the events of the night before were temporarily forgotten in the need to come up with a strategy to defeat Tarw. By midday the plans were made and as the men set about preparing for the campaign, Gerald joined Godwin upon the ramparts behind the palisade.

'So,' said Godwin, 'what are your thoughts?'

'On what, the plan?'

'No, what to do about Owain.'

'To be honest, I have focused on the campaign only. There is no room for that man until this task has been completed.'

'But you cannot just let him go?'

'He enjoys the king's favour, Godwin, and as such falls under the protection of the Crown. Even if I was to challenge him to arms, should I emerge the victor I would answer to Henry. No, I have to push him to the back of my mind and when this is over, perhaps petition the king to be allowed to right the wrongs this man has inflicted on my family.'

'The Gerald of old would have cut him down as soon as he saw him,' said Godwin.

'Perhaps so, but I am older and wiser these days so let us just look towards the battle before us. After that, well, whatever will be, will be.'

'As you wish,' said Godwin, and the two men returned to their own troops to continue their preparations.

The Forests between Builth and Hen Domen

July 20th, AD 1115

Tarw lay just behind the crest of the ridge, enjoying the sun's warm rays. The past few days had been a nightmare as far as the weather was concerned and his men had been drenched to the skin, so much so that they had sought shelter in the farms still loyal to the Welsh cause. Eventually the weather had changed but it meant they were days behind schedule and had to move the site of the ambush further north.

Now they were in place, all they had to do was wait until the English caravan entered the steep-sided valley and unleash their steel against it. Tarw's spies had informed him of a particularly valuable wagon within the caravan and with their supplies in the Cantref Mawr running low, they needed a good hoard to fund their continued campaign.

'Tarw,' whispered a voice, and the prince looked up to see one of his men crouched beside him.

'Connor, what is it?'

'Our scouts have spotted the caravan just under two leagues from here. They'll be here within the hour.'

'Were they seen?' asked Tarw, sitting up.

'Of course not. I've told our men to get to their positions.'

'Good,' said Tarw, getting to his feet. He tightened his sword belt and looked across the valley, watching several dozen archers deploying amongst the shelter of the boulders on the rocky slopes opposite. To his right, the single track climbed the flank of the hill, and it was from this direction the enemy caravan would come. To his left, the track disappeared down to the village of Brown-water Bridge, and behind him, a heavily wooded slope guarded his back.

'Are they aware of the signal?' asked Tarw.

'You know they are,' said Connor. 'Don't worry, Tarw, everything is in hand but we need to get into position.'

'I'm ready,' said Tarw. 'Let's go.'

An hour later, Tarw and Connor stood amongst the trees alongside the track at the bottom of the valley. In front of them a cart blocked the path as two of Tarw's men pretended to replace a damaged wheel. In the forest behind, fifty men lay hidden, waiting for the signal.

'Here they come,' said Connor.

Tarw looked up the path and saw the first English wagon enter the valley. Beside the cart rode two armed men, obviously mercenaries under the pay of the caravan master, and as more carts appeared, more guards could be seen.

'Come on,' said Tarw quietly to himself, 'keep coming.'

The caravan continued halfway down the track before the lead rider held up his hand, calling it to a halt. The twelve wagons rumbled to a standstill, while four horsemen rode forward to see what was happening.

'Get down,' whispered Tarw, and he and the rest of the men near to him lay prone amongst the undergrowth.

'What's happening here?' came a loud voice from out on the track.

'My lord,' replied one of the men repairing the wagon, 'we lost a wheel this morning but have just about got it fixed.'

'How long will you be?'

'A few minutes, nothing more.'

'Show me the broken wheel,' said a second voice.

'Over there,' said Tarw's man, pointing at a shattered wagon wheel leaning against a rock. 'Luckily we brought a spare.'

'Get a move on,' said the rider, 'we need the road.'

'A few moments, my lord,' said the rebel, 'and we will be out of your way.'

'You have until our caravan gets down here,' said the rider. 'If you are not on your way by then, we will tip it down the bank.'

'That will not be necessary, my lord,' said the rebel, 'we are almost done.'

Tarw heard the horses ride away and breathed a sigh of relief. He had anticipated the caravan would be guarded and though he and his men were prepared for a fight, he needed something blocking the path to stop the carts escaping when the attack started.

'So far so good,' he whispered as he peered through the undergrowth. Further up the path the caravan resumed its journey, with all the carts lumbering closer and closer.

'I count a dozen guards,' whispered Connor, 'no more. Easy fodder for our archers.'

Tarw didn't answer but just stared at the lead cart as it crept ever closer.

'Tarw,' said Connor, 'they are almost upon us. Give the signal.'

'Wait,' said Tarw. 'Something is wrong.'

'What do you mean?' asked Connor. 'They have fallen for the ruse completely.'

'See the wagons,' said Tarw. 'They are heavy on their axles. Too heavy.'

Connor looked up at the wagons and it was obvious the teams of mules struggled to pull their heavy load.

'It means nothing,' said Connor. 'It could be stores, weapons or even people. Many travellers pay handsomely for the protection such a caravan offers these days.'

'They do,' said Tarw, 'but they could be anybody. Even men-at-arms.'

Connor turned to look at the caravan. It was now less than fifty paces away from Tarw's men on the track and he could see them glancing nervously towards the trees waiting for the signal.

'Tarw,' hissed Connor, 'you need to decide. Do we attack or call it off? Whichever it is I will support you but we need to know now.'

'What is your counsel?'

'I say we do it. We have come too far and suffered too much to ride away now.'

'And if there are more armed men in the wagons?'

'Then we fight,' said Connor. 'We are well armed and have numbers on our side.'

Tarw paused but finally nodded his agreement. Getting to his knees he waved towards the men next to the cart on the path and without further ado, each took an axe and started smashing the spokes of the wheels, ensuring it could not be moved.

Further up the path the lead rider called a halt again and stared at the men destroying the wagon.

'*What do you think you are doing?*' he roared, and followed by ten other riders he spurred his horse forward.

The men with the axes saw the danger and ran into the forest, their work done. The riders circled the damaged wagon nervously, knowing it could be some sort of a trap.

'Whoever you are,' shouted the lead rider, 'show yourself, for we ride under the banner of Henry himself.'

Tarw stood up and walked out into the open, followed by Connor and eight of his own men. They stopped fifty paces away from the riders.

'Who are you and what do you want?' shouted the rider.

'My name is Tarw,' came the reply, 'and I want your caravan. Take your men and any passengers back the way you came and I promise there will be no bloodshed.'

'You are but ten men, and I am equipped with ten mounted knights, each hardened on the battlefields of France. I suggest you yield the road else I have your head displayed atop a lance to feed the crows.'

Tarw sighed and held up his hand. The rider turned to see all Tarw's archers reveal themselves from the rocks at the base of the slopes. Another signal summoned another fifty well-armed men from amongst the trees, each staring coldly at the riders on the path.

'As you can see,' said Tarw, 'you are well outnumbered. Even with your undisputed fighting skills, you have to agree the odds are not in your favour. My archers will drop you within moments and as the carts can't retreat up the path, it is inevitable that we will win the day. Now for the last time, withdraw or face the consequences.'

For a few moments the two men stared at each other, before the rider's face broke into a smile.

'Well, Tarw,' he said with a hint of menace, 'I guess you are going to have to do your worst.'

Tarw's eyes narrowed and his heart missed a beat. There was no doubt he had the advantage, yet this man challenged his position. That could mean one of two things – either he was very stupid or very confident.

'Well,' said the rider, 'what are you waiting for?'

'You invite your own death,' said Tarw. 'Why would you do that?'

'We all have to die sometime, Tarw, but today I believe is not my time.' Without another word he held up his own hand and a horn echoed around the valley. Every rebel looked around nervously and their hearts raced as line after line of archers appeared on the ridgeline higher up the valley. Up at the wagons, men-at-arms poured from the backs of the carts, quickly assembling across the road, and behind them, another twenty mounted men rode into the valley, spreading out to prevent escape.

Tarw looked in horror. Within moments the tables had been turned and he and his men were now severely outnumbered.

'Do you know who I am?' asked the rider as the trap closed.

'I know your face,' replied Tarw, 'but your name escapes me.'

'I am Godwin,' said the rider, 'comrade and right-hand man of your brother-in-law.'

'Gerald?'

'Indeed. The wind has changed, Welshman. Now you are faced with the same choice as I was just moments ago. Yield or suffer the consequences.'

Tarw thought furiously. He knew he had been bettered but if they were captured, he knew every man would be executed as a rebel. There was only one thing for it: they would have to fight their way out. His hand crept to the handle of his sword.

'Don't do anything stupid, Tarw,' growled Godwin.

'To die on the end of a rope is stupid,' said Tarw, drawing his sword, 'to die fighting for freedom is a privilege.' He turned to face the hill.

'*Archers*,' he roared, 'cut them down.'

In an instant, the Welsh archers let loose upon the English men-at-arms but had only got two arrows away before the English archers responded in kind. Men fell amongst the rocks and screams echoed throughout the valley. Tarw's men-at-arms immediately charged the enemy, knowing that the only hope of survival was to go on the offensive. The English riders spurred their horses and rode headlong into the enemy, their swords cutting the Welsh foot soldiers down like scythed hay.

Desperately Tarw looked around and to his dismay saw yet another column of riders galloping up the path from further down the valley, cutting off their obvious means of escape. The only way out was into the forests but to do so meant they would be spread out and easier for the English to chase down. Without any other option he roared his command.

'*Men of Wales, to the trees!*'

All around him men broke off from the fight and fled headlong back into the forest. With a victorious roar, the English soldiers chased them up the wooded hill, knowing the fight was won. Amongst them rode Godwin, his horse frothing at the mouth, eyes staring wildly.

'*After them,*' roared Godwin, and he threw himself from his horse to join in the chase. All around him his men were dispatching any Welsh stragglers and screams echoed amongst the trees as men were slaughtered without quarter. For the next few minutes, the forest resounded with the noises of battle as men fought desperately hand to hand.

Godwin stopped, leaning on a tree to catch his breath, when another man appeared beside him.

'You look exhausted, my lord,' said the soldier. 'Leave this to us and get that wound sorted.'

Godwin looked down and saw his leggings were saturated with blood. His thigh was cut open and in the heat of battle he hadn't even noticed. The knight nodded. It was pointless pursuing the Welshmen any further as they were in their element amongst the trees and anyway, though they didn't yet know it, there was one last surprise awaiting Tarw and his men at the top of the hill.

'Come on,' gasped Connor, 'we're almost there.' He pulled Tarw up over the ridge and both men fell to the ground exhausted.

'We can't stay here,' Connor said after a few moments' rest, 'they are right behind us.'

Tarw got to his feet and looked around. No more than a few dozen of his men had made it up and many of those carried wounds.

'Oh, by the Devil's breath . . .' gasped Connor. 'Look.'

Tarw followed Connor's gaze and saw more riders coming through the trees. 'There's no way they could have ridden the horses up there – they must have been waiting here all this time. We have been out manoeuvred, Connor, it is us who have been ambushed.'

Both men turned to run but before they had gone a hundred paces, Connor cried out in pain, struck by an arrow between the shoulders. Tarw stopped and turned to help his friend but it was obvious there was nothing he could do.

'Leave me,' Connor choked, 'I am done.'

'Connor . . .' started Tarw.

'Shut up, Tarw, and save yourself. You need to survive to lead the fight another day.'

Tarw gripped his friend's shoulder in one last farewell but as he got to his feet, a horse smashed into him from behind and he fell to the ground. All breath had been knocked from his body but still he got to his feet, determined to sell his life dearly. He looked around for his sword but the knight smashed him across the head with his boot, sending him sprawling once again. This time there was no getting up, and as Tarw lay on his back, gasping for breath, the knight dismounted before walking over and pinning Tarw to the ground with his foot.

Tarw looked up, his eyes blurred. He heard the sound of the man's sword being unsheathed before feeling the point of the blade against his chest.

'Well, look who we have here,' said the attacker, 'if it isn't the man himself, Gruffydd ap Rhys Tewdwr, one-time prince of Deheubarth.'

'My name is Tarw,' came the response. 'At least have the decency to use it.'

'Oh, I know who you are, Tarw. Our families were once very close. In fact, I believe we once shared games at your father's castle when we were young boys.'

'Who are you?' asked Tarw, his eyes narrowing.

'Don't you recognise me?' asked the man. 'I am Owain ap Cadwgan, prince of Powys.'

'I don't understand,' said Tarw slowly. 'If you are indeed he, why do you hold a blade against my breast? Surely we are brothers in arms.'

'A year or two ago, perhaps,' said Owain, 'but things have changed and I now ride under the banner of Henry.'

'*You fight for the English*,' gasped Tarw. 'But why?'

'I took the amnesty, Tarw. Something you should have considered.'

'You sold your soul to the devil, Owain. Heaven help you.'

'Oh, it won't be for long,' said Owain, 'just until Henry returns our lands to our family. After that I will reclaim the kingship of Powys.'

'Even so, as a fellow Welshman you should let me go.'

'I'm afraid I can't do that,' said Owain.

'Why not? Are we not kindred spirits?'

'Perhaps, but unfortunately there is rather a high price on your head and if I claim the bounty, who knows where it may lead. Henry may even grant me lands in Deheubarth – after all, you will have no further need for them.'

'Don't do this, Owain,' said Tarw. 'If you turn away from your heritage now, then you will surely rot in hell.'

'Hell has no fears for me, Tarw,' said Owain, 'so unfortunately your warnings fall on deaf ears.' He adjusted his grip on his sword and prepared to thrust it downward into Tarw's heart. 'Any last words for your dear sister?'

'Just do it, Owain,' said Tarw. 'And may your forsaken soul rot in hell for evermore.'

'So be it,' said Owain, but as the pressure increased on the blade, Tarw heard a thump and Owain's eyes widened in disbelief. The killing thrust from his blade never came and instead, Owain dropped the sword before staggering to one side and falling to his knees, an arrow sticking out of his back.

Tarw looked over to see his saviour but was confused to see two more Englishmen sat astride their horses. One was obviously a knight and was in the process of returning a bow to the other, an archer.

'Be gone,' said the knight to the archer, 'and forget what you saw here on pain of death.'

'Aye, my lord,' said the archer, and he rode back into the trees.

The knight dismounted and walked across to Owain, who was struggling to breathe, one lung having collapsed from his wound. The knight knelt down in front of his victim and lifted the young man's head so he could look into his eyes.

'Gerald,' groaned Owain, 'I don't understand.'

'Of course you do,' said Gerald. 'Even you must have known I could not let your actions pass unavenged.'

'God will judge you,' gasped Owain.

'And Satan you,' said Gerald. He leaned forward and placed his left arm around the young man, whispering into his ear. 'This is for Nesta.' He pushed his blade slowly into Owain's stomach before twisting the blade and thrusting it upward. Blood spurted over Gerald's hauberk as Owain writhed in agony but still he held the man close, listening to him die.

Eventually he lowered the dead man to the ground before getting to his feet and walking over to Tarw. Tarw gazed up at the imposing English knight, hardly believing what he had just seen. Gerald stared back down before replacing his blade in his sheath and walking away.

'Wait,' said Tarw, 'what is this about? Where are you going?'

'I have Welshmen to kill,' said Gerald.

'But I don't understand.'

'You may be my enemy, Tarw, but I can't ignore the fact I am married to your sister, and though we fight under different flags, it would be wrong to avenge her embarrassment with one hand, then kill her kin with the other.'

'You are letting me live?'

'Just this once, but from this day forward there will be no quarter.'

'But what about my men? Will you let them live also?'

'They are rebels, Tarw, and know the price to be paid. Now I suggest you be gone for I have had my fill of killing princes for one day.'

The Cathedral of Saint David

July 30th, AD 1115

Ten days had passed since Tarw had fled the slaughter at Brown-water Bridge, heading westward back towards Deheubarth. At first he had ridden hard but when his horse had fallen and broken a leg, he had to slit its throat and carry on by foot, seeking out the lesser-known paths and hidden ways of the dense forests of Mid Wales. With no food or water, he had to live off what he could steal from outlying farms and drink directly from the streams, knowing full well that as far as his pursuers were concerned, he had killed Owain ap Cadwgan before making his escape. Consequently there were English patrols everywhere, and though Tarw still had friends loyal to his cause, most doors were closed to him, their occupants fearful of retribution.

With nowhere to go he had considered seeking help from Nesta but he knew that in the circumstances, he would be putting her life at risk, and that was something he would never do. Finally, in desperation he knew there was only one place he could go and know he was safe: the cathedral of Saint David.

The last five days had taken its toll on Tarw. He had no food, his feet were heavily blistered, and to top it off, he had badly twisted a knee after falling into a stream. Despite this he knew he had no other choice but to continue, for he was a wanted man and it was only a matter of time before someone saw him and told the English where he was. Exhausted, he finally emerged from the low-lying forests near the cathedral, and after waiting for the anonymity darkness brought, limped the final few leagues towards its sacred walls.

Knowing he had neither the strength nor the skill to climb the walls surrounding the cathedral grounds he realised he had no option but to throw himself on the mercy of the guards manning the gatehouse. Slowly he staggered forward, desperately hoping the patrol he had seen earlier was nowhere nearby, until finally he fell against the heavy timber door beneath the stone archway. Using the last of his strength he banged his fist repeatedly against the oak, desperate for a response.

'Who goes there?' shouted a voice eventually, and Tarw looked up to see a priest leaning out of a window.

'Sanctuary,' gasped Tarw. 'Please, I beg of you, open the gates.'

'Tell me your name, stranger,' said the priest, 'and state your business for there be brigands about and it is known they favour religious treasures.'

'I am no brigand, Father,' said Tarw, 'I am a prince of Deheubarth and need the protection of God's walls.'

For a moment the priest looked down, before disappearing from sight. Tarw collapsed against the wall to await his fate, too tired to care any more. Ten minutes later a hatch slid open in the gate and the priest's voice spoke again.

'Are you still there, stranger?'

'Aye,' said Tarw.

'Then come close so we can see your face.'

Tarw got to his feet and stumbled over to the gate. The priest held a lamp up to the hatch and Tarw's eyes narrowed against the bright glare.

'Is this him?' asked the priest to someone else behind the gate.

For a few seconds there was silence, until finally a familiar voice brought waves of relief to Tarw's heart. 'Aye, that is he. Open the gates.'

The sound of locks being withdrawn was followed by the creak of the giant hinges and as Tarw stumbled through the opening, he fell into the arms of a man he hadn't seen for many years.

'It's all right, Tarw,' said Hywel, holding his brother tightly, 'you're safe now.'

———

For the next few days Tarw was nursed by the staff of the cathedral, drifting in and out of consciousness as the milk of the poppy took effect. Hywel stayed at his side, ensuring he was given the best of care, and eventually Tarw was strong enough to sit up and take some soup. Soon he was back on his feet and he and Hywel walked around the walled grounds of the cathedral, each sharing their adventures since they had last met. Tarw's mood was sombre as he recalled the outcome of the battle at Brown-water Bridge, and the realisation he had lost all his followers haunted him like the worst nightmare.

'They knew the risks,' said Hywel as they walked, 'and at least lived the lives of free men before they fell. Many never enjoy that privilege.'

'Yes, but I should have known,' said Tarw. 'I knew there was something wrong yet ignored the signs. My success over the years bred a feeling of superiority and I naturally assumed we would emerge victorious.'

'You had every right to feel confident, brother,' replied Hywel. 'You are a great warrior and leader of men. Your reputation precedes you and your name is spoken with fear at many English manors.'

'Ha,' sneered Tarw. 'Whatever reputation I may have had now lies blood-sodden at Brown-water Bridge. I think it may be time to end the dream, Hywel. Perhaps this time I have gone too far.'

'*No*,' said Hywel sharply. 'You must continue.'

Tarw stopped walking and stared at his brother, surprised at the animosity in his voice.

'Hywel,' he said eventually, 'I am only discussing the options and to be honest, it is very easy for someone to preach violence from behind the safety of the cathedral walls. Why are you so determined I continue?'

Hywel stopped walking and took a deep breath before turning around to face his brother. 'I'm sorry,' he said, 'I did not mean to offend. Of course you have the right to choose your own path but you should also realise that you are more of a risk to the English than ever.'

'And how do you make that out?'

'Because they know they had you cornered yet you escaped. The English have no idea there are no more rebels in the Cantref Mawr and I suspect they sleep even less these nights knowing you are still at large. Is not a bull more dangerous when wounded?'

'Pretty words, brother, but I am a single man and can do nothing alone.'

'You are not alone, Tarw, you have me.'

Tarw smiled. His brother had spent most of his life as a prisoner of the English, suffering terrible injuries as a result, and though he had been a guest in the cathedral since being rescued by Tarw years earlier, he still had a slight frame and no battle skills.

'And a fine fellow you are, Hywel,' said Tarw, 'but even together there is little we can do. Perhaps we should go to Ireland, at least while I lick my wounds.'

'You can't go to Ireland, Tarw,' said Hywel. 'The English expect you to take that route and all the ports are being watched.'

'They know I am here?'

'Probably. There are spies everywhere. I doubt Gerald's men will break the rules of sanctuary but it is only a matter of time before some brigand will chance his arm. After all, there is an attractive price on your head.'

'So there is no way out,' said Tarw. 'I am to wait here like a frightened hare until the hunters flush me out.'

'Not necessarily. There is another option.'

'I am listening.'

'We could go north to Gwynedd. King Gruffydd has a strong army and is feared by the Marcher lords. We could petition him for men to ride back with us and continue the struggle.'

'Gruffydd would never do that, Hywel, for to do so would invite the wrath of Henry.'

'Perhaps not, but he could give us financial aid, and with enough money we could hire mercenaries.'

'Why would the king of Gwynedd even contemplate risking his own peace to help a southern kingdom?' asked Tarw. 'You make no sense.'

'*Because he owes us,*' shouted Hywel. 'Don't forget, our father aided him when he was outnumbered at Mynydd Carn, and when they emerged victorious, he promised he would be there to help should our family ever need his aid. Well, this is such a time, Tarw. It is time to collect on the debt.'

Tarw stared at his brother, knowing his words had merit. No freedom fighter ever gave up because things had gone wrong; they simply reorganised and started again. However, there was something in Hywel's eyes that he had not seen before, a hardness and determination that he did not recognise. It made Tarw slightly uneasy.

'Even if we pursue this path,' said Tarw, 'how do we escape this place without being seen?'

'Leave that to me,' said Hywel. 'My time here has not been wasted.'

'To be honest,' said Tarw, 'I was beginning to wonder how you knew so much about the situation outside of these walls.'

'My influence stretches further than you may think, Tarw, and one day I will share my story with you, but until that day, just focus on getting well.'

'I am already feeling much stronger,' said Tarw. 'I believe that in a week or so, I will be able to ride again.'

'Good. So are we going north?'

'Aye, brother,' said Tarw, grasping Hywel's wrist, 'that we are.'

Aberffraw

August 25th, AD 1115

Gwenllian and her brothers rode hard across the vale, yet again testing each other's strength on horseback. Spittle flew back from their steeds' mouths and Gwenllian's hair blew loose about her shoulders. The look on the girl's face was determined and she spurred her horse to greater effort, desperate to better the others.

'To the ridge,' shouted Cadwallon, and they all wheeled to push their horses even harder up the slope. But Cadwallon already had the advantage and he crested the slope with a shout of triumph.

'You used trickery,' gasped Gwenllian, reining in her horse beside him. 'The route was easier to your flank.'

'Does a king whine about trickery when he is outflanked,' asked Cadwallon, sliding from his saddle, 'or would he admire his opponent for seizing the advantage?'

'You know what I mean,' said Gwenllian, dismounting. 'Battle is one thing but a race should be equal to all concerned.'

'What's the matter, dear sister?' laughed Cadwaladr, joining them on the ridge. 'Are your feelings hurt by being bettered?'

'I can take losing as well as winning,' said Gwenllian, 'as long as the contest is fair.'

Both boys laughed and tied the reins of their horses to a low-hanging branch before walking up to the rocking stone overlooking the valley.

Despite her denial, Gwenllian was indeed vexed at her loss for it meant constant teasing by her brothers for at least the next day or so. It was thus in many things and though she was now eighteen years old, it meant she had to train harder and longer than any of her brothers to maintain a competitive standard. It was hard work for although mentally she saw herself as an equal, physically she was undoubtedly weaker. Whereas her brothers' strengths were visible in the way their bodies grew, her own frame, no matter how hard she fought or how heavy the training sword, seemed to soften as she changed into a woman. This incensed Gwenllian but though she knew there was nothing she could do about it, the one thing she feared more than anything was the prospect of being married off to some stranger in the name of powerful alliances. Many was the time her mother had broached the subject but the standard response of shouting and swearing usually meant it was shelved for a different day.

Gwenllian had no interest in men, unless they were a training partner or recounting tales of valour and battle. At these times she was transfixed and could listen to them talk all night, but the thought of kissing one made her feel sick to the stomach. Every night she silently cursed the day she had been born a girl, for battle and glory lay only in the hands of men and it seemed she would be denied the opportunity.

Still sulking, she walked away from her brothers and along the ridgeline towards the next valley. Soon she was out of sight and sitting on a rock to watch the eagles soar above the higher peaks. But she was there for only minutes when the sound of voices reached her on the breeze. Always aware of the potential danger of brigands out in the mountains, she quietly drew her sword, but rather than return to her brothers, she decided to see for herself who was responsible for the ruckus. Slowly she approached the edge of the ridge and looked down into the valley below. Just below her position she could see two horses tied to a tree and beyond them, a mountain stream tumbling from an overhanging rock and plunging into the pool below. Carefully she crawled down the slope and took position behind a thick bush to see what was happening.

The originators of all the shouting soon became obvious as she saw two men taking the opportunity to cool down in the water, jumping from a higher rock into the pool. One of the men still wore leggings, while the other was totally naked. Gwenllian found her gaze lingering on the unclothed man for though she was not unfamiliar with the male form, this was the first time it had had any effect on her. For a few moments she stared, surprised at her reaction, but she soon snapped out of it and relaxed as she watched the two strangers enjoying themselves in the clear spring water.

Their enthusiasm was infectious and Gwenllian watched with glee, often covering her mouth with her hand to stop any laughter escaping, but when one of the men slipped on the rock and tumbled head over heels into the pool, a snort of laughter gave away her presence.

The man who had fallen emerged from the water coughing and spluttering, still winded from the fall. He staggered to the shallows, cursing, but soon saw the look of warning on his comrade's face as he looked towards Gwenllian's hiding place.

'What's the matter?' he asked, holding his side where he had hit a rock on the way down.

'There's someone there,' said the second man. They both stared towards the bush.

'Are you sure?'

'I heard him laugh. Reveal yourself, stranger,' he shouted. 'At least have the decency to show who it is that finds enjoyment in another man's misfortune.'

Gwenllian stifled another laugh for the man looked ridiculous just standing naked in the shallows of the pool.

'I am a prince of Deheubarth, stranger,' shouted the naked man, 'and if you laugh again, I swear I will drag you out and beat you to within an inch of your life.'

Gwenllian took a deep breath and stood up. 'If you are truly a prince,' she said, struggling to contain her mirth, 'then introduce yourself formally for I am the daughter of a king and I would be glad to make your acquaintance.'

'My name is Gruffydd ap Rhys,' came the reply, 'and I am commonly known as Tarw.'

'And he?' asked Gwenllian, nodding towards the man in leggings.

'This is my brother, Hywel, and we are on our way to meet with King Gruffydd ap Cynan. Do you know of him?'

'I do, for he is my father.'

'Then perhaps you can take us to him.'

'I could,' said Gwenllian, 'but there are certain standards to be observed in my father's court, clothing being one of them.'

Tarw glanced down and realised he was still naked and standing in front of the daughter of the most powerful king in Wales. His hands moved to his front to cover his manhood.

'It's a bit late for modesty,' she laughed. 'You have been stood there as naked as the day you were born since I stood up. At least your brother has the decency to wear leggings.'

'You had me at a disadvantage,' said Tarw, 'and were surely spying upon us like a vagabond child.'

'I was doing no such thing,' said Gwenllian, wiping away tears of laughter. 'I thought you were brigands out to rob travellers on the path through Gwynedd. It was my duty as a loyal subject of my father to check out any potential dangers.'

'Well, you have had your fun, now please allow us to get dressed.'

'Feel free,' said Gwenllian, shrugging her shoulders.

'We can't,' said Hywel.

'Why not?'

'Because our clothes are in front of the bush you used to hide your presence.'

Gwenllian looked to one side and saw the two piles of discarded clothes.

'I still don't see the problem,' said Gwenllian mischievously. 'I'm not going to stop you.'

'My lady,' said Tarw, 'you have had your fun, please let us end this farce and get dressed.'

Gwenllian smiled and just sat on a rock, folding her arms in defiance. 'You have nothing I have not seen before, Sir Prince, for I have grown up amongst a host of brothers and warriors. Of course, if the presence of a girl concerns you, I will gladly withdraw.'

'I'll get your clothes,' said Hywel. He started to walk out of the pool.

'Wait,' said Tarw, 'if she wants to play her game, then we shall play along.'

His hands fell to his sides and with a deep breath he walked out of the pool towards Gwenllian.

As he approached, Gwenllian could see he was very handsome and a fine specimen of a man. He stopped a few paces before her.

'Your presence does not concern me, dear princess,' he said calmly. 'I was only worried for your own embarrassment. Now, if you don't mind, please stand aside so I can get clothed.'

All signs of Gwenllian's initial confidence disappeared and she stared into his eyes furiously, afraid that her own might glance downward of their own accord. 'Of course,' she stuttered, 'I only meant . . .'

'Like I said, you have had your fun. Now is the time to end such mischiefs.'

Gwenllian turned and faced the other way as both men got dressed. Finally, Tarw announced they were once again decent and she turned to face them once more.

'So,' he said, 'shall we start again?'

Before Gwenllian could answer they heard a shout and they all turned to see her brothers riding furiously down from the ridge, swords drawn. Tarw and Hywel picked up their own swords as they approached but Gwenllian ran forward and held out her arms.

'Stop,' she called. 'I am not at risk; these men are allies from the south.'

Cadwallon and his brother slowed their horses but circled Tarw and Hywel, their swords still drawn.

'Who are you,' asked Cadwallon, 'and what are you doing here?'

'I am Gruffydd ap Rhys, prince of Deheubarth,' replied Tarw, 'and we have come here to seek an audience with your father.'

'You are Tarw?' asked Cadwaladr, recognising the name.

'I am, why?'

'They say he was killed a few weeks back near Builth.'

'Then they are wrong,' said Tarw, 'whoever they may be.'

'Can you prove it?'

'What do you want to know?'

'Do you have your kingdom's seal?'

'Of course not. We have only just escaped the English with our lives and have ridden here to seek aid from Gruffydd.'

'What about you?' said Cadwallon. 'What is your name?

'I am Hywel,' came the reply, 'brother to Tarw.'

'If you are truly he, then you must be the one who was mutilated at the hands of the English as a boy?'

Hywel just stared at the man, shocked that someone who lived so far away from his home could know of his shame.

'Oh, don't look so surprised,' said Cadwallon, 'your tale is known across the country. Is it right that they cut off your balls?'

'That is no business of yours,' growled Hywel.

'Oh, but it is,' responded Cadwallon, 'because if you remove your leggings, your castration would prove who you claim to be.'

'It would,' said Hywel slowly, 'but that is not going to happen.'

'My friend,' said Cadwallon, pointing at Hywel with his sword, 'you are at a disadvantage here. You will do whatever I say or suffer the consequences.'

'We want no conflict,' said Hywel, 'and came here as allies, but I have suffered enough shame for a hundred men in my lifetime and will suffer no more even if it costs me my life.'

Cadwallon glanced across at his brother. 'What do you think?'

'Even if he is who he says, it does not prove the identity of the other,' said Cadwaladr.

'Enough of this nonsense,' interrupted Gwenllian. 'All we have to do is take them to Aberffraw and let them speak to Father. He was close friends with Tewdwr so will soon find out if these men tell the truth.'

'And if they be assassins?' asked Cadwallon. 'What fools we would be to take them into our father's house.'

'I'm sure our father's guards will see that he is never put at risk.' She turned to Tarw. 'You will accompany us back to Aberffraw but if at any time I detect the slightest sign that you are not who you claim to be, then it will be my blade that sheds your blood. Understood?'

'Clearly,' said Tarw, resheathing his sword.

'You stay here with my brothers, while I get my horse,' continued Gwenllian. 'When I return we will take you to meet the king. You will ride close to me.'

'I would have it no other way,' said Tarw with a disarming smile. As Gwenllian walked back up the hill to the ridge, she realised that for the first time in her life, she was blushing furiously.

A few hours later, they rode through the gates into the grounds of Aberffraw. Several guards manned the stone walls surrounding the palace, and in the courtyard dozens of men practised their sword skills against their comrades, the edges of the practice swords dulled. Everyone dismounted and Cadwallon walked into the main house to find his father, while Cadwaladr and Gwenllian stayed to guard their visitors.

'This is a magnificent place,' said Hywel, looking around. 'Never have I seen anything like it. To build such a place in stone must have cost a king's ransom. Your father is obviously a very wealthy man.'

'My father's finances are none of your business,' snapped Cadwaladr.

'The observation was intended as a compliment,' said Hywel.

'You would do well to keep your musings to yourself,' replied Cadwaladr, 'and just hope you can convince the king you are who you claim to be, otherwise you will be fed to the dogs by nightfall.'

Tarw smiled at the forced aggression displayed by Cadwaladr. Young men often put on such displays of bravado thinking it was needed to convince any potential adversary of their grit and courage, but in reality it led to nothing except the amusement of the recipient. He considered baiting the boy in an argument but decided against it. Cadwaladr was only doing what he himself probably did at his age. He turned to Gwenllian.

'So, my lady,' he said, 'this is your home?'

'It is. Do you not have a similar one in Deheubarth?'

'Alas, no. My family home was the castle at Dinefwr but since Deheubarth fell under the control of the English, it lies abandoned and now falls into disrepair.'

'So where do you live?'

'My hearth is often in a different place each night. My bed is made from the dried leaves of the forest, my roof is the sky and my candles are the stars.'

'You told me you are a prince,' said Gwenllian. 'Even if you have been ousted from your home, there must be many who would give you a room and a hearth.'

'I am a wanted man with a price on my head,' said Tarw, 'so though there are many who would offer such a gift, for their sakes I must avoid their hospitality, for if the English found out, my hosts would soon face the gallows or a life beside me as a rebel in the Cantref Mawr.'

'Do you really live the life of a rebel?' asked Gwenllian, her interest piqued.

'I do. Does that concern you?'

'Not at all. In fact, I admire men such as you for it is they that keep the flame of freedom alive. They are few and far between these days and I am forced to listen to stories from men who haven't raised a sword in anger for many a year.'

'I don't understand,' responded Tarw, looking around. 'By the looks of this place and from what I hear on the road, Gwynedd is a free kingdom. Why would you need the help of rebels?'

'Because Wales is bigger than Gwynedd,' said Gwenllian, 'and if we are to see her free again, then we need all such kingdoms to stop leaning against each other and unite against the English. Oh, I know Henry would respond with all his might but even he can't subdue a united country determined to gain its freedom. Our landscape alone prohibits all-out warfare and his treasuries would soon be emptied if he pursued such a course.'

'You speak like a committed rebel,' laughed Tarw, 'yet are graced with the face of an angel. I struggle to know which one I am addressing.'

'It is my heart not my appearance that should hold your attention,' said Gwenllian, 'for it is as cold as ice when it comes to tricksters or the invaders. Like my brother said, I hope you can convince my father of your true identity.'

'Well, we'll soon find out,' said Tarw. 'Here he comes.'

Across the courtyard, Gruffydd ap Cynan walked out of the manorhouse doors flanked by his son and his second-in-command and walked across to stand a few steps in front of Tarw. For a few moments, nobody spoke as the king looked Tarw up and down.

'They have been disarmed,' said Cadwallon, 'but even so, should they prove to be imposters I will have them hanged.'

'There will be no hangings this day,' said Gruffydd, his face breaking into a huge smile, 'for if this isn't the son of Tewdwr, then God has seen fit to make a man in my friend's image.' He walked forward to greet his visitors, and as Tarw bowed his head in respect, Gruffydd embraced him as if he was a long-lost son.

'My boy,' he said, 'I have not seen you since you were a child yet I know you as if you were my own. You are the image of your father and are welcome in our home for as long as you want.'

'My lord,' said Tarw, 'thank you. We have travelled a long way but are truly refreshed at the warmth of your welcome. Indeed, the welcome from your sons and daughters has also been very . . . shall we say enlightening.'

Gruffydd laughed out loud. 'Blame them not, Tarw,' he said, slapping the young man on the shoulder. 'Unlike your father and me, they have never experienced war's sharp bite and I hope they never do, but alas, we must always prepare for such days for they will come as surely as winter follows autumn.'

'I fear Deheubarth already suffers the chills of war,' said Tarw, 'and that is why we are here, to seek whatever aid we can from a man who my father counted amongst his greatest friends.'

'Your father was a gift from God himself,' said Gruffydd, 'and if it wasn't for him my corpse would be feeding the worms beneath the soil of Mynydd Carn, but let us talk of such things later. I'm sure you must be hungry and thirsty after your journey.'

'Indeed,' said Tarw, 'and refreshments would be greatly welcomed.'

Gruffydd turned and summoned a man standing to one side. 'Master Steward, please find our guests some hot meat and cold ale but feed them not too much for I feel the need to feast in their honour. Do we have the means within the kitchens to do them justice?'

'Indeed, my lord,' said the steward. 'There is a hind hanging as we speak, caught only two days ago.'

'Excellent,' said the king. He turned back to Tarw. 'Eat lightly my friend,' he continued, 'for tonight we will do damage to that deer and talk of great things, both past and those yet to be. Does that suit you?'

'It does, my lord,' said Tarw with a smile. 'I shall look forward to it.'

'Then follow the steward and he will see to your needs.' He turned to his daughter. 'Gwenllian, your mother awaits you in the lesser hall. Something about embroidery.'

'*Father*,' hissed Gwenllian in annoyance.

'Don't take your anger out on me, my girl,' laughed Gruffydd. 'I may be the king but it is your mother who wears the crown in Aberffraw.' With a wink at Tarw he turned away and led his family over to the manor house, leaving Tarw and Hywel staring in his wake.

'Quite a character,' said Hywel quietly.

'He is,' said Tarw, 'and something tells me there is a lot more to see of this king.'

'My lords,' interrupted the steward, 'please follow me.'

Later that evening, Tarw and Hywel were guests of honour at the evening meal and they listened with fascination as Gruffydd recounted tales of how their father fought alongside him against far superior numbers at Mynydd Carn. Ale flowed freely and soon the hall was alive with laughter and merriment. Gwenllian managed to seat herself close to Tarw and when he made his excuses to go and check his horse, she immediately offered to show him the way.

'I think he can manage to find his way to the stables,' laughed Gruffydd. 'The stink alone will show him the way.'

'On the contrary,' said his wife, placing her hand on her husband's arm, 'it would be rude to allow a guest to wander unaccompanied. I think it's a wonderful idea.'

Gruffydd stared at his wife with surprise and was about to pursue the argument when he received a kick on his ankle, causing him to almost choke on the chicken in his mouth.

Angharad turned to Gwenllian. 'Of course you should escort our guest,' she said with a smile. 'It may also be nice to show him around the estate while there is still light.'

'Thank you, my lady,' said Tarw with a slight bow. 'Your home is indeed grand and I would be honoured to see it in all its majesty.'

'Then tarry no longer,' said Angharad. 'Gwenllian will show you the way.'

As Tarw and Gwenllian left the noise of the hall behind them and walked out into the courtyard, Gruffydd stared at his wife. 'What was all that about?'

'Don't act the fool, my love,' said Angharad. 'Surely you could see our daughter is attracted to this man?'

'Nonsense,' said Gruffydd, 'she was interested in his tales of warfare, nothing else.'

'Really? Then answer me this. When was the last time you saw our daughter wearing a pretty dress?'

Gruffydd's mouth opened to answer, but he could not. Slowly he turned to stare at the door by which they had left. If his wife was right, as she usually was in such matters, their lives were about to change dramatically.

The Palace of Aberffraw

October 24th, AD 1115

The next two months flew by for Gwenllian. For the first time in her life she found herself attracted to a man, and overwhelmed with the strange feelings, endeavoured to spend as much time as she could in his company. Tarw also found himself being distracted from his military purpose and often caught himself thinking about Gwenllian when his mind should have been on matters of warfare. Day after day they spent together, often riding out at dawn and not returning until late, much to the chagrin of Gruffydd, but Angharad was much more pragmatic about the whole thing and calmed the king's ire whenever he came close to administering any kind of admonishment.

One night when both were still absent, Gruffydd paced around his quarters like a caged lion. 'He has gone too far this time,' he growled.

'Relax,' said Angharad, focusing on her needle as it passed through a tapestry, 'she is with Tarw.'

'That's what I am worried about,' said Gruffydd. 'That man is far too old for her.'

'The age difference is similar to our own,' said Angharad without looking up.

'Maybe so,' he replied, 'but the sun is already down and there is still no sign of them. I'm in good mind to turn out the guard.'

'Do that and she will never forgive you. Gwenllian is a young woman, Gruffydd. She is no longer your little girl.'

'She is naïve, Angharad, and knows nothing of the ways of men.'

Angharad sighed and placed her embroidery on her lap. 'My love, she is eighteen years old. I was fifteen the first time I lay with you.'

'What do you mean?' asked Gruffydd. 'Are you casting doubt on the character of our own daughter?'

'All I am saying is, I'm sure she knows more than you give her credit for. You declare she knows nothing about the ways of men, when actually I believe it is you who perhaps knows little about the ways of young women. Leave them alone for if you forbid them spend time together, they would do it anyway but behind your back. At least this way we know she is safe.'

'But what if she falls for him completely? What will become of her?'

'What will be, will be, Gruffydd, but at least she is with a prince. It could be so much worse.'

'He is a prince without a crown,' said Gruffydd. 'What does he have to offer?'

'Perhaps nothing, but we will worry about that when it happens. For now, just be glad that your daughter is happier than I have ever seen her. Surely that in itself is a worthy outcome?'

'I suppose so,' said Gruffydd, dropping into a chair. 'But I still say he should bring her home earlier.'

'I will have a talk with her,' said Angharad. 'Now have some more ale and worry about something else. Your daughter is in good hands.'

⌣

Not very far away, Gwenllian and Tarw lay back on a blanket in the haystack in the barn. Both were naked and exhausted from their evening of passion.

313

'You are a wanton mistress, Lady Gwenllian,' said Tarw, 'and I fear I cannot keep up with you.'

'That is because you are an old man,' said Gwenllian with a hint of mischief in her voice.

'I am only sixteen years older than you,' said Tarw defensively, 'and in the prime of my life.'

Gwenllian smiled and rolled over to look into his eyes, tickling his face with a piece of hay held between her teeth.

'Stop it,' said Tarw, waving away the offending stalk.

'Oh, stop being such a misery, old man,' laughed Gwenllian. She squealed in delight as he grabbed her and wrestled her back into the hay. For a few moments he looked down at her beautiful face in silence, until finally Gwenllian spoke gently.

'Tarw, what is to become of us?'

'I don't know,' said Tarw, 'but I do know this: I cannot see a life without you.'

'Then you must approach my father and ask for my hand.'

'I fully intend to do that, Gwenllian, but at the moment I have nothing to offer but my love.'

'That is all I want,' said Gwenllian. 'The rest will come.'

'I know, but it may not be enough for your father. He is a mighty king and has a duty to his children. What sort of message would he be sending out if he allowed his only daughter to marry a pauper?'

'You are not a pauper. You are a prince.'

'In name only.'

'But that is enough. We can stay here and live as man and wife under my father's wing. I'm sure he wouldn't mind and my mother would think it wonderful.'

'I don't know,' said Tarw. With a sigh he rolled onto his back. 'What about Hywel? What about Deheubarth?'

'Hywel is happy enough,' said Gwenllian, 'though it is a shame he is unable to enjoy the company of women. He busies himself with looking after my father's destriers and spends his evenings drinking with the garrison. As for Deheubarth, well, it will still be there in a few years and, who knows, by then you will have won respect and influence with my father. He may even let you have men to reclaim what is rightfully yours.'

'I can't see him doing that,' said Tarw, 'for it will break the truce he currently enjoys with Henry, but I see merit in your plan. Perhaps I will approach him and seek permission to marry you. After that, we will let the fates take us wherever they will.'

'When?'

'Soon, I promise.'

Gwenllian leaned over Tarw and kissed him deeply. 'Do that and you will make me the happiest woman who ever lived,' she said eventually.

'Then that is my quest,' said Tarw. 'Now come back here. There is life in this old man yet.' He pushed her gently back onto the blanket where they had lain for hours, both unaware that their world was about to crash down around them.

Forty leagues away, two riders handed over their horses to a groom in the bailey of Hen Domen Castle and ran up the steps of the motte. A couple of guards at the keep gates presented their pikes and demanded they make themselves known.

'Our names are unimportant,' said the first man, 'so just tell your master the king's messengers are here.'

'Let them through,' said a voice from behind the guards, and they turned to see Sir Broadwick standing in the shadows.

'My lord,' said one of the guards, 'we have not been told about any messengers for the castellan tonight.'

'I am telling you now,' said Broadwick. 'Let them through.'

The two guards stood aside and the messengers rushed past, keen to fulfil the king's will.

'Where is the castellan?' one demanded.

'He will meet you shortly in the lesser hall,' said Broadwick. 'Come with me.'

They followed him into the dining hall and removed their riding cloaks as a servant poured warmed ale. For several minutes they made small talk with the English knight, until finally Baldwin de Boulers entered the room and walked over to shake the first man's hand.

'Edward, it has been a long time.'

'Indeed it has,' said the messenger. 'Too long.'

'It is good to see you again but I am at a loss why the king would send his own steward just to deliver a message.'

'The message is of such importance it could not be written down, my lord, so he sent me with the spoken word knowing full well I would gladly die before repeating it to those who should not hear.'

Baldwin's eyes opened wide at the revelation. He turned to dismiss the servants before turning back to the steward. 'Please, be seated. My mind is racing as to what content is so important the king's favourite is put at risk.'

'What about him?' asked Edward, nodding towards Broadwick.

'Sir Broadwick is my right-hand man and as such knows everything there is to know about me and my business. Whatever it is you have to say can be said before him.'

'But the king said . . .'

'Let me worry about the king, Edward, for even if I send this man away, I will brief him before you reach your quarters tonight.

The steward glanced at his comrade, who nodded his head in acceptance.

'So be it,' said Edward. 'My lord, you will have heard that a few months ago Gerald of Windsor ambushed a column of rebels under the command of the man known as Tarw.'

'I heard the reports,' said Baldwin, 'and I have to say it was a masterpiece of strategy.'

'Perhaps not as great as you have heard,' said Edward.

'What do you mean? The enemy was wiped out to a man, with hardly any casualties of our own.'

'One man did escape, my lord, the greatest prize of all. Tarw.'

'Tarw escaped,' gasped Broadwick, stepping forward. 'We were told he was killed by Owain ap Cadwgan, who was then killed himself in the battle.'

'A version told for political purposes only,' said Edward. 'The truth is that Tarw killed Owain and then escaped into the Cantref Mawr. Our men searched for him but he simply disappeared. For the past few months we have had no idea where he was, until now.'

'You know where he is?' asked Baldwin.

'We do, and that is the purpose of my visit. The king wants you to send a column after this man with all haste. It is to be as strongly armed as you can arrange but unfortunately, its purpose must remain secret.'

'But why?'

'Because if it became known Tarw was still alive it could bond any rebels left across Deheubarth. The king wants you to find him, kill him and destroy the evidence. It's as simple as that.'

'And where is he hidden?'

'Tarw and his brother currently enjoy the hospitality of Gruffydd ap Cynan in the north. As you know, there is a truce between Henry and Gruffydd, but the king is so incensed you are given free rein to use whatever force you need. The main thing is that the fact they are still alive needs to be kept secret, so when they are finally killed the status quo in the south will remain.'

'But don't the people of Gwynedd already know?'

'No, for Gruffydd knew their presence could compromise his truce with Henry, so few know they are there. That is why we must move quickly.'

'I still don't see the importance,' said Baldwin.

'I do,' said Broadwick. 'Tarw already had a strong following throughout the south, as well as a network of safe houses and sponsors. At the moment they all think he is dead, as indeed did I, so imagine the joy if suddenly their prince arises from the grave. The surge of misplaced patriotism would be huge.'

'Exactly,' said the steward, 'and that is why we must move swiftly. So, can you do this task or not?'

'I'm not sure,' said Baldwin. 'Like many other castellans my garrison has been weakened by Henry's campaign in Normandy.'

'I will do it,' interrupted Broadwick.

All the other men in the room turned to stare at the knight.

'Why?' said Baldwin. 'You have already spent two years searching for Diafol, with nothing to show for your efforts. What makes you think you can succeed this time?'

'This is different. If this rebel's location is known, I can fall upon him with great force. There will be no escape.'

'I don't know, Broadwick,' replied Baldwin. 'It seems to me this could again turn out to be a fool's errand. Besides, it is not really our fight.'

'It is mine, my lord. I owe that man retribution for what he did to my brother knights. I have to do this, even if I go alone.'

'Your honour will get you killed one day,' sighed Baldwin, 'but I will not see you go unsupported.' He turned back to the steward. 'Edward, we will put you up tonight and see you are well looked after. In the morning, take fresh horses and ride back to the king with all haste. Tell him that by the time he hears your words, Sir Broadwick here will be well on his way to Aberffraw and before this month is over, both brothers will be rotting in a shallow grave.'

Edward smiled and lifted his tankard. 'And that, my lord, is exactly the response he will want to hear.'

The Palace of Aberffraw

November 28th, AD 1115

Gwenllian looked out of the window of her chambers, wondering what the commotion was all about. Since waking there had been the sound of voices in the courtyard, as well as the comings and goings of several horses. Finally, the sound of men shouting roused her from her bed and she walked over to open the shutters, peering into the courtyard below.

Usually there would be the bustle of men going about their business or taking the opportunity to practise their sword skills, but something was different today and there seemed to be a feeling of awkwardness about the whole place. Men stood together in groups, whispering like common conspirators, while others glanced up at the higher levels of the house, as if knowing something untoward was about to happen.

Gwenllian frowned and realised their attention seemed to be aimed at her own windows, and she stepped back, unsure about what was happening. Quickly she donned a robe and left her quarters to descend the stairs to the lesser hall. As she entered, she could see her mother talking in subdued tones to other ladies of the court.

'Mother,' said Gwenllian, 'what's happening?'

Angharad broke off her conversation and walked quickly across the floor to meet her daughter. Gwenllian could see she had been crying and immediately her heart raced in fear.

'Mother,' she said, 'what's the matter?'

'Gwenllian,' said Angharad, reaching out to hold her daughter's arms, 'come and take a seat. I have some bad news.'

'What is wrong, Mother?' asked Gwenllian as she was led to a bench. 'Is Father well?'

'Your father is fine,' said Angharad, 'as are your brothers. Sit down and I will explain.'

'Mother, you're scaring me.'

Angharad took a deep breath and stared into her daughter's eyes. 'Gwenllian,' she said, 'it's Tarw.'

Gwenllian's legs weakened at the sound of his name and she immediately feared the worst. She lowered herself into the chair and stared at her mother.

'What's happened to him, Mother? Has he been hurt?'

'No, he's not hurt but there have been developments and, well, your father has had to take some drastic action.'

'Mother, you're not making any sense,' said Gwenllian. 'Just spit it out.'

Angharad took another breath. 'Your father has had to arrest Tarw and his brother on the king's command.'

'*What?*' gasped Gwenllian. 'What do you mean? Father *is* the king.'

'No, I mean on the command of King Henry.'

Gwenllian stared at her mother in disbelief. 'That is ridiculous,' she said eventually, 'Henry holds no jurisdiction in Gwynedd. Father must let Tarw go immediately.' She got to her feet but her mother grabbed her arm.

'Gwenllian, wait. This is bigger than you realise. Henry has found out that we are harbouring Tarw and his brother and has sent an ultimatum that they are handed over immediately. There is a column riding here from Hen Domen as we speak and we have no other choice than to do what Henry says.'

'Why?' shouted Gwenllian. 'Since when do we bend a knee to that son of a Frenchman?'

'Since he threatened to march on Gwynedd and annexe our kingdom to England.'

For a few seconds there was silence as Angharad's words sunk in.

'He can't do that,' said Gwenllian. 'There would be a war, a war he could not sustain.'

'Perhaps, but in the meantime there would be death and destruction on a massive scale. Many people would die and everything we as a family have worked so hard towards over all these years will be gone, and for what? For the life of one man who doesn't even hail from Gwynedd. I know it is hard, Gwenllian, but surely even you can see the futility in such a gesture.'

Gwenllian shook her head slowly. 'Actually I can't,' she said, 'for he is more than just a man, he is one of our own, a true-born prince of Wales who spends his life fighting against the injustice of occupation. What have we become, Mother? Years ago the very mention of an enemy column upon Gwynedd soil would send our men racing to the armouries, yet here we are, with not an Englishman in sight, already quivering in our skins like a beaten slave. If that is the price of our so-called freedom, then lead me to the Cantref Mawr to live amongst the rebels for I cannot countenance life as a coward.'

She got to her feet and again Angharad grabbed her arm.

'Gwenllian . . .'

'No,' said Gwenllian, pulling out of her mother's grasp, 'I will hear no more. Just tell me where Tarw is. I need to see him.'

'He has been locked in the corn stores,' said Angharad with a sigh. She watched her daughter storm away in a temper.

Adele placed her hand on her mistress's shoulder. 'She will come around, my lady.'

'I think not, Adele,' replied Angharad to her maid. 'I think this is not going to end well.'

Gwenllian stormed across the courtyard to the corn stores, only to be blocked by a guard on the doors.

'Let me through,' said Gwenllian.

'My lady, I can't do that,' said the guard.

'Master Willis,' said Gwenllian, 'I have known you all my life and have oft thought of you as my brother but I swear if you do not move aside, you will have to cut me down with that pike.'

'My lady,' said the guard, 'please don't do this. You know as well as I that I can't let you through. It is your father's command and as much as I think of you, I have to obey my king.'

'We'll see about that,' said Gwenllian, and she ran across to the stables. A few moments later she emerged with a sword and faced the guard once more. 'I have no more time for games, Master Willis. Now let me through or defend your life.'

The guard was in a quandary, a situation he could not win. If he let Gwenllian through, he would be disobeying the king but if not, he would be forced to fight her and though he was confident he would be the victor, any injury upon her would no doubt cost him his life. Finally, he took a big sigh and stood aside.

'Be quick, my lady,' he said, 'or I may be joining them on the gallows.'

'Nobody is going to hang, Willis,' said Gwenllian, barging past him, 'trust me on this.'

'Gwenllian,' said Tarw, looking up as she stormed into the corn stores.

'Tarw,' she said, looking down at the chains around his feet and wrists, 'by the Devil's teeth, I am so sorry about this.'

'This is not your fault, Gwenllian,' said Tarw, 'so don't for one minute think you are in any way to blame.'

'Oh, but I do,' said Gwenllian, kneeling beside him. 'If we had not become involved, you would probably be back on the road to Deheubarth by now. I just can't believe my father would act like this.'

'He had no choice, Gwenllian, and I'm sure he took no pleasure in his actions, but sometimes a king must make decisions that weigh heavily against his better judgement.'

'So what has he said to you?'

'We haven't seen him. All I know is we woke this morning with swords resting against our throats and we are to be handed over to an English column sometime tomorrow.'

'We'll see about that,' said Gwenllian. She stood up.

'Where are you going?'

'To find my father and get you released.'

'He won't listen to you, Gwenllian, the needs of his people out-weigh the death of two rebels.'

'Not in my eyes,' said Gwenllian. 'And if you think my father, king or not, will ignore what I have to say, then you have a lot yet to learn about me. Be patient, Tarw, I will get this sorted.'

Without another word she stormed out of the corn stores and back to her room to get dressed.

Despite her ire, Gwenllian was unable to talk to her father as he was nowhere to be found. Instead she stormed around the palace grounds in a foul mood, taking out her temper on anyone unfortunate enough to get in her way. Servants were chided and many warriors challenged as she struggled with her anger until, eventually, Angharad summoned her to the solar.

'What do you want?' asked Gwenllian, standing in the doorway, her hands on her hips.

'Come in, Gwenllian,' said Angharad. 'We need to talk.'

'I have nothing to say, Mother, not until I speak to Father.'

'*You will do as you are told*,' shouted Angharad, much to Gwenllian's surprise, 'and for once in your life, you will listen to what I have to say.'

Gwenllian was shocked. She couldn't recall a time when her mother had ever raised her voice in anger, and after a few moments' hesitation, she walked over to sit in the chair opposite Angharad.

'Now you listen to me, my girl,' continued Angharad in the same vein, 'this behaviour has to stop. I know you are angry but since when does that give you the right to admonish those below your station? You may be born of a king but at the moment you act like the lowliest of fisherwomen and for the first time in my life I am ashamed of you.'

Gwenllian swallowed hard. All day she had struggled with her emotions and whenever they threatened to surface, she had reacted in the only way she knew – to verbally lash out at the nearest person. Deep inside she knew she was wrong but it was only now, as her mother laid bare Gwenllian's failings, that she realised how bad she had been.

'Furthermore,' continued Angharad, 'I found our beloved Adele in tears earlier, having been on the wrong end of a tongue-lashing from you in the kitchen. How dare you raise your voice to her? She has been at my side since I was a young woman and she has been like a second mother to you since the day you were born. You may be my daughter, Gwenllian, and I love you dearly but I will not allow this behaviour to continue an instant longer. Do you understand?'

If Angharad was expecting the usual terse response from her head-strong daughter, she was very much mistaken. Instead, she watched as tears welled up in Gwenllian's eyes and before she could speak further,

her daughter did something she had never done in her life. She burst into tears.

'Oh, my dear girl,' said Angharad, walking over to take Gwenllian in her embrace, 'I didn't mean to hurt you but you have to understand, these are matters of kingship and sometimes there is little we can do to affect the outcome. I am just concerned you are heading along a path that will only bring you pain.'

'But I love him,' sobbed Gwenllian. 'I have never felt this way about any man and for the first time in my life I could see a future as a wife and a mother. To have this taken away from me now is just too cruel.'

'Oh, Gwenllian,' said Angharad, tightening her embrace, 'I am so, so sorry. I never realised.'

'He is everything to me,' said Gwenllian, wiping her eyes. 'I cannot lose him. Surely Father can't hand him over to the English when he knows the depth of feeling we share.'

'I don't know, Gwenllian,' sighed her mother, 'there is a lot at stake here, but I promise I will talk to him as soon as he returns.'

'Where is he? I have asked those amongst the garrison but nobody will tell me where he is.'

'That is because we cannot risk you riding out there and interrupting matters of the king.'

'Out where? Where has he gone?'

'Gwenllian, your father has ridden out to meet with the envoy of King Henry. A knight by the name of Sir Broadwick is currently encamped on the other side of the river along with two hundred mounted men. It is his messenger who informed us of the whim of the English Crown.'

'Two hundred men are not an army, Mother. We could swat them away like a fly.'

'It's not as simple as that, as well you know. First of all, we only maintain a basic standing army and should they attack Aberffraw before we had chance to call upon the villages to provide men-at-arms, we would probably struggle to match them. Secondly, even if we did, win or lose Henry would see it as a declaration of war and that is a situation we cannot contemplate.'

'So why has Father gone out there?'

'To see what leniency there is in this matter, if any.'

'So his mind is not yet set upon handing Tarw over?'

'I didn't say that. We will just have to see when he returns.'

'When will that be?'

'Within the next few hours. You go and freshen yourself up and perhaps we can talk to him together, but you must promise me two things: one, you will go and apologise to everyone you have upset today; and two, when we talk to your father you will keep your decorum, no matter what the outcome. The last thing we need is you losing your temper, for to do that will raise the king's ire and then there will be no talking to him. Agreed?'

Gwenllian nodded.

'Good. Now go about your business and we will see what we can do.'

Several hours later, Gwenllian and her mother sat at the table, picking on cold meats and losyns as they waited for Gruffydd to finish his meal. It had been a long day and though outwardly he projected his usual confidence, both women could see that inside he was deeply worried. Osian sat opposite him and they talked quietly, sharing a flask of ale as they finished their meal. Finally, the king belched and sat back in his chair, replete.

'That's better,' he announced, finishing his goblet of ale.

'Are you done here?' asked Angharad.

'I am done with the meal, my love, but there is business to attend so I may not be with you for several hours yet.'

'Before you go,' said Angharad, 'could you please let us know what is happening with regard to Tarw?'

Gruffydd looked at both women in turn and saw that they both showed signs of upset. He knew this conversation would be coming but had studiously avoided it since returning. Realising it could no longer be put off, he let out a deep sigh and walked over to sit on a chair opposite his wife and daughter.

'What is it you want to know?' he asked. 'But make it quick. There is men's work to be done.'

'Father,' said Gwenllian before Angharad could speak, 'I want you to release Tarw immediately. He has done us no wrong and to hand him over to the English would be an act of betrayal against every man that ever bore a weapon in defence of this country.'

'Gwenllian, please,' said Angharad, a warning tone in her voice, 'we agreed you would be civil.'

'It's all right,' said Gruffydd calmly, 'I understand why she is upset.' He turned to his daughter and smiled gently. 'Gwenllian, I know how you must be hurting but you have to realise there are bigger things at risk here. All my life I have fought and bled for this kingdom and many times I came close to death, but through perseverance and the spilled blood of many loyal men we finally enjoy the fruits of our endeavours. At last we live the lives of free men in our own lands. Our subjects are healthy, our fields are fruitful and we enjoy a treaty with the English that guarantees this arrangement will carry on long past my death. This being the case, you can see why I must tread carefully with Henry when it comes to Tarw for if we awaken the beast, he could overrun Gwynedd within months and everything we have will be gone.'

'I understand that, Father, but surely patriotism and loyalty have a place in your heart. This man is only trying to do what you did when you were a young man. How would it have been if someone had betrayed you all those years ago?'

'Gwenllian,' said her mother, 'that's unfair. Your father has betrayed no one.'

'Oh yes, he has,' said Gwenllian, staring her father in the face, 'he has betrayed me.'

'Now you are being insolent,' said Gruffydd, his voice lowering. 'Be careful, Gwenllian, for I will not take lessons in kingship from a mere girl.'

'Is that what I am to you?' asked Gwenllian, standing up. 'I thought I was more than that. I assumed I was your loved and trusted daughter. I assumed I was someone groomed to defend your legacy. I also assumed I was an integral part of this family but obviously I was wrong on all counts.'

She turned to walk away and Gruffydd jumped to his feet, his face red with rage, but before he could call out, Angharad grabbed his arm. 'No,' she said quickly, 'it will do no good. Let her go.'

'That girl will be the death of me,' growled Gruffydd, dropping back into his seat.

'She thinks she loves him,' said Angharad, 'so you have to tread gently.'

'Don't you think I already know that?' asked Gruffydd. 'I am not blind, Angharad. I see the way she looks at him and in different circumstances perhaps it could have been a good match, but there is nothing I can do.'

'What do you mean? Did not the meeting with Sir Broadwick go well?'

'No, it did not,' said Gruffydd with a sigh. 'Anyone would have sworn it was he who was the king and I just a humble knight, such was his manner.'

'I hope you showed him personal scorn.'

'I had to be careful with my words, Angharad, for he carries the full weight of the English Crown and he made sure that I was fully aware of what that implies.'

'What do you mean?'

'I tried to reason with him but it was of no use. Unless we hand Tarw to this man, we will be at war with England.'

For a few moments there was silence. Eventually Angharad spoke again. 'So what are you going to do?' she asked, fearful of the answer.

'There is nothing I can do,' said Gruffydd. 'Tomorrow morning at dawn, I will hand over Tarw and his brother to the English Crown. I just pray God will have mercy on his soul.'

The Palace of Aberffraw

November 28th, AD 1115

Tarw and Hywel sat against the wall of the corn stores, their bodies stiff from the cold and heavy chains. Outside the night was as black as pitch and the palace grounds as silent as the grave. Beside them was a tiny candle burning on a clay plate, alongside a flask of water and a hand of stale bread.

Hywel dozed fitfully while Tarw just stared at the wall, contemplating his impending fate. Gruffydd had at least had the decency to come and explain everything to the brothers and though it was not what they wanted to hear, Tarw could understand the reasoning. A kingdom should always come before the life of one man, no matter who he was.

Tarw wasn't afraid of dying, just sad that it meant the love that had grown between him and Gwenllian over the last few months was never going to reach its full potential. He sighed and adjusted his position to ease the aches in his bones but jumped when a piece of slate fell from the roof and shattered on the floor just across the room.

For a few seconds he stared in confusion but then looked up as he saw another slate being moved. Several more followed until eventually he saw a pair of legs dangle through the newly created hole. Tarw held his breath as the intruder dropped to the floor and ran across the room.

'Gwenllian,' he gasped, as her face was revealed by the candlelight, 'what are you doing here?'

'You didn't think I was going to stand by and watch you get killed, did you?' she asked.

'I don't know what I thought,' said Tarw, 'but I certainly didn't expect you to descend from the ceiling in the middle of the night.'

'There are guards on the door,' said Gwenllian, 'so I had to come this way.'

'Why are you here?'

'To get you out, stupid.'

'How?'

'With this,' she replied, producing a key from inside her leather jerkin.

'Is that the key for the locks?'

'No,' she said, 'it's the key to the kitchens.'

Tarw stared in confusion again.

'Of course it's the key to the bloody locks,' she hissed. 'Don't be a fool. Now hold up your hands.'

Tarw did as he was bid and Gwenllian released his chains. With his hands free, he took the key and set about the other locks, while Gwenllian crept to the door and listened carefully. When she came back, both Tarw and Hywel were free from their bonds and looking at the young woman expectantly.

'What now?' asked Tarw.

'Now we climb,' she said. 'There are two guards on the door but none behind these stores. Once we are on the roof, be as silent as you can and lower yourself into the courtyard at the rear. I have horses waiting down by the stream.'

'How do we get past the outer defences? Surely you don't have the gate key as well?'

'This is my home, Tarw, not just some fortified castle guarding the Marches. Of course I have access to the keys. There is a postern gate in the western corner already unlocked. Just be aware that a guard patrols the palisade above the postern, so wait until his back is turned.'

'Understood,' said Tarw.

'We should go. Ready?'

'Ready.'

'Good. You go up first and then pull me and Hywel up behind you. We haven't got much time.'

'Thank you, Gwenllian,' he said, pulling her to him to kiss her passionately.

'There will be time for that later,' hissed Hywel. 'Let's go.'

Tarw released Gwenllian and reached up to the rafters to pull himself up. Moments later all three were sat on the roof, their heads kept low to avoid creating a profile.

'Down there,' whispered Gwenllian, and they lowered themselves to the rear of the building before making their way to the postern gate, keeping low in the shadows.

The sound of slow footsteps on the palisade above their heads made them cower lower in the shadows but as soon as they died out, Gwenllian eased open the gate and squeezed through, followed by the two men.

'This way,' she whispered. They followed her along the wall until they reached a path heading down a slope into a gulley. Again they waited for the guards on the palisade to pass before crouching low and running down to the stream.

'Made it,' gasped Gwenllian as they made their way into the relative safety of the trees. 'The horses are just along here.' Moments later they walked into a clearing and saw the mounts tied to a branch. Tarw stopped and stared, his mind racing as Hywel and Gwenllian set about untying the reins.

'Come on,' hissed Gwenllian, 'what are you waiting for?'

'There are three horses,' said Tarw.

'Of course there are,' said Gwenllian. 'There are three of us.'

'You can't come with us, Gwenllian,' said Tarw. 'It's not your place.'

'My place is by your side, Tarw,' she replied, 'and if you try to stop me, you will see a side of me you haven't experienced.'

'You have a home and a loving family here. If you come with me now, you will be saying goodbye to all that forever.'

'Don't you think I know that?'

'Of course, but I urge you to carefully consider your actions here. Once this journey is started, there is no turning back.'

'I have thought of nothing else since learning of your incarceration, Tarw, and I know what I want. I love you and need to be at your side, no matter what that entails or where our journey leads.'

'And I love you, Gwenllian, and don't want to put you at risk. Stay here and if I reach safety, I will petition your father to let you come to me.'

'That will never happen. He will lock me away first or have me sent to a convent. I am coming with you and anyway, how do you expect to leave Ynys Mon?'

'The same way as we came, via the bridge.'

'The bridge is heavily guarded, Tarw, and you will never get across. There is, however, another way. One that has no guards.'

'And where is that?'

'I'm not telling you,' said Gwenllian, 'not unless you agree to take me with you.'

'Gwenllian . . .' he started, but deep inside he knew she would not change her mind.

'Well?' she asked. 'What's it to be?'

Tarw looked at his brother, who shrugged his shoulders in reply. 'It seems like she has all the answers, brother,' he said. 'Let her come.'

Tarw turned back to Gwenllian. 'So be it,' he said eventually, 'but if there is any sign of trouble, you must promise to ride to safety as fast as you can. I would surely rot in hell if you came to any harm.'

Gwenllian raised herself up onto tiptoe and kissed his cheek.

'I knew you would come around,' she said with a smile. 'Now mount up. We have a long way to go.'

Angharad was fast asleep when a knock came on the door of her chambers.

'Who is it?' she asked, sitting up in bed.

'My lady, it's Adele,' said the voice quietly. 'I need to speak to you.'

Angharad looked down at her husband, who was still snoring quietly. 'Just a second,' she replied, getting out of bed to walk over to the door. She lifted the bar and peered out. 'Adele, what's the matter?'

'My lady, I'm so sorry to bother you but it's your daughter.'

'What about her, is she ill?'

'No, my lady, she's gone.'

'What do you mean, "gone"?'

'She's not in her room, my lady. I heard her door close quietly an hour or so ago and I thought she had just gone to spend some time with Tarw before he is handed over on the morrow, so I wasn't too concerned.'

'Perhaps she is still there.'

'Possibly but I don't think so. I fell asleep and when I awoke wasn't sure if she had returned, so I went to her room. Her bed hasn't been slept in, my lady, and her armour has gone.'

'Her armour,' said Angharad. 'Why would she wear her armour?'

'I don't know, my lady, but something seems very wrong.'

Angharad thought furiously. The only reason her daughter would wear her leathers was if she was training or going on a long journey. 'Adele,' she said quickly, 'go to the corn stores and check on the prisoners. Also, alert the captain of the guard. I want her found immediately.'

'Yes, my lady,' said Adele, already running down the stairs.

Angharad turned to stare at her sleeping husband.

'Gruffydd,' she said loudly. 'Wake up. We have a problem.'

———

'How much longer do we have to wait?' mumbled Hywel. 'Every moment we linger is a moment our escape could be discovered.' He held his hands out to the small fire they had allowed themselves on the stony beach of the strait separating Ynys Mon from the mainland.

'Not long now,' said Gwenllian, staring out over the narrow strip of water. 'The tide is almost at its ebb.' All three looked across the channel. On the far side they could see the occasional flicker of candlelight from the windows of distant farmhouses and further along the bank, the lights of several burning torches illuminating the well-guarded bridge.

'Are you sure about this?' asked Tarw. 'That water looks pretty dangerous to me.'

'Trust me,' said Gwenllian, 'there is a period of time when the tide is at its lowest, during which we can ride almost all the way across. There will be rock beneath the hooves of our mounts and we can be on the mainland within minutes.'

'Almost?' said Hywel.

'Sorry?' replied Gwenllian. 'Did you say something?'

'You said we can ride *almost* all the way across. What does that mean, exactly?'

'There will still be a narrow channel in the centre where we will have to swim,' said Gwenllian, 'but the horses are used to it. Just slip out of your saddle and hold on tight. My brothers and I have done this many times.'

'In the dark?'

'No, but . . .'

'Fully clothed?'

'Stop fretting, Master Hywel. We will be fine. Just show some of the resilience that got you through the years of imprisonment. Besides, there is no other way. Dawn is not far off and when our escape is discovered, my father will set his men after us. We need to get to the other side and lose ourselves in the hills as soon as we can.'

Tarw got up and walked over to a nearby tree to relieve himself. He was on his way back when something caught his eye in the darkness.

'What's that?' he asked.

Gwenllian and Hywel got to their feet and followed his gaze. In the distance, a line of fiery torches lit up a distant ridge like a line of stars.

'It looks like riders,' said Hywel, 'and they are moving fast.'

'They are coming from Aberffraw,' said Gwenllian. 'The alarm must have been raised.' She spun around and faced the two men. 'Discard anything we don't need – saddlebags, blankets, food, even your cloaks.'

'Why?' asked Hywel.

'Because we have to go now and the extra weight will drag the horses under.'

'You mean we are going to try and swim across that?' gasped Hywel, looking back at the still-large expanse of water. 'But the tide isn't fully out yet.'

'There's no other way,' said Gwenllian. 'Once they realise we haven't crossed the bridge they will check down here. Just keep urging your horse forward but go with the flow of the current. We should be fine.'

Tarw stared at Gwenllian for several moments, knowing she wouldn't be suggesting such a dangerous course of action if she wasn't confident it could be done.

'Well,' she said, 'are we going or not?'

'We are,' said Tarw eventually, 'and may God go with us.'

Sir Broadwick was fast asleep on his furs when his second-in-command banged hard on the fabric of his campaign tent.

'My lord,' shouted his fellow knight, 'wake up.'

Broadwick sat up immediately, his hand reaching out to touch the reassuring hilt of the sword by his side. 'I'm awake, Cliffdon,' he said loudly. 'State your business.'

'My lord, our scouts report that a column of riders just galloped from Aberffraw heading southward.'

'Do we know why?' asked Broadwick, getting to his feet.

'Not yet, but we do know it was led by Gruffydd himself.'

'Come in,' said Broadwick, and his comrade pushed aside the flap to enter the tent. 'Why would Gruffydd lead an armed column in the middle of the night?' continued Broadwick as he pulled his shirt over his head.

'I know not, unless he is using darkness to help Tarw escape.'

'No,' said Broadwick, reaching for his chainmail, 'he would be risking the wrath of Henry. Gruffydd may be a lot of things but he is not stupid. There must be another reason, unless . . .' His eyes widened as he realised what must be happening. 'Cliffdon, sound the alarm, I want every man mounted immediately.'

'Do you suspect there is treachery afoot?'

'Not treachery,' said Broadwick, 'but unless I am mistaken, I believe our quarry may have escaped and Gruffydd has set out to chase them down. If that is indeed the case, I want to catch them before he does. Have my squire prepare my horse, Cliffdon, there is a race to be run.'

'As you wish,' said Cliffdon as he ran into the darkness to summon the rest of Broadwick's column.

'Keep going,' shouted Gwenllian to her horse, 'come on, Starlight, you can do it.' The horse's eyes were wide with fear and it kicked hard against the freezing water, with Gwenllian hanging onto the saddle for dear life. Her eyes stung from the salt water and she knew that if her hands slipped off the pommel of the saddle, the weight of her leather armour would take her to the bottom of the strait.

'*Almost there*,' she gasped as she felt the horse lurch as the first of its hooves struck solid ground. 'That's it,' she panted, 'keep going.' Moments later the horse found its footing and lurched out of the water to stand exhausted on the shore. Gwenllian let it go and turned to see Tarw and Hywel not far behind. 'Come on,' she hissed, glancing along the bank towards the bridge, 'you're almost there.' Finally, the two men staggered out of the water and stumbled towards the safety of the treeline. Hywel dropped to his knees to be violently sick, spewing up a vast quantity of salt water.

'Are you all right?' asked Gwenllian with concern.

'No, I'm bloody well not all right,' replied Hywel. 'I'm half drowned. Don't tell me you and your brothers do that for fun?'

'Many times,' said Gwenllian, 'though not usually when the tide is that strong.'

'I'm freezing,' said Hywel. 'We need a fire to dry off.'

'There's no time,' said Gwenllian. 'The riders are already upon the bridge and it won't be long before they go down to the fording point. Dawn is almost upon us and as soon as it is light enough, they'll pick up our trail and realise we swam across. We have to move now while we still have an advantage.'

The Llyn Peninsular

November 29th, AD 1115

Tarw peered through the branches of the thicket where they were hiding. The sun was high and the three fugitives had been riding hard all day. Finally, they had sought the shelter of a heavily wooded copse to rest the horses, and while Gwenllian and Hywel went to buy food from a nearby farm, Tarw watched the road from their hiding place, knowing full well their pursuers couldn't be far behind. He heard a noise to his rear and turned to see his comrades coming back from their task. Gwenllian carried a basket, while Hywel nursed a goatskin and a sack of oats.

'Wine?' asked Tarw hopefully.

'No such luck,' said Hywel. 'It is nought but weak ale, but it will have to do.'

'What have you got?' asked Tarw, turning to Gwenllian.

'Some bread,' said Gwenllian, placing the basket on the ground, 'as well as some cold potage and roasted chicken.'

'You've both done well,' said Tarw. 'It's almost a feast.'

'It didn't come cheaply,' said Hywel. 'Gwenllian had to trade a necklace in return.'

'Did they know who you were?' asked Tarw.

'Alas, yes, but they promised not to tell anyone that we passed this way,' said Gwenllian. 'However, we made a point of saying we were riding south in case they were not true to their word.'

'Any sign of anyone following?' asked Hywel.

'Not yet,' said Tarw, 'but we can't be too careful.'

'My father has some excellent scouts,' said Gwenllian, 'so we can linger no more than absolutely necessary. As soon as the horses are fed and watered, I suggest we continue west.'

'What makes you so certain there will be a boat in this place we are headed to?' asked Hywel.

'It is a fishing village well known to my family. All our fish comes from there and I have a cousin who owns a skiff in the dock. If I ask, I'm sure he will transport us south with no questions asked.'

'I hope you're right,' said Tarw, breaking a leg from the chicken. 'I don't think your father will give up this chase easily, so the sea is our best hope of getting away.'

'I agree,' said Gwenllian, 'so eat up and we will be on our way. I'll see to the horses.'

A few leagues away, one of Sir Broadwick's scouts rode back down the path to meet the English column, coming to a halt beside the waiting English knight.

'My lord,' said the scout, removing his helmet to wipe the sweat from his eyes, 'the Welsh are no more than a league in front of us. Their pace is slow as they are following a trail.'

'Excellent,' said Broadwick. 'We will follow but maintain our distance. Remain alert for as soon as they indicate they are near our prey, I want to pounce on Tarw like a cat upon a mouse, seizing our prey from beneath the very gaze of the Welsh king.'

'Aye, my lord,' said the scout. He went to re-join his unit far to the front of the column.

Broadwick turned to Cliffdon. 'Have the men remount. We will advance slowly. We don't want to alert the Welsh king we are almost upon his back.'

Cliffdon nodded his assent and signalled to his men to mount their horses. As silently as they could, each man climbed into his saddle, and with a minimum of fuss, the whole column started to advance slowly along the track left by the Welsh less than an hour earlier.

The three fugitives pushed their horses onward and, after cresting a hill, could finally see the coastline a few leagues ahead.

'Another hour or so and we'll be there,' said Gwenllian, staring at the distant fishing village. 'Hopefully, by this time tomorrow we can be headed south.'

'We need to be gone long before then,' said Hywel. 'The hounds are upon us.'

Tarw and Gwenllian turned to see Hywel looking back the way they had come. In the distance a column of men was emerging from the trees.

'They carry the banner of your father,' said Tarw quietly. 'His scouts must have found our trail.'

'There's not enough time,' said Hywel. 'Even if we ride hard, we will never find a boat and get it launched before they are upon us. It is over,' he continued, 'we are done.'

'I refuse to give in as easily as that,' said Tarw, 'and will sell my life dearly.' He turned to the young woman at his side. 'Gwenllian, you have done what you can but now it is time for you to save yourself. Ride back to Gruffydd – I'm sure he will forgive you.'

'I will not leave you, Tarw,' said Gwenllian, 'and if I must raise my sword against my father, then so be it.'

'I will not allow you to do that, Gwenllian. Your father is a good man and his hands are tied in this matter. Go home and never blame yourself. The angels will surely testify before God that you acted always with compassion and love.'

Gwenllian shook her head. 'Never,' she said, 'and this day is not yet over.'

'What do you mean?'

'There is one more thing we can do, Tarw, but I don't have time to explain. Spur your horses and follow me.' Without waiting for an answer she turned and urged her horse down the far slope of the ridge. Tarw glanced back and saw Gruffydd and his men were now galloping towards them as hard as they could.

'Well,' shouted Hywel, 'what do we do?'

'You heard the girl,' responded Tarw, 'this day is apparently not yet over. Follow in her dust, Hywel, for in the short time I have known her, there is one thing I have learned: never, ever underestimate her mettle.' Without another word both men spurred their steeds and galloped after Gwenllian, with King Gruffydd and his men hot on their heels.

Another league back, the English scout once more reined in his horse alongside the English knight.

'My lord,' he shouted, 'the quarry is cornered and Gruffydd closes in as we speak.'

Broadwick stood up in his stirrups and shouted back along the column.

'To arms, men of England! Lighten your loads and prepare to ride as fast as the wind.' He turned to his second-in-command. 'This is it, Cliffdon,' he said, fastening his helmet strap beneath his chin. 'Mark this day well for before nightfall we bring to an end not only King Henry's task, but a personal quest to avenge the death of a brother. Lead us out, Cliffdon, and spare not the horses.'

The Village of Aberdaron

November 29th, AD 1115

Gwenllian, Tarw and Hywel drove their horses onward, desperate to outrun the pursuing column. Foam whipped from the horses' mouths and the riders knew they couldn't keep up the pace much longer.

'Which way is the port?' shouted Tarw, riding alongside the young woman.

'Forget the boat,' shouted Gwenllian. 'There is no time. Follow me.' She turned her horse off the track and headed down a slope towards a nearby building encircled by a small wall. Moments later she reined in her horse and slid from the saddle, turning to face her fellow fugitives. Less than a few hundred paces behind them were the lead riders of her father's column.

'Quickly,' she shouted. 'Dismount and bring your mounts through the gate.'

'What are we doing?' shouted Tarw. 'This is madness. How can a wall as high as my knee keep out an army?'

'This is no ordinary wall, Tarw,' said Hywel. 'Can you not see?'

Tarw looked around and saw a wooden cross attached to the wall beside the door. 'A church?'

'Aye,' said Gwenllian, 'but not any church – this is Saint Hywen's and has been granted the powers of sanctuary by the Pope himself. Once inside the perimeter, no man, king or pauper can take us against our will lest he be excommunicated by the church.'

'I'm not so sure,' said Tarw, 'but I suppose we are about to find out.' All three looked up as the pursuing column reined in their exhausted horses close by. The first four men dismounted and ran towards the wall, but Gwenllian stepped forward and pointed her sword towards them.

'Hold there,' she shouted, 'for this is sacred ground and you will surely be damned if you break the laws of sanctuary.'

The four men came to a stop at the wall, a few paces from their quarry. They looked around in confusion and saw the crucifix by the door. Nervously they crossed themselves and looked back at their captain, not sure what to do.

Gruffydd's second-in-command rode forward.

'Gwenllian,' said Osian, 'I don't know what you were thinking, but this madness has to end. Come out of there and let us take care of business.'

'I'm not coming out, Osian,' she said, 'and neither is Tarw or Hywel. We claim sanctuary in this place and should you breach that, then you will risk the wrath of God himself.'

'And how long do you intend to stay?' asked Osian. 'For you have to come out eventually.'

'We will stay as long as it takes my father to realise he sends one of his own to the grave.'

'There are bigger matters to take into consideration,' said Osian, 'things you have no knowledge of.'

'That may be so,' said Gwenllian, 'but I do know this: I will not leave Tarw's side. We are safe here and enjoy the shield of sanctuary.'

'Actually,' said a voice, 'that's not quite true.'

Gwenllian looked over Osian's shoulder and saw her father approaching.

'You know this is true,' said Gwenllian nervously, 'for is this not the very place where you yourself sought sanctuary when you were defeated in the battle of Llyn, before I was born?'

'It is indeed,' said Gruffydd, walking his horse right up to the small boundary wall, 'and, of course, you are right about the consequences of breaking the laws of sanctuary, but there is something you have forgotten. To enjoy sanctuary, you first have to request it.'

'What do you mean?' asked Gwenllian nervously. 'We are within the church boundary.'

'Yes, but you have to ask for, and be granted, the privilege from a man of God within this church, and alas, I see no such man.'

'Father,' said Gwenllian, 'please don't do this.'

'I have to, child,' said Gruffydd. 'The prosperity and safety of an entire kingdom outweighs the life of one man, no matter how highborn his father.'

'He was your friend,' hissed Tarw, 'and fought alongside you at Mynydd Carn. He once told me you swore that one day you would return his favour. Well, that day has come, Gruffydd. Is this how you repay your debts?'

'I promised your father, not you,' replied Gruffydd. 'The debt died with him.'

'No,' shouted Gwenllian as Gruffydd turned to Osian. 'Don't do this, Father, I beg of you.'

'Arrest them, Osian,' said Gruffydd, 'and take them back to Aberffraw.'

Tarw and Hywel drew their swords as several men climbed up onto the wall.

'Put your weapons away,' said Osian. 'We don't want to hurt you.'

'You may kill us,' said Tarw, 'but I swear that some of your men will join us in the journey.'

Gwenllian stepped forward, brandishing her sword with tears running down her face.

'Is this it, Father? Is this how it ends, with daughter fighting father?'

'You will not be hurt, child,' said Gruffydd, 'but my hands are tied. The pledge has been made and these men must be delivered to Henry, dead or alive.'

'Then there will be three bodies here today,' said Gwenllian, resuming her place alongside Tarw. 'For I will not live without him.' She turned to face Osian. 'Make your move, old friend, the point of my sword awaits.'

For a few moments, nobody moved and before Osian could react, a voice spoke out from behind the soldiers.

'Sheathe your blade, sweet Gwenllian,' it said. 'There will be no bloodshed this day.'

The soldiers parted to let the man pass, and he walked through the gate before standing beside the princess and turning to face the king's man.

'And who are you?' asked Osian.

'You know who I am,' said the man, pushing the hood back from his face, 'for I have been drunk with you on many occasions.'

As the hood fell away, many of the men gasped as they recognised Cynwrig the Tall, the man who had ridden alongside them for so many years. Osian looked across at Gruffydd, whose face was bright red with anger.

'My lord,' said Cynwrig, bowing his head, 'welcome to our church. I will gladly welcome you in, but alas, your men must wait outside.'

'Cynwrig,' said Gruffydd eventually, 'I had forgotten you had taken up residence here. I assume you now enjoy the full benefit of priesthood.'

'Indeed I do, my lord, and as such, am able to grant sanctuary to your daughter and her comrades, should it be requested.'

'Yes,' interrupted Gwenllian, grabbing his arm, 'we do request it.'

Cynwrig was about to respond when Gruffydd shouted out, 'Wait. Cynwrig, I know I owe you a great debt for if it was not for you, I would probably be dead. But this is not about us, it is about the people of Gwynedd, many of whom will die if you grant sanctuary to these two men.'

'The politics of the world are no longer of interest to me, my lord. I only care for those who seek the comfort of our saviour Jesus Christ, in whatever form that may take.'

'You don't know what you are doing, Cynwrig,' said Gruffydd. 'Do this and you may force me to break the laws of sanctuary.'

'You won't do that, Gruffydd,' replied Cynwrig. 'For you were once in their position, and to do so would surely damn your soul to everlasting hell.' He turned to face Gwenllian and the two brothers, and after forming the sign of the cross in the air with his hand said, 'I grant you the protection of the Lord's house as decreed by the laws of sanctuary. Please, come inside.'

With the king and his men looking on helplessly, Cynwrig opened the door to the church and walked inside. Gwenllian, Tarw and Hywel followed him in, still shocked at the priest's timely intervention. The door slammed behind them and all three looked around the sparse church, the gloom illuminated only by a few candles.

'Cynwrig,' said Gwenllian eventually, 'I don't know how to thank you.'

'There is no need to thank me, Gwenllian,' said Cynwrig. 'I'm just glad I came when I did.'

Gwenllian was about to reply when Cynwrig's body jerked forward and he staggered forward in shock, an arrow sticking out of his back. Gwenllian stopped him from falling and lowered him gently to the floor. Tarw brandished his sword, as did his brother, but before they could move, several men stepped out of the shadows, each holding a crossbow.

'One more step,' said a voice from the furthest part of the church, 'and the girl gets killed first.' A man emerged into the candlelight, and Tarw screwed up his eyes to see who it was.

'Hello, Diafol,' said Sir Broadwick slowly, 'at last we get to meet.'

———————

Tarw stared at the knight for a few seconds, recognising the face but struggling to recall where and when they had met before. Finally, his memory cleared and his own face screwed up with anger.

'I know you,' he said quietly, 'you are the man responsible for killing my mother.'

'I am,' said Broadwick, 'but in my defence, her death was an unfortunate accident. The arrow was meant for the man at your side as, if you recall, he was nought but an escaped prisoner and deserved the justice of the Crown.'

'I was, and still am, an innocent man,' said Hywel, 'as well you know.'

'It is irrelevant,' said Broadwick. 'We are where we are. There is business to attend here and I will be honest with you, it does not include a happy outcome for either of you.'

'You harm a hair on his head,' said Gwenllian, 'and my father's men will fall upon you like a deadly plague. One scream from me and they will burst through this door in a heartbeat.'

'I don't think so,' said Broadwick, 'and anyway, it is not you I am interested in, it is Diafol, the murdering filth who mutilated a fellow knight.'

'Why do you insist on calling me Diafol?' shouted Tarw. 'I am not that varlet and have no idea who or where he is.'

'Who said I was talking about you?' asked Broadwick.

'But . . .'

The church fell silent and Tarw saw Broadwick staring coldly at Hywel.

'Him?' said Tarw eventually. 'But that's just stupid.'

'Is it?' asked Broadwick. 'Why not ask him yourself?'

'Because it is impossible,' shouted Tarw. 'Not only is my brother hardly able to wield a sword, such is the legacy you left upon him, but he has also spent the years since his escape recovering in the Cathedral of Saint David. Tell him, Hywel, tell this idiot he makes a fool of himself.'

Again there was silence.

'Well,' said Broadwick quietly, 'do you deny my accusation, Hywel ap Rhys?'

Tarw turned to stare at his brother, who in turn was staring at Broadwick steadfastly.

'Hywel!' shouted Tarw. 'Stop this foolery. Tell him he is mistaken.'

'He is not mistaken, brother,' said Hywel quietly, 'I am who he says I am.'

'But that's impossible, you are . . .'

'I am what?' asked Hywel. 'A cripple, incapable, a weakling? What am I, brother? Spit it out.'

'I only meant that you are not the sort of man who would carry out the atrocities they speak of. I have heard Diafol's men killed indiscriminately. Surely you would never do such a thing.'

'Tarw,' said Hywel, 'they mutilated me as a child and kept me prisoner in their dungeons for most of my life. They starved me, tortured me in ways you will never understand and finally killed our mother with an arrow meant for me. How could I not carry a burden of vengeance?'

'But you were ill and had no money. Even now the very effort of raising a sword leaves you as weak as a babe. How could you possibly have fought the English in your state?'

'I didn't say I did these things with my own hands, Tarw, and mercenaries are cheaper than whores.'

'You paid for men to kill on your behalf?'

'And if I did, what is so wrong with that? Every life they took in my name was linked in some way to this man.'

'So,' said Broadwick, 'there you have it. A confession from the man himself.'

'I don't believe it,' said Tarw, 'it can't be true.'

'Oh, it's true,' said Broadwick, 'for I have tracked this devil on many occasions but always he kept just one step in front. Many thought you were the one responsible for the atrocities, Tarw, and it served my purpose to let the suspicion fall upon your shoulders, but I knew better. I wanted the real culprit for myself, but while he hid himself away in the cathedral, he was beyond my reach, so when I heard he had joined you in Gwynedd, I knew that at long last I would have my vengeance.'

Before he could say any more, the door flew open and Gruffydd burst into the church, accompanied by Osian and several Welsh knights. The English bowmen lifted their crossbows to aim at the newcomers, but Broadwick lifted his arm in restraint.

'Hold,' he shouted, 'there is no need for any deaths in this holy place.'

'What goes on here?' shouted Osian, drawing his sword. 'And who are you?'

'It's Henry's ambassador,' said Gruffydd, pushing past him to get to his daughter, 'the man the king sent to kill the brothers.'

'Father,' gasped Gwenllian. 'Thank the Lord you have come.'

Gruffydd looked down at his daughter. 'We found horses behind the church,' he said, 'and then heard the shouting. Are you hurt?'

'No, but Cynwrig is wounded. We need to get him out of here.'

Gruffydd turned to face the English knight. 'Explain yourself, Broadwick,' he snarled, 'for to me it looks like not only have you wounded a priest in his place of worship but your men hold bows aimed at my daughter. Think well on your next actions.'

'Your daughter is not at risk, Gruffydd,' said Broadwick, 'and if God is truly on his side, the priest should survive, but as for these two, well, let's just say I have got what I came for.'

'It wasn't supposed to be like this, Broadwick. They were supposed to be given a fair trial.'

'The time for trials is over,' snapped Broadwick. 'These men are now in my custody, so I suggest you take the girl and the priest before this gets out of hand.'

'Are you threatening me, Broadwick?' asked Gruffydd. 'My own men are but a heartbeat away.'

'Do you really think I would come here unprepared?' sneered Broadwick. 'Take a look outside, Gruffydd, and think carefully about your next decision.'

For a few moments everyone stared at each other, until Osian turned and walked back to the door. Seconds later he returned and spoke to the king. 'My lord, there are over two hundred mounted men spread out along the top of the hill. We are heavily outnumbered.'

'You are,' said Broadwick, 'and there could only be one outcome should this end badly. Now, I will ask again. Take your daughter, King Gruffydd, and return home in peace. I will deal with these two rebels and within a few days, all this will be forgotten. The priest will heal, your daughter will find a better suitor and we can all get on with our lives.'

Gruffydd was stuck. He knew the English knight had the upper hand and anyway, there was no way he could risk the whole of Gwynedd for the sake of two men. He turned to his own two soldiers.

'Take the priest outside and get him to a physician.'

As the task was carried out, Gwenllian got to her feet and turned to face Gruffydd. 'Don't do this, Father,' she said, her voice breaking. 'Your conscience will haunt you forever.'

'I have no choice,' said Gruffydd. 'Go and join the rest of the men outside.'

'I will not,' she said. 'My place is with Tarw.'

'*You will do as you are told*,' roared the king, his patience failing him. 'Osian, have her taken away.'

Another two men grabbed Gwenllian and dragged her screaming from the church, leaving Gruffydd and Osian to face Broadwick and his men alone.

'Well,' said Broadwick, 'what is it to be?'

'If I do as you request, will you allow me and my men to leave peacefully?'

'Of course.'

'And what of you?'

'When we have dealt with these men, we will return to Hen Domen, Henry will be informed and Gwynedd can continue to savour the peace she has enjoyed for so many years. The choice is simple, Gruffydd. These two men or your kingdom. It is as simple as that.'

***

Outside the church, Gwenllian struggled valiantly against her captors but was no match for their strength.

'*Let me go*,' she screamed again, the tears rolling from her eyes.

'I cannot do that, my lady,' said the sergeant as he tied her hands behind her back, 'or it will be my own head in the noose.'

'Noose?' said Gwenllian. 'What noose?'

The soldier glanced over to a tree in the far corner of the church grounds. Broadwick's men had already secured two hanging ropes from one of the stronger branches.

'No,' gasped Gwenllian, shaking her head. 'They can't. My father won't allow it.'

Before the soldier could answer, Gruffydd and Osian came out of the church and strode towards their men.

'Mount up,' shouted Osian. 'Prepare to ride.'

As the Welsh made their way to their horses, Gruffydd approached Gwenllian, his face etched with sadness. 'Gwenllian—' he started, but was interrupted by his daughter.

'*No*,' she gasped again, 'please say you didn't let them take him. Father, what have you done?'

'I have no choice, Gwenllian,' he said, 'just look around you. We are outnumbered two to one. Even if I agreed with you, which I don't, and we fought and defeated Broadwick, we would eventually pay the price at the hands of Henry. I cannot do that to Gwynedd, Gwenllian – there has already been too much blood spilled in pursuit of freedom. All we can do now is hope the death of Tarw will be the last.'

'No,' gasped Gwenllian, grabbing at his tabard. 'Please, it's not too late.'

A noise from the church made them both turn their heads and they saw Tarw and Hywel being marched out at the point of a sword. Their hands were tied before them and they were forced over to the cart waiting beneath the ropes. Gwenllian stared in horror as both men were manhandled up onto the cart to face the noose. Tarw looked over at Gwenllian and gave her a poignant smile.

'*No!*' screamed Gwenllian, pulling free from the guard before running over to the cart, closely followed by two of Gruffydd's soldiers.

'Hold,' shouted the king, 'there is nothing she can do. Let her say her goodbyes.'

Gwenllian reached the cart and looked up at Tarw, tears running down her face.

'Tarw,' she gasped, 'this cannot be. Surely even God can see this is so wrong?'

'Be strong, my love,' he said. 'It will soon be over and you will return to the arms of your family.'

'I have no family,' sobbed Gwenllian as her father and Osian approached to stand a few paces away. 'What family allows an enemy to murder one of their own?'

'He means well, Gwenllian,' said Tarw. 'Forgive him.'

'*Tarw*,' sobbed Gwenllian as one of the English climbed up onto the cart to secure the nooses, 'I love you.'

'And I love you,' said Tarw. 'Say a prayer for us, Gwenllian, and we will surely be together in the next life.'

Gwenllian turned to face Gruffydd. '*Father*, please, don't let them do this.'

'I have to,' said Gruffydd, his own voice breaking. 'Don't you understand? In the eyes of the English he is nothing more than a brigand.'

'What about my eyes?' sobbed Gwenllian. 'What about my heart?'

'He is the first man you have ever had feelings for, Gwenllian. There will be more.'

'But—'

'Gwenllian, it is time to go,' interrupted Gruffydd. 'Osian, bring her to my horse.'

Osian stepped forward as Gruffydd turned away. For a moment the king's eyes met the cold stare of Broadwick.

'Finished now?' asked the knight.

'Don't gloat, Broadwick,' said Gruffydd. 'You have the day but God will never forgive you.'

'We will see,' said Broadwick. He looked over to the cart. 'Executioner,' he shouted, 'continue.'

As Gruffydd walked away, Osian grabbed Gwenllian's arm and dragged her behind him.

'*Father*,' shouted Gwenllian, but Gruffydd kept on walking back to his horse. '*Father*,' she shouted again, '*you have to listen to me.*'

'There is nothing more to say,' replied Gruffydd over his shoulder. 'It is done.'

'*Father*,' screamed Gwenllian for the last time. '*I am with child!*'

The Village of Aberdaron

November 29th, AD 1115

Gruffydd stopped dead in his tracks. For a few seconds his eyes closed as Gwenllian's words sunk in. Silence fell around the churchyard and even the birds seemed to hold their breath. Slowly he turned around and looked at her. Despite her leather armour, all he could see was a frightened child, the daughter he had doted on since the day she was born.

'Gruffydd,' said Broadwick nervously, breaking the silence, 'it makes no difference. These men are still rebels and will pay the price demanded of them. Don't do anything stupid.'

Gruffydd didn't take his eyes off his daughter, just stood there as if he had the weight of the world on his shoulders.

'*Father*,' sobbed Gwenllian again, as she sank to her knees, 'I beg of you, please help them to live. I carry your grandchild inside of me. Rebel or not, Tarw's blood is now as much a part of this family as mine. Let them kill Tarw and I swear, you will be killing me.'

As her words died away she finally broke down and lay on the floor, sobbing like there was no tomorrow.

Gruffydd looked up and gazed around. His daughter lay on the ground between him and the wagon containing the two condemned men, while to his left stood Osian and two of his men-at-arms. Behind

Osian were the rest of his column, a hundred mounted men waiting nervously for a command. Broadwick stood to his right with half a dozen archers and though his own horsemen vastly outnumbered the Welsh, they were high on the ridge, unaware of the drama unfolding far below.

'Oh, sweet Jesus,' mumbled Gruffydd at last, '*what have I become?*'

'Gruffydd,' said Broadwick, his voice rising in warning, 'the girl may be lying. Think well on your actions.'

'My daughter does not lie, Broadwick,' said Gruffydd quietly as he walked towards Gwenllian. 'She is the best daughter any man could ever want.' He dropped to his knees and lifted her chin, smiling gently into her eyes. 'My sweet, beautiful Gwenllian,' he said softly, 'I am so, so sorry. When you were but a babe, you used to hold your arms out to me seeking comfort and I would sweep you up with joy in my heart. Today, you held your arms up to me again and I almost turned away. May God forgive me.'

'*Help us,*' she begged, her voice barely audible through her tears.

'I am your father, Gwenllian,' whispered Gruffydd through his own tears, 'of course I'm going to help you.' He produced his knife and cut the bonds around her wrists. 'Do you remember your tenth birthday,' he continued, 'the time when we came here and I taught you how to fish off the rocks?'

'I do,' said Gwenllian.

'And do you remember when I chased you and you ran away? Do you remember where you hid?'

'I do,' said Gwenllian again.

'Then I want you to play that game again, but this time keep on running. Do you know what I am saying?'

Gwenllian swallowed hard and nodded her head.

'I love you, sweet child,' said Gruffydd, 'and one day, if God sees us through this day, I will cradle your baby with all the love any man can muster. Until that day comes you must place your trust in God and the father of your child.'

'What are you going to do?'

'I am going to do what all fathers are born to do, Gwenllian. Protect my own.'

'I don't understand.'

'Just be ready, sweet girl. Seek the warrior within for though you are equal in arms to any of my men, that training will be needed if you are to survive this day. Do you understand?'

'I think so,' said Gwenllian. 'And Father?'

'Yes?'

'I love you too.'

'I know,' said Gruffydd. 'Be happy, sweet child.' Without another word he stood up and spun around to face his men.

'*Men of Wales, to arms!*'

———

Broadwick roared with fury and turned to face the wagon.

'*Kill the prisoners*,' he shouted, but as one of the executioners drew his sword, Tarw kicked him as hard as he could in the groin, sending him backward off the cart. One of the Welsh archers accounted for the second executioner with an arrow to the throat and as the two brothers jumped from the wagon, Gwenllian ran forward to plunge her knife into the heart of the first executioner. Arrows flew both ways and within moments, the few English archers lay dead or dying around Broadwick. The knight and his second were unharmed.

'*Hold your fire*,' shouted Osian, and everyone fell still once more.

'You will pay for this, Gruffydd,' growled Broadwick, 'as God is my witness I swear you will endure the wrath of Henry for your treachery.'

'There is no need for more death, Broadwick,' said Gruffydd. 'Take your men and leave these lands. Tell your king, this is Gwynedd and I am the rightful ruler here. No man, be he pauper or king, will tell me who lives or dies in my kingdom. Is that understood?'

'You are signing your own death warrant, Gruffydd,' spat Broadwick, 'and Henry will burn Gwynedd to ashes before this year is out.'

'If he does, he will be the first to ever achieve such a feat,' said Gruffydd. 'Us Welshmen don't die as easily as you think.'

As the two nobles stared at each other, Gwenllian cut Tarw's bonds and the prince walked over to stand near Gruffydd.

'My lord,' he said, 'this man came here to kill me. Why not allow him the chance to do what he craves so much.'

Gruffydd turned to stare at the prince. 'What do you mean? I have gained you your freedom, now take it before it is too late.'

'My lord, this man imprisoned my brother for many years and killed my mother. I request a trial of arms.'

'*Tarw, no,*' shouted Gwenllian, but the prince just stared at the Welsh king, waiting for an answer.

'Let him come, Gruffydd,' sneered Broadwick. 'We both have scores to settle but as his brother is no more than a cripple, I will fight Tarw as his champion.'

'And if he emerges the victor?'

'If that is the outcome, then my men will withdraw and leave you in peace.'

'How do I know you will keep your word?'

Broadwick turned to his second-in-command. 'Cliffdon, ride up to the men. If I should fall, I order you to ride back to Hen Domen without delay. Is that clear?'

'Understood,' said Cliffdon.

'Let them through,' shouted Osian, and they all waited as Cliffdon galloped up the hill to join the English lines.

'Well,' said Broadwick, turning back to Gruffydd, 'are we agreed?'

'We are,' said Gruffydd, watching as both men walked out into the space before the wall.

Broadwick swung his heavy sword back and forth like a giant pendulum, his fingers flexing as he savoured the weight of his weapon.

'Make your move, Welshman,' he said, 'for this farce has gone on long enough.'

Tarw made the first assault, his sword crashing into Broadwick's own, and though he was the smaller man, his technique and training came as a surprise to the English knight. Instantly, Broadwick fell back under the onslaught but he was an experienced warrior and only used enough energy to parry the heavy blows. Tarw continued his attack but as Broadwick knew they would, the strength of the Welshman's blows soon weakened and the knight saw an opening. With a sudden and unexpected counter-attack, he ducked below Tarw's head shot and swung his own blade sideways, smashing it into the Welshman's hauberk, forcing jagged chainmail into the wound. Tarw gasped and staggered backward. Broadwick followed up with a kick to Tarw's midriff and the prince fell backward, sprawling in the dirt. He quickly regained his feet but the pain was immense and he guessed one of his ribs was broken. Desperately he fought on but, crippled with pain, there could only be one outcome. Broadwick forced him back until he was against a tree and after punching Tarw's wound with his free hand, the knight forced his opponent to drop his sword. Breathing heavily, he lifted the point of his own weapon to Tarw's throat.

'Short but well fought, Welshman,' he said. 'Under normal circumstances you would be offered quarter but this is not that day.'

'Just do it, Broadwick,' gasped Tarw, 'for one more minute in this life while you still breathe is a minute I can no longer endure.'

'As you wish,' said Broadwick, but as he was about to plunge his sword into Tarw's throat, he felt a blade against his own and he froze in fear. Behind him, Hywel had pulled back the knight's head, pressing the blade of his dagger against the knight's unprotected flesh.

'Hywel,' gasped Tarw, 'what do you think you are doing?'

'Finishing what you could not,' said Hywel, 'avenging our family.'

'Hywel,' said Tarw slowly, 'the fight was fair. I lost and the price must be paid.'

'War is not fair, Tarw, neither is torture or murder. This man is guilty of all three.'

'You will rot in hell for this,' gasped Broadwick.

'Hell has no fears for me,' whispered Hywel into his victim's ear, 'for I am the Diafol, remember?'

Before Broadwick could answer, Hywel dragged his knife across the knight's throat, carving deeply through flesh and cartilage.

Tarw knocked Broadwick's sword to one side and the knight fell to his knees, clutching at his throat. His eyes bulged with hatred and Tarw walked over to stand beside his brother to watch the English noble die. Gruffydd stared in disbelief but before he could say anything, Osian called out, 'My lord, look to the hill.'

The king turned and stared upward. Broadwick's second-in-command had seen the treachery and all two hundred riders were galloping down the hill, fully armed and hell-bent on revenge.

Gruffydd roared out his commands. 'Men-at-arms,' he shouted, 'take position behind the walls. Present shields. Archers, form two ranks and prepare for volley fire. Osian, gather ten men and get ready to take down the horses. We may be outnumbered but the ground is in our favour.'

As men ran everywhere, Gruffydd turned to see Gwenllian staring in fear at the approaching enemy.

'*Gwenllian*,' shouted Gruffydd, 'you know what to do. Take Cynwrig with you, we will hold them here as long as we can. If we should fall, remember this day to your children.'

'*I love you, Father*,' shouted Gwenllian above the noise.

'And I love you,' shouted Gruffydd, 'now *run!*'

Gwenllian turned and shouted over to the brothers.

'Tarw, Hywel, follow me.'

'Where are we going?'

'Down to the boathouse.'

'We'll never make it to the dock,' shouted Hywel, 'we will be run down by their horses.'

'The boathouse is not in the dock, Hywel, it is in a cove at the bottom of the cliff. No horses can get down there.'

'Perhaps not, but their foot soldiers can.'

'Take ten men with you,' shouted Osian. 'They will fight a rearguard action as you descend.'

'What about Cynwrig?'

'I will have him brought down on a stretcher, but wait no longer than you have to. Men will die here today, that much is certain, but if you should fall after all this, then they will die in vain.'

Gwenllian turned and ran towards the cliff edge, followed closely by Tarw and Hywel. Behind them, ten men left the defensive lines and after picking up Cynwrig's stretcher, followed as fast as they were able.

At the wall, Osian and the king marshalled their men the best they could in the short time available.

'Archers, ready your bows,' shouted Osian. 'I want arrows in the air faster than you have ever done before. Ready?'

'*Aye*,' roared the archers in response.

'Wait,' shouted Osian as the English horses thundered towards them, 'wait . . . *Now!*'

The air filled with willow and the arrows fell amongst the riders like hail.

'*Second rank*,' roared Osian, 'loose! First rank, ready, *loose*!'

Over and over again the arrows flew through the air, and though the English responded with their own, from horseback their aim was poor at best and few fell on target. Despite this they still came, and Gruffydd turned to his foot soldiers standing fifty paces behind the churchyard wall. '*Shield wall!*'

The front rank knelt, digging the bottom edges of their shields into the soil before leaning their shoulders against them. The second rank lapped their own shields over those at the front and braced themselves for the imminent impact.

'Archers,' shouted Osian, 'upon my command, drop to your bellies and prepare to turn inward.'

A few more arrows flew towards the English but within seconds the cavalry were at the wall, each galloping horse clearing the wall with ease as they charged the Welsh defenders.

'*Down*,' roared Osian, and every archer dropped to the floor as the horses soared through the air above them. A few of the riders with lances stabbed downward as they passed, killing some of the men below, but most just sailed over, focused on the shield wall.

'On your feet,' shouted Osian as the last rider passed, 'target the horses.'

Again the Welsh archers fired volley after volley into the English, but the enemy had already smashed into the shield wall, and the battle proper commenced.

———

'Here it is,' shouted Gwenllian, finding the path that led down to the cove. 'Quickly.'

'The English are upon us,' shouted Hywel.

'*Keep going*,' bellowed the sergeant in charge of the men sent by Osian. 'We'll hold them back!'

The fugitives and the two men carrying Cynwrig's stretcher descended the path as fast as they could, eventually reaching the shore.

'Over there,' shouted Gwenllian. They could see a ramshackle boathouse built into the rocks, with a timber quay reaching out into the water. Alongside it, a boat bobbed gently on the swell and as they ran towards it, two men emerged from the boathouse.

'You there,' shouted Tarw, 'we need your boat in the name of the king.'

'What king?' asked one of the fishermen, his eyes screwing up in mistrust.

'King Gruffydd,' gasped Gwenllian as they reached the boat, 'my father.'

The fisherman's eyes opened wide with surprise. 'Lady Gwenllian,' he said, 'is it truly you?'

'Aye, it is,' replied Tarw, 'and her life is at risk. An English army is on our trail and if you don't help us now, she will be dead within the hour.'

'Of course,' said the man, 'climb aboard. We'll get you away from here.'

Gwenllian and Hywel climbed into the boat as Tarw and the second fisherman ran back along the shore to help the two exhausted stretcher-bearers.

'Quickly,' shouted Gwenllian, 'they are coming down the cliff.'

'*Cast off,*' roared Tarw from further along the shore, 'we will wade out to meet you.'

The first fisherman pushed his boat from the quay and grabbed a set of oars, propelling it out into deeper water.

'Get some oars,' he shouted, 'we need to move faster.'

'I have never rowed a boat,' replied Hywel.

'Nor I,' said Gwenllian.

'It matters not, just do as I do, it all helps.'

The three rowed as hard as they could, while further along the shore, the four bearers waded out into deeper water, the waves splashing over the stretcher as they went. Behind them, six Englishmen ran into the sea but stopped thigh-deep. Two of them retrieved crossbows from their backs but the swell of the sea meant Tarw and his comrades were difficult targets and none of the bolts hit home.

Though they could still touch the bottom with their feet, the water was now chin-high on the Welshmen and they stared at the approaching boat, desperate to be pulled aboard.

'Gwenllian, stay down,' shouted Tarw as it got closer, knowing the boat was a much easier target for the crossbows.

The experienced fisherman brought the boat alongside and everyone was pulled aboard to lie exhausted in the bottom. Tarw looked up at Gwenllian and saw the horrified look on her face. He followed her gaze and could see they had a clear view of the unfolding battle above. What he saw made his blood run cold.

———

Gruffydd fought furiously, his sword swinging in all directions. The English had broken through the shield wall and now both bodies of men fought man to man, with neither command nor formation to guide their actions. On the English side, the soldiers were more disciplined and well trained, while the Welsh had the advantage of a feral approach, learned from years of fighting a guerrilla war from the forests of the North Wales mountains. Men fell on both sides and the battle spilled over onto the grassy slope leading down to the cliff edge. Quarter was neither asked nor given and soon the slope was dotted with individual fights, each man labouring from exhaustion.

Unable to employ their bows lest they hit a comrade, the Welsh bowmen ran amongst the carnage, administering death with their knives, and though for a while it seemed the English would gain the day, the effect of the bowmen proved the difference and soon the tide turned in favour of the Welsh.

Green grass was stained red as far as the eye could see and bodies lay everywhere, the cries of the wounded echoing across the field. A few fights remained, and as Osian pulled his sword from an opponent's chest, he looked around for the king, knowing that to lose him now would be unthinkable.

Down on the cliff edge, Gruffydd was being forced back by two English men-at-arms and though he fought valiantly, Osian could see he was spent. Frantically he ran down the slope to help Gruffydd and as one of the king's attackers turned to face him with sword outstretched, Osian increased his speed and crashed into him, impaling himself on the enemy sword. Despite the mortal wound, his momentum carried both himself and the enemy swordsman over the edge of the cliff to crash amongst the rocks far below.

The second swordsman was distracted for the smallest of moments but it was enough and from his position on his knees, Gruffydd drove his sword upward through his opponent's groin and into his chest. The Englishman's head tilted back and he screamed in agony as blood poured from the wound over Gruffydd's face. Slowly the swordsman fell backward and Gruffydd gasped in relief. He pulled his sword clear and, looking up, saw that the remainder of the English had broken off the attack. Some were running towards the high ground, while others sought whatever horses remained alive.

Those Welshmen who remained standing watched them go, unable to pursue, such was their exhaustion, and many just looked around, confused as to how they had emerged victorious. Slowly, one by one, they saw their king and as Gruffydd dragged himself to his feet, the remainder of his men walked down the hill to gather around him. For a few moments they stood around their blood-soaked king in silence, too tired to celebrate. Gruffydd turned and looked down into the cove, seeing the small skiff containing his daughter sailing slowly out to sea, and as she sailed away to a new future, he finally lifted his sword high in the air in celebration.

'*Live long and live free, Gwenllian,*' he roared, '*and make Wales remember your name!*'

The Welsh survivors up on the hill each raised their own swords and bellowed their own victory cries, the magnificent sound echoing off the rocks of the bloodstained cliffs.

Down in the boat Gwenllian stood with her hand over her mouth, tears streaming down her face. She had watched as her father defeated an overwhelming enemy in an effort to save her, and as the skiff carried her out of the cove to an uncertain future, the last thing she saw was King Gruffydd ap Cynan, stood atop a cliff edge with sword held high, his body and soul soaked . . . *in the blood of kings* . . .

Author's Notes

The storyline in this novel is loosely based on actual events from around the times reflected. Information is very scarce and facts are disputed, but overall, the stories included in this series of books are far too good not to be told. As you can imagine, on occasion some dates, places and even names have to be altered slightly to make the story work as smoothly as possible for the reader. However, where this was unavoidable, I have tried to keep it to a minimum.

The Abduction of Nesta ferch Rhys

Around Christmas time in 1109, many historians believe that Nesta was abducted from a castle by Owain ap Cadwgan, the son of the Welsh rebel prince, Cadwgan ap Bleddyn.

Records show that while attending a celebration near Cenarth Bychan Castle (probably the site of Cilgerran Castle today), Owain became aware of her presence and was infatuated by her beauty. That night, along with approximately fourteen or fifteen men, Owain accessed the outer walls of the castle and set the buildings alight. He and his men then trapped Gerald of Windsor, castellan of Pembroke Castle, in Nesta's chambers but before the attackers could capture him, Gerald escaped through the garderobe, the chute used as a toilet. Owain then forced entry but finding Gerald gone, turned his attentions to Nesta.

Some reports say that he raped the princess in front of her children, while others say she was a willing participant. Whatever the truth, it appears that she was taken as his prisoner (willing or otherwise) and stayed with him for several years.

During this time, Nesta managed to secure the release of her children, who were sent back to Gerald unharmed. Various reports also say that Nesta went on to have one or possibly two children fathered by Owain during this time, but these reports are often disputed.

Owain ap Cadwgan

After Owain ap Cadwgan abducted Nesta, Henry was incensed and Gerald sought to release his wife from Owain's clutches. Pressure was put on the rebel from all sides and eventually he had to flee to Ireland in fear of his life. There doesn't seem to be any record or account of how or when Nesta was finally released.

Owain was eventually offered amnesty by Henry and fought for the king in France. It would seem that Henry was so impressed with the young man's fighting prowess, he knighted him. Sometime later, Owain was given a mission by Henry and found himself on campaign alongside Gerald of Windsor, Nesta's husband. Gerald must have still borne a grudge for it is claimed he subsequently took his revenge by killing Owain, probably in the heat of battle.

Gwenllian ferch Gruffydd

Gwenllian was a real character and the daughter of the king of Gwynedd, Gruffydd ap Cynan. Her beauty was renowned throughout the land, as was her prowess with arms. We can only imagine her growing up amongst her brothers as a tomboy, relishing the chance to train and one day fight in the many battles of the time. When Tarw arrived seeking help from Gruffydd, he fell in love with the beautiful Gwenllian and they eventually eloped together and returned to Deheubarth (South-West Wales) to raise a family and continue the struggle against the

English. History seems to be quiet as to whether she left at the same time as Tarw or joined him later.

Saint Hywen's Church

Saint Hywen's Church in Aberdaron, North Wales, is a real place and was the church where Gruffydd sought sanctuary in 1094 during his long campaign to retrieve the kingship of Gwynedd. Ironically, the same church was used by Gruffydd ap Rhys (Tarw in our story) in 1115 while fleeing the attentions of Gruffydd, who, under the orders of King Henry, tried to detain the Welsh prince to be tried as a rebel. The priesthood apparently protected Tarw under the laws of sanctuary and enabled his escape via a boat. Whether that was with Gwenllian at his side or whether she joined him at a later date is unclear.

About the Author

Photo © 2015 Steve Powerhill

Kevin Ashman is the author of seventeen novels, including the bestselling Roman Chronicles and highly ranked Medieval Sagas. Always pushing the boundaries, he found further success with the India Sommers Mysteries, as well as three other standalone projects, *Vampire*, *Savage Eden* and the dystopian horror story *The Last Citadel*. Kevin was born and raised in Wales and now writes full-time. He is married with four grown children and enjoys cycling, swimming and watching rugby. Current works include the highly anticipated Blood of Kings series, of which *Rebellion's Forge* is the third and final instalment. Links to all Kevin's books can be found at www.KMAshman.co.uk